Shop On The Corner

Books by J.L. and Lin Stepp

The Afternoon Hiker
Discovering Tennessee State Parks
Exploring South Carolina State Parks
Visiting North Carolina State Parks
Coming next --Traveling Georgia State Parks

Books by Lin Stepp

The Smoky Mountain Series

The Foster Girls	*Tell Me About Orchard Hollow*
For Six Good Reasons	*Delia's Place*
Second Hand Rose	*Down by the River*
Makin' Miracles	*Saving Laurel Springs*
Welcome Back	*Daddy's Girl*
Lost Inheritance	*The Interlude*

The Mountain Home Books
Happy Valley
Downsizing
Eight at the Lake
Seeking Ayita
Shop on the Corner
Coming Next--The Red Mill Bookstore

Christmas Novella
A Smoky Mountain Gift
In *When the Snow Falls*

The Edisto Trilogy
Claire at Edisto
Return to Edisto
Edisto Song

The Lighthouse Sisters Series
Light the Way
Lighten My Heart
Light in the Dark
Coming Next ---The Light Continues

Shop On The Corner

A MOUNTAIN HOME BOOK

LIN STEPP

Cover design: Katherine E. Stepp
Interior design: J. L. Stepp, Mountain Hill Press
Editor: Elizabeth S. James
Cover photo and map design: Lin M. Stepp

Library of Congress Cataloging-in-Publication Data

Stepp, Lin
Shop On The Corner/ Lin Stepp

ISBN: 979-8-9877251-2-2
First Mountain Hill Press Trade Paperback Printing: March 2024

eISBN: 979-8-9877251-3-9
First Mountain Hill Press Electronic Edition: March 2024

1. Women—Southern States—Fiction   2. North Carolina - Smoky Mountains- Fiction
3. Contemporary Romance—Inspirational—Fiction. I. Title

Library of Congress Control Number: 2024900969

This book is dedicated to all my fans and readers in the Western North Carolina area, who kept encouraging me to write a book set in the Waynesville - Sylva area. I listened, and I truly enjoyed all my visits to this area working on my new *Mountain Home* book.

ACKNOWLEDGEMENTS

I first visited the small town of Waynesville, NC, for a book signing for my first published book. The charm of the city captivated me and I returned to Waynesville and the nearby area for many book events in the years since at Blue Ridge Books in Waynesville, City Lights Bookstore in Sylva, and at Malaprops and Barnes & Noble in Asheville. My thanks to all these fine bookstores for bringing me to Western North Carolina and for carrying my book titles.

Thanks also to the friendly staff members in Waynesville businesses who provided me with helpful information, including the Waynesville Visitor Center, the Chamber of Commerce, and Re/Max Realty on Main Street. I so appreciate the maps, brochures, and information they sent to help me with my book. I am also grateful to the Haywood County Arts Council. Their staff answered many questions about Waynesville's art scene and I am pleased to feature the Arts Council Gallery on Main in several scenes in my novel. Waynesville offers many colorful events during the year, too. like Art After Dark at participating galleries, including the Arts Council Gallery, and I enjoyed spotlighting this event and the wonderful International Festival held in the city every summer. Thanks to all those in Waynesville who work hard to make these events happen every year.

Grateful acknowledgement also to the shops, restaurants, historic spots, and churches peppered throughout my story, like Bocelli's Italian Eatery, the Sweet Onion, the Haywood Smokehouse, Clyde's Restaurant, Church Street Depot, Birchwood Hall Southern Kitchen, The Patio Bistro, and many others. Gratitude, also, to wonderful sites around the Waynesville area, included in my story, like Junaluska Resort and Conference Center, Biltmore House and Gardens, and the Great Smoky Mountains National Park.

Special thanks to Becky Fain at the Inn at Iris Meadows on Love Lane who graciously answered many questions about the town for me. You will find mention of the Iris Inn in my book and Becky allowed me to model my fictional dog Zoey after her dog of the same name. Check out this beautiful Bed-and-Breakfast Inn if you are in the Waynesville area.

Acknowledgements to all those who helped with this book:

_ Elizabeth S. James, copyeditor and editorial adviser
_ J.L. Stepp, production design and proofing
_ Katherine Stepp, cover design and graphics
_ And ongoing gratitude to the Lord, who helps me with all my books.

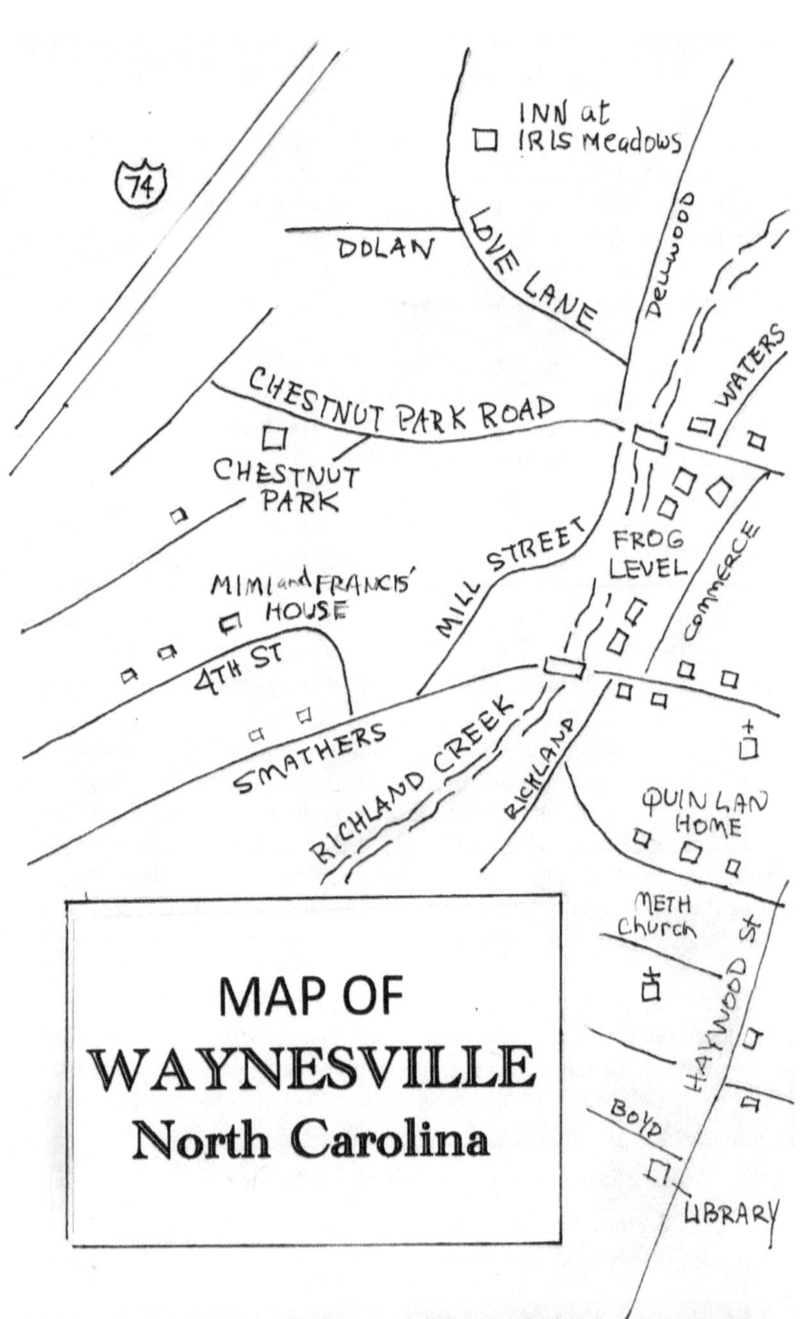

MAP OF
WAYNESVILLE
North Carolina

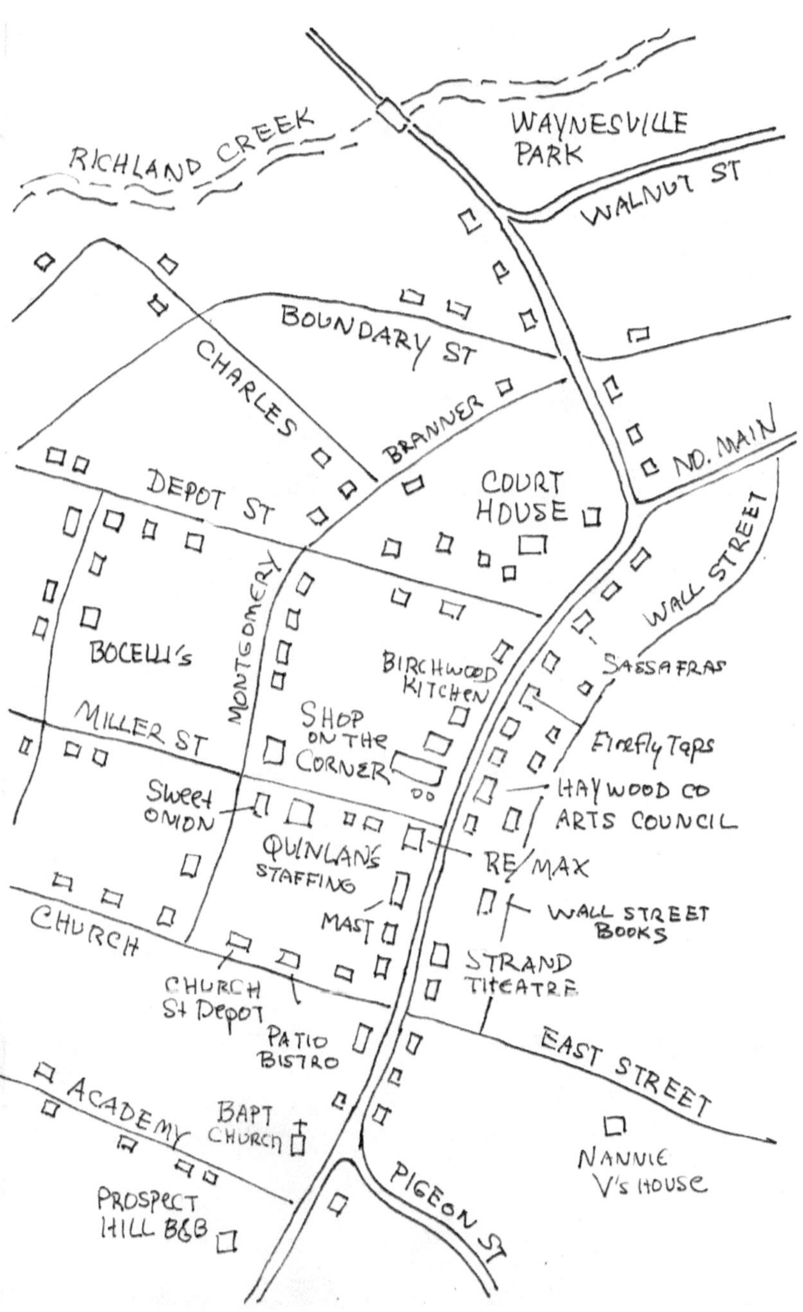

RICHLAND CREEK
WAYNESVILLE PARK
WALNUT ST
BOUNDARY ST
CHARLES
BRANNER
ND. MAIN
COURT HOUSE
DEPOT ST
WALL STREET
MONTGOMERY
BOCELLI'S
BIRCHWOOD KITCHEN
SASSAFRAS
MILLER ST
SHOP ON THE CORNER
Firefly Taps
HAYWOOD CO ARTS COUNCIL
Sweet ONION
QUINLAN'S STAFFING
RE/MAX
MAST
WALL STREET BOOKS
CHURCH
STRAND THEATRE
CHURCH St Depot
PATIO BISTRO
EAST STREET
ACADEMY
BAPT CHURCH
NANNIE V's HOUSE
PROSPECT HILL B&B
PIGEON ST

CHAPTER 1

$\mathbf{L}$aura shivered as she started coffee brewing in the kitchen. It was cold this January morning in Amory, Mississippi, the temperature in the low forties after dipping below freezing last night. She even saw a little frost on the windows. In the older house she rented, the insulation wasn't everything it should be, but with a few space heaters she stayed snug enough.

She got eggs out now, deciding on scrambled eggs and toast before she headed to work. She'd already set a plate at the little dining table off the small kitchen, put out butter, jelly, and fruit beside the newspaper she'd rescued from the front porch.

Turning at a sound, she saw her sister Georgina hesitate in the kitchen doorway, wrapping her robe tightly around her. Actually, it was Laura's robe; she wondered where it had disappeared to.

"It's freezing in here," Georgina said, scowling. "And it's even colder downstairs."

"I'm surprised you're up so early," Laura said, turning back to the stove. "You and Chance stayed up late."

"We got into an old movie," she said, settling on a kitchen stool. "But the smell of your coffee woke me up."

"Do you want eggs, too?" Laura asked. "It's no trouble to scramble another and pop a second piece of bread in the toaster."

"I'll just have coffee." She wrinkled her nose. "I can't believe you eat at this time of day anyway. It's only seven."

"You know I open the shop at nine." It seemed ridiculous to explain this to Georgina. The upholstery business Laura ran now, since their father's death five years ago, had kept the same operating hours since the day her father opened it.

Georgina shrugged. "You pay people to work for you. They could open the store so you don't have to go in so early."

Laura cracked her eggs into the skillet, deciding not to answer.

"I can't believe when I look around this kitchen how many of Mother and Daddy's old things you kept." She laughed. "You still have those tacky rooster dishes we ate on when growing up—plus the matching glasses and canisters. Chance totally cracked up when he first saw them. Why in the world did you keep those old things when we sold Daddy and Mother's house?"

"I like them," she answered, putting her eggs and toast on a plate and carrying them with a cup of coffee into the little dining area.

Georgina followed her, sitting down across from her at the small table to nurse the cup of coffee she'd fixed herself.

Laura watched her out of the corner of her eye while she ate. Her sister was beautiful even with her hair mussed, no makeup, and dressed in one of Chance's old shirts under her robe. Laura could tell Georgina had something on her mind, too, from the way she kept picking at her nails nervously.

"You probably remember Chance and I have another gig with the band this weekend. We're going to leave this afternoon to drive to Memphis, and we're staying with one of Chance's friends through the weekend. We probably won't be back until late Monday." She offered a smile. "It's a first-class club we're playing at, and of course I'll be singing, too. Chance said some important people in the industry often drop in at this club. It could open a good opportunity for us."

After a few minutes she added, "Everybody says the Mississippi Ramblers are going to be really big some day like Alabama or The Oak Ridge Boys. Somebody said, when we were playing down at Jackson last weekend, that when Chance and I sing together we sound kind of like Trisha Yearwood and Garth Brooks."

"You've always had a beautiful voice," Laura decided to say.

Georgiana picked at her nails again. "Well, it takes time to grow and develop in the industry. You have to work hard at it and keep believing one of your songs will catch the attention of a good agent or someone in the industry one day. Then you take off."

Laura tried to think what to say. This had been Georgina's dream for years now, ever since she quit college to run away with Chance Richardson and his country music group.

"I need to borrow a little money for this weekend," Georgina said then. "The winters are always a little slow and we're short right now." She offered Laura another smile. "You know we'll pay it back."

Laura knew instead she'd be lucky if she ever saw a penny of this or any of the rest of the "little loans" Georgina and Chance had borrowed from her since they showed up at her house before Christmas. They'd been here for over six weeks now and continued to answer evasively when they planned to go back to Nashville.

Laura had felt excited when Georgina called before Christmas to suggest she and Chance come to stay with her for the holidays.

"We haven't seen each other for a long time," Georgina said. "I thought it would be nice if we came for the holidays, especially since Chance and I have a show or two scheduled in that area. Would it be okay if we come? I think you said you had an extra bedroom in the new house that you're living in now."

Laura hesitated answering for a moment, letting Georgina babble on about Christmas plans. The truth was Laura wasn't fond of Chance Richardson. She never had been, and she wasn't comfortable having the two of them in her home, unmarried as they were. She only had one sister though and their relationship had been strained for years, ever since their mother died and especially since Georgina ran off with Chance Richardson, walking away from a full four-year scholarship in voice at Old Miss.

Laura finally answered. "I could clean out the workroom downstairs for you, Georgina. There's a queen size sofa bed there and a bathroom in the laundry room. Keep in mind my place is small though; it won't be like the house we grew up in." Laura still missed the lovely family home Georgina insisted they sell after her father was killed one rainy night when his delivery van skidded off the road.

"I'm sure it will be fine," Georgina put in quickly.

Apparently, it had been fine. Whenever Laura quizzed Georgina about when they planned to head back to Nashville, her sister's comments seemed vague and indefinite. "Chance and I decided to let our old place go in Nashville and we have some friends helping us look for another one. I'm sure we'll track something down soon."

In the meantime, they'd freeloaded on Laura, not paying a penny toward expenses or groceries or helping with any cleaning around the house. They also drank too much, and the downstairs smelled like booze and the subtle scent of marijuana. Laura was pretty naive about that sort of thing, but she'd seen all too clearly when the two of them—and especially Chance—were high on one thing or the other. While she worked every day, they hung around the house watching television or listening to music between the weekends when they met up with the members of Chance's band to perform. It seemed obvious that Georgina and Chance didn't plan to leave any time soon, and Laura had soon learned not to leave money around the house. She'd also locked up her jewelry and anything else of value after a few things mysteriously disappeared.

She studied her sister now, trying to decide what to say about yet another loan. "I think it might be a good idea if you or Chance, or both of you, got a part-time job to make a little money for your expenses."

Georgina tossed her head. "You don't need to be mean just because we're having a slow spot. And we need our time between jobs right now to work on new songs. We've written several good ones together. I thought you'd be happy to help us with our work and our dream." Her eyes narrowed. "It's not as though you're going after any dreams of your own to understand. You've always just worked at the shop with Daddy, and then he left it to you. Chance says that really wasn't fair. It should have come to both of us, like the house."

"Daddy knew you'd push to sell it."

"So? Wouldn't that have been right? You could have gotten a job in any little upholstery shop in any Podunk town around Mississippi or anywhere else. I mean it's only a small-town store, Laura. You're too sentimental about things."

"It's our family business and I love it," she answered.

"Well, fine. But you can give me a little help with my business. You're my only sister. I'd do it for you if you asked me. If you'd ever had any kind of real dream, I would have helped you to achieve it, too. Chance says you don't really believe in us."

The words hurt, and Laura knew they were partially true. She had her doubts about Chance and she worried about the path and the dreams he fed to Georgina. What should she do?

Glancing at the clock, she said, "I need to head to the shop." She picked up her purse from the chair nearby and opened her billfold, peeling out several twenties. "I have a hundred dollars you can have for your weekend. I hope everything goes well."

"Thanks," Georgina said, smiling now and adding graciously. "I'll clean up the kitchen."

At the shop later, Laura sat at her desk, looking through her mail while indulging in a bout of tears. She tried to wipe them away as Lillian Greeley let herself into the store.

"Good morning. It's cold as all-get-out in Mississippi today, isn't it?" She walked into Laura's office. "Bobby dropped me off and said to tell you he's going to deliver that sofa and chair we finished to the Beckers before he starts his day."

She paused catching sight of Laura's face. "Bless your heart. It's a rare thing to see you cry. What's the matter? Did you get another of those letters reminding you of when we have to get out of this building here?"

Relieved at Lillian's question, Georgina answered, "Yes, I did get another reminder."

"It sure was a shock to us, and to everyone else around here, when the government came in and held those hearings to let us know they were taking ten buildings in that imminent domain thing to widen the highway that runs through town. It was a heartache at first to hear it. I remember a lot of people tried to fight it, but there's not much you can do about a thing like that."

Lillian sat down in the chair across from Laura's desk. "But honey, we've known this was coming for almost two years now. And, blessedly, they're giving you more than fair price for this old building your family has owned all these years. You can easily buy another one with that amount and have money besides to put away."

She sipped on the coffee she'd brought into the store with her. "I know you've been looking around for another location and talking to Bobby and me about it. Didn't you find a building over on Third Street you feel good about, the one that used to be a ballroom dance studio? You said it had a big back room we can easily convert for our upholstery shop, a front office and entry area, storage in the back and a rear entrance and parking places to keep our delivery truck. I thought you'd settled your mind to it."

Laura sniffed and blew her nose on a tissue. "I guess it will be all right for the shop, but it's not the same."

"Well, it might not be the Shop on The Corner anymore, especially with the new location settled between two buildings like it is, but it's a nice enough place."

"I know." Laura looked down at the letters in front of her. "I also know I need to talk to the realtor to start finalizing the sale. This last letter said that the money will be released Monday and then I'll only have thirty to sixty days to vacate."

"It won't take us more than a few days to pack up and move, and like they've told you, there will be moving and relocation money, too. You've known worse heartaches than this, honey, losing your parents young and then having all this trouble with your sister. Are she and that deadbeat boyfriend she's hooked up with still staying at your house?"

Laura felt the tears well again.

"Those tears tell me yes, and it's my guess she's talked you out of more money again, acted nasty, and caused you more heartache.

Has she?"

"Yes. They're going out of town for another long weekend to play at some club in Memphis and she wanted to borrow more money for their expenses. They have another gig next month, too, and I'm sure she'll be hitting me up for more money then."

Lillian put her hands on her hips, provoked. "Did you suggest to her that they both need to get themselves a real job? It's awful how they showed up, acting like they wanted to spend Christmas with you, making you feel loved and cared for, and then stayed on and on, showing they really only wanted to use you. I shouldn't say it but I really hate them for that."

She got up to pour herself more coffee from the machine in the corner.

Laura sighed. "I'm worried that if Georgina finds out they're taking the shop and that I'm getting money for the building and money to cover a move, that she will want a big part of it. She and Chance have said a number of times they think it was wrong that Daddy left me the shop rather than leaving it to both of us."

Lillian came to sit back down with her coffee. "You've been working here and learning this business since you were a girl. Your daddy, Mason O'Dell, knew you'd continue the shop he started, and he knew Georgina would sell it out from under you if he left it to you both. So he left her money and part ownership in the family house. And she made you put your family home on the market as soon as you'd buried Mason next to his sweet wife Carolyn, not even caring she left you homeless at a hard time. Honestly, your mother is probably turning over in her grave, and Mason, too, to see all that girl is putting you through. Mason told us once he felt glad sometimes Carolyn hadn't lived to see what a mess Georgina was making of her life. Carolyn was so proud of that girl, of her talent, her scholarship. I well remember she carried that girl from state to state for years to pageants, contests, and other performances, proud as a peacock of her."

"I remember that, too. Georgina inherited all of Mother's musical gifts and her pretty blond looks. It was natural Mother would be excited to help her develop her talents."

Lillian crossed her arms. "There were times she spoiled the girl, too—probably part of the problem now. I watched Georgina grow up, if you remember. She was pretty and talented, for sure, but stuck on herself. She liked the whole wide world swirling around her. You know it's true, and you were always so sweet and nice about it."

"I wasn't jealous of her."

"No, and everyone could see that. You had your own life, your own interests, and you loved working here at the shop from the time you could toddle around." Lillian laughed. "I always feel like a second mother to you, since I got to spend so much time with you growing up. I helped to teach you to sew, to upholster—Bobby did, too—and your father was so proud at how gifted you were with every aspect of the business. You gained more expertise, too, getting your degree at the community college and learning all those good computer skills."

Laura looked around her. "It just seems so sad to me that our building will be torn down, and that the business will have to move. Nothing is the same anymore."

Lillian grew quiet for a moment. "There's nothing that says you can't make a change in your life about now either. Maybe that would be good for you." She hesitated. "Actually, Bobby and I have been thinking about retiring from full-time work for some time but we didn't want to leave you on your own after your daddy passed. Anyway, I don't want you thinking for a minute you need to be staying here in Amory, Mississippi, taking care of us."

She paused and turned to Laura with a little smirk. "You know, I just got a picture in my mind of how fun it would be if you bought yourself a little shop far away from here in another city and simply slipped off and left your sister and her freeloading partner behind one weekend—with no forwarding address—while she was off spending your money on one of her little trips."

Laura looked up, shocked. "Where would I go?"

"Honey, the world's full of lots more small towns than Amory,

Mississippi. If I was you, young and unencumbered, I'd look around at pretty tourist towns, down at the coast or over in the mountains of Georgia, Tennessee, or North Carolina. I'd seek out an adventure. Years ago, Bobby and I saw some real nice places camping on our vacations. I'd often picture myself living in some of those spots, imagining a brand new life. But we had the kids and the farm outside of town, plus a lot of family here."

She leaned forward. "Why don't you get on that computer of yours and start looking at little retail sites in small towns around the south? Places that look pretty to you when you Google them. See what you can find."

Lucille crossed her legs. "Those government people said they'd pay to help you relocate to wherever you needed to go. Maybe it ought to be somewhere else besides Amory, Mississippi. Maybe that's why you can't settle your heart into moving over to the building on Third Street. You know, God sometimes speaks to us with a restlessness when we need to think about a move. A mother eagle will start pulling the feathers out of the nest under her young when she wants them to fly, letting those thorns underneath prick them when the soft down is pulled away."

"You're sweet to care so much about me, Lillian."

She grinned. "Honey, if you move somewhere pretty, Bobby and I can take us a nice trip to come to see you."

Laura laughed. "We both need to get to work now. I have that set of dining room chairs to reupholster for Bernice Harvey and you have that wing chair to work on."

"You're right." Lillian glanced at her watch. "It's time to open the shop, too." She stood and then hesitated. "I really do think you ought to look around for other possible properties this weekend before you sign on buying the new building in Amory. Will you promise me you'll just look? It might be right fun for you anyway. I know the lease on your house has to be re-signed soon, too, although I forget the date."

"The lease on the house is up at the end of April."

"Well, you see how the timing of everything is kind of lining up,

Laura? After you finish your chairs today, you head over to sit on that bench by your parents' graves and pray over this. See if the good Lord doesn't talk to you." She grinned at Laura again. "You tell him I'm sorry, too, over how delighted I felt to imagine your sister coming home to a house about empty and her gravy-train meal ticket cut off."

"Maybe she and Chance will move on soon."

"And maybe pigs might fly." Lillian snorted.

With a little pushing from Lillian and Bobby at noon, Laura left early for the day. She drove by the building on Third Street she'd been considering for the shop. She parked to walk around it. It would work and be an adequate location, but for some reason she simply felt discontent with it. Remembering Lillian's advice to pray, she went to the big Methodist church where she'd grown up instead, slipping inside to sit on a back pew.

How many times had she sat in this church on Sundays with her father, listening to her mother play the piano for the service, watching Georgina sing in the choir and perform solos, both of them so musically gifted. Georgina was wrong that Laura hadn't been proud of her—and of her mother. She had been, but she'd also been proud of her father, of his solid goodness, his giftedness with his hands, his kindness to all he served in his business. She knew she'd been a Daddy's Girl just as Georgina had been her mother's favorite. Not that she and Georgina hadn't been well loved by both their parents. But similarities breed a certain affinity, even between kin.

She closed her eyes. "Lord, I've got a real situation here in my life I could use Your help with. I need to vacate the Shop On The Corner that was my dad's business and I could use some advice about what to do next. I also need help knowing what to do about my sister. It's hard to realize your own sister would take, and take some more, and even steal from you, caring so little for you and being so unkind. She and Chance Richardson both. It's hard not to let it hurt."

Trying to think what else to pray, she reached down to pick up an old Sunday bulletin off the floor. Under the pretty picture on the front were the words: "Ask and it shall be given you; seek, and ye shall find; knock, and it shall be opened unto you."

She smiled. "I guess if that's some quick advice from You that it wouldn't do any harm to seek and knock a little. I'm the steady, homebody sort that doesn't like to make changes, but I'll try to heed Lillian's and Your counsel and look around some."

She headed home then to fix a sandwich for lunch and to do a little housecleaning. Georgina and Chance kept their space in the basement always in a mess, and Laura tried to tidy it up whenever they were gone.

The house she rented, only a few blocks from the shop, was small with only a kitchen, dining room, living room, one bedroom, and a bath on the main floor. Downstairs was a partially finished basement with a laundry-bath combination and an open room she'd used as a work area before Georgina and Chance came. When she knew earlier that they planned to come for Christmas, she'd worked to fix up the room, bought a nice rug and a few pieces of furniture to create a bedroom at one end of the downstairs space. Now the entire area was a mess—clothes strewn everywhere, many of them her clothes that Georgina had borrowed without asking. Old pizza boxes and cola cans sat here and there and papers, with the scribblings of song lyrics on them, lay scattered about. The bathroom was nasty again and Laura was alarmed to find random bottles of pills lying around and a syringe in the trash. How had her sister come to this? Their mother had always seen to it that they cleaned their rooms and helped with chores around the house. How could Georgina have changed so much?

"It would serve her right if I did move off," Laura said out loud in a huff.

She looked around, considering the idea for the first time. "I could leave the bed and furnishings here for them, towels, sheets, and a few dishes, and I could bring the sofa and chairs in the shop's entry to put in the living area upstairs. If they wanted to renew the lease and stay on they could. Or they could take what I've left to a new place. It would be more than they deserve."

Laura gathered up her own clothes she'd found while cleaning, a pair of slacks and a blouse, a pink sweater, and her robe. She took them back upstairs with her. Then she sat down with her laptop at the dining room table and began to search Internet sites for "retail businesses for sale in small southern towns." She soon narrowed her search to retail shops in specific states like Georgia, Tennessee, and the Carolinas. She liked Lillian's idea of living near the mountains, and she remembered a happy vacation she, her mother, dad, and Georgina took there one summer.

She followed up on any downtown shops that took her fancy, calling the realty company to get particulars, reading about the town if she found the property interesting. That night, well into her search and enjoying herself, she called Lillian to ask if she and Bobby could handle the shop tomorrow on their own so she could look more. Over coffee the next morning she settled in again.

When she called Lillian to check on the shop later, she said, "I admit it's been fun looking at stores. I'm finding some really cute little towns and some nice properties—one in Dahlonega, Georgia, I like, one in Greenville, South Carolina, and another in Maryville, Tennessee. Thanks for pushing me to at least look around. Even if I stay here, I'm going to go visit some of these places some day on vacation."

"Look at some of the small towns in Western North Carolina, too. It's pretty there."

"I'll do that," Laura promised, and a short time later she located possibilities in Boone, Sylva, and Waynesville. One shop in Waynesville especially appealed to her, situated right on Main Street downtown with cute awnings over the door.

She called the realty number and was connected with the agent Becky Ray.

"That store is a nice space," Becky told her. "It's been a craft shop, and our main street in downtown gets heavy local and tourist traffic. What sort of business do you hope to start in Waynesville?"

"I own a family upholstery business I need to relocate, and I decided to consider looking at other small towns and possibly moving."

"That's interesting. I have another property you might want to consider, too," she said with an amused laugh. "It actually is an upholstery business—or it was until two years ago when the owner, Benton Renfree, died. He had no family and his only sister, who lives in an assisted living facility in California, just wants the property sold. It might be perfect for you. Mr. Renfree was well known here in Waynesville and he ran a prosperous business for many years. Would you like me to send the specs on it and some photos?"

"Is the building downtown like the other property?" Laura asked.

"Yes, it is. It's a block off the main street right on the corner of Miller and Montgomery streets."

Laura put a hand to her heart. "It's on the corner?" she asked, saying the words slowly.

"Yes, and it's a cute place with entrances on both Miller and Montgomery and with blue awnings over the doorways."

"I love the awnings so many of the businesses in Waynesville have."

"Waynesville is a great place to live and work, but I'm probably prejudiced since I've lived here all my life." Becky paused. "Another thing you might like, since you mentioned you were single, is that there is a full apartment above the shop. It's part of the building property for sale and Mr. Renfree lived there. Actually, the bulk of Renfree's furniture is still in the apartment and most of the upholstery equipment, fabric, machinery, and other furnishings are still in the shop. We were waiting to see if a new owner wanted to negotiate for the furnishings or if we should sell them through an auction company. Would you like me to send interior photos, too?"

"I would," Laura replied. She laughed then. "This seems like a lot of coincidences to me, Becky. Our family upholstery business here in Mississippi is called the Shop on the Corner."

Becky laughed. "Well, if you like the business and decide to buy it, bring your sign. I'm sure we can get someone to hang it up for you right where the Renfree's sign is now."

Less than an hour later Laura was poring through photos of Renfree's Upholstery Shop in Waynesville and looking through the lovely photos of Benton Renfree's apartment above the store. It seemed almost too perfect to be true. The price, in comparison to many retail properties she'd looked at, was also surprisingly reasonable.

She called Lillian a little later to tell her about it.

"Oh, honey, I know where that little town is," Lillian said with enthusiasm. "It really does seem like a sign to me that the business location was already an upholstery shop, and on a corner, and that you'd have a nice place to live right above it. Pack up your computer and bring it over here and let me and Bobby look at everything with you. I'm getting excited just thinking about it."

It only took Laura fifteen minutes to pack up everything and get to the store. Bobby and Lillian were soon exclaiming enthusiastically over everything they saw. While Lillian helped a customer a short time later, Bobby helped her evaluate the equipment, think about what the store in Waynesville already had, and what she might need to take from the Amory shop.

"You'll be wanting a lot of your own things you're comfortable with from our store here, no matter if this new place has replicates." He tapped a few pictures as he spoke. "Upholsterers are artisans and we get used to and comfortable with our own tools and equipment. Our own ways and methods we've learned."

Her eyes filled with tears, looking at his kind face. "What will I do without you two?"

"You'll be fine," he said, pushing his glasses up over his nose. "There are always folks around who can do a little upholstery work. If they don't know all they should at first, you can teach them."

Lillian came back to join them. "Think of it as an adventure, Laura." She sat down and began to scroll through the pictures again. "Look what a pretty place this is, too. A lot nicer than the shop here, no offense intended."

"It is a little more posh," Laura agreed. "So is the apartment compared with my little rental house."

"So will you do it?" Lillian asked, her eyes bright.

Laura looked between them, realizing for one of the first times their ages, seeing their white hair and other signs she'd seldom noticed. "If I decide to do this, what will you two do?"

Bobby turned from the club chair he'd been working on. "I've got an extra garage out at the farm, the perfect size for a small business for the two of us. If you'll let me negotiate for some of the equipment, tools, and such you won't need to move, I'm thinking Lillian and I might open a part-time business of our own. We can keep in touch with the old customer base and do jobs as we want to."

"We have been talking about it," Lillian admitted. "But as long as O'Dell's Shop on the Corner was here we wouldn't have wanted to compete or to leave you."

Laura looked around the store. "If I say yes, the realtor, Becky Ray, I've been working with in Waynesville, says that with a cash sale I can close and move in by the first of March—unless we run into any difficulties. Would that be too quick for you two? I can delay the move a little more if that would be better. But I need to vacate by the end of March at the 60 days date they set."

"We'll help you with everything," Bobby said, reaching over to give her a hug. "We'll miss you for sure though."

She bit her lip. "Do you think Daddy would have minded if I move?"

Bobby shook his head. "No, not with all that's happened and with the old place being torn down. Your dad would have felt like you—that it wouldn't be the same locating O'Dell's someplace else. I agree with Lillian, too, that it might be a really happy thing for you to get away and start fresh. You've had one too many losses here, carried more responsibility than a young girl ought to."

"Well?" asked Lillian, leaning forward. "What do you think?"

Laura frowned then. "I have one more problem I need your help with. Because of Georgina and my problems with her and Chance, I want to move without her knowing where I've gone."

She dropped her gaze to her lap. "She's been borrowing money from me for a long time even before she even showed up at the house near Christmas. I don't know how she blew through all her inheritance and the money from the sale of the house as quickly as she did, but I do know from papers I accidentally saw in their trash that they were evicted from their apartment in Nashville. That's why they came to me, not from fondness or wanting to spend a holiday with me like Georgina said. I think they're both doing drugs of some kind, too, and I think they might follow me or keep contacting me for money if they know where I move. I hate to say it, but I think I need to sort of disappear from them for a time."

"We'll keep as quiet as two little mice about where you've moved," Lillian assured her. "We'll act like we're as surprised as her, not sure where you even moved off to."

"If you want to keep it quiet where you're moving, you'll need to tell as few people as possible where you're going for a time," Bobby said. "That could be hard for you. I'm sure the first thing your sister will do is quiz your landlord, your friends, your neighbors, your minister, and any members in your mama's or your daddy's family."

She frowned. "I hadn't thought of that."

"If you're a little quiet with this move and tell only a few people you can trust where you're going and why you don't want your sister to learn of it, I'd say she'll move on from Amory pretty quickly. You'll need to pay out your house lease before you leave. That will give her and Chance two months to sort themselves out and figure out where they want to go next. My guess is once a little time has passed you can contact old friends and family more safely. But she'll be mad at first and looking for you."

"I know that." Laura sighed. "But she would have gotten mad, anyway, when she realized I got money for the business and didn't give her what she and Chance would decide is her due."

Bobby nodded. "I'd say you're right about that, and from what I know about folks that start having problems with drugs, it changes them. The love of drugs starts to mean more to them than the love of others, even their own family, and they can soon start to justify all sorts of wrong ways to satisfy their cravings."

"It worries me for Georgina," Laura said. "Even for Chance."

Bobby put a hand on one hip. "Well maybe they'll have a Come-to-Jesus moment and get themselves straightened out. Those ways usually lead only further and further downhill. They might decide to look up after a while. It happens."

"We'll pray for that," Lillian said. "Deep down Georgina has been raised right. I remember when she gave her life to the Lord as a girl and joined the church. I don't know much about Chance's background, but I know about Georgina's. Your mother and dad raised her with good morals. I'm hoping she'll find her way back."

Laura sat thinking for a moment, looking through the photos on her computer again. "Well, I think I've made up my mind," she said with resolution. "I'm going to do it. I'm going buy this new Shop on the Corner and move to Waynesville, North Carolina. It will be a new life and a new start."

CHAPTER 2

Glad to see warmer weather with March finally here, Mitchell Quinlan whistled on Monday morning as he worked getting ready for the weekly staff meeting. The employees at Quinlan Staffing Services always met on Mondays at eight before the business opened at nine. It was their traditional time to talk out problems and ideas, share updates, and go over the week ahead. Sometime in the past—Mitchell couldn't remember exactly when—his father started bringing in breakfast to the meetings.

"It's a way to give back to a good staff," he once said.

Mitchell's mother lifted an eyebrow at his words. "It's also an excuse for you to cook and make that breakfast casserole you love," she'd said with a smile. "Besides I believe sharing a real breakfast is healthier than filling up on junky donuts or fried pies."

As a boy, Mitchell had often watched his dad put together his breakfast casserole of eggs, sausage, hash browns, and cheese on Sunday nights. Now, with his father gone, he made the casserole on Sunday evenings and thought of his dad every time he did.

His heart still hurt they'd lost his dad seven years ago. Gosh, Mitchell had only been twenty-three, fresh out of college. Even though he'd worked in the business since high school years, it was a huge responsibility to take over Quinlan's at such a young age. But life was what it was and with support and help from his staff he'd managed and Quinlan's was as strong as ever. He thanked God for that. He'd always wanted to take over Quinlan's one day, and expected to, but not quite so soon.

"Thinking of you, Dad," he said out loud as he carried the casserole downstairs to the break room at the back of the Quinlan offices. The staffing business had operated in this building the family owned since 1946, when his grandfather started it not long after the end of World War II.

Mitchell glanced around the break room as he sat the casserole on the counter. He'd started coffee earlier, put a bowl of fruit on the counter, pulled mugs from the shelf, put out plastic plates, silverware, and napkins. Some Mondays he also made biscuits, not the real thing but the frozen ones he could bake with the casserole, but Rosemarie had called last night to say she wanted to bring homemade muffins today. She or Norma often did that, and sometimes Kent stopped by the Buttered Biscuit or the Orchard Coffee Shop to pick up bakery items. All the staff loved their Monday breakfasts.

With everything ready, Mitchell walked up the hallway now flicking on lights along the way. The Quinlan building was a long, narrow one tucked between several other businesses on Miller Street. Miller was a short downtown road off Main Street with tree-lined sidewalks, benches, and flowers in spring. Over the Quinlan doorway hung a red awning with the store's name, and the year it was established, on it. Immediately inside was a welcoming entry area where Rosemarie Fowler greeted everyone with warmth and skill. Off the hallway behind the entry on the right were bathrooms, a long testing room, and Norma Burdett's office, at the end of the hall. On the left, were the break room at the far back, an employee bathroom, and Kent Atkinson and Mitchell's offices nearer the front.

In a small-town business, like Quinlan's, the four of them could handle the staffing services for the area, helping employers fill their needs for temporary, temp-to-hire, and full-time employees.

"Good morning," he heard Rosemarie call as she let herself in the back door this morning. "We're getting nicer weather with March settling in."

"Hi, Rosemarie." Mitchell walked back down the hall to join her.

"I saw some bulbs trying to peek up in my yard," she added, putting a plastic container piled full of hot muffins on the counter.

Norma and Kent came in almost right behind her. Kent paused to lock the door while Norma walked into her office to drop a pile of papers on her desk before coming back to join them.

"I saw bulbs sprouting in those front flower beds along the sidewalk on Friday, too," Norma added. "It sure is nice to see spring again."

With familiar ease, they each helped themselves to a plate of breakfast food, poured coffee and juice, and settled at the table, catching up on odds and ends of news as they started their breakfast. Rosemarie, red-haired with glasses and the chattiest of the three, had been with Quinlan's for fifteen years. She'd studied nursing originally, worked in hospital staffing, and brought that expertise to the business, handling all the medical and healthcare placements as well as running the front office. Norma, grey-haired with a grandma look and a no-nonsense business-like manner, had been at Quinlan's twenty years. She handled all the books, payroll, helped with finance and accounting placements and supervised much of the company testing.

Kent, the newest on their team, had worked at Quinlan's eight years now, replacing Raymond Sellers when he retired. Dark-haired with black glasses and a quiet demeanor, Kent had grown up here in Waynesville. After finishing college and working for a year or two out of state in a big city company in computer graphics, he came back home to work at Quinlan's, bringing his technical skills to the business. Like Raymond before him, Kent handled all the trade, industrial, and technical placements, while Mitchell took care of the retail, sales, office, and professional ones. They each had their areas of expertise, but pitched in to help each other according to work demand. Mitchell's dad had been skillful in selecting the right kinds of employees for his business, just as he'd always used the same skill for placements in the local community.

When Kent finished eating he said, "Did ya'll see the news this morning about the flag being stolen from in front of the courthouse?" He grinned. "I had to drive by to see the sight before I came to work and before they had time to hoist down the Jolly Roger pirate flag some prankster put up."

Mitchell laughed despite himself. "You're kidding."

"No and I took pictures, too." He pulled out his cell phone to locate the photos, passing his phone around.

Rosemarie put a hand on one hip. "That is so disrespectful. Whoever would do that?"

"Some folks with too much time on their hands or with a grudge." Norma frowned at the photos. "How did they get away with this right in front of the city courthouse?"

"It happened in the middle of the night, from what I heard on the news," Kent added. "Nobody saw anything or heard anything. But the big American flag is a loss to the city. I heard the incident made the mayor, the aldermen, and everyone mad, too."

Glancing at the big clock on the break room wall, Mitchell said, "I guess we'd better go over a few business items before we need to open." He paused, looking down at the notes on his iPad. "With spring coming, tourism will pick up. That may put demand on a number of the businesses we work with and give us opportunities to pick up new clients, too. Perhaps each of us can take time from the office to go out in the field to check in with employers we work with and find potential new ones. At Quinlan you know we've always tried to make in-person visits whenever we can. A face with a name makes a memory and it sets us apart from competitors."

"We can alternate outside visits like we've done in past on days that are slower," Norma added. "Swap out answering incoming calls for each other."

They talked about different clients they worked with then, problems they'd been having with some, positive reports on placements with others.

Norma suggested a new Aptitude Test she wanted to order and try, and then added, "I know we use the Harver personality questionnaire to reveal some strengths about personality to our employers. They like quantifiable results along with our own opinions about applicants, but I wanted to add that using the Myers-Briggs self-scoring tests in the office has really been a good idea, too."

"It has," Rosemarie put in. "I think the best result of using those tests is in helping the applicants understand their own strengths and weaknesses more clearly. Several told me the test gave them words to better describe themselves in interview situations."

"I like that we picked up a number of the actual Kiersey and Tieger books about the Myers-Briggs types that our clients can sit and read through after taking the test, too," Kent said. "The Kiersey book details all the temperament types in a helpful, easy-to-understand way but the Tieger goes further, talking about the kinds of careers best suited to each type. A lot of the people I work with have given me positive feedback about both."

"I've heard comments like that, too," Mitchell confirmed. "Several of our larger employers use the Myers-Briggs in their business as well to help employees get along better. They also use them in the hiring process to decide between candidates. They really like that we're administering the tests here, even in a more informal way."

"Some of our applicants grumble at having to take tests to identify either personality or cognitive skills. They feel it's invasive of their privacy. Some even grumble at having to take basic skills tests," Norma shook her head. "They think we ought to simply take their word for typing and keyboard, data entry or spreadsheet skills."

"I hear you," Kent added. "I get complaints about that, too. They think their word and their resumes should be enough for us or for any employer. A number of my big industrial companies ask me to give basic reading comprehension and writing tests now, too. Many of my applicants really grumble about those."

"None of them like having to get a drug test, either." Rosemarie laughed. "Polly Overland about chewed me out over that the other day. She said, 'I've lived in this town all my life and gone to church with you. You ought to know I don't need a drug test. I resent you even asking me to drive across town to get one.'"

Norma laughed, too. "It takes time to try to calm some folks down about the tests we ask them to take."

"Well, remember to explain in a low key, upbeat way that the employers expect us to administer the tests before they will interview potential applicants," Mitchell added. "Remind them, too, that if they went directly to the employers they'd eventually have to take the same tests there. Always put a positive spin on it all. Let them know the tests, and all our talks and visits in the office, allow us to get to know them better and to help them gain access to good employers and jobs they probably wouldn't find on their own." He grinned. "I always tell them we're like matchmakers, helping to match them to a job they'll really like and to an employer that will really like them."

They went over other issues then about payroll changes, some new forms required, and appointments set for the week. After an initial interview at an applicant's first visit, background checks were conducted, skills examined from an employee's application and resume, and results from drug tests received. If all checked out well, a second interview was set and needed tests scheduled to get the applicant ready for outside employer interviews. It always took longer than applicants realized or wanted, most eager to start work immediately, needing the work and the income.

After the Quinlan staff finished their meeting they cleaned up the break room and then headed to work. Mondays were almost always busy at Quinlan's.

Mitchell took calls, answered emails, and completed several interviews over the morning. Rosemarie stuck her head into his office at about noon. "Nolan and Rita Harbeck are here, hoping to see you for a minute. Do you have time to talk to them?"

"Sure," he said. "Send them back. I have a few minutes before I take lunch."

He stood to welcome the Harbecks, a local couple he'd known since he was a kid. Nolan, an affable, talented man in his sixties now, picked banjo in a group called The Waynesville Boys. His wife Rita, dark-haired and friendly with a million-dollar smile, often sang with the group and worked in all sorts of philanthropic organizations around the city and with many of Waynesville's festivals. Mitchell liked them both.

"Hey," he said, shaking hands with both warmly. "What brings you by to see me?" He gestured to the chairs across from his desk and they all sat down.

Nolan leaned forward. "We learned today through Becky Ray at Re/Max that someone's bought Renfree's Upholstery across the street. You know we both worked there with Bennett Renfree for almost twenty years, ever since I got out of the service. I started right after Bennett opened his place. I'd worked with my dad doing upholstery on the side back in Tennessee so I knew the work. I began teaching Rita, since she was good with a needle and could sew. She started doing part-time jobs at home while our boys were small and then came to work full-time, too, when they started school. Since Bennett died two years ago and the upholstery shop closed, we've been trying to keep up some work with old clients, but with the shop opening back up again, most of those folks will probably take their business to the store again."

Rita joined the conversation. "We walked by the store just now. You know it's right across the street from your place on the corner. Becky Ray told us a woman bought the store who had owned an upholstery store in another state. We couldn't get much more out of Becky, but we'd love to get our old jobs back. Since you know us as well as you do, we were hoping you'd go pitch us to the new owner. We can fill out applications and all with you, give you references galore, even bring you photos of work we've done."

"See here's the thing," Nolan put in. "We're in our sixties now. A lot of folks think you're over the hill then, ought to be thinking about retiring. But Rita and I are feeling stronger and better than ever at this age. You know we aren't letting any grass grow under our feet and we're not the rocking chair types either. But this woman, she might need someone besides us telling her that. Putting in a good word about how active, strong, and healthy we both are."

Nolan hesitated. "Age discrimination is a big thing in the

world today although folks don't talk about it. When I was a kid, employers just told people, 'We think you're too old; we want someone younger.' Today with all the new legal-flegal out there, employers won't say that out right. They'll say someone else was more suitable or more qualified. We've seen it happen with a lot of our friends, and it's happened to us."

"I hear you," Mitchell said, steepling his fingers. "I deal with it a lot."

"Will you help us?" Nolan asked. "Go scope this woman out, see what you think of her and if you think we'll like her and if she'll like us? We really enjoyed working with Bennett all those years and we got along well with him, even if he was a little sweet—if you know what I mean. We didn't care about that. He was good and gifted. He had an innate sense for what people needed and wanted for their upholstery work, what would suit them best. He found great fabrics to keep on hand in the store, always bought good equipment to work with. He was neat as a pin, too—almost picky neat—in the store and in his apartment upstairs."

"His apartment sure was decorated real pretty," Rita interrupted. "Did you ever see it?"

"Yeah, I did a number of times," Mitchell replied." It was a nice place—a lot of red in the décor, not the usual man's choice in color or style."

"We've really missed our work at the shop," Rita put in, shaking her head. "It's happy and satisfying work for us. We both like busy hands and we like seeing an old furniture piece come to new life after we work on it."

"We thought about just walking in to see this new woman, but decided it would be better to work it through you." Nolan ran a hand over his short beard. "She might have brought her own people. We don't know, but I think she's come here to Waynesville on her own. The folks at the Sweet Onion restaurant said she's stopped over to eat a time or two with them, always by herself. They said she's sorting, cleaning out the place, working to get it ready to open. If she's on her own, it won't take her long to see she'll need help. Renfree's was always busy. If she does good work, treats people fair and right, and is friendly and reliable like Bennett was, she'll do well here."

Rita smiled. "She's calling the place Shop On The Corner. She took down the old Renfree's sign and put up a new one on the corner this morning. Becky said she's going to live above the shop like Bennett did."

"I'll see what I can do," Mitchell told them. "Tell Rosemarie to give you the paperwork you need and leave me all your references. Send Rosemarie some photos of some of your work by email so she can print them out, too."

Nolan smiled and stood. "Thank you, Mitchell. I don't mean to be rushing you, and I know you're busy, but go put in a word real soon that we'd like to come back to the shop. I don't want anyone else getting the edge on us."

Mitchell nodded, seeing them both out. Nolan Harbeck's father and Mitchell's dad had been good friends, and his dad had loved Nolan's music. It should be an easy task to go talk to the new owner and make a recommendation that she consider rehiring the couple who'd worked for Bennett. It was sensible to at least weigh the idea. Everyone knew the Harbecks and liked them.

Later when Mitchell walked two doors down to the Sweet Onion restaurant to get a catfish sandwich for lunch, he looked across the street. He could see the new sign hanging near the corner of the building. It hadn't been there yesterday, and he could see other work going on now that he studied the storefront more closely.

Doormats had been put out at both entrances again, potted trees beside the doors, the old black wrought iron tables and chairs set back out on the sidewalk, the awnings and windows cleaned. Someone was settling in to do business. He needed to meet the new owner, too. Rosemarie jokingly called Mitchell "Waynesville's Welcome Man" since he made it a practice to call on any new business in town. It was a long-standing Quinlan business practice and Mitchell found it paid off. People still appreciated common courtesy.

Closing the office and locking the front door later, Mitchell looked across the road to see lights on at the upholstery store—both upstairs and downstairs. The owner was working late. He'd had a chance to look through the Harbeck's paperwork. Maybe he'd walk over and say hello, offer a welcome to the neighborhood, and drop a hint that Nolan and Rita would like to come back to work. If he liked the new owner, of course. He wouldn't want to see Nolan and Rita get into a job situation that would be unhappy for them.

He ran some copies of the Harbecks' paperwork, references, and work photos, folded them into an envelope and then went upstairs to find one of the store's Welcome to Waynesville boxes. His mother, an artist, had painted the design they used on the cover of all the white boxes. Inside were a few thoughtful gift items—a Waynesville mug, a candle, a jar of local honey, some of his mother's gift cards, a jar of mixed nuts, a few tourist brochures and wrapped candies. It was the thoughtfulness aspect people liked and remembered more than what was in the box.

His mind made up now, Mitchell zipped upstairs above the store to his apartment. He couldn't remember a time there hadn't been a family apartment above Quinlan's two-story building. His grandfather Eldridge and his wife, Viola, had lived there for a short time, when they first opened the business, before they bought their two-storied home on East Street where Viola, or Nannie V to him, still lived. At the top of the stairs were also storage rooms, several closets, two extra offices—one Mitchell had converted into a personal office—and the apartment looking out over the street with a large open living room, dining area, kitchen, big bedroom, and a bath.

From time to time over the years the family had rented out the small apartment or loaned it to someone going through a rough patch in life. But after finishing high school, Mitchell claimed the place for himself. He had shifted in and out of the place several times since. First, he'd moved back to live with his mom in their family home when his dad died. He stayed on—when he might have moved back—when his sister and her husband were killed in a traffic wreck, and when he and his mom took in Alise's children Mackenzie and Charlie.

Only when the kids started to school did Mitchell finally move back to the apartment again. Even now he constantly rotated between his place and the family home on Church Street not far away. His mom worked, like he did, and he needed to help out a lot with his niece and nephew. Mackenzie had only been four and Charlie two when they'd brought them home from Alise and Hudson's home in Asheville. It hurt his heart to remember that time. He and his mother had both leaned on each other through these years, not easy ones for either of them.

All the hard years since had left little opportunity for more than work, family, and occasional times with friends when he could cram it in. As Mitchell had learned, for some people life simply created situations that thrust them into responsibility and adulthood early. He was definitely one of those.

With the weather nice now and the worst of winter past, Mitchell decided he'd walk to Bocelli's for pizza for supper after he stopped to drop off his welcome box at the upholstery shop. Maybe he'd run into someone he knew there, hang out for a little while. With that in mind, Mitchell cleaned up, pulled a sweater on over his shirt, and spritzed some cologne on for good measure. Not a fancy sort of guy, he liked a simple citrus-musk with a hint of lime to it. It worked good with his skin. Colognes were like that; some worked for you, some didn't.

Throwing on a lightweight jacket, he stuffed the employment envelope in a deep pocket of his coat, picked up the welcome box, and headed downstairs and out to the street, locking the door behind him. It had been one of those warm days for March in the high fifties but the temperature was dropping now.

Crossing the street, Mitchell walked past the brick wall of Davis Furniture to the upholstery shop. He could still see the light on downstairs, so hopefully the new owner would come to the door if he rang the bell. A few minutes later he saw a woman walking through the vestibule, pausing to peer out the glass door. He waved a friendly greeting, smiling and holding up the welcome box.

She opened the door then, smiling back, her eyes meeting his, and he felt a jolt and a rush of physical attraction right down to the soles of his feet.

"Hi, can I help you?" she asked, her voice low and melodic.

He smiled, trying to collect himself enough to speak. Wow. He'd read once that it took only one second for attraction to hit you, but he hadn't felt a jolt like this since he fell for Patricia Smithwood at church camp one summer. How old had he been then? Fourteen?

Collecting himself and finding his voice again he said, "I'm Mitchell Quinlan. I own Quinlan Staffing Services across the street, the business with the red awning." He gestured behind him, smiling wider. "I stopped by to bring you one of our welcome boxes."

"Oh, how nice." Her eyes widened, and when she looked at him, he saw her move a hand toward her heart without seeming to notice, her breath quickening, too. Obviously, she felt a similar attraction. He could tell.

They stood there for a moment, taking each other in. She had rich brown hair drifting down over her shoulders, with a touch of red in it, much like his in color, and her eyes were a light honey brown with dark rims circling the irises. Her face and figure were soft and feminine, her makeup minimal, and she had the sort of wholesome, outdoor look he'd always liked.

She smiled at him again. "I'm Laura O'Dell and I'm so pleased to meet you."

He reached out a hand to shake hers, tucking the box under one arm. "Welcome to the neighborhood, Laura O'Dell."

As he took her hand the attraction kicked up an extra notch and he watched Laura's eyes widen, saw her bite her lip just slightly. She felt that kick, too.

"Would you like to come in?" she offered after a minute, withdrawing her hand. "It's a little cold standing here in the doorway." She hesitated. "I haven't opened the shop yet as you can see. Things are still topsy-turvy with boxes scattered around. But do come in for a minute if you'd like. You're the first person I've met here except for Becky Ray at the realty who helped me buy the store."

"Thanks." He stepped into the vestibule, following her around the corner and into the hallway, catching a waft of a light, subtle smell like fresh oranges in her wake.

"There's a table in the salesroom, where we can sit down for a minute while I open your box." She turned to flash that warm, sweet smile at him again, sending another rush over him. "This is really so nice of you. And look at all the colorful Waynesville storefronts painted on the cover of the box. I love the artwork."

"My mother painted the design and we had it printed on our boxes. She's a well-known regional artist here in Waynesville."

"Oh, my, she's really gifted," Laura said, gesturing to him to sit down at a table in a side room off the vestibule and pushing a few boxes to the side.

Mitchell hadn't been in the store's salesroom, where customers picked out upholstery fabrics, for a long time. Colorful rolls of fabric lay stacked in shelves reaching high toward the ceiling and hung on long spools along the wall. Piled on the other tables in the room were fabric books and multi-colored stacks of upholstery swatches.

He looked around with interest. "Everyone was glad to hear the store sold at last, and it's especially nice someone wants to reopen the place as an upholstery shop again."

"Thank you," she said. "Do you believe in fate?"

He almost grinned at her question with the attraction between them still rolling around the room in waves.

She leaned forward. "My family's upholstery shop in another town was scheduled to be demolished, along with other buildings and businesses, for the widening of a highway. I looked at other places but nothing felt the same, not like our old place. So on a whim I started searching for retail shops on the internet. After a day or so of looking, while talking with Becky Ray about a store for sale on Main Street in Waynesville, she told me she actually had an upholstery shop for sale on a corner nearby. It seemed like destiny the more I learned about Renfree's."

"The store has a good reputation, too."

"Becky told me that." Laura opened the welcome box and began to take out the items packed in shredded excelsior, oohing and aahing over each one, so gracious over small things. He liked that about her.

Mitchell watched her pull the items out of the box. It was a kick to him to be as physically attracted to her as he was, but of course they really didn't know each other yet. His life hadn't offered much time for dating over the last seven years, or even now. Most girls he'd started dating got quickly annoyed at how much time he spent with his niece and nephew.

"It's not like you're their father," Christy Gamble pronounced one day with a pout when he'd told her the children would be coming with them on a planned trip to Biltmore. "You really spend too much time with them. You need to think of yourself more." He realized then that was mostly all Christy Gamble thought of—herself—and he'd quietly stopped taking her out after that.

He refocused on Laura as she said, "I've never received a box like this. It really does make me feel welcome when a little lonely so far from home. Thank you. It was such a kind gesture."

Mitchell saw her glance at her watch, a signal for him to go.

"Listen," he said. "Have you had dinner yet? I was going to walk down to Bocelli's for a pizza after leaving here. Would you like to go with me?"

She hesitated, glancing down at her slacks and flicking some dust off her shirt. "Well, I don't know. I've been working."

"I'll wait if you want to run upstairs and pull a sweater on." He grinned. "That's what I did. You'll want a jacket, too. Even though the day was warm today, the temperature is dropping fast now that night is falling."

He watched the emotions shift across her face and could almost hear her thoughts wondering what to do.

"It's only dinner," he said quietly. "Bocelli's is a casual, family place. I work across the street from you and have grown up in Waynesville. I'm just a regular sort of guy. I don't carouse or drink. You don't need to worry about walking up the street or back with me to have dinner. Besides, I can answer a lot of questions you might have about Waynesville."

"All right," she said, blushing a little at his words. "Let me run upstairs and pull on a sweater, get my purse and coat."

While Mitchell waited on her, he thought back on the moments since Laura opened the door. He'd always been a people person, and reading people was an important part of his job. Like his dad, he'd always been good at it. too. But the sudden attraction he felt the minute he saw Laura O'Dell was something totally different. Surprising, a little mysterious, an instant thing that hit him like a jolt of electricity, switching his whole body on and swamping him. He'd read about physical attraction like this, heard about it, even watched it happen sometimes to others. But he'd seldom experienced it. It was a trip—that was for sure.

He shrugged at his thoughts and grinned to himself. Sometimes life just happens, he decided. It delivers you what it delivers you. He'd learned that often enough, and he knew you simply had to ride the wave of it, whatever came. That's what he'd do with Laura O'Dell. See what would happen, see how the attraction played out, and if it continued. He grinned again. Maybe he'd even enjoy the ride.

CHAPTER 3

Upstairs in her apartment, Laura had a moment to catch her breath while she took a soft pink sweater out of a drawer to pull on over her shirt. She whisked some upholstery fabric off her slacks with a lint roller, brushed her teeth and hair quickly, and dashed on a little pink lip gloss before slipping on her corduroy car coat and draping her purse over her shoulder. Moving quickly didn't keep her from wondering again if she should have said yes to having pizza with this new neighbor.

She glanced at her flushed face in the mirror. Gracious, he made her heart race and the blood rush to her head. She felt silly at her age experiencing such a sudden physical attraction for a man. It seemed like he'd felt it, too, from the way he looked at her, the way he hesitated when he reached to shake her hand and then held it a few minutes too long.

"Come on, Laura," she told herself in the mirror. "You're not a silly high school girl anymore. You may not have dated much or know a lot about guys, but you're almost twenty-six years old, a businesswoman, and a store owner. You can share a pizza with a new neighbor and get acquainted. His business is across the street, after all. You'll obviously run into him often, and you know you want to have good relationships with everyone in the community—like you've always had."

She started for the front door, still talking to herself. "Besides you don't even know this man. He might be married with several children. You might not even like him much once you get to know him. That spark you felt might fizzle out quickly. It certainly has often enough before."

Coming back into the showroom to find Mitchell, they exchanged a few pleasantries and then she followed him out the door, strolling along Miller Street and up Haywood for about a block to the restaurant. They didn't talk much while walking, but once she caught the sound of Mitchell whistling. Somehow the sound relaxed her, easing some of the tension from the air.

Near the restaurant, Mitchell stopped to talk to a man walking his dog, chatting in that easy, warm, and comfortable way of his. That confidence and friendly ease about him pleased her, and she liked how he took time to talk with the elderly man, even squatting down to pet and talk to his dog, knowing both their names, and introducing her in a casual way that didn't make her feel awkward.

Bocelli's was a picturesque place, tucked back from the street. The restaurant had a courtyard in front, with twinkling lights strung above wrought iron tables, ivy twining up the walls, and with outdoor statuary and potted plants adding ambience.

"It's nice to sit outside here in the courtyard when the weather is warm," Mitchell commented, opening the front door for her. "But it's a little chilly for it tonight."

Inside the entry area, Laura giggled at a cute chef statue, grinning and holding up a chalkboard that read: Welcome to Bocelli's! Enjoy!

"My niece and nephew love this little guy." He smiled at her. "They call him Gus and talk to him every time they come here."

"He is memorable," she replied.

When a waiter walked over to seat them, Mitchell pointed to a table by the window. The waiter seemed to know Mitchell and chatted freely to him as he seated them, bringing menus and iced tea after Mitchell got an okay from her on a beverage. Often a little shy in new situations, it was pleasant to be with someone so easy with themselves and with the world.

As she started looking over her menu, Mitchell said, "Bocelli's Best Pizza is my favorite one on the menu. It has a little of everything—pepperoni, beef, sausage, mushrooms, green peppers, onions, black olives and extra cheese. If that sounds good to you, I think a medium pizza will take care of both of us along with a couple of side salads."

"That sounds perfect. Pizza with everything is my favorite, too," she said, happy to let him help her with a dinner choice.

He chatted with the waiter again when he came back and waved at someone across the room as they left, comfortable and at ease.

"I'm glad you said yes to coming out to eat with me, Laura."

"It's nice to start to learn the neighborhood," she answered. "And it was nice of you to invite me."

"I did have a second ulterior motive for inviting you."

She knew her eyes widened.

"Now, don't let your mind go wandering in a twisted direction, Laura O'Dell. I told you I was a nice guy. Ask the waiter. I helped him get his job here."

The waiter brought their salads then. Teasing her, Mitchell asked the man to confirm his words, which he did with obvious enthusiasm.

"Feel better?" he asked with a twitch of a smile as the waiter left.

She picked up her fork to take a bite of her salad. "So what was your other motive?" she asked after a minute.

He pulled a fat envelope out of the pocket of his coat that he'd draped over the back of his chair. "I'd like to recommend two possible employees to you for the Shop on the Corner if you're planning on hiring anyone to help you with the business. Nolan and Rita Harbeck worked with Bennett Renfree for almost twenty years before he died from flu that went into pneumonia. Everyone liked Bennett in Waynesville; it was a loss to the community when he died, but especially to Nolan and Rita. They have a good character and excellent references for you to look at if you might consider hiring them." He handed her the envelope.

Laura opened it and looked over the paperwork while she ate her salad. "You've included photos of their work and of them. That isn't usual."

"The Harbecks are good friends of my family. Nolan Harbeck

and my dad, especially, were long-time friends. They often went fishing together. My dad loved to fish." He finished off his own salad.

She let her eyes move over the paperwork again. "They seem very qualified and I will need someone to help at the store. A couple worked for me at my other upholstery store and they became like family to me."

"It happens when you work with people for a long time."

"Well, I will be happy to talk with them. I had planned to hire at least one person to work with me at first, maybe a second if needed. My idea was to ease into it. People here in Waynesville don't know me yet or the kind of work my shop can do. I've been doing upholstery since I was a girl. I have some certificates and coursework credentials, but in the upholstery business it's really skill and time on the job that best teach you. Also, some people have a natural gift for it, for helping customers pick fabric, sensing what they want and how to please them, working out unexpected problems while handling the jobs, making their old pieces sing again. I like doing that."

He watched her eyes light up over the words. "You love what you do. I can tell that from hearing you talk."

"I do love it. It was hard walking away from our old store, knowing our building would be taken down for a highway and that there was nothing I could do to save it."

"Couldn't you have stayed? Relocated to another location?"

She looked out the window, trying to decide how to answer. "Nothing I looked at felt right. I'd lost my mother years back, and my sister, older than me, had another life. Then my dad died, too, five years ago. It suddenly all seemed sad in some way. But even then I only really started looking at other retail locations out of state on a whim. Then the store here simply seemed to call to me."

He met her eyes and some of that attraction flashed between them again.

The waiter came with their pizza, breaking the tension, giving them something to do besides stare at each other in that awkward way. How did other people handle this sort of thing? Laura wondered and wished, suddenly, she had more experience with men to know what she ought to do. Georgina had always seemed to handle this sort of thing so easily, boys always flocking after her. She'd even flirted with Laura's boyfriends, when they were five years younger than her—like Laura was—seeming to enjoy attracting them, like a sport or game. Georgina had always been like that, liking attention and wanting to be the center of attention. Laura knew she had often faded into the background of Georgina's dominant personality, her strengths never noticed as much as her sister's.

"Penny for your thoughts," Mitchell said in a quiet voice.

Laura looked up to see him watching her.

"I guess I was wool-gathering." She rubbed her neck, a little embarrassed. "Tell me about your business, your family."

"The Quinlans are an old Waynesville family. You'll see one of the historic family homes on south Main Street—the Charles and Annie Quinlan House, a bed and breakfast now called Prospect Hill. Charles and Annie Quinlan, who built the house, and Charles's dad before him, were my grandad's people, lumbermen who came from up north and stayed to become bankers and politicians. My mother's people, the Dawsons, are an old family, too. Both my grandfathers are gone now, like my dad who died young, but my two grandmothers are still living, my Nannie V Quinlan and my grandmother Mary Dawson we call Mimi. My mom still lives in our family home a few streets away on Church Street, too, where I grew up with my sister."

Laura watched a shadow cross his face. Knowing family pain, she recognized it in others. "You mentioned a niece and nephew. Are those your sister's children?"

"Yeah." He finished a last piece of pizza before continuing. "Alise was seven years older than me. When I was six and starting school, she was already thirteen and a teenager. But we were still close. She went away to college, studied to be a nurse, and met a young doctor, Hudson Jacobs, at the Asheville pediatric clinic where she worked. After a time they got married, bought a house in Asheville a year before Mackenzie was born. Then Charlie came two years later. Alise and Hudson were good people, great parents, dedicated in their work. They were killed in a freeway wreck when a drunk hit them. Mom and I brought the kids home to our place then. We've raised then since. Mostly Mom, although I've tried to do my part. Last year, with both kids older and settled into school, I moved back to the apartment above the store again. Mackenzie is nine now, Charlie seven. I still run back and forth to the house often; I spend a lot of time with the kids."

Laura reached across the table to put a hand on his. "You've known loss and sorrow. I know about that, too. It changes you. I'm sure Mackenzie and Charlie look to you like a dad. And I bet you're a good one."

He turned her hand over to hold it, his fingers playing with hers a little. "You're a very nice person Laura O'Dell and a very attractive woman."

"Thank you," she said, unsure what else to say.

Laura studied him shyly—a tall man with red brown hair, hazel eyes, a strong chin with a touch of beard like so many young men had now, and those serious eyes that could turn merry and quirk at the corners when a smile lit his face. He was attractive, too.

He let her hand go somewhat reluctantly at last. "Well, it's nice we're going to be neighbors," he said, trying to move their conversation back to a more casual tone.

Laura picked a piece of pepperoni off a pizza slice to nibble it. "Tell me about Quinlan Staffing Services," she asked.

He took a breath and she imagined he was glad for the change of subject.

She liked him but she didn't want things to move too fast with them. Casual would be best. She had so many changes behind her, so many more ahead. And she really needed to keep a lot of her personal information to herself for now. She certainly wasn't ready to share with this man she'd only met tonight, no matter how kind he was.

The waiter brought the check and Mitchell said, "Let me pay our tab and I'll tell you about Quinlan's on our way back."

Laura noticed he helped her into her coat when she stood. He was the type of well-schooled Southern man that opened doors and guided her gently with his hand on her back, too. She liked that, and his good manners and natural charm drew her. She could admit that easily to herself.

As they walked down the street in the dark, he picked up the conversation again. "You probably saw on the awning above our storefront that Quinlan's started in 1946," he said. "My grandfather built the business, my father inherited it, and then me. We handle temporary, temp-to-hire, and full-time staffing in and around the Waynesville area. Three employees work for me. We stay busy. We're honorable and we work hard to make good placements. That's about all there is to say. Come over one day and I'll give you a tour around the store, introduce you to some nice people." He paused. "Let me know when you'd like to talk to the Harbecks, too, and I'll set a meeting up."

Laura pulled her coat snugger around her. The temperatures were colder here in the mountains than in Mississippi.

"Do you think they could come tomorrow on Friday?" she asked after considering his request. "Is that too soon? They might be able to answer some questions for me about the business, having worked for Bennett Renfree for so long. If I feel a good connection with them, I'll talk with them about working with me. You can usually tell when you sit and talk with people for a while if there's an affinity, a connection. Do you know what I mean?"

"I do, and I'll see if they can come over tomorrow. What time would be good?"

"Maybe one or two. Either time would be fine with me." As they got to the store, she paused to reach into her purse. "Here's one of my business cards." She passed it to him. "I just picked them up this week. It has the business phone on it and my cell, too. You can call me in the morning to let me know if they'd like to come. If that doesn't work, we can look at Monday or Tuesday next week.

I'm pretty flexible right now."

"I really appreciate you being willing to talk with them, Laura."

She nodded. "I can't promise anything, but I will talk with them. If I like them and they like me we might start with a trial period, maybe part-time working into full-time as the business gets going. Do you think they would be open to that?"

"I do, and I think they'd understand that arrangement."

She looked down at the keys in her hand she'd also pulled from her purse to open the door. "It doesn't usually take too long to sense if you're going to get along with someone."

He reached out a hand to touch her face, surprising her. "Sometimes in only a moment you know you've met someone special. It can happen."

She knew she blushed and turned to fumble with unlocking the door. "Thank you again for the welcome box and for dinner. It was a pleasure to meet you, Mitchell."

"The pleasure was mine." He pulled a card from his pocket. "Here's my business card, too. If you ever get scared or have a problem, remember I am right across the street. It's nice to have good neighbors. We all watch out for each other here, especially those of us who live downtown."

"Thanks. I appreciate that." She opened the door and turned. "I'm sure I'll be seeing you again soon."

"You can count on it," he said with a soft voice, leaning toward her as if he thought to kiss her but then he pulled back, stuffing his hands in his pockets and turning to leave. "Sleep well, Laura O'Dell."

"You, too," she replied, slipping into the store and locking the door, feeling oddly restless then, not sure if she'd wanted any more or not from their goodbye.

Her phone rang later in her apartment, surprising her. Few people knew her new business or personal cell numbers. She hesitated before answering. "Hello?"

"This is Mitchell. I hope I didn't wake you, but I thought I'd call and say I already talked to the Harbecks. They're looking forward to meeting you tomorrow. I thought it might help your planning to know tonight that they could come at one o'clock."

"That's good," she said, smiling despite herself to hear his voice again. "Should I call to let you know how it goes when I talk with them? Should I make even a tentative offer or talk about money with them before speaking with you? I haven't ever worked with an employment agency."

"In this case, with friends, I probably won't handle this through the agency." He chuckled. "The only reason they didn't come to you directly was because they thought I could help them over any age discrimination issues, put in a good word for them."

She laughed at that. "The Greeleys, who worked for me before, are older than the Harbecks by about ten years at least."

She heard him chuckle again. "Well, be sure you tell them that."

"I'll try to find a way. Thanks again for calling."

He sighed. "I think I was looking for an excuse. I kept looking across the street thinking about you."

Laura's mouth dropped open and she wasn't sure how to answer.

"Look out your window in a minute and I'll blink my lights to tell you goodnight." And then he hung up quietly before she could answer.

Still holding her phone, she walked into the living room of her apartment where she could see across the street to the buildings on the other side of the road. Even in the dark she could see the shadow of the awning over Quinlan's entry and lights on in the second story. The lights blinked then, off and on three times before stopping.

Laura smiled at the charm of saying good night this way, and she moved to her own light switch to send him back a three blink off and on reply.

In acknowledgment he sent back only one blink before the lights dimmed out totally.

Smiling, she made her way back to the bedroom. This had been a nice day, and as she got ready for bed she looked over the Harbecks' paperwork and photos once again. She hoped they would be nice people. She'd need help to run the shop, and it would be a distinct advantage to her—if she liked Nolan and Rita Harbeck—to have locals like them, who already knew the business, to work with her.

The next morning, she spent time trying to sort things out a little more in the shop and to clean up some before the Harbecks arrived. At five minutes to one she heard the front bell ring, a good sign. She liked people who knew how to arrive on time.

Laura opened the door. "Hi, you two. Come on in. I'm Laura O'Dell and I'm happy to meet you."

Rita's mouth dropped open. "Gracious me, you're pretty as a picture and only a girl." She shook her head. "Somehow I was imagining a much older woman and I worried you might be real sophisticated and stern-looking."

Nolan laughed. "Well, I guess you can see already Rita sort of says what she thinks. We're just plain people, Laura, and not very good with knowing interview etiquette."

"That's all right." Laura almost giggled.

"I didn't mean to speak out of turn," Rita said. "But Mitchell didn't give me a clue as to what to expect here."

She handed a basket into Laura's hands after they stepped inside. "I hope it's all right if I brought you a loaf of my homemade banana bread," she said, "plus some of my lemon squares and chocolate fudge. I thought with you just settling in, you might not have had much time to bake yet."

Looking at the basket covered in a red-checked cloth, Laura smiled and shook her head. "I'd planned for us to have a nice formal interview at the table in the salesroom, but after seeing this basket, I wonder if you'd mind if we had the interview upstairs in my apartment. I made coffee and iced tea, thinking I might bring some down later, but if we go upstairs, we can all have sweets with it, too. I really love homemade banana bread."

"Well, that would be real nice," Rita said, pleased. "And I'm dying to see how you've changed out Bennett's apartment."

As they cut through the upholstery workroom toward the back hallway and the stairs leading up to Laura's apartment, Nolan stopped in the middle of the room.

"I sure have missed this old place," he said looking around. "Becky Ray said Bennett's sister was open to sell all the upholstery equipment and everything with the store sale, but I wasn't sure that was true until now." Nolan walked over to a worktable to pick up a few tools one by one. "When a man does upholstery he gets attached to his own tools. They become like old friends."

"I understand that, Nolan. I brought a lot of my own tools and equipment with me, even after reading the inventory sheets of the shop," Laura said. "I'm fond of my own worktable, my old staple gun, a rawhide upholstery hammer that was my dad's, and especially my Sailrite sewing machine. I understand that sentimentality."

Rita had wandered over to the sewing area to look around. "That's a fine red Sailrite machine you brought with you. That old green Sailrite there in the corner was always my baby. I guess you think we're carrying on like a couple of old ninnies, but we haven't been in the place for two years since it closed and got shut up. It sure is nice to be here again."

Nolan walked over to join them. "Becky Ray said the real estate company pretty much left the shop, the vestibule, the office, and the salesroom as is until they could learn if a buyer wanted to buy any of the furniture and equipment with the building. If not, they planned to have an auction company come in and pack it up to see if they could sell any of it for Mr. Renfree's sister."

"And you bought it all with the building?" Rita spoke the question with wonder.

Nolan looked around. "Heck fire, we could start work tomorrow making money with everything still here like it is."

"The place is dirty, though," Laura put in. "I have piles and stacks of boxes and equipment still unpacked from my other store, too. Everything needs to be sorted through and the shop cleaned well before I can even think about doing business here. The salesroom is almost as bad. She gestured toward the back of the big upholstery workroom. I brought a lot of fabric, fabric books, and swatches. It will take me a lot of time before I'm ready to reopen. I spent the first week working in the apartment, deciding what to keep and what to let go of among the things Bennett left there. I thought I might need to do some painting, but Mr. Renfree left everything in pretty good shape."

Laura hesitated, looking around. "I've worked since I came to set up the office, and I've gone through files and old paperwork. I'm trying to get familiar with the filing system Bennett Renfree used and trying to learn to read his handwriting."

Rita laughed. "He wrote like a chicken scratching in dirt sometimes. But after a while we got to where we could read his scratchings pretty well."

Nolan rubbed a hand up his arm. "If we get on and if you like us after a little visit, Rita and I could sure help you clean up this place and get it ready for business. I guess you read that we worked here nearly twenty years. The old place is like another home for us. We could be a good help to you, Laura." He hesitated. "You'd be a help to us, too, if you saw fit to let us come back to work here. We've missed the work and, admittedly, the money."

Laura smiled at them. "Then let's go upstairs and talk about everything and have some of Rita's banana bread."

CHAPTER 4

On Saturday, with Quinlan's closed for the weekend, Mitchell went to have breakfast with his mom and with his niece and nephew Mackenzie and Charlie. The family home was only a couple of blocks away and Mitchell liked walking the short distance, except in foul weather. He enjoyed seeing the familiar scenes along the way, as he strolled up Miller Street and south on Haywood, before turning on Church Street. The home he grew up in sat just around the corner, a big, white, two-storied traditional home with black shutters. The house sat comfortably among lush shade trees and well-established shrubbery with a long back yard.

Mitchell followed the driveway around to the back door. The kitchen was empty when he let himself in, giving him a minute to look around and enjoy the sweet sense of home that always washed over him when he came into the old house.

His mother, Evelyn, an artist, loved the peace and serenity of the color blue and her house showed it throughout. The big family kitchen, white with gray tiled floors, provided the perfect backdrop for the blue delft China his mother collected. The patterned pieces mixed nicely with the blue stoneware the family used for every day

Seven-year-old Charlie and nine-year old Mackenzie came running into the room then to welcome him with hugs, followed by the family dog, a part border collie, named Zoey, demanding her share of attention, too.

"Uncle Mitch, Uncle Mitch," Charlie cried, climbing on Mitchell's back when he leaned over to pet the dog. "Are we still going to the movies to see *Doolittle?*"

"That's the plan," he answered, wrestling Charlie off his back to tousle his hair.

The boy grinned up at him, a smattering of freckles across his nose, his hair the same color as Mitchell's, eyes the same hazel.

"He looks so much like you at the same age," Mitchell's mother said, coming into the kitchen. She crossed the room to give him a hug, and he enjoyed the scent of her familiar cologne.

Mackenzie smiled at her. "I think I look like my mother Alise when she was a girl. She was pretty. Great grandmother Mimi showed me pictures and said I inherited the looks of the Dawson women."

"Well, don't tell your other grandmother, Nannie V Quinlan, that," Mitchell's mother said, moving into the kitchen toward the stove. "She's convinced you look exactly like she did as a girl."

Mitchell laughed. His two grandmothers had a warm-hearted rivalry for the children's affection, both having spent so much time helping to raise them.

"Uncle Mitch, Grammy made us breakfast pie today," Charlie announced, changing the subject.

Evelyn smiled. "As you well know, Mitchell, that means I made quiche with cheese, bacon, and ham. There are also strawberries on the table, and I'm popping cinnamon toast into the oven now. It will only be a few minutes until everything is ready." She turned to the children. "You two take Zoey out in the yard for a few minutes and then come right back. She's standing by the door, looking at her leash longingly."

"Okay." Charlie dashed toward the door, Mackenzie following.

"Both of you put on your jackets hanging in the mud room as you go out, too," she called after them. "It's cold this morning."

Mitchell settled on a stool by the kitchen counter. "I'm sure you know that Charlie and Mackenzie are probably two of the only children I know who love quiche."

"It's all a matter of how you present things." She smirked.

"Yeah, I remember the day you asked them if they wanted to

help you make breakfast pie. They were so excited at the idea, and they still think of raisins as raisins candy, brussels sprouts as baby cabbages, and broccoli as magic trees that will make you stronger."

"Well, you need to use a good imagination with children."

He laughed. "You've done a great job with them, Mom. Alise would have been so proud."

"I think of her every day when I look at them." She turned from the counter where she was sprinkling buttered bread slices with cinnamon and sugar. "You were my rock through all those years, too, Mitchell. I was still grieving the loss of your father when that wreck happened taking Alise and Hudson's life in a moment. I don't know how I would have made it through everything without you." She frowned then. "I worry though that it's stolen a big part of your young-single-carefree years. You've hardly dated anyone in months. You should. Have you met no one who interests you?"

"Maybe," he answered.

Catching the word and his tone, she turned, lifting an eyebrow. Mitchell wondered if she knew how beautiful she was, with a lovely mature beauty, her long dark hair streaked with silvery white, her eyes keen, her ways always graceful. In every aspect of her daily life her artistry showed in all she did, not just in her paintings and teaching.

"What does maybe mean?" she asked, popping the toast into the oven under the broiler for a few minutes.

"I met someone yesterday." He hesitated, trying to decide how much to tell his mother. "Remember when you told me once that the minute you and dad met something happened between the two of you?"

She smiled. "It felt like the sky above shifted and a zip of lightning passed between us." She closed her eyes, remembering. "It didn't matter for even one minute that your father was ten years older than me either. I knew he was the one."

"I remember hearing that story from dad, too." He paused. "One day last year while doing some research on personality for the business I read the results of a study that said it only takes one single second when meeting a person to know whether you're attracted to them or not. One second. I didn't believe it when I read it."

She turned from the refrigerator, where she'd gotten a pitcher of orange juice out, to study him. "Do you believe it now?"

"I'm considering it." He knew his lips twitched in a smile.

"Well, how nice," she answered, taking the juice pitcher to place it on the kitchen table by the bay window. "Do I get any details?"

"It's the woman who bought Renfree's Upholstery."

"Really? I heard someone bought the building and the shop. I guess I assumed she was older, probably married and staid. I assume that isn't the case?"

"Hardly. I went to talk to her Thursday night about possibly hiring Nolan and Rita Harbeck to work at the shop again. They'd come and asked me if I would put in a word for them with her."

"Did she hire them?"

"She did. They hit it off when she interviewed them yesterday."

"And did she hit it off with you, too?"

He laughed. "There was definitely a jolt in the air. It hit me for a loop, Mom. I think it surprised her, too. I pushed it a little after we met and I took her out to get pizza with me at Bocelli's."

"Hardly an impress-me-with-a-first-date sort of place." She smirked.

Mitchell frowned. "I'd already planned to walk over there after stopping by to see her. It was sort of an impulse thing to ask her to go along."

"I'm only teasing you. Did you have a good time?"

"Yes," he admitted. "And I keep thinking about her. A lot."

"Is that a problem?" she asked.

He crossed his arms. "I don't know. Most girls seem to be looking for that carefree single guy you were talking about, a good time party boy. That's not me."

She shook her head. "You're wrong about that, Mitchell. You've simply dated that sort of girl more in the last years, like that silly Christy Gamble. I honestly thought the girl had a cognitive disorder. Silly, toddling around in those outrageously high-heeled shoes, obsessed with shopping, and she had the most boring conversation. My smile nearly froze on my face sometimes. I have to admit I was glad when you stopped dating her. The children weren't fond of her either."

"That always worries me—you and the kids."

"You mean, whether the children and I will like your girlfriends?"

"Well, yeah." He scowled. "You, Mackenzie, and Charlie are my family. Anybody who doesn't like you, well ..." His voice drifted off and he got up to help his mother carry quiche and toast to the table and then walked across the kitchen to the counter to pour himself a cup of coffee.

She was quiet for a moment. "You're taking Mackenzie and Charlie to the movies today, aren't you? And then to lunch and to the park?"

"Yeah, I kind of promised them a day."

"Well, call and invite this girl to go along."

He knew his mouth dropped open. "Mom, it's the Saturday morning children's matinee at The Strand. We're seeing *Dolittle*—the movie about Dr. Dolittle's voyage to get a cure for Queen Victoria."

"So?"

"It's a kids' movie and I'll have Mackenzie and Charlie with me all day."

"Exactly." She went to get herself a cup of coffee, too. "Anybody who doesn't love Dr. Dolittle books or movies is not our kind of person, Mitchell. And anybody who can't have fun with a couple of great kids like Charlie and Mackenzie isn't our sort of person either. If you take her with you, you'll learn a lot about her quickly. What is her name anyway?"

"Laura O'Dell."

"Nice name." His mother smiled. "Anyway, taking Laura O'Dell with you today will tell you more about her than a dozen formal dates at fancy restaurants or clubs."

"I don't know, Mom." He ran a hand over his neck. "The kids

can be pretty active and candid, and I gathered from Laura she hasn't been around family much—her dad and mother both gone, her sister living another kind of life, she said."

"If she's our kind of person she'll be hungry for real family. If not, you'll know quickly, and not lose any more sleep tonight mulling the idea of her over and over." She started toward the door. "I'm going to go call the kids in for breakfast." She glanced at the clock. "It's not even nine o'clock; Laura O'Dell would have plenty of time to get ready if you call her now."

She gave him a kiss on the cheek as she walked by him. "Give it a chance, son. Your father took me to meet his mother on our first date together. And yet here I am." She laughed on the way toward the mudroom. "Family won't run off the right person."

Mitchell stood looking after her. "Oh, what the heck," he said to himself after a few minutes. "I guess I can give it a whirl."

He went into the living room for a minute, away from the kitchen, to give Laura a call.

When he came back to join his mom and the kids now sitting at the breakfast table filling their plates, his mother said, "What did she say?"

He scowled. "She said yes."

She turned to the children. "I talked your Uncle Mitch into taking Laura O'Dell, the new girl who bought Renfree's old upholstery shop, to the movies and lunch with you today. She's new in town and all by herself. She doesn't know anybody and hasn't ever been to The Strand, or to the Church Street Depot for lunch, or to the park or anything."

"You mean she hasn't ever been to the Depot for burgers and a shake? It's the best place to eat ever," Charlie said, his eyes wide.

"I think she'll love *Dolittle*," Mackenzie added. "We saw the first Dr. Dolittle movie on television and I can't wait to see this one, too." She hesitated. "Is Laura nice, Mitchell?"

"Yes, she is," he said, still surprised Laura said yes when he called impulsively to invite her to join them for much of the day.

His mother smiled, forking up a bite of quiche. "Bring Laura by to meet me when you drive the kids back and before you head to your apartment."

Mitchell groaned.

His mother paid no attention to his obvious reluctance. "I'll be painting upstairs in the studio all day, getting that new Waynesville scene done that I'm working on."

"All right," he conceded, digging in to his breakfast.

The movie *Dolittle* was nearly a two-hour show, and by the time Mitchell, Laura, and the children went to lunch at the Depot after it, and then on to the Waynesville recreation park for the kids to play on the swings, slides, and wooden fort, it was nearly four o'clock when he brought Mackenzie and Charlie back home.

The kids ran upstairs to find their grandmother in her studio as soon as Mitchell parked his Bronco in the driveway. He followed, bringing Laura and stopping to introduce her to an excited Zoey along the way.

"We had the most fun," Mackenzie was saying as they walked in his mother's studio. "We all loved the *Dolittle* movie."

Charlie grinned. "Laura hid her eyes when the tiger was going to eat Dr. Dolittle though," he added. "It was a scary scene."

Laura smiled. "Well, there were some tense moments now and then. I read the book *The Voyages of Dr. Dolittle* years ago, along with others in the series, but seeing the story come to life on the screen was certainly more exciting." She walked over closer to Mitchell's mother. "Hi, Mrs. Quinlan, I'm Laura O'Dell, which I guess you've figured out by now. I'm so pleased to meet you."

"Please call me Evelyn," his mother said, taking Laura's hand and patting it. "I'm delighted you were willing to spend time with my son and my grandchildren today."

"Oh, I loved every minute," she replied.

"Laura's really fun, Grammy," Charlie said. "She liked the Church Street Depot, too, and got a hamburger, fries, and a strawberry shake."

"Which were excellent," Laura confirmed.

"Laura can swing really high on the swings, too," Mackenzie

added. "She taught us a fun Hide-and-Seek game at the park, called Sardines. One person hides and everyone looks. If you find the person hiding, you scrunch in and hide with them, so soon everyone ends up all scrunched up like sardines until the last person finds them. Some of the other kids at the park played with us, too."

Mitchell saw his mother give him a satisfied smile. "It sounds like you all had a truly wonderful day."

Laura walked over to study the painting Evelyn had been working on, a large watercolor of ladies in swirling, lavishly decorated skirts on one of the streets in Waynesville. "This is beautiful."

Evelyn pointed to an array of photos taped on a bulletin board beside her work area. "I took photos this summer at the Folkmoot International Festival, held every year in Waynesville. I especially loved the women in these lavishly colored long skirts who danced and marched in the parade, so I decided to do a painting of them. A lot of tourists come to Waynesville for the parade and other international events, and if I make prints, I may well sell several during the festival. I have a couple of shops I can count on to display them, too."

Laura leaned closer to study the photos. "Look at the lavish fabrics in these dresses, rich blues, bright reds and yellows, vibrant oranges and greens, and all the decorative bands of color around the skirts."

"I imagine as an upholsterer you have a special eye for fabric," Evelyn said.

Laura smiled. "I do admit I tend to notice fabrics more than most."

"Folkmoot is a really fun festival, too," Mackenzie put in. "We love the parade. Maybe you can watch it with us this year."

Laura's eyes brightened. "I'd love that."

Mitchell's mother smiled at her. "We'll make a point of inviting you in July and we may try to get you to volunteer for one of the festival committees now that you're a local."

"I'd be honored to help," Laura said.

"Well, I'm looking forward to coming to see your shop when you open later," Evelyn told her. "I had many pieces in my house done at Renfree's, and I know everyone has missed having the store there."

"I admit I took a peek at some of the gorgeous fabrics you've used in your home as I walked by your living and dining area." Laura sighed. "I love all the rich blues mixed with the tans, browns, and whites in your house. The wallpaper I spotted here and there is fabulous, too."

"Well, I like color. Not everyone does."

"Most people are afraid to use it," Laura replied. "They don't have the confidence or sense of artistry to utilize rich colors wisely."

Evelyn smiled. "Well, I will take that as a compliment." She turned to the children. "If you two go to the den, you'll find some Dr. Dolittle books on the game table that I found for you to read, since you've seen the movie. Charlie, maybe Mackenzie will help you with some of the big words you don't know or read the books to you. I also bought you Dr. Dolittle coloring books I found in a little shop downtown last week. I put crayons and pens on the table. I thought it would be fun for you both to color scenes you saw in the movie and to read the books now."

Mackenzie's eyes lit up. "Thanks, Grammy!"

Excited, she and Charlie turned to head out of the room.

"Whoa! What do you say to Mitchell and Laura for spending their Saturday with you?" Evelyn reminded them.

"Thanks, Uncle Mitch and Laura," both echoed before they headed down the hall.

Evelyn looked after the children and commented, "I always try to link every event to reading and learning if I can."

"How well I remember." Mitchell grinned. "You did it with Alise and me, too."

"So I did." Evelyn turned to Laura. "I imagine you're worn out from a long day with the children and would like to get back home. I hope you will come back and visit with us again another time."

"I'd love that," she replied.

"Thank you for helping to make a nice day for Mackenzie and Charlie." Evelyn paused. "What did you do with Bennett Renfree's apartment over his shop? He had some incredible pieces of furniture there, used a lot of rich reds, gorgeous lamps and chandeliers, and lovely art and collectibles. I think Becky Ray said no one in the family wanted to take his things and that if the new owners didn't buy the furnishings, Renfree's sister planned to have an auction company come pick it all up. Did you keep any of it? I've wondered."

"I've chosen to live in the apartment over the shop," Laura answered. "I thought the realty company's offer to buy the shop and apartment furnished was reasonable. I needed the additional equipment and furnishings for the shop, not wanting to move any more than I needed to from my other store. I also really liked the photos of the furnishings in the apartment." She smiled. "My favorite color is red and my own small apartment had a lot of furniture and decorative pieces in red. I've found the two melded well together."

"How wonderful," Evelyn said. "Let Mitchell come up to see your apartment so he can tell me about it. If I recall, Bennett Renfree had one or two of my paintings in his place. I'd love to know if they're still there. Later when I'm in town one day, maybe you and I can have lunch and you can show me how you've redecorated the place. I was fond of Bennett. I know he'd be happy to think someone was enjoying all the beautiful things he collected. He was quite an artisan in his own way and did a lot to support the arts in Waynesville. I'm hoping maybe you might fill some of his old roles. We always need volunteers at the Haywood County Arts Council on Main. It's just around the corner from your shop. I'll take you over to meet some of the staff one day."

"I'd like that."

Evelyn turned back toward her painting. "With the children busy for a time I might get this painting finished this afternoon if I get back to work. You two have a blessed afternoon."

Mitchell led the way back downstairs, marveling as he always did at his mother's skillful ways of orchestrating his life. Not that she couldn't keep her oar out when needed but she'd always had a keen sense about people and a way of moving individuals and events around in an artful way, like a person would formulate moves in a chess game.

"Your family has a lovely home and yard," Laura said as they walked out onto the back patio near his car.

He glanced toward the deep back yard. "In the spring the yard will come alive with dogwoods, yellow forsythia, tulips, and daffodils." He pointed to a path by the back hedge. "Through the shrubs a side path winds behind the Episcopal church to a pretty Memorial Garden. The flowers and shrubs are nice on the garden walkway in the spring and summer. I used to slip over there to play as a kid, and I take Mackenzie and Charlie now."

"You have a wonderful family, Mitchell," she said, climbing into the car as he opened the door for her. "You're really blessed with that. Your mother is so gracious and the kids are smart and fun with really good manners."

He walked around to climb into the Bronco and started the ignition to back out of the driveway. "I'm glad you had a good time today, Laura." Alone with her now he could feel that little sizzle and draw floating in the air. It always made him want to touch her.

"If you have time, Mitchell, maybe you can come up to see my apartment, like your mother suggested. You can look around to see if I have any of her paintings. I guess I didn't look at the artist names under the different ones on the walls carefully. It would be lovely if I own one of her works. She is so talented."

Mitchell smiled at how his mother had orchestrated this opportunity. "Maybe I can take you to dinner after as a reward for putting up with my niece and nephew all day. I promise something nicer than hamburgers and shakes."

He saw her twist her hands in her lap. "You don't have to do that, Mitchell."

"I know but I'd like to," he replied. "You can show me your place, what you've been doing in the shop, and over dinner maybe you can tell me how you're getting along with the Harbecks."

She hesitated in replying and Mitchell felt that reluctance in her again, even though he believed she really wanted to spend more time with him. What troubled her? Something did. And something held her back. She obviously had secrets of some sort.

CHAPTER 5

Laura had impulsively said yes to Mitchell's invitation to spend most of her Saturday with him and his young niece and nephew. She was, admittedly, eager to get to know him better but also reluctant to spend too much time with him one-on-one. A day in the company of his family sounded fun and more casual. She wanted to get out and see more of Waynesville. With the shop not open yet, her days were filled mostly with work. A break would be good.

At the end of the day now, as Mitchell drove her back to her apartment, Laura felt glad she'd said yes to his invitation. She'd enjoyed a great time with Mitchell, Mackenzie, and Charlie, loved how fun and relaxed he was with the children. She liked his mother, too, and felt confident in an odd way that the two of them would get along if they got together for lunch later, both loving and appreciating art. The upholstery business was more artistic than most people realized—or it could be for some. It certainly was for her.

Thinking over Evelyn Quinlan's words about Bennett Renfree's apartment, Laura was eager to look at her paintings more closely now to see if she owned one of Evelyn's works. She felt excited, too, about Evelyn helping her to get more involved in the community. She wanted that, wanted to be useful, and wanted to make more friends.

Mitchell parked his car behind his store and they walked around to Miller Street to cross to her shop. She unlocked the front door.

"There's an entrance to my apartment directly off Montgomery Street, too, by the parking lot," she told Mitchell. "But this entrance is closer for us."

He followed her inside, glancing around. "The vestibule and waiting area look much the same as I remember."

"They both do." She turned to grin at him. "Nolan said whenever Bennett got bored that he redecorated the vestibule, recovered the chairs, painted or papered the walls, and switched out the paintings. I had to dust and sweep everything, of course, but I thought the entry area looked beautiful as it was—certainly more so than the entry at my old shop."

Laura opened the door on their left. "I might re-do the office though to make it more my own style." She gestured at the vibrant art on the walls. "I'm not very fond of modern art like this, but I do love the furniture and the antique rug. What do you think?"

"Hmmm. The modern art here is a little surreal and abstract for me, too," he replied. "I like more realistic art. I know many people love art exactly like this, though."

She nodded and then giggled. "Nolan said I could put these paintings in the upholstery workroom, that they would brighten the place up."

"I can see that working well." He leaned his head to one side. "You know, these look sort of like Paul Klee's colorful buildings and surrealistic art."

She lifted an eyebrow.

Mitchell spread his hands and grinned. "I was raised by an artist. You tend to pick up artists' names and remember them."

Laura walked over to look at the prints on the wall more closely. "These are prints of Paul Klee's." She turned to him. "I'm impressed."

"Come show me how the shop and the salesroom are coming along. Nolan and Rita said they worked some on Friday afternoon to clean both up a little more."

"Honestly, they all but begged me to stay and work."

"They're like that; I don't think you'll be sorry you hired either of them."

"I don't either and I'm already glad they wanted to come back." She led the way from the office and vestibule into a hallway. "The salesroom, where customers can look at fabrics for their upholstery jobs, doesn't look much different from the day when we sat at the table there to talk," Laura said. "But I'll show you the big upholstery work room." She led him to the right into a large room that filled the entire end of the building.

Mitchell followed.

"This is a great work area," Laura said, stopping to gaze around. "There will be plenty of room for all three of us to work on different projects here, and I love the partitioned sewing area Bennett created. It's large enough so Rita and I can both sew if needed. Renfree's business space is bigger than my shop was back home."

"And where was your shop?"

"In a little town in the deep South you've probably never heard of." She shrugged. "Let me take you upstairs now. I want you to look around to see if I have one of your mother's paintings."

Laura felt sure Mitchell noticed her evasive answer about her old shop location, and her quick change of subject, because he gave her an odd look. But he didn't question her further.

A door from the shop led into the hallway of the back entrance. To the left a wide door led outside to the parking area behind the store, and to the right stairs led upstairs to her apartment.

Laura stopped to unlock her front door as they reached the entry area, and then she ushered Mitchell inside.

"The place looks a little like I remember," he said, pausing inside the doorway.

"The whole apartment was decorated in rich reds, creams, and white, with a touch of yellow and green, but I toned down the strength of the colors and the elegance of the place to make it cozier and more comfortable for me."

He smiled. "I can see some of the changes, especially chairs and pillows in red-checked fabric and many of your own things scattered around. The place looks nice."

"Thanks." She took off her coat and draped it and his on a coat rack by the door. "I admit I spent most of my time here the last two weeks working to make the place more a home for myself. It was a little posh and elegant for my tastes, and many of Bennett Renfree's things were still here. I packed up his personal items, clothes, and books in boxes. I'm not sure what I'll do with them yet."

"We have a couple of thrift stores that would love to take any of the things you don't think you can resell."

"That's a great idea. I've been trying to decide what to do about everything. I also wrote Bennett's sister. I thought she might like some of the personal photos I found tucked away."

"That was nice of you." Mitchell walked around, looking into the dining area to see changes she'd made and glancing into the kitchen. She knew he could see a host of feminine changes throughout, especially in her bedroom with the floral pillows, red and white quilts, and girly items scattered about. She'd even papered her bathroom in a cute floral wallpaper and in Bennett's old office she'd added colorful pillows and red checked drapes.

Mitchell walked over to a side wall in the office. "Ah, here are my mother's paintings." He gestured toward them. "These two paintings of scenes in downtown Waynesville are Mother's and the one of the town-scape, with the mountains rising in the background behind it, is one of hers, too."

Laura walked over to study them closer. "Your mother will be pleased to know Bennett had three pieces of her work. And they're wonderful."

"I wish I could say Alise or I inherited some of her artistic talent, but Mother thinks Mackenzie is showing promise. Sometimes talent skips a generation."

Mitchell walked back to the living room. "When Mother comes over, she'll be able to tell you more about all the paintings in your apartment. Bennett enjoyed buying local art."

He glanced at his watch. "It's nearly 5:30. If you'd like, we can go on to dinner. The restaurants get busy if you wait until later on Saturday evening."

"Okay. Let me tidy up for a minute." She glanced down at her brown slacks, white shirt and tan sweater. "Do I need to change clothes?"

"No," he said. "You're fine. I'm not changing either. Casual clothes are okay where we're going. I thought we'd walk over to the Firefly Taps & Grill on Main. It's only about two blocks from here. Have you been there yet?"

"No, but I've seen the brown awning and the cute restaurant front."

"They have good food—trout, sirloin, ribeye, several chicken entrees, country fried steak, nice salads, and sides."

"It sounds perfect. I'll go zip in the bathroom, brush my hair, and be right with you."

A few minutes later, they headed back downstairs to let themselves out of the shop and walked up Miller to the main street that ran through downtown Waynesville.

"Have you met the people in the big Davis Furniture store behind you yet?" he asked.

"I honestly have worked so hard to settle in that I haven't been anywhere," she answered. "Just getting out today was a treat."

Mitchell pointed out different shops and places as they walked along, telling her local facts, keeping her entertained. As they stepped inside the restaurant, several people waved at him and one man across the restaurant stood to walk toward them.

"Hey cousin," he said, grinning at Mitchell. "Becky Ray and I just sat down to have dinner. Will you guys come and join us?"

Mitchell glanced at Laura for an okay.

"That would be fine," she assured him. "Becky and I are already friends. She helped me buy the shop and she's stopped by a time or two to check on me already."

The young man, about Mitchell's age, reached out a hand to take hers. "I'm Rob Killian. Mitchell and I are cousins on the Dawson side of the family, and we went to school together."

"This is Laura O'Dell," Mitchell said, making the introduction. "She bought Renfree's old upholstery shop and building across the street from Quinlan's."

His eyes lit. "Ah. Becky was telling me someone bought the building. Glad to meet you."

They walked over to join Becky at a round table near the middle of the room.

After greetings were exchanged, Laura settled into a chair, studying Becky with her curly dark hair, her smile as friendly as always. She wore a jeans skirt, casual shirt, and boots. Rob was casually dressed, too, in jeans and a flannel shirt. His height was similar to Mitchell's but his hair darker and he had dimples that flashed when he smiled.

"I'm pleased you've met Mitchell although I'm not surprised." Becky grinned. "He tends to get around to meet any new business owners in town."

Mitchell laughed. "Well, what I'm surprised about is to see you two out for a date. I seem to remember you two had a long running grievance going between you."

Rob frowned at him and turned to Laura. "You may not know it, but all three of us went to school together here in Waynesville. Becky and I dated in high school and then I foolishly ticked her off by running around with another girl our senior year. We went off to college after but whenever I ran into Becky, here in Waynesville later, she tended to avoid me."

"I totally avoided you. No tending to about it," Becky added, grinning.

Rob rolled his eyes. "Well, anyway, I finally talked her into helping me find a house through Re/Max, and while we spent time driving around checking out houses in the area, I apologized. Abjectly, too." Rob looked across the table at Becky and winked. "We found that while we spent time together, that 'old good feeling' we had in high school kicked up between us again."

Mitchell laughed. "I always thought you'd been foolish to let Becky get away."

"Here, here." Becky agreed.

"Well, I've made amends," Rob added.

The waitress came to drop off menus and take drink orders then.

They chatted amiably while they looked over menu options and then ordered. Mitchell ordered steak and Laura decided to try the salmon. Their drinks came in cute mason jars, and the ambience in the restaurant was cozy, with wood floors, a beamed ceiling, and soft lighting.

Laura enjoyed listening to the casual banter of Mitchell, Rob, and Becky, obviously long-time friends.

"I'm sure you both heard about pranksters taking down the flag at the courthouse and hoisting that Jolly Roger pirate flag, didn't you?" Rob asked.

They nodded.

"Well, last night someone stole the old historic bell in front of the high school," he continued.

Mitchell looked up in surprise. "Really? I missed hearing that one. But I took Mackenzie and Charlie to the movies and the park today. I dragged Laura along and I guess we were so caught up with the kids we didn't pick up on the news. What happened?"

"Like the other time, someone came in the night, unscrewed and detached that big bell from its concrete base and simply carried it off," Rob told them. "No one saw or heard anything."

"Everyone in town is so upset," Becky added. "You know that bell used to be on top of the first school in Waynesville and it was rung to call the kids to school. Over time, the old bell has been saved and moved whenever a new school was built. It was at the old high school and then moved to Tuscola High School when it opened. Tuscola still rings it on the first and last day of school, when they win a ball game, or for any other major event. It's a part of our town's history. Everyone is in an uproar over this. You can't replace something like that old bell."

"Who'd want to make off with an old bell?" Laura asked. "Is it valuable?"

"Probably not, and if someone tried to sell it, they'd be tracked down," Mitchell added.

"I can't figure out who's doing these things. Or why." Rob shook his head. "A lot of people are getting mad at the mayor, the town aldermen, and the police for letting these things happen."

"Well, Waynesville has a lot of history and they're proud of it," Becky put in. "People are getting worried about what could be targeted next. The town is full of historic businesses, buildings, churches, and homes on the Historic Register. A lot of them have statues, artifacts, museum rooms, and more. People are worried if this is going to become a crime trend. The flag theft seemed like only a prank, but this tends to show it might be the beginning of a broader problem."

Their dinner arrived, and they changed their conversation to more easy chatter, catching up on their lives, sharing bits and pieces about happenings in the town that Laura enjoyed hearing about.

"This has been fun," Becky said as they finished their dinner and began to get ready to leave. "We need to get together another time soon."

"Yeah, let's do that," Rob added. "It was a pleasure getting to know you, Laura. I hope you'll enjoy living in Waynesville."

It was dark now as Laura and Mitchell made their way back to the shop.

"You were a little quiet tonight," Mitchell commented.

She laughed softly. "With three old friends, all sharing memories of the past, I just enjoyed listening."

"I've seen you're good at that." He reached over to take her hand as they walked along. "I hope we'll enjoy more good times together like we've had today, Laura. I really like being with you."

She tried to think what to say. "I appreciate you sharing your day with me. And thank you for taking me out to lunch and dinner."

"It was my pleasure," he said as they arrived at the shop door.

She wondered if she should ask him in again.

"I'll blink the lights for you again later to say goodnight." He grinned at her and then stood looking at her in the moonlight. "Whatever this is between us sure is sweet, Laura. I know you feel it, too." And this time Mitchell leaned in to kiss her.

Laura felt a little pleasure jolt flash through her and she thrilled at the feelings when he pulled her closer, letting his fingers drift into her hair and his lips slide over her eyes and cheeks.

He stood back after a time, breathing heavily, and smoothed a hand down her cheek. "I won't ask you to invite me in," he said huskily. "But this has been a sweet day. We'll just see how this goes, Laura O'Dell. Sleep well."

He leaned over to give her one more kiss, winked at her, and then walked away. As Laura let herself in the door, she could hear him whistling in the dark.

CHAPTER 6

March slipped away, after dumping a late snowstorm on Waynesville near the end of the month, which made April even busier catching up. It seemed like the first of the month was always one of the busiest times at Quinlan's.

"I guess with the spring here, everybody's decided to get out of the house and find a job." Rosemarie laughed at her own words as she brought Mitchell a pile of new mail. "We sure have been busy these first weeks of April. How'd your interview go with Howard Childers?"

"I had to give him a pretty stern talk. His casual attitude about every job we've found for him is wearing thin with me. In the last two jobs we placed him in, he was late so often—with so little repentance—they let him go. The word is getting out around town that he's an employee to avoid."

"That's a shame, because he's so well-educated and personable when he puts a mind to it. I wish he'd quit self-sabotaging himself."

Mitchell shook his head. "Some days I feel more like a psychiatrist than a staffing agent or recruiter."

"Well, get ready for another challenge. Betsy Moreau is here for her second interview with you. She's the one we found with a smattering of false information on her paperwork. Norma found it while checking her references and her educational credentials."

He shook his head. "Why do people do that? Don't they realize with the Internet the way it is today, that any incorrect data will be ferreted out?"

"I think they hope most people won't really look at their references and credentials closely, and you know many employers don't. You read all the time about some attorney practicing law who falsified passing the board or some doctor in practice without an appropriate medical degree."

"It does take time and money to check references, educational credentials, and backgrounds closely. Most employers work with us, and keep working with us, because we do check well. Saves them potential problems and lawsuits as well as time."

Rosemarie turned to leave. "You want me to send Betsy in now?"

"Yeah. I'll try to get a sense for why she lied like she did, see if we can still work with her or not."

He glanced through Betsy's paperwork that Rosemarie had placed on his desk earlier. Most of the problems on her application were with overestimating the years she'd worked at certain jobs, but the worst was noting she finished a training program she never really completed. He'd need to talk with her to discern why she decided to fudge on her credentials. One of his applicants had used that very word: fudge. "I just fudged a little to make myself look better on paper," he'd explained. "Everybody told me you should do that."

Mitchell shook his head looking at the notes Norma had made throughout Betsy's paperwork. He liked giving people a second chance to get it right, but he worried about the attitude and ethics of people who would basically lie on their applications. If they lied and crossed ethical boundaries at their work site later, it would come back on Quinlan's and make the business look bad to the employers they worked with.

He met with Betsy a few minutes later, who got mad and hateful when he pointed out the discrepancies in her paperwork. He smiled and told her he didn't think she was a good fit for Quinlan's at this time. She left in a huff, telling him she'd find herself a job on her own. He hoped she would and he also hoped she'd realize in future that she needed to be more honest about her credentials and training.

"You did the right thing," Rosemarie said to him, coming around the corner. "She was a nasty piece of work, left talking hateful like we'd done something wrong rather than the wrong being on her own door step. You can't do anything with people who won't acknowledge when they're in the wrong." She shook her head. "She's young though. Maybe life will teach her some needed lessons as she goes along."

"I hate dealing with issues like this some days." He scowled.

"Remember other people's problems aren't your problems unless you let them be." She smiled at him. "Reed Barlow just popped in the door and wanted to know if you had a minute to say hello. Can I send him back? Maybe he'll cheer you up."

"Sure. Send him back."

He heard Reed laughing before he came in the office.

"Hello stranger," Mitchell said, getting up to shake Reed's hand. "What brings you into town today?"

Reed grinned. "It's good to see you, boy. You're looking good. I know your daddy would be happy to see how well you've done taking over his business."

Mitchell sat back down and gestured Reed to a chair. The man, who lived out in the country beyond Hazelwood, was dressed, typically, in an old green T-shirt tucked into work overalls. Crammed on his head was the battered felt hat he usually wore and rarely took off, even indoors. However, looks were deceiving in Reed's case. All the Barlows, if rough around the edges, were smart. Reed, his brother Crockett, and their sons, along with Reed's dad Obion Barlow, managed a successful construction company and owned acres of land outside Waynesville. They also owned a wide array of rental homes tucked around the mountains nearby that they'd bought at auctions and foreclosures over the years and fixed up to put on the rental market. Their business office near Hazelwood sat near the Old Balsam Road not far from the gun and ammo store. Reed's wife Leona ran it with a tough iron hand and a brusque manner, but underneath it, Mitchell knew she had a heart of gold.

"I sure miss fishing with your dad," Reed said leaning back in his chair to prop a booted foot over his knee.

"Dad loved getting out in the backwoods to fish with you." Mitchell's thoughts wandered back in time. "I still remember how you and Crockett found Dad that day, out on the bank by the reservoir, when he'd had a heart attack and how you brought him home to us."

Reed shook his head. "There's a bad memory I don't care to recall. I saw him leaning up against that tree on the bank and thought he was asleep. He'd hiked a long way to the backside of the reservoir to fish. My dad said he stopped by the house earlier to ask if he could cut through our property."

"None of us even knew where he'd gone that day. He simply left a note to say he'd gone fishing, wanted to get outdoors."

Reed looked out the window for a moment. "A lot of days Crockett and I went with your dad fishing. You probably remember we all three went to school together. We'd known each other since we were kids."

He rubbed his neck. "That's why it hurt so much to find him." He paused. "Sometimes when my mind wanders back to that day, I like to think your dad at least died happy, doing what he loved. Even if we all lost him too young. I think of him whenever I fish back on the reservoir."

"We'll always be glad you and your brother decided to go fish yourself later that day and found him, Reed. If you and Crockett hadn't brought him back, it might have been days before anyone tracked him down him out there."

"Aw, we just did what anyone would do at a time like that."

Mitchell shook his head. "No, that's not true. Most people would have called the cops and not gotten personally involved. You brought Dad home to us though, stayed with us, and helped us call the funeral home. Your wife Leona sat with my mom, comforted and hugged her while she wept. We won't ever forget it, Reed."

He waved a hand. "Well, that's the past and this is today. We move on." He pulled a flier out of his back pocket. "Me, Crockett, and the Waynesville Boys are playing next weekend at The Strand's stage on Friday night. I was across the street giving Nolan Harbeck some fliers to put around and he suggested you might put one up on your front door or beside it. We're hoping for a good turnout now that spring is here."

Reed, his brother Crockett, Reed's son Gideon, Nolan Harbeck, and another local man named Skeener Tate all played together in a bluegrass group. Mitchell's dad had gone to see them play whenever he could and usually Mitchell tagged along when allowed.

Reed winked at Mitchell as he stood to leave. "Nolan says you're dating the girl at his shop. Bring her along. Introduce her to some good bluegrass and mountain music."

"I'll do that," Mitchell stood to see Reed out. "Did you read about the courthouse flag and the old school bell being stolen?"

Reed gave a disgusted snort. "We read the papers. You couldn't miss hearing of it. Folks everywhere are talking about it."

"What do you think is behind pranks like that?

"Heck, I don't know. Maybe some kids with nothing better to do, maybe some weirdo that collects historic artifacts, or someone with a grudge against the mayor or the city. I've heard a lot of ideas on it."

He turned to leave. "Leona said for me to tell you to not make yourself scarce. She said to tell you to stop by the house sometime or by the business when you're out our way."

"I'll try to do that," he said.

Mitchell's mind turned to thoughts of Laura as Reed left. He imagined she'd enjoy going to The Strand for one of the local events the theater held. He and Laura had been dating somewhat regularly now, but he still felt she was keeping things from him. Even when they'd gone out again with Rob and Becky last week, he could tell from looks she and Becky exchanged, when Rob asked her a few questions about where she'd lived before, that Becky knew more about Laura's past than he did. Why? He couldn't figure it out.

Laura ought to realize that with him the owner of a staffing service, it was easy for him to do a background check on her, to find out where she'd lived before, if she had a troubled past or a criminal record. But all he'd learned in checking was that she'd come from a small town in Mississippi called Amory. He found some newspaper notes on the imminent domain order that took a group of downtown businesses to widen the highway. He'd located the address and saw old photos of the Shop on the Corner. She hadn't lied to him about anything from what he learned, but he couldn't figure out why she wanted to be secretive about her past—simple as it was. It made him uncomfortable.

His mother stuck her head in his door. "Do you have time for lunch, Mitchell? I've been teaching a class over at the Arts Council and thought I'd get a salad or something at the Sweet Onion before I head home. Rosemarie said you didn't have another appointment until two."

Mitchell nodded and shut down his computer. "That sounds good, Mom." He was glad she'd missed Reed Barlow's visit. His mother knew and loved the Barlows, of course, but seeing Reed would have brought back a sweep of sad memories.

At the Sweet Onion Restaurant two doors from Quinlan's, they were soon seated at a table for two by the window. "I'm glad to look out at the sunshine after that snow last month. I still can't believe we had four inches of snow in late March." She smiled. "The kids loved it though. They got out of school and had a blast sledding with you and Laura."

"Laura had rarely seen snow where she lived, even in the winter months."

His mother frowned. "I took her to lunch one day and over to the Arts Council to meet everyone. I can't seem to remember where she said she lived before though."

He made a face. "That's because she hasn't said where she lived before. Not even to me, but I think Becky Ray may know. She handled her real estate transactions."

"That's odd." She lifted an eyebrow. "However, knowing you, I imagine you've checked her out."

Mitchell felt a guilty twinge of conscience at her words. "It's not hard to find out a few basic things about anyone these days."

"Especially if you run an employment and staffing service and run checks on people every day."

The waitress stopped by, saving Mitchell from an immediate response.

His mother smiled up at the waitress. "I want the salad with the smoked chicken, cheese, bacon, and cranberry sauce," she told her. "Leave off the jalapeno though. And just bring me water with lemon to drink."

"I'll have the BBQ sandwich with coleslaw and iced tea," Mitchell said when the girl turned to him. "And add a side of macaroni and cheese to my order, too."

"They make the best macaroni and cheese here." His mother sighed.

He grinned at her. "Why don't you order some? But if you don't, I'll give you a bite of mine."

"Life is wretchedly unfair that you can eat anything you want and never gain weight."

"If it makes you feel better, I don't eat out most of the time. And you know I'm active."

She changed the subject as the waitress left. "I visited at Laura's shop last week after her grand opening. Everything looks good. Rita said old business is returning and a lot of new people are stopping by."

The waitress brought their drinks and his mother stopped to squeeze lemon into her water and take a few sips. "Laura took me upstairs to see her apartment, too."

"I like the three paintings of yours she owns. Your Waynesville scenes are some of my favorites. You know we have them all over the office here, too."

"Laura seemed pleased with them, asked me questions about each. I talked to her about the artists I knew who had done a few of the other paintings and prints she owns." She looked out the window toward Laura's shop across the street. "Why do you think Laura is being secretive about her past?"

"I don't know."

"Have you asked her specifically? The two of you are growing close now. There really shouldn't be big secrets between you."

"I hear you." He drank some of his tea and looked across the street again. "I guess I haven't pushed on her to tell me more about her past. I simply assumed she would as we got to know each other better. Instead, she's been oddly silent about her past."

"Hmmm. Invite her to church for Sunday and to Nannie V's for lunch. After Laura has spent much of the day around your family, simply confront her in a natural way, and ask her about her past more specifically."

"What if she evades my questions again?"

"If Laura evades your questions again, you'll need to be more direct. Be candid and tell her you've noticed she's shied away from answering any personal questions about where she lived before she moved to Waynesville and about her family. Remind her she's met most of your family and that you've been open with her. If you want, tell her it hurts you that she isn't sharing with you, that you've noticed even Becky seems to be more in her confidence than you are. Tell her you'd like an explanation."

He considered her words.

She raised an eyebrow. "I wouldn't mention that you checked her out, though. She might resent it."

"I'm falling for Laura pretty hard," he told his mother after the waitress brought their lunch.

"So are the children, and I'm rather fond of Laura myself."

They ate in silence for a few minutes before Mitchell added, "It does hurt though that she's keeping things from me."

"Well, then it's time to talk about it," she said matter-of-factly. "Speaking of talking about something, I meant to tell you that Sam Jacobs, the children's grandfather and Hudson's father, wants me to bring the children down to Savannah for spring break. You know he still has the house where Hudson grew up on Tybee Island. He has plenty of room and the children love the beach. I've taken them there a few times before to stay. He wants to keep a relationship with them. When Alise and Hudson died, he was kind and supportive about us taking the children to raise, with Hudson's mother gone. Working as he does and traveling in pharmaceutical sales, it would have been difficult for him to raise them."

"I like Sam. I don't see any problem with you going if you want to."

"Well, I think I can arrange to get away, but you'll need to take care of Zoey again, either stay at the house with her or take her over to your place."

"I can do that."

"Well, good." She finished off the last of her salad while they talked about mundane things.

Mitchell's mind was partly diverted, considering his mother's advice about Laura.

"You let me know if Laura can come to Nannie V's for lunch, even if she doesn't care to go to church with us."

"I will after I talk to her."

Mitchell picked up the tab the waitress brought.

"I invited you to lunch," his mother argued, reaching for the ticket.

"Yeah, but it was my pleasure to spend time with you. Let me pay, Mom. You feed me often enough at the house."

"Well, if you want." She gave him a smile and a hug before they left.

As Mitchell started back toward Quinlan's, he paused and looked across the street to Laura's shop. Maybe he'd walk over at the end of the day and invite her to church and to dinner on Sunday. The weekend would be a good time for a more candid talk.

CHAPTER 7

Laura looked with satisfaction at the wing chair she'd been working on most all day in the shop. The new turquoise linen fabric made the old chair look fresh and pretty again.

"I like how that chair is turning out," Rita commented. She stepped back for a moment to check to see if the stripes, on the armchair she was reupholstering, were aligned correctly before cutting fabric for the chair's cushion.

"It was nice of Vern and Claudia Lawrence to let us redo all the pieces in their living room," Nolan said from across the room where he was working on a large Chesterfield sofa. "Three chairs, an ottoman, and this sofa. It's nice to get a whole room to do." He rubbed his neck as he bent back to his work. "These tufted backs and the piped accenting around the chair and sofa arms sure do take some time though, don't they?"

Laura looked across the room to smile at him. "They do at that."

"Well, we're blessed to get this job, though," Rita put in. "Vern and Claudia Lawrence entertain a lot and Claudia belongs to a lot of those women's groups around town. People will see the work, the Lawrences will talk about it, and it will help bring in more business."

"We've done well since the shop opened at the first of April," Laura said, beginning to measure and cut piping for the chair arms. "I'm really pleased at all the work that has come in for us."

"We've been as busy as three beavers and that's a fact." Nolan picked up a bottle of water to take a drink.

"Well, I think we'll get all of these pieces finished by tomorrow and then we can start reupholstering the outdoor furniture for the Hamlins. With spring here, a lot of people may bring us more porch pieces to recover."

"Weather is hard on furniture." Nolan started back to work.

"I tried to encourage Mrs. Hamlin away from some of the fabrics she was considering that would fade more quickly in the sun." Laura pulled fabric off the big roll on her work table to cut long strips to go around the piping she was working on.

"Well, look at the time," Rita said with surprise. "Can you believe it's nearly five o'clock already? This day sure has gone by fast."

Laura glanced at the big clock on the workroom wall. "Why don't you two clean up and head home. It's time to close. We can finish all this tomorrow."

Rita started tidying up her work area. "I really love these aprons you brought us from your other store." She smoothed a hand down the navy apron with the words Shop on the Corner embroidered at the top. "It saves me having to wash our clothes as much and always mending Nolan's shirts where he's snipped them with the scissors accidentally."

Nolan laughed. "I like the aprons, too, especially the big pockets in them where I can tuck in a few tools I'm using. It's nice how you could keep the name of your old store and bring so much from it to this place—like the sign you hung out front, these work aprons and such."

"I think my dad would have been pleased to see the name of his store continue even if the old building got torn down."

"I'm sure he's smiling in heaven to see all you've accomplished to get this new place set up," Rita said. "I imagine he looks down from that big upholstery shop on high and smiles even wider to see the fine work you do every day."

Laura glanced across at her two employees who had quickly become friends. "Thanks. Those are kind words."

"Just true ones," Nolan hung his apron on a peg by his work area. He glanced at Rita. "You ready to head to the house?"

"I am, but I want to stop at the seafood market down the street to pick up a couple of pieces of fish to fry for dinner." She began to hunt for her purse. "Laura, have you gotten fish and seafood there yet? It's always fresh and you can walk to the market from here."

"No, but I keep hearing about that shop. I need to visit one afternoon. It has a funny name, doesn't it, the Wicked Fresh Seafood Company?"

"Yes. Mr. Gray doesn't close til six, too. That's a help. If you go by one day, be sure to tell him we sent you his way."

"I'll do that."

As the Harbecks left, Laura put the closed sign on the front door, locked the shop for the night, and headed into her office near the front of the store to check email and make a few calls before she called it a day. She smiled looking around to see the new paintings of old Victorian houses now hanging on her office walls. They were prints of Evelyn's that Laura found at one of the galleries downtown. Most of the people who stopped in the office recognized the old historic homes around Waynesville she'd painted, and Laura thought paintings of local buildings better suited to an upholstery store than the modern art there before.

She smiled to find a text from Mitchell on her phone. 'Thinking of you; I may stop by later for a minute."

Laura hoped he would but she felt a wince of conscience, too, as her thoughts moved his way. She hated that she was still keeping her past from him. It didn't feel honest or right now that they were getting more involved.

With Mitchell on her mind now, she scrolled through photos of him on her phone she'd snapped when they'd spent time together. She really enjoyed Mitchell's company and she knew her feelings for him were deepening. Even now that old sweep of attraction still hit her whenever he walked into a room, looked at her in a certain way, or touched her sometimes. It felt school girl silly, but she loved it, too. She'd never felt this kind of attraction with someone and with so much rich friendship, trust, and ease.

A niggling of guilt that she wasn't being honest with Mitchell washed over her again. He deserved better. She closed her eyes thinking about it and then decided to call Lillian in Amory. Maybe she could learn more of what had happened with Georgina and Chance from her. All Laura knew from talking with Lillian a few weeks ago was that Georgina and Chance were still living in the house. Lillian said Georgina had called their home once, hoping for a phone number for her, but that Bobby evasively told her he didn't have one yet or an address. When Georgina pushed for more, Bobby cheerily told her he felt sure you'd contact her in time. Laura hadn't heard from anyone else in Amory about her sister, naturally, since no one really knew where she was. But she wondered.

She dialed Lillian's number and grinned as she heard her familiar voice answer. "Oh, hi honey. I saw your name and phone number pop up right on my television screen. Isn't that the most innovative thing today?"

"Lillian, it's good to hear your voice."

"You, too, sweet girl. How are things going there?"

"Fine, and the weather is getting lovely with spring here at last."

They chatted for a few minutes catching up.

"Have you heard any more from Georgina?" Laura finally asked. "Even as awful as she's acted sometimes, she is my sister, and I keep thinking about her."

"Well, I hated to bring the subject up as much sorrow as you've experienced with her, but she came by here this week."

"Really?"

"I'd like to say it was a nice visit but it wasn't. She looked as pretty as always but acted as mean as a snake to us. She said she felt sure we knew where you were and she pushed us to give your address and phone number to her."

Lillian paused a minute. "Bobby told her he had no intention of passing along any of your personal information to her. She started getting mad then and claimed she had a right to know where you were, that she'd learned the store was being torn down and that you'd gotten money for the building that should have been partly hers. She sure talked spiteful and mean after that. I don't even want to share her hateful words. We surely were shocked. I'll tell you that."

"Oh, Lillian, I'm so sorry."

"Honey, her ugliness isn't your fault. It sure made us glad though that you'd made a change in your life. That boyfriend of hers actually got out of the car and threatened us, cursed at us and called us some real ugly names." She heaved a sigh. "Bobby got right up in his face after that and told him a thing or two, and then he asked them to leave."

Laura winced at her words.

Lillian continued, "Bobby told Georgina she didn't deserve a kind sister like you, who'd give her money all the time and let her mooch off her without helping out any. He told her he knew good and well you'd left the house furnished for them and paid the rent through the end of April just to be nice. He asked Georgina what in the heck more that she thought you owed them."

Laura began to cry. "I hate that they came out to your home and acted like that to you and Bobby."

"Well, it sure showed us what they were both like—selfish and ugly and thinking of nobody but themselves. Bobby said it must grieve Mason and Carolyn O'Dell in heaven to see what one of their own children has come to."

"Did Chance and Georgina leave then?"

"They did. Our big ole' Shepherd dog Ajax came out growling and acting kind of aggressive about that time, hearing all the hollering and picking up on the anger and aggression. He's a real protective type. It sent Georgina and Chance backing away from us and getting in their car to leave. I gave Ajax a lot of sweet talk and two dog bones after they left for helping us to get rid of them."

"Do you think I should call Georgina? I don't want them bothering you two anymore."

"Oh, honey, they've left town now. I was getting to that part." Lillian paused. "Your landlady, Betty Humphries, called us yesterday to tell us one of the neighbors let her know they'd moved out. Knowing the situation with them, she'd had them watching the house for her. They loaded up everything you left behind in one of those little moving trucks and took off. The neighbors said a couple of young men helped them. I figure it was some of the boys in Chance and Georgina's band. I don't know where they've gone. Probably back to Nashville. They knew the lease was about up and Betty said she'd been pushing them to sign a new one or give her a date when they planned to move. She said they left the place a mess."

"I'm so sorry about that for Mrs. Humphries. She was always nice to me."

"Honey, Betty knows it wasn't your fault. Don't worry over that. She's already had the house cleaned and found a new renter."

Laura felt relieved to hear that.

"Now, don't you be getting yourself upset over this. I worried about telling you but I knew you needed to know about what's been going on. Georgina has moved on and we'll all keep praying that in time she'll have a good wake-up call and get her life straightened out." She chuckled. "My grandson Tim said it sounded like she'd sold out to the Dark Side. He watches a lot of Star Wars."

Laura tried to think what to say. "I'm really so sorry my problems caused you this trouble."

"Now, you quit apologizing and just keep having yourself a good life there. I think Nolan and Rita sound like fine folks. Bobby and I have been thinking about coming over that way for a vacation later in the summer or in the early fall to see you."

"Oh, I'd love that. There's a sofa in my upstairs office that makes a nice bed. You can stay with me."

"Well, I think we'll bring the camper. It's got everything we need in it, and we've been wanting to take some more trips now that we're not working all the time. We thought we might go to a nice campground we like near Townsend in the Smoky Mountains for a week and then come over your way for a few days before we start back home. You look around for a good campground nearby where we can stay."

"I'll do that," she promised.

After a few more words, they hung up, and then Laura burst into tears. She was so embarrassed at how her sister had acted to Lillian and Bobby. How could she act like that to them? They'd worked for her father since she and Georgina were only little girls, had been sweet to them whenever their mother or father brought them to the shop. Given them birthday presents and graduation gifts.

It hurt Laura's heart so much to see what her sister had become. She'd been so gifted, always so talented. When they were little, she and her sister had been close, too, even with the age gap between them.

Laura was hunting through her drawer for another tissue when she heard the doorbell at the front door. A text popped up on her phone from Mitchell. "Hi. I saw your light in the office. Come let me in."

Trying to mop at her face, she made her way into the vestibule to the front door to open it a small crack. "Listen, this isn't a good time. Maybe you could come by tomorrow."

He pushed the door open, his face concerned. "No, I'm coming in right now. What's happened?"

CHAPTER 8

Mitchell was shocked to see Laura's tear-streaked face when she eased open the door slightly. He didn't think he'd ever seen Laura cry before, and it tore at his heart to see her so upset. Despite her objections and her desire to send him away, he had no intention of leaving her at a time like this.

She looked away from him in embarrassment as he shut the door behind him.

"Look, I'm okay, Mitchell," Laura assured him. "I simply had an upsetting phone call from home, but I'd rather be alone for a little while if you don't mind. You can come by tomorrow."

He walked closer to her and lifted her face. "I'm staying, Laura. You don't walk out on people you love when life hurts them. Besides I don't want to be shut out of your life anymore. If you care for me, you need to let me in."

She burst into tears then and he pulled her into his arms.

Mitchell let her weep for a few minutes and then said, "Why don't we go upstairs? You need to sit down. We don't want people walking by the shop and hearing you crying."

Her eyes widened at that thought and then she shrugged in a resigned way. "Okay, let's go upstairs. I do need to sit down. My legs feel shaky."

Mitchell locked the front door and wrapped an arm around her waist as they made their way through the downstairs of the business, turning off lights in the store, setting the alarms, before starting upstairs to her apartment.

He opened the door there with her key, and then helped her across the living room to the sofa to sit down. She started crying again then, hiding her face in her hands.

"Honestly, Mitchell, this is really a bad time for me," she said between her tears. "Just let me be by myself to have a good cry. It's so embarrassing to have you here."

"I'm used to being around crying women. Don't worry about it." He snagged a box of tissues from a nearby shelf, handing them to her. "I'm going into the kitchen to fix some coffee. I can make hot tea for you if you prefer it."

"No, coffee would be good."

He left her for a few minutes to go rustle around in her kitchen. He'd been here often enough now to find his way around, and it didn't take him long to locate the coffee maker and a can of coffee on the pantry shelf.

Mitchell started the coffee and then came back to sit beside Laura on the sofa while their coffee brewed. He snuggled her close under his arm without saying anything. Sometimes a little quiet was a good thing. He'd learned that lesson often enough through all the sorrows he'd passed through. It wasn't always what you said to someone at a hard time, it was simply the fact that you were there for them.

When the coffee finished brewing, he went to the kitchen to pour a cup for both of them. He remembered she liked a little creamer, nothing else. So did he. Digging around in an old-fashioned bread box on the counter, he found some of Rita Harbeck's banana bread and cut off a couple of slices for them, putting each with a fork on two small plates he found on a shelf.

He brought coffee and a plate to Laura and then went back to get one of his own.

"Thanks," she managed to say.

He studied the rooster on his cup and plate and couldn't help grinning.

"I wouldn't say anything about my rooster dishes right now if I were you," she said in a quiet warning tone.

"What? I like them," he replied, grinning again.

"Just now I'm feeling a little testy; that's all."

"So drink your coffee for a minute and then we're going to talk. It's long overdue between us, and you know it. I'm sorry you had a hurtful call from home, but I want you to share about that call with me. You've avoided sharing about your past with me for a long time. I could understand that when we first met. You didn't know me. You didn't owe me any explanations about your past life. But it's different now." He lifted her chin to look at her. "I'm a part of your life now, Laura. I don't want to be pushed to the outside anymore."

"You're making this night harder for me." She pulled away from him, sniffling again.

"It doesn't need to be harder. Let me in. I want to be a part of the good and the bad with you. I don't only want a superficial relationship between us."

"It might be easier to talk about things another day when I'm not so upset."

"If I had a bad day and was upset, would you be there for me? Would you want me to share with you or put you off?"

She sighed. "That's really not fair."

"Isn't it?" He stirred his spoon around in his coffee. "Even Becky Ray knows more about you than I do. I've noticed the looks between you two."

"I've been trying to decide when to talk with you sometime about things," she said in a small voice.

"Well, now is a good time," he replied.

He heard her draw another deep breath and close her eyes.

"I have some family problems," she said at last.

He waited.

"You have such a lovely family, Mitchell—your mom, the kids." She hesitated.

"I also lost my dad, my sister Alise, my brother-in- law, and one of my uncles in the military. I know about hurt in families."

"It's not the same. You know my mother died young, too, and

my father."

Mitchell tried to remember if she'd mentioned any other family members. "You said you had a sister, living another kind of life."

The tears started again, so he figured that must be where part of the problem lay.

"Is she in trouble?" he asked.

She leaned her head back against the sofa. "Yes, but she doesn't see that. Oh, Mitchell, she was so talented, so gifted. It hurts so much to see what she's become."

Through tears and with a little encouragement along the way, she opened up and shared with him finally about all the problems she'd had with her sister.

"I feel so ashamed about her," she said after telling him about Lillian's call tonight. "I still can't believe Georgina would act so mean to our long-time family friends. They're such good people. They don't deserve to be treated like that."

"Neither did you before," he added.

"Do you think I was wrong to move away and leave? Was it cowardly?" She sniffed. "I've thought about that a lot since. Maybe I should have confronted Georgina and Chance, insisted they move out of my house, been tougher."

"Would you have stayed in Amory, signed the lease for the other shop or bought it, if they had moved away?"

She shook her head. "I don't know. Nothing was feeling right somehow. I'd put off for weeks signing any paperwork for the new store, knowing I risked losing the space."

"Was it only because of your sister that you didn't make a commitment about the new building you'd located?"

Laura considered his question. "No. If I'm honest, no. I felt restless from the time I first learned the government was taking away the building, tearing down the place I'd always known. I'd already lost the family home."

She looked down at her lap. "Daddy left the house to me and Georgina. He hoped she might straighten out, want to come home to live with me there. I don't think he ever imagined she would make me sell it to get her share of the money as soon as he was buried. It was such a pretty place. Mother and Daddy were so proud of it. It had old shady porches, beautiful trees and shrubs in the yard—kind of like your family home—but more Southern in looks. I'll show you a picture of it someday. It broke my heart to see it sold."

She took a breath. "Daddy wasn't unfair about the money either. He actually left Georgina much of his savings, leaving me the business instead. I didn't have enough to buy out Georgina's share of the house without going into heavy debt. Then it took all my energy and time afterward to clean out the house when it sold, find a small place to rent, get resettled and keep the business going, pick up all the work Dad used to do. It was a lot to handle even with Bobby and Lillian's help in the shop."

"I know that feeling. I remember the load of responsibility that fell on me when my dad died." He set his cup on the coffee table. "I'd just moved to the apartment above the shop to be more independent but I moved back home with Mom then. The shock and grief was hard for both of us. Mom managed in part by pushing on with her teaching and painting. She'd never worked in the business, never wanted to. She came in to help in what ways she could at first but, like you, I had good people at Quinlan's to help me through. Then a few years later Mom and I had to meet the additional sorrow of Alise and Hudson's death and taking on the children, only four and two."

Mitchell laced his fingers in Laura's. "Taking on responsibility like we both did makes you grow up earlier, doesn't it? I didn't see myself as more carefree before but I realized quickly after Dad died that he carried the load of the business. I just worked there."

She gave him a small smile. "I know what you mean. I felt overwhelmed at first when Daddy died. I think I almost forgot how to date until I met you."

"I'm glad you did meet me." He leaned over to give her a kiss on the cheek. "Do you ever think that maybe you were meant to come here? That there was a Greater Hand at play in your life?"

"You mean God?"

He nodded, realizing they'd never really talked much about faith together.

"Lillian told me that maybe all my restlessness was from God, that He was stirring up my nest to make me want to fly—like the eagle stirs up her nest to get her young ready to leave that snug safe place. I'm a real homebody type. I get attached to people and places. To things." She grinned at the cup in her hand. "These were my mom and dad's dishes with the roosters on them. I kept them and many of their things. I'm sentimental and I know I resist change. Even when it's needed."

"I remember that Bible story about the eagle. It's in the Old Testament. It painted a pretty word picture of the mother eagle stirring up her nest to encourage the baby eaglets to fly." He smiled at her. "Have you ever seen an eagle's nest? They're usually on a narrow ledge high up on a rocky mountainside or in the very top of a high tree. Any little eagle looking over the edge of the home nest would be scared silly to leap out. Yet that mother eagle knows they need to fly and she pulls the soft down out of the nest so the sharp sticks underneath poke the babies, making them uncomfortable."

"After Lillian talked about that story, I looked it up. It's in Deuteronomy. The other sweet part of the story is that when the little eagles do finally leap out of the nest, she flies above them so the updraft of her big wings holds them up and keeps them safe."

"Until they sort of get their own wings and can fly safely on their own?"

"Yeah, isn't that sweet? I guess that's how God so often takes care of us in hard times, bearing us up, lifting us above problems and helping us."

"That's a nice thought." He propped a foot on the coffee table. "I think I've always loved eagles. Mom did a painting of eagles for me for my birthday once. I have it in my apartment."

"You need to invite me up so I can see it," she said.

He shrugged. "I thought you might think I was putting too big a rush on you, asking you to my place."

"Well, you've been to mine often enough."

He grinned. "Your place is a lot bigger than mine and more colorful. I'm a plain tans and neutrals kind of guy. But you're welcome any time."

She twisted her hands in her lap. "Thanks for pushing me to talk and share tonight. I was so embarrassed when you came by. I hate people seeing me cry, and I knew you didn't know anything about my sister and all my problems yet. But I admit it's been good having you here, Mitchell."

He glanced at his watch. "I'd hoped to take you out to eat tonight. It's getting late. Are you hungry?"

"I am, but I don't want to go out."

"I could go pick something up and bring it back," he suggested.

She glanced toward the kitchen. "No. Let me fix something here for us. You're always taking me out and won't ever let me pay. Let me make dinner for us. It will be good for me to do something useful." She paused. "I have frozen shrimp in the freezer and the makings for shrimp with linguine. Would that be okay with you? I like it with edamame beans as a side, and I can slice one of those nice tomatoes I picked up at the market. What do you think? I'm actually a pretty good cook. I had to learn when Mama died. Georgina was off at college and Daddy was really pretty helpless in the kitchen."

"That sounds great. I'm handy in the kitchen, too. Will you let me help?"

"Okay. We'll work on dinner together."

Mitchell spent the next hour congenially working with Laura in the kitchen to make dinner. She seemed less upset now and he felt glad he'd pushed her to let him stay and pushed her to talk with him. She'd had a rough and disappointing time with her sister and he could tell how much it hurt her.

They sat down in Laura's little dining room beside the kitchen when everything was ready. As he forked into the shrimp and linguine dish he could tell she'd underestimated her cooking skills.

"This is great, a really good dish." He glanced at the beans. "I've never had these beans before, kind of like limas. How did you pronounce the name?"

"It's pronounced eh-da-MAH-may. It's a vegetable type soybean. When cooked, they're really good for you, high in fiber and vitamins."

They ate for a while, both hungry.

After a time, she said, "The main reason I didn't tell you about my sister was because I thought you might think I was cruel to simply run off and leave her, without leaving an address. Basically, leaving her only a Dear John letter."

He looked across the table at her. "What did you tell her in the letter?"

"That I was sorry we'd become so different in so many ways. I told her I hadn't been happy with them staying with me, not helping out in any way, always borrowing money they never repaid, making fun of me, and never thanking me for cooking for them and cleaning up after them. I was honest and said I hadn't liked them drinking and doing drugs in my house. I told Georgina it had really hurt me, too, how she'd acted and all the things she and Chance had said to me. I explained that when I decided to move to another town with Daddy's shop closing, I also decided it would be best for us to not keep in touch for a time. That my heart needed some time to heal. I told her I loved her and that I hoped her life would be happy."

"That sounds honest."

"I tried to be." She sipped her iced tea, obviously thinking back. "I told her I knew she might think it cowardly of me to leave without talking to her first, but that all the times I'd tried to talk to her before hadn't worked out well. I explained that all the furniture I'd left at the house she and Chance could have, that I'd paid the rent for March and April for them, and all the other bills, like the utilities, and that if they wanted to renew the lease and stay they could. I gave them the name and number for the landlady, told Georgina the amount of the monthly rent. It was reasonable."

Laura looked away then. "I also left her a thousand dollars. I didn't even tell Lillian that. I knew they'd been evicted from their place in Nashville. I thought if they didn't want to find work and stay in Amory that they could use the money to help them move to wherever they wanted to go."

"You didn't have to do that. It sounds like you'd done enough already and only been exploited, unappreciated, and taken advantage of."

"That's probably true, but I wanted to look back and think, that despite all, I had been generous and kind. I really love my sister, even after all the unkind things she's done. She's the only close family I have now. I think that makes it all feel worse. I wish we could be close, and I'd like to at least think she likes me. But, apparently, she doesn't. She says I haven't done much with my life, that I don't know what it's like to have a dream. Maybe I don't."

Mitchell reached a hand across the table to take hers. "Don't be so hard on yourself. You were running from a difficult situation that wasn't going to improve. I heard, mixed in with your story earlier, that they were both often high on drugs and drank heavily. Those problems can become addictive and distort and change people's lives. I hope, as your friend Lillian says, that Georgina has a wakeup call in future. Despite any talent that she or Chance have, an involvement with drugs and alcohol will ruin their chances for any real success or joy."

"That's the part that scared me the most then, I think. I didn't know how to deal with those things, what to do or say."

"If you'd been candid in every way with your sister, she would still have been angry with you. She wanted money, even what was legitimately yours. Her heart wasn't right, Laura. You can't fault yourself for that. If you'd told her where you were going, I think she and Chance would have continually bled you for more money. You weren't wrong to shield yourself from that in some way. The situation might have become nasty, too."

"I didn't want it to end that way, becoming nasty, me having to contact the police to get them out of my home, to tell the authorities how my sister and her boyfriend stole money and things from me. After Lillian put the idea in my head about just leaving, it seemed the best solution somehow." She bit her lip. "I had to take Becky partially into my confidence, to ask her not to tell people about my problems and where I'd come from. She was the realtor who handled the sale of the shop, so there were things I had to tell her."

He nodded. "You do know that if Chance and Georgina really want to find you they probably can. Not telling people around here where you came from or being evasive about your family and your past won't really protect you, Laura. I work in the staffing business. Every day we track down people's background information to see if they're being truthful for jobs. It isn't that hard."

"Do you think she'll try to find me, try to track me down?"

"Probably not for a while. She's moved away, resettled somewhere. She's probably mad, too, right now." He stopped to think. "Had you ever visited here before? Do you have family around this area that will make her think you might have come here?"

"No. Daddy's people came from the Montgomery, Alabama, area. Many of them still live near Montgomery in a little town called Dothan, although my grandfather is gone now. Daddy's mother lives near my dad's older sister, my Aunt Dorothy. We used to drive over there to see them sometimes." She ate a last bite of shrimp. "Mother's father was a Methodist minister. They moved around a lot, but when Grandad Baylor retired, he and my grandmother moved to live in Gulfport, Mississippi, in a retirement community near their son Tom. It was fun to go down there for visits and to go to the beach. When we vacationed, it was usually to family in Alabama and Mississippi. I'd never been to Waynesville or even to North Carolina before I came here."

She made a face. "I started looking at retail places far away from family, knowing Georgina would expect me to go to live near them. That she might call or bother them looking for me. She might have already. I know I'll need to let my family know in time where I've moved."

He smiled at her. "It was brave of you choosing a place you'd never even visited for a new home."

She smiled back at him and he was glad to see her smiling a little again. "The pictures on the Internet of the town with all the cute awnings over most of the businesses simply charmed me, and the mountain scenes looked so pretty."

She paused for a minute thinking back. "I called Re/Max about a retail building for sale on Main Street originally. Then after Becky began to ask me a few questions, she told me she actually had an upholstery shop for sale. As she talked about it and mentioned that it sat a block off Main Street and right on a corner it just seemed like a sign or something. The more I learned about it and saw the pictures of it, the more it seemed custom made for me."

Laura smiled at the memory. "So I did one of the first impulsive things ever in my life and bought it. The government paid well for the building I owned on the corner in Amory. I was easily able to afford the cost of Renfree's, even with all the furnishings. Becky teased me and said I should bring my store sign Shop on the Corner so I did. The movers also brought our store van, with the name on the side of it, and I packed the store's work aprons and other items with Shop on the Corner written on them, too. I brought a lot of the old family store in Mississippi to the new one here."

"Well, it seems to me like you were meant to come here, Laura O'Dell." He winked at her. "If only to meet me."

She laughed. "I admit that has been a perk."

"Well, I'm glad you're feeling better now after I pushed my way in on you tonight."

Laura got up to take their plates to the kitchen. "I have some Neapolitan ice cream in the refrigerator. Do you want some?"

"Yes, one of my favorites. Did you know that Neopolitan immigrants, who came to the U.S. from Naples in the 1800s, first introduced ice creams with multiple flavors molded together? Their first concoction was spumoni, with chocolate and pistachio layers of ice cream with fruit and nuts between."

"I didn't know that. I always wondered at the name though."

"I take no credit for finding that knowledge. Mother looked it up and told me."

Laura got the ice cream out of the freezer and began to scoop out some for each of them. "I really like your mother. She came by here to visit, see the shop, my apartment and her paintings, and she took me to the Art Council to meet some the staff and her friends."

"Actually, one of the reasons I dropped by tonight was because Mother wanted me to invite you to come to church with us this Sunday and then over to Nannie V's for lunch. That's Dad's mother, Viola Quinlan. I think the plan has expanded now to also include Mother's mom, Mary Dawson—who we call Mimi—and her sister Frances Killian, that she lives with. After both their husbands died, my Mimi moved closer into town to live with her sister Frances. They're a case, those two. Will you consider it?"

She brought their ice cream back to the table. "They will probably all ask about my family, about where I'm from. It's only natural. What should I say, Mitchell?"

"Well, I think you've evaded people long enough. It makes people imagine the worst scenarios. I think I'd just tell people a simplified version of the truth."

She frowned. "Like what?"

"Tell them you inherited the family upholstery shop and building in downtown Amory, Mississippi, where you grew up but that the government decided to widen the highway and took many businesses by imminent domain to do it, including yours. Say that with both your parents gone and your sister away, and not involved in the business, that you decided to look around at retail sites in other Southern towns and fell in love with the shop for sale in downtown Waynesville."

"That's mostly all true except for my sister being away."

"Well, she was away when the domain order first came and she is away now."

Her mouth twitched in a smile. "Will people be happy with that answer?"

"Sure. Most people don't really want a detailed life history when they ask about you. I try to tell our applicants that all the time. Often, they tell an employer far more than they need to know or act twitchy and guilty in an interview worrying that an employer wants to dig out all their personal home and family problems."

"I guess you've learned a lot about people in your business."

"I'm sure you have, too," he said, digging into his ice cream.

"Answers to problems always seem simpler when they're for someone else, too."

"That's for sure."

They sat for a minute finishing their ice cream.

"Can I tell Mom you'll come on Sunday? She said you could come only for lunch if you didn't want to join us for church."

"What church do you go to?"

"The big Baptist church downtown that the Quinlan family has gone to for generations. Mimi and Francis go to the old Methodist church for the same reason. I guess we could go to either or to some other church if you'd like. I'm comfortable going to different churches if you have some other preference. I've visited around a lot with friends." He grinned. "It provokes my grandmothers when I tell them there will be only one church in heaven, and that it helps me get ready to mix in to visit around."

She laughed. "Well, I was raised in a Methodist church, but going to the Baptist church with your family will be fine. My mother played the piano at our church every Sunday, and Georgina sang in the choir and sang a lot of solos, too, when she got older."

"Does she have a really good voice?"

"A blessed and gifted voice. That's the sorrow of it. She got a full ride scholarship in voice in the Music Department at Ole Miss and then walked away from it with Chance Richardson before she graduated."

He winced. "That does seem a shame. Did you go to Ole Miss, too?"

"No, I worked in the store and went to the small community college in town for an associate degree in business, and I drove over to a small college near Montgomery to get some upholstery certificates. I didn't go away."

He grinned. "Neither did I. I worked, too, in our business with Dad and I drove back and forth to Western Carolina in nearby Cullowhee to get a business degree."

"In some ways we have a lot in common."

"That's true, but in some other vital and excellent ways, we are really very different." He sent her a wicked and suggestive grin that made her laugh again.

She glanced at her watch. "You know, we both have to work tomorrow, and it's getting late."

"And you're getting worried about that last lecherous statement of mine." He laughed. "Don't worry. I'll head home after I help you clean up the kitchen, but I won't promise I won't heartily kiss you goodnight before I go. That old feeling is already circling in the air again." He winked at her as he picked up some of the last dishes on the table. "I'll blink my lights to say goodnight later, too."

CHAPTER 9

$\mathbf{L}$aura had to admit it had been a relief to finally talk to Mitchell candidly about her past last night. She'd been embarrassed when he stopped by, hated for him to see her crying and tried hard to get rid of him. But she was glad now he'd pushed to stay. He'd helped her and given her good advice about her situation.

They were all sitting on the big front porch of Mitchell's grandmother Nannie V's house on East Street now. It was a gracious old two-storied farm style home sprawled across a large hilltop lot. The children were running around in the yard playing with the family dog Zoey that Evelyn stopped to pick up after church.

As usual in a crowd, Laura enjoyed just listening to the conversation, adding in a few comments now and then. Following Mitchell's advice, at lunch she'd given them the simple and truthful explanation he suggested about her past and they'd accepted it readily. She noticed Evelyn passed a look to Mitchell across the table however. Evidently, they'd talked before about Laura's reluctance to share much of her past life.

Surprisingly, no one really asked her for more details either, more interested in the shop and how she'd been enjoying living in Waynesville. They all offered suggestions for things she should do and see.

Mitchell's Nannie V was a gracious, silver-haired lady, with a poised bearing. Mary Dawson, or Mimi, Evelyn's mother, was more casual, talkative and fun loving, as was her sister Francis. Both, with short white hair, glasses, and a bubbling humor, seemed to constantly have a story to tell, many of them making Laura laugh.

"I can't believe there has been another of those thefts," Francis said now, pushing herself back and forth in the old rocker she sat in on the porch. She turned to Mitchell. "You just went to a Chamber of Commerce meeting this week. The mayor and a number of the aldermen usually come. What are they saying about these things?"

Mitchell shrugged. "They're upset, like everyone else is, but all the investigations so far haven't uncovered any real clues as to who is behind the incidents."

"Hmmph," Nannie V said with a frown. "I'd hardly call them incidents when they've been thieving our town monuments. First the flag, then the old historic school bell, and now a huge bronze statue of a Revolutionary War militiaman right off the Courthouse lawn."

"How in the world did anyone haul that big bronze statue off?" Francis asked. "I watched that statue put up in 2019 on the Fourth of July. They used a crane."

"It would take several people and a big truck to move that statue," Evelyn put in. "But I've seen larger pieces moved easily with enough hands and the right equipment. The big question is why—why are our town memorials being targeted?"

"It's bringing some real criticism to the Waynesville government, to the Mayor, the aldermen, and the police," Mimi said.

"Do you think that's a factor in this, bringing embarrassment to the city government?" Nannie V asked. "Does someone have a grudge against Waynesville for something?"

"It's odd, that's for sure." Evelyn picked up her glass of iced tea to take a sip.

"Those children sure are having a good time playing and throwing that ball for the dog," Mimi commented, looking out at them in the yard.

Evelyn looked at Mitchell then. "If you still plan to take Mackenzie, Charlie and Zoey walking at Junaluska this afternoon like you promised, you might want to head that way before the kids get too worn out and start getting cranky. They still have school tomorrow, too. I'd like you to get them back home by about five. After this big dinner, I'm only making a light supper, but they both have homework to do."

"I'd almost forgotten I promised to take them walking around the Lake Trail at Junaluska this afternoon," Mitchell said.

"Well, they haven't forgotten. Unless you want to be in the doghouse with them for breaking a promise, you'd better take them. It isn't far to the lake, and I imagine Laura would like to tag along to see Lake Junaluska." Evelyn looked Laura's way. "Have you ever been to Lake Junaluska Conference and Retreat Center?"

"No, but I've heard about it."

Mimi leaned forward smiling. "Oh, honey, it's a pretty place. You'll love it, and it's a nice day for a walk. The roses on the Rose Walk won't be in bloom yet, but with April moving along now you'll see some wildflowers along the trail, I'm sure."

"I can take you home if you'd rather not go," Mitchell said to her.

She glanced down at her long blue dress and Sunday flats. "I'm not dressed much for walking."

"Neither am I," Mitchell replied. "I'll run us both by our apartments so we can change into walking shoes and something more casual." He motioned to the children in the yard as he stood to leave. Evelyn had thought to bring play clothes for them and they'd already changed at Nannie V's after church.

While Mitchell rounded up the children and the dog, Laura said her goodbyes and offered Viola Quinlan thanks for hosting the meal.

"I want you to come by the house one day so I can talk to you about reupholstering some furniture for me," Nannie V said. "I love this old place but some of the pieces are getting a little shabby now. Do you think you might help me figure out if they could be reupholstered?"

"I'd love to. Daddy taught me well how to look at older furniture and evaluate it. Many times older pieces are better constructed underneath than newer pieces made today." Laura smiled at her.

"I'll give you a call and plan to stop by this week."

Mitchell made a quick trip to Miller Street so he and Laura could change clothes and then they headed toward Junaluska. He followed North Main into the Asheville Road, swinging under the Expressway to enter the Lake Junaluska grounds at the east end, soon winding along Lakeshore Drive beside the lake.

"It only takes about ten to fifteen minutes to drive over here," he told Laura. "It's a great place to come for a walk. The shorter loop around the lake, that I take when the kids are with me, is only 2.3 miles, the longer loop is closer to four miles."

"Oh, it's beautiful here." Laura looked across the blue lake that spread before her.

"Our walking trail goes all the way around the lake," Charlie told her. "How big did you say the lake was, Uncle Mitch?"

"Two hundred acres," he answered, pulling into an empty parking spot.

"I'll put Zoey's leash on," Mackenzie said, giggling. "She's excited."

They got out and after Mitchell locked the Bronco, they started off down the paved trail by the lake, the children walking along ahead of them, pointing at familiar sites.

Mitchell spoke to Zoey and she fell into pace beside him.

"She's well-trained to walk so nicely beside you," Laura said.

He smiled. "It takes work to train a dog but it's worth it. Mother was always a stickler about training any of our dogs over the years."

"I noticed your Nannie V has cats," she said, making conversation as they walked along the trail.

"Yes, those two Siamese hid pretty quickly after they saw Zoey and the kids come in the door." He laughed. "Nannie V calls them Leah and Simon. They're both pretty and can be rather vocal, like most Siamese cats. They provide her good company."

"I like both your grandmothers and your Aunt Francis," she said. "You're blessed to have so many of your family members living close by."

"I am," he agreed. "Although sometimes Charlie and I feel

outnumbered with so many women around us."

The trail curled around the side of the lake and Laura could see a bridge ahead spanning across the water. The children waited for them there, looking out over the rails at the expanse of lake before them.

"Grammy likes to come here to paint sometimes," Mackenzie told Laura. "There are lots of pretty garden spots around Lake Junaluska. Grammy paints the flowers and some of the old buildings, too."

"Your grandmother is a gifted artist."

"She's teaching me to paint. I like it more than Charlie. Maybe I'll be an artist someday."

"I want to be a doctor like my dad was," Charlie put in. "He was a kids' doctor. What do you call that Uncle Mitch?"

"A pediatrician."

"Yeah, that's it or maybe I might be a doctor for animals." He squatted down to scratch Zoey behind her ears. "I like animals, all kinds."

"Charlie loves the Nature Center in Asheville," Mackenzie said. "Have you ever been there Laura?"

"No there are a lot of places I haven't visited yet. Like the Biltmore. I've been reading about it though. And I want to go on some hikes in the mountains."

"We go to Biltmore a lot," Mackenzie said, walking on across the bridge. "We have family passes. It's fun to go there at different times of the year, like at Christmas."

"Can I hold Zoey's leash?" Charlie asked.

"If you keep her walking beside you," Mitchell answered.

"I will," he said, taking the leash and talking to the dog as he did.

"He'll walk her for a short time and then bring her back," Mitchell said as the children moved ahead of them again. "He and Mackenzie don't like the discipline of walking Zoey very far. They'd rather climb on benches, pick up pinecones, or toss rocks into the lake."

"They seem to be having a good time."

"They love it here." He turned to her as they walked on. "Do you really like to hike?"

"I hiked in nearby parks with my friends in Mississippi and always walked a lot. One of the reasons I felt attracted to the mountains was because of all the trails here. I picked up a lot of brochures at the visitor center and I found a few books about some of the trails near Waynesville and in the Smoky Mountains nearby."

"I love to hike. I'll be glad to take you on some trails. This is a great time of year to hike right now. The weather is perfect, the wildflowers are blooming, and the summer tourist traffic hasn't really hit yet."

"I'd love to go. Don't pick too tough a trail for our first hiking trip, though. Remember I'm from the flatlands of Mississippi. I know some of the mountain trails involve steep climbs."

"I'll make it easy on you at first. There are some great trails near Maggie Valley and in the Cataloochee valley nearby. Maybe next Saturday when we're both off work, we can go if the weather's good."

"I'd like that."

They caught up with the children again, who obviously knew not to run or walk too far ahead without stopping to wait for them. Charlie gave the dog's leash back to Mitchell and they walked on around the backside of the lake, enjoying the afternoon. The trail crossed another bridge and wound around past a big cross and amphitheater.

"That's Inspiration Point up there where the big cross is," Mackenzie told Laura, skipping along beside her. "It lights up at night and it's really pretty."

"I would imagine so," she said, looking up at it.

"People like to stay at that big inn on the hill there behind it, too." Charlie pointed behind the cross. "You can see all across the lake and to the mountains from the patio. Can we go up there, Uncle Mitch?"

"Not today," he said.

"Then can we stop at the bookstore café to get an ice cream?"

he asked.

"I'm sorry sport, it's closed on Sundays."

"We could go to the Big Dipper." Charlie sent an appealing look Mitchell's way.

"Not today, when Grammy's looking for you both back by five," he said, ruffling the boy's head. "But maybe we can drive up to the Dipper next weekend sometime."

Mackenzie looked back at them, her eyes bright. "Next weekend is Easter, Uncle Mitch. We have the egg hunt at church and Easter Sunday and then we're going to Grandad's place in Savannah and to the beach for our spring break with Grammy."

"Oh, cool. I almost forgot." Charlie sprinted ahead to catch up with Mackenzie, the ice cream temporarily forgotten.

"To fill you in, the Big Dipper is an ice cream store in Waynesville, Laura, a great spot to stop to get a waffle cone. And Mackenzie and Charlie's grandfather, Samuel Jacobs, lives in a house right outside Savannah on Tybee Island near the beach. Mom is taking the kids down there so they can spend some time with him for their spring break the week after Easter."

The four of them and Zoey circled on around the lake toward the spot where Mitchell had parked the car earlier, passing lodging facilities along the way, the big auditorium where events were held, other buildings and a café, before arriving at the car.

Laura paused to look at the long row of roses along the lakeside near where they'd parked. "I image this is a gorgeous place when these roses bloom."

"It is. There are over 200 different varieties of roses here on this Rose Walk section of the trail. I'll bring you back to see it in the summer. I come here a lot to walk Zoey."

The children chattered with excitement about their upcoming beach trip and Easter plans on the way back home.

"Do you have a new Easter dress?" Mackenzie asked. "Mine is yellow and I have an Easter hat, too."

"Mitchell hides Easter eggs for us in our yard," Charlie added. "Maybe you can come to hunt with us."

"I'd like that," she said.

When they finally dropped the children off and started back toward Miller Street, Mitchell turned to Laura and laughed. "You're really a good sport to put up with Mackenzie and Charlie like you do. Nine and seven are pretty active, talkative ages for kids."

"They're a joy to be with," she said. "Stop making it out to be a trial. I love time with them." She sighed. "I always thought Georgina would marry before me, being so much older, and that I'd get to be in her wedding, and maybe play with her kids."

"Don't you want kids yourself when you get married?"

She looked away from him, feeling a little embarrassed at the question. "Yes, I'd love that someday," she answered with honesty. "Do you want a family?"

"I do." He smiled at her. "Helping to raise Mackenzie and Charlie has really shown me that. I've enjoyed watching them change and grow since they were only little." He frowned. "Charlie doesn't really remember his dad or Alise at all. He was about two and a half when they died, so little, and Mackenzie only four. We've showed them so many pictures and home movies that Alise and Hudson took, though, that they both feel like they remember their parents more than they really do."

'That's good, isn't it?"

"Yeah, it is. Mom and I have tried hard to keep their parents' memories alive for them." He paused, his voice dropping. "That first year after Alise and Hudson died was a really hard year, though. Death is never easy, but two little kids that young don't understand well when their parents are suddenly gone."

He turned into the parking lot behind Quinlan's. "You want to come up and see my place? I'll make us a couple of bacon and tomato sandwiches for dinner if you do. After that big Sunday lunch, a sandwich will do it for me." He hesitated. "I borrowed a movie Mom recommended to watch called *The King's Speech*. It's a British historical drama about King George VI who had to cope with a stutter. Somehow, I missed it when it came out originally and Mom said it was really good. We could watch it, too, if you have time.”

“I’d like that,” she said and smiled at him. “And if you don’t have popcorn, I can run over to my place to get some.”

He grinned at her. “I always keep popcorn. You gotta have popcorn with a movie.”

Laura followed him in the back door of Quinlan’s. She’d already stopped by to tour the business and to see Mitchell’s office before, but as he’d mentioned the other night, she hadn’t been upstairs yet to see his apartment.

She walked around in his place with interest after he let them in, eager to see where he lived. His apartment was neat and immaculately clean, and, like he’d told her, decorated in mostly neutrals—tans and browns with touches of cobalt blue. On the walls were many of his mother’s paintings, mainly outdoor scenes, painted in rich acrylics rather than her usual watercolors.

Laura stood studying the eagles painting he’d mentioned, hanging in his office. “I thought your mother painted only in watercolors.”

“She paints mostly in watercolors. It’s her favorite media and the paintings she does in watercolors sell well, but she takes seasons when she likes to work in acrylics. I talked her out of these for my place. I like the feel of them.”

“I do, too. They’re glorious.”

They walked back to Mitchell’s living room, and she noticed he was acting odd and antsy. She turned to look at him and Laura felt that sweep of attraction hit her again, exactly like at the first. It was a heady feeling.

She walked closer to put a hand on his face. “I’m so glad you came into my life,” she said softly. “You’ve been such a blessing to me.”

“Well, your blessing would like to get a little closer for a minute.” He pulled her into his arms and kissed her, easing off some of the tension in the air. Some, but not all of it.

“You’ve turned my well-ordered life upside down, Laura O’Dell,” he said against her lips after a minute.

“I hope that’s a good thing,” she whispered, threading her hands into his hair.

"Oh, yeah, it is." He kissed her again, long and well.

She felt passion rising and a new gentleness in his kiss this time.

"You know I'm falling in love with you, don't you?" he asked after a time. "I've experienced a few relationships that grew serious for a short time, but nothing like this, Laura. I'm on all new ground with you."

"I hope that's good."

"Yes, it's good." He kissed her again and Laura felt a warmth roll right through her heart she'd never known either.

"I think maybe I'm falling in love with you, too, Mitchell Quinlan."

"Well, then this is a moment to remember." He kissed her again long and deep before stepping back and taking a breath. "I think it might be good for us to make bacon sandwiches now. Too much of a good thing is starting to take my mind down a much warmer path than I think we're ready to travel yet."

She smiled, trying to settle her own heartbeat, too, and turned toward Mitchell's kitchen to put some space between them. "Let's go check out your kitchen to see what we can find for dinner. I was so nervous meeting all your family that I didn't eat much."

"They were nice to you, though, weren't they?"

"As sweet as could be," she said, pausing to lean against a counter. "What if my sister and Chance show up some time, Mitchell?"

"Then we'll deal with the situation together, like anything else that comes along for us." He pulled a package of bacon out of the refrigerator. "Your problems are my problems now, kiddo, and my problems are yours, so settle your mind to it."

She giggled a little. "You always make me feel better."

"Good. Now come cut tomatoes and put mayonnaise on some bread for us while I work on this bacon." Laura moved into the kitchen, marveling at how her life had turned from such a hurtful season to this wonderful time of falling in love with Mitchell Quinlan.

CHAPTER 10

It was the first Friday evening in May now, and Mitchell, Laura, Becky Ray, and Rob Killian made their way into one of Waynesville's downtown restaurants, the Birchwood Hall Southern Kitchen. Fortunately, knowing the owners and making a reservation ahead, they'd snagged a nice booth for dinner. The four of them had been enjoying the Art After Dark event in downtown Waynesville.

"Good thing you made a reservation, Mitchell," Becky said, sliding into the booth. "It's crowded tonight in town with Art After Dark beginning again." She looked across the table at Laura. "The event shuts down during the winter. Tonight is the first Friday since last year for it, which explains the crowd."

"The shirt-sleeve sunny weather helps, too," Rob added.

They ordered sweet tea and then studied the menu.

"What do you like to order here?" Laura asked. "This is my first visit to Birchwood."

"Everything is good," Becky replied. "But after nibbling hors d'oeuvres at so many of the galleries we popped into, I'm ordering something light. I love the tomato pie here with tomatoes, herbs, cheeses, and a biscuit crust. I'm ordering that and I'm adding a small house salad."

"That sounds good to me, too," Laura said, as the waitress came back. She and Becky gave their orders.

Mitchell watched a waiter walk by carrying a plate loaded with a big hamburger and fries. "That looks good to me. I'm getting the Pimento Cheese Burger with fries."

"I love those burgers. I'll have the same," Rob said as they handed their menus back to the waitress. He grinned at Mitchell. "Whoever thought of that idea was a genius."

Becky smiled at Laura. "How did you enjoy our evening at Art After Dark, poking around in all the participating art galleries in Waynesville?"

"It was wonderful. The small Mississippi town where I grew up doesn't have anything like this, but then it doesn't have many galleries or craft shops like Waynesville."

"Waynesville grew up catering to tourists with shops and entertainment. It's always been a part of our history." Rob leaned back in the booth to get comfortable.

"The entire downtown area, bounded by Main, Walnut, and Beech, is now a Historic District," Becky added. "As is the Frog Level Historic District along Richland Creek. You do know the funny story of how that part of Waynesville got its name."

Laura laughed. "Yes, Nolan entertained me with that story one day at the shop, telling me that locals often said the creek there sometimes flooded to frog level, and that the name stuck."

Mitchell listened to Rob and Becky share other funny stories about Waynesville's history with Laura. He was glad the four of them got along so well; he and Rob, as cousins, had always been close.

"We should go the Frog Level Brewing place one evening, order some burgers, and sit outside by the creek," Rob suggested.

"I've explored many of the shops in Frog Level," Laura offered, "especially because several thrift stores are in that area. Sometimes I find wonderful fabrics at those stores or old furniture pieces I can pick up to reupholster."

"I noticed you were putting some pieces for sale in the big window on the Montgomery Street side of your store," Becky said.

"Yes. It draws people in so they see the showroom area, examples of our work, and learn more about the shop. I find that if people can see the kind of work you do, it inspires them to consider getting some of their own furniture reupholstered."

"I know you have a lot of fabric in the showroom, but what if it isn't what people are wanting for the pieces they want to have done?" Rob asked.

"I give them an estimate of the fabric they'll need and refer them to a couple of the fabric outlets around the area where they can find more options," Laura answered.

Their food arrived and the topic of conversation shifted to a discussion of the gallery events they'd visited that evening. Mitchell's mom had been a guest artist at the Twigs and Leaves Gallery, although she also had paintings at the Haywood County Arts Council as well, where she sat on the board and taught classes. They'd run into Nannie V there helping with hors d'oeuvres and talking to visitors. She'd been a long-time supporter of the arts in Waynesville.

"Who's keeping the kids tonight?" Becky asked him.

"They're with Mimi and Frances."

"Did they have a good time at the beach on their Spring Break?"

"Yes, they did," he answered. "They came back tanned, excited, and full of stories of all the places they'd visited around Savannah. They really love spending time with their Granddad Sam."

Mitchell thought Sam Jacobs would find little time to spend with his mom and the children on their break, but, evidently, he'd been able to take off more time from work than originally planned. For the first time Mitchell wondered about all the time his mother spent at Samuel Jacobs' home with the children. It seemed silly to wonder about it, with them both older adults and widowed. The two were on their own a lot though, whenever Evelyn took Mackenzie and Charlie to Sam's place in Savannah or when Sam came through town and stayed at their house on Church.

He frowned at the thought.

"What?" Laura asked, catching his eye.

"Nothing, just wool-gathering." He grinned at her.

"What did you think about the latest town theft?" Becky asked, introducing a new subject. "This makes four now—first the flag, then the bell, then the statue, and now Harold Jacobson's convertible."

Laura wrinkled her nose. "What does an old convertible have to do with the other historic items taken?"

"It's not just any convertible," Mitchell explained. "It's the classic aqua blue 1950s Chevy convertible the mayor always rides in for Waynesville's parades, like at Christmas or the Fourth of July."

She nodded. "So all of these thefts seem to be linked more and more to the town of Waynesville's government in some way, don't they?"

"That seems particularly obvious now," Rob said. "My dad's on the Board of Aldermen right now and they really talked about this at their meeting on Tuesday night."

Becky jumped in to explain more about Waynesville's government to Laura. "The Town of Waynesville officials, like the Mayor, and the Board of Aldermen on the Council, are elected to serve four-year terms. The board usually meets monthly to determine budget directions, policy, and to oversee day-to-day operations of the town and its departments."

Mitchell turned to Rob. "Did they come up with any ideas as to why any of this is happening?" he asked. "Did they remember any big policy changes, legal actions, or arguments that might have instigated a sweep of revenge acts like we've been seeing?"

Rob shrugged. "Dad said nobody could think of anything more than a few minor grievances." He smirked then. "If you'd ever sat in on their meetings and listened to some of the items they discuss with the townspeople, you'd be even less likely to imagine any major grievance behind this. They hear complaints of workmen scaring someone's cats, trampling someone's roses, or grumbling about fines or ongoing roadwork noise."

Becky laid down her fork after finishing off most of her pie. "Maybe it's more personal—an ugly divorce or a betrayal of some kind relating to someone in a government position, someone getting fired from a city job, or maybe someone exploited or cheated in business by an official in the government in some way."

"They've tried to consider every possible angle, Becky," Rob replied. "Even in some private meetings, held to probe more into each other's personal lives, they've found nothing. I admit, though, that people can get kind of crazy about personal issues and wrongs they feel were done to them."

"I've seen that in the staffing business and occasionally seen some retaliation but never anything to this extent." Mitchell shook his head. "These thefts involve a team effort, too. One person alone couldn't haul off a big statue or a historic bell."

"Well, it's upsetting and it's hurting the town's image because no answers are being found." Becky tapped a fingernail on the table. "It worries me, too, that someone may get hurt in this. So far no one seems to have been around on the nights when these thefts occur but what if someone is one night? Harold was out of town when the thieves broke into his barn and hauled off his convertible. He loves that old car and he's not happy about this. What if he'd have been home? You know he'd probably have done something foolish."

"That's a good point, "Mitchell put in. "These thefts seem to be carefully orchestrated for times when no security, witnesses, or people are close around. But that luck can't last."

"Dad said they realize the theft acts must involve team work, planning, a big truck or van, and skills to even remove and move some of the things they've taken." Rob stopped to talk to the waitress who'd brought their checks.

"Does anyone want dessert?" he asked.

"No." Becky groaned. "I am stuffed, and I need to head home. I have an Open House starting early tomorrow morning and Saturdays are always busy for me at the realty."

"I don't usually work on Saturdays myself but I have a meeting with a client at the bank tomorrow, too, about some changes in their investment program. It's the only time we could connect and we need to act on this opportunity now or not at all," Rob said, fishing out his credit card from his wallet. He was a Financial Advisor at a bank on Russ Avenue.

After paying their bills, Laura smiled at everyone. "I've had such a wonderful evening," she said with her usual warmth and gratitude. Mitchell always liked that about her.

"Me, too," Becky added, giving her a hug.

A short time later, Mitchell and Laura walked down Main Street from the restaurant and turned the corner to start down Miller, passing the Old Mountain Music sculptures in front of the brick wall of Davis Home Furniture.

"Those big statues always make me smile." Laura paused to look up at the two statues, hovering over them in the darkness. "How tall are those things anyway?"

"About fifteen feet tall each, the bass player taller than the banjo picker. They're made of recycled steel and were created by a sculptor named Stefan Bonitz. I met him once with Mom at an art event. He lives in the Western Carolina area, grew up in Asheville. He does a lot of whimsical work like this."

"Well, I love that they're on our street. People are always stopping to take pictures here with the statues."

"Yeah, it helps to bring business our way," he replied as they walked on.

"I always think of Nolan now when I see those statues, now that I've heard him play with his bluegrass group."

"The Waynesville Boys. I enjoyed their show last month. Didn't you?"

"I loved it. Nolan practiced his banjo some at the shop on his breaks ahead of time, entertaining Rita and me while we worked."

"Did Rita sing? Even though she doesn't sing with the group all the time, she has quite a voice."

"She joined in sometimes. She does have a great voice." Laura sighed as she dug out her keys.

"Thinking of your sister?" he asked.

"Yes. It's hard to not know if she's okay, if life is going well for her." She started inside. "Do you want to come up a minute for a cup of coffee?"

"Sure." He followed her upstairs and into her apartment.

Still noticing she was overly quiet, he asked. "Do you ever Google the group your sister sings with, to see where they're traveling, to see if there's any news of how well they're doing."

"I admit I've looked a time or two. I've never seen more than a brief announcement of the Mississippi Ramblers being at a local club somewhere." She shook her head. "I don't think they're doing well."

He sat down on the sofa while she started coffee, flipping through a pile of magazines and fliers in a stack of mail on the table. "You sure get a lot of upholstery and fabric catalogs."

"That shouldn't surprise you."

He paused at a personal envelope with a Nashville postmark on it.

As she came back to join him, she seemed to pick up on his change of mood.

"You got something from Nashville, hand-addressed." He passed her the letter.

Laura sat down beside him to study it. "It's not Georgina's handwriting. She writes with a flowery hand and puts circles over all her "i's" and little curlicues on many of her other letters. She has a distinctive hand."

"Are you worried about opening it?" he asked, watching her hesitate.

"I don't know, but I have a bad feeling about it. I can't think right off of anyone else I know well in Nashville."

"Well, you don't have to open it now if you don't want to."

"No, I'm being silly." She slit the envelope with a nail, pulling out a sheet of paper to look it over.

Mitchell heard her gasp and cry out, and then saw the letter drop from her hands.

"What?" he asked, picking it up to look at it as he saw the tears welling in her eyes.

He read the words quickly that were scrawled across a plain sheet of paper. "I know where you are. I won't forget how you dumped out on Georgina and me and treated us like dirt. So watch your back."

Laura put a hand to her mouth, beginning to cry.

Mitchell reached for her and pulled her into his arms. "It's only an idle, ugly threat, Laura. I told you Chance and Georgina could track you down if they spent some time looking. Don't let this worry you. It's unlikely you'll hear from him or your sister again unless they hit you up for more money."

"Why would he write something ugly like that to me?" she asked.

"To get exactly the reaction he did. To upset you, to let you know they know where you live, or at least that he does." He studied the scribbled note again. "Does this feel like something your sister would write or approve of?"

"No." She reached for a tissue to blow her nose. "We had our differences and she hasn't been kind to me these last years, but she's never threatened me before. I can't imagine somehow that she would."

"There's no return address on the envelope," he noted. "Chance might have just poked around on the Internet, located you, and sent this as his little form of vengeance. From everything you've shared with me, he's an ugly type that your sister may later regret getting involved with."

"What do I do if I hear from them again or if they show up here?"

"Call me. And know this: They will never stay with you again and you should never give them money again." He lifted her chin to look into her eyes. "Don't let them bring you their problems. They need to find their own way, get their lives straightened out in their own way. If they try to use you or make trouble for you again, I have good friends on the police force we can contact."

"This scares me." She looked at the letter, not wanting to even pick it up again.

"Laura, let me put this letter away to keep for you. If for some reason Chance sends you more notes we can track him down, the same way he found you. I imagine if I ran background checks I might find some problems in his past or his present. He can be dealt with—if need be by the police. It's a serious federal crime to use the mail to threaten a person. Here in North Carolina it's a Class 1 misdemeanor. I've dealt with it before with a few applicants we helped to find jobs that wrote hateful and threatening notes to employers after being fired. It doesn't happen often, but it happens. Most people just do it impulsively because they have problems themselves or they're drunk or mad. They often don't realize it's a crime. A few words spoken to them or a legal arrest by a police officer usually wakes them up in a hurry."

She began to cry again. "I guess moving away didn't really solve my problems."

"Don't say that. You're only upset." He gathered her close to hold her again. "This has been a good happy move for you in many ways. You have often told me how much you love it here in Waynesville, how much you love your shop and the friends you've made. I really think, as we've shared before, that God wanted this change for you."

He kissed her forehead. "We met, too, because you moved here. That's a positive."

She tried to smile. "I know you're trying to make me feel better."

"I am and you can be sure I will take care of you no matter what ugly, stupid little threats like this come your way. I've been in business for a long time, and I've often seen people with problems try to create them for others, say ugly things when mad, even make nasty threats. Those actions don't prosper." He took her hands. "Here's another thing to remember, God takes care of His Own. He watches over us and protects us from harm. Those who bring hurt to others without cause get the rewards they deserve in time."

She looked at him. "Like Karma?"

He considered her words. "There are a lot of scriptures that assure us of God's protection, that tell us not to seek vengeance for wrongs that come our way, but to leave any recompense to Him. However, people open the door to Satan to have a heyday in their lives when they do wrong to others without remorse. They blow a big hole in their own hedge of protection. You know it's true."

"You're making me feel better." She sniffed.

Mitchell wiped a tear off her cheek. "Dad used to remind me of that a lot of times when I got mad and wanted to get even with some applicants or employers who treated us shamefully. He'd remind me that God promises with the good and the pure hearted that the same will come back to them but for the perverse and crooked that the ways they mete out will return to them, too."

He took her hands. "We're going to have faith that God will right this and we're not going to get into fear. That's not from God. Neither is worry or anxiety."

She gave him a small smile. "I didn't know you could be such a comfort. I also didn't know you had this deep spiritual side."

"Well, it didn't happen overnight." He shrugged. "If I have grown stronger in that way, it was because I was fortunate to have good teachers along the way."

Mitchell glanced around. "Do you have a Bible? This is a good night to sit and read the Psalms before you go to bed. Nannie V taught me to do that when life gets tough. A lot of times she made me sit down and listen to her read the Psalms or whatever other scriptures she thought I ought to hear."

He chuckled. "She had a way of letting God chastise and rebuke me that way rather than fussing at me a lot herself. It was effective. It's kind of hard to argue when you're sitting reading 'Thus saith the Lord.'"

Laura laughed and he was glad to hear it.

She took a deep breath after a minute. "I'm really glad you were here with me tonight, Mitchell. Thank you." She glanced toward the kitchen. "We forgot about our coffee."

"I think I'll pass on that and get on home. Will you be all right now?"

She nodded. "I will. I think I'll pass on the coffee, too, put on my pajamas and read the Psalms in bed."

"Good plan." He picked up the letter to take with him, purposed to hunt up Chance Richardson tomorrow to know where he was, to be ready if necessary to take action for Laura if he needed to.

He also thought he'd talk to Jack Salter tomorrow, one of his high school friends who was on the police force. Mitchell didn't like the idea at all that anyone was writing threatening notes to Laura.

CHAPTER 11

Laura woke up a few times that night, troubled over the note she'd received, but by the next morning she felt better. When she thought about it reasonably, she couldn't imagine that Georgina, or even Chance, would really do anything to harm her—even if annoyed at her right now.

The good thing was that she could now contact family in Alabama and Mississippi, and old friends in Amory, to let them know where she'd moved, to pass along her address and phone. She didn't need to worry about staying hidden from Chance and Georgina any longer since they both knew where to find her now. She hadn't moved totally to run away from them anyway. It just seemed like time for a change. And it had been a good change.

In the shop, Laura waited on several customers, getting acquainted and talking about potential upholstery jobs. In between, she ordered supplies and more fabric for the store. In addition to reordering fabrics that had already sold well since she opened Laura decided to also add a few lighter fabric colors to their stock that she thought would be appealing with spring here. After finishing her orders, she walked back to the workroom to check on Nolan and Rita.

"Did you get that new white fabric reordered?" Nolan asked. "I'm using the last of the roll today on this sofa." He frowned. "I can't make any sense of fashion trends sometimes. Back in the day everybody was upholstering in avocado green and harvest gold, then bright orange kicked in and all kinds of animal prints and fur fabric. Now it's gray or white. I think gray is drab when there's too much of it—looks like a prison or something. And all this white makes me think of hospitals. How come people with kids and dogs and an active family want their sofas and chairs upholstered in white? One dog with dirty feet hopping up on a white sofa and it would be a mess, even with supposedly easy-to-clean fabrics."

Rita laughed. "Chester Wilson told his wife that he can't even be comfortable in his own house anymore since she redid everything in white. She even painted all the kitchen cabinets white, reupholstered nearly all their furniture in white fabric, and bought white comforters for their beds."

Laura picked up a scrap of the white upholstery fabric on Nolan's work table. "Most people don't feel comfortable unless they are dressing themselves and their homes in whatever is the most popular fashion. But look on the good side of it, Nolan. Every time people change out their homes, we get more business."

He chuckled. "Well, now that's a practical businesslike view."

"You heading out for that appointment now?" Rita asked.

"Yes. I have a meeting at Viola Quinlan's to help her decide on fabric to reupholster her living room furniture and a set of dining room chairs. She preferred me to bring some selections to the house where she could see them in the rooms. Sometimes I push for people to come here to the showroom where I have so many more fabrics for them to see, but Viola is older." She hesitated. "She is also Mitchell's grandmother."

"She's a good, sweet lady, too, and a fine Christian," Rita added. "You go on over there. We'll be fine here. I'll listen for the bell in case anyone comes in."

Laura smiled. Rita was a warm, friendly, smart and business-like woman herself, who worked well with the public as well as in the workroom doing upholstery. Laura had learned, since buying the shop, that Rita and Nolan had handled the bulk of the workload during the years they were employed for Bennett Renfree. He seldom did any actual hands-on upholstery work like Laura did, and when the store got busy, he hired a local man to help fill orders who liked part-time hours.

Gathering up the materials she planned to take, Laura carried them out to her car. She didn't need to take the shop van today since the store wouldn't be picking up the furniture yet. Her own car was a Subaru Outback with a nice pop-up back that let her load various fabrics and show-books into it easily, along with rolls of fabric, items found on buying trips, or even an occasional small piece of furniture.

It took only a few minutes to drive to Nannie V's on East Street. Laura had walked to the house easily with Mitchell and the children before. The old house, built by Mitchell's great grandfather in the early 1900s, sat on a hillside on one of Waynesville's quiet side streets. The white house with a farm style look, had long windows, a gray roof and gray shutters, a front gable, and a wide covered front porch. Old trees and shrubs and a sweep of green lawn gave the house a welcoming look. The house wasn't pretentious in looks or size, but it offered a gracious, home-like feeling.

Viola Quinlan walked Laura around the house on her last visit, so Laura knew the downstairs held a living room, dining room, kitchen, a sitting room or family den, a small half bath, and Viola's bedroom and adjoining bathroom. Upstairs were three more bedrooms and two additional bathrooms. A long screened-porch spanned the back of the house where Viola liked to sit on quiet afternoons to enjoy the backyard and her flower gardens. Laura parked her car in the driveway beside the garage now, the garage separate from the house but matching it in design.

As she started up the steps to the front porch, Viola opened the door before she could knock. "Come in, Laura. I heard your car." She held the door open. "Can I help you with those things?"

"No, simply suggest where I might put them."

Viola pointed to the left. "Why don't you lay them out on the big dining room table?"

Laura carried them into the room. "That's a good idea. We'll have lots of space here to spread things out and with good light." She smiled to see a beautiful embroidered tablecloth on the table and a big vase of peonies.

"Are those flowers from your garden?"

"Yes, I have a couple of pink and white peony bushes that always bloom pretty this time of year. I love to mix the pink and white blooms with a little green ivy trailing from the sides of the vase." She straightened a few flowers as she spoke. "You must get Mitchell to take you over to Wildcat Ridge Farm in Clyde. It's North Carolina's largest peony farm. I got my plants there, but it's a lovely place to simply stroll this time of year during the farm's 'Festival of Peonies in Bloom.'"

Viola gestured to a chair. "Sit down, dear. I know it's a working day for you, and I don't want to take too much of your time. It was kind of you to bring fabrics here for me to look at. I know we already talked about ideas and you've seen the furniture pieces I want to have done. I'm sure you brought some nice fabrics I'll love."

"I hope so. If not, you can come to the shop to see more options or get Evelyn to drive you to the big fabric outlet in Fletcher."

Viola leaned over to pick up a piece of blue fabric with a subtle stripe in it. "Oh, I really love this blue fabric."

Laura smiled. "I hoped you might like that one. It's a Covington antique blue Jacquard woven with cotton and polyester. The two tones of blue, with that subtle ribbon-like stripe in the weave, gives it a rich look, I think." She unfolded the big fabric piece she'd brought so Viola could see it better. "This would look gorgeous on those two matching chairs in your living room and possibly on your dining room chairs here as well. I know you like the old fabric on the chairs there, and this fabric has a similar blue weave."

"You have a good memory, Laura," she replied. "What else have you brought for me to see?"

"Well, I agree with you that the sofa should stay a solid color, so I brought a warm light beige with a low luster." She pulled out a fabric sample to show Viola. "This beige color will tie in beautifully with the flame stitch pattern I brought for the big chair and ottoman in the living room." She laid the fabrics next to each other. "You can see that the flame stitch, a beautiful linen fabric, has a rich look like hand-embroidery, and it carries the same warm beige and the two tones of blue in the other fabrics. If you like this flame stitch, we can cover that other side chair in the living room with it, too."

Viola felt of the fabrics, smiling. "How clever of you to know exactly what I might like and what would look good in my old home without me changing too much. Can we take these pieces into the living room and lay them out so I can see how they might look?"

"Of course." Laura gathered up the fabric pieces. "I knew you'd recently had the walls painted in that soft cream and I remembered the beautiful painting over the fireplace had many of these colors in it. Actually, the colors in your living room now are beautiful, but the fabrics are simply getting worn and frayed."

As they walked around the corner into the living room, Viola's two cats looked up from the sofa where both were curled in a pile sleeping.

Viola smiled. "Well, you can see that Leah and Simon make themselves quite at home here. I've taught them not to scratch, but they do shed a little and sometimes knead." She looked around the room. "I've had all these old furniture pieces for a very long time. I do like them. I was pleased when you said my chairs and sofa were exceptionally well made and that I wouldn't regret reupholstering them."

"You won't, Viola. The construction is wonderful and you can't find pieces like this anymore. They so suit your home, too."

She smiled and went over to stroke the cats. "I think my old house would find it offensive to be filled with some of the new modern pieces out now." She wrinkled her nose. "It simply wouldn't do."

"I think every house has its own individual character. So many times people spoil that, inside and outside, by trying to make the homes something they were never intended to be."

Viola studied the fabric pieces as Laura laid them out. "I think you would have made a very good interior designer, Laura, if you had wanted to pursue that path."

"Possibly. I took a few extra courses in design while I worked on my associate degree in business. But I love making old things new again. It gives me joy to see a beautiful piece of furniture restored." She paused, studying the effect of the blue fabric on Viola's chair. "If I expand more in the business, I'd like to find old pieces, reupholster them, and resell them. I'm trying a little of that now."

"Well, good for you, taking initiative to try new things."

They talked about the upholstery work to be done and then Laura showed Viola some other fabrics she'd brought.

She studied them all and then said, "Dear, I think the fabrics we looked at first will be perfect for the living room and I would like you to use the blue stripe for the dining room chairs as you suggested. It will help to unify the two rooms, and I'm very fond of that blue fabric, too." She picked up each of the fabrics again to study them. "Could you make some pillows from each of these fabrics, too, that I can use around the room? My old ones won't suit now."

"I can take your old pillows and rework them with the new fabrics I'm using. Most are well made, and I can fluff them up as I work on them."

"Well, I'm simply so pleased with everything." Viola smiled. "I was worried about making changes, used to my familiar things. But the colors you've picked are so similar in many ways that I'm going to feel right at home with them, I'm sure."

Laura began to gather up the fabrics to take them back to the dining room.

"I'm going to the kitchen to get out the lunch I fixed for us," Viola said. "I thought we might eat out on the screened porch since the day is so pleasant. While I'm getting the lunch things out, you can put your fabrics and books back in the car if you like."

"Won't you need help?" Laura asked.

"No, it's only a light lunch. I made everything earlier before you came."

As Viola suggested, Laura loaded all the fabrics and her materials back into her car, pleased that Nannie V had liked her choices so well. Returning to the house, she made her way back to the kitchen.

"Here, take these two plates out to the glass table on the porch," Nannie V said, handing two plates to Laura. "I made each of us a chicken salad sandwich on croissant, a little spinach salad with mandarin oranges and a nice homemade dressing, plus chopped strawberries and blueberries. Will that be all right with you?"

"Oh, it looks lovely. These plates are so pretty, too."

"That's my old wedding China, a Noritake pattern from the 1950s called Colby. I always loved the blue edges, gold trim, and pretty flowers. Evelyn says it's a collectible now, that you can't find the pattern anymore." She followed Laura out to the porch to a pretty round table covered with a pink cloth and with more peonies in a small vase in the middle of the table. Each seat was already set with silver, cloth napkins, and glasses of iced tea.

Laura put the plates down and waited until Viola put two pieces of pie near each of their lunch plates and seated herself before she joined her.

Viola offered a short sweet blessing and then picked up her fork to eat, signaling in the Southern way that Laura could follow suit.

"Everything looks so beautiful," Laura said. "Thank you for fixing such a nice lunch for us."

"I love to entertain and I've been eager to get to know you better since Mitchell is seeing so much of you now."

Not sure how to answer, Laura focused on enjoying her lunch.

"Viola, I think you told me that your husband's father and mother built this house," Laura said after a short time, moving the conversation in a new direction.

"Yes, the Quinlans are an old Waynesville family. They built a number of homes around the area, including Prospect Hill, the historic home on South Main that belonged to Charles Eldridge Quinlan and his wife Annie. Most of the Quinlans are linked back to that family. My husband's father Theron, and his wife Lucia, lived here until they passed away. When Lucia died, far too young,

Eldridge and I moved over to the house here with his father. I had our boys by then, Charles Eldridge, often nicknamed C.E, and my younger son Dean, who died after he was grown in the military, so my life was busy with my husband, two little boys, and Eldridge's father Theron to take care of."

"I remember Mitchell telling me he'd lost his uncle. I'm sorry you lost him."

"Life seems to hold its tragedies for everyone." Viola stopped to eat a little more lunch. "I've been happy in this old place through the years. When Eldridge's father passed away, we moved downstairs to the big bedroom on the first floor—although as you saw, the three bedrooms upstairs are very large. It makes it easier for me to stay in this old place alone with everything I need right on one floor."

"It's a beautiful old house," Laura said.

"I'm glad you like it. Mitchell does, too. I've always planned to leave the old place to him one day. It's already beginning to be too much for me to care for now that I'm in my upper eighties." She poured them both more iced tea from the pitcher on the table.

"When Evelyn's mother Mary Dawson's husband passed away, " she continued, "she owned a big home, too. Her husband Edward had been a very successful doctor here in Waynesville. However, since neither of her sons Garrett or Julius wanted her home, both living out of state with their own lives, and since her daughter Evelyn was well settled with my son in their nice place on Church Street, Mimi sold her place and moved in with her widowed sister Francis closer to downtown. The two had always been close."

"I'm learning a lot about the family from you."

"Did you notice the old painting in the dining room of Mitchell's great grandparents and the framed photo of my husband Eldridge and me when we were young?"

"Yes, I did and that wedding picture of you was simply lovely." Laura ate a last strawberry on her plate. "I actually think Evelyn looks a lot like you did when younger even though she is not your daughter."

Nannie V chuckled. "You're not the first to comment about that. We've always gotten along very well, too." Viola stood up. "Let me take your plate, if you're finished, and then we'll eat our pie before you head back to the shop."

"What is this pie called?" Laura asked when Viola came back.

"It's Peanut Butter Pie, one of the children's favorites." She settled into her chair again. "They're coming over to stay with me this evening while Evelyn has an art event to attend. She teaches at Western Carolina University nearby in Cullowhee as well as at the Arts Council downtown. Mimi, Mitchell, and I alternate keeping the children on nights when Evelyn teaches or has meetings or events related to her work. As you probably know though, Mitchell is traveling with his cousin Rob to a bachelor party in Asheville tonight for one of their college friends who is getting married."

"I think I remember him mentioning that." Laura tasted the pie. "Ummm. How do you make this?"

"Actually, it's very easy. Most of the best things are, I think." Viola replied. "I'll write down the recipe for you. You simply combine cream cheese, confectioner's sugar, and peanut butter, stir in half the whipped topping, and pour it into a graham cracker crust. Over the top you spread the rest of the whipped topping, sprinkle it with chopped up peanut butter cups, and then freeze the pie overnight. I like to drizzle a little chocolate over each piece when I serve it, too."

Laura ate more of the pie with pleasure. "I'll definitely have to try this recipe."

"Mitchell is fond of it, too." She smiled at Laura. "He says you're a very good cook."

A little embarrassed, Laura wasn't sure what to say.

Viola reached a hand across the table to pat hers. "All of us in the Quinlan family are very fond of you, Laura, and we're delighted you and Mitchell are dating. I do want you to know that."

"Thank you," she answered, feeling herself blush at the compliment. "I'm fond of all Mitchell's family, too."

When they finished their pie, Nannie V wrote down the recipe for Laura on a floral recipe card, and then they said their goodbyes. Laura had been a little concerned that Viola Quinlan might probe further into her life or push her to discuss her feelings for Mitchell, but she'd only been gracious and hospitable. Laura drove back to the store, smiling.

Since she and Mitchell wouldn't be going out tonight, she planned to contact many of her relatives and friends in Mississippi and Alabama. She'd bought some cute "I've Moved" cards, too, and planned to send those in the mail on Monday, adding personal notes and tucking one of her business cards into each.

CHAPTER 12

It was Saturday night, and Mitchell and his cousin Rob had driven to Asheville for a bachelor party for one of their old college friends, Gavin Conway. They'd had a great time seeing old friends, enjoying a guys' night out of laughter and celebration. Rob had driven them in his car over to Asheville but Mitchell insisted on driving back, knowing Rob had kicked back a few drinks. Mitchell stopped drinking alcohol totally after his sister Alise and her husband Hudson were killed by a drunk driver. On that night, a group of teens, laughing, speeding, and drunk, had roared into the wrong turn lane on the freeway, crashing into Alise and Hudson head on. It was a tragic and stupid thing to happen, but a more common accident than most would think on busy freeways.

At Rob's place later, Mitchell stayed a little longer talking and lingering over a good evening before starting for home. Rob offered to let him drive his car back to his apartment, but Mitchell chose to walk instead. It wasn't far from Rob's home on Welch Street to Church and then to Main. Once on Main Street, Mitchell started east through downtown Waynesville, passing The Strand and other familiar businesses, all shuttered and closed now at after two in the morning.

He enjoyed the quiet as he walked through town, thinking back over the evening. He passed the Nest Home Goods Store, Massie Furniture, a couple of small businesses, and started past the big Mast General Store. But then he slowed at the muffled sound of voices. Moving closer against the side of the store and more out of sight, Mitchell peered ahead in the darkness. He could see some movement around the big steel statues of the Mountain Musicians at the corner of Main and Miller just ahead. With the heavy night darkness and the tree cover along Miller Street at this hour of the night, Mitchell couldn't see much, but he couldn't figure out why anyone would be hanging around the statues at this time of night. It wasn't exactly the time for a souvenir photo.

Mitchell moved with caution past the Mast store, staying in the shadows under the awnings of the Re/Max realty, edging his way closer to the street corner. Still noticing furtive movements around the statues, he pulled out his cell phone, deciding to call 911 to give the police an alert. He'd heard a sound like tools clanging and he could see the shadow of two men leaning over the base of the statues. Hearing the police dispatcher answer, Mitchell started to quietly give his name and an alert, but was whacked with force over the head and in the chest simultaneously as a shadow darted out from the sheltered doorway of the realty. Everything went black then.

When Mitchell woke up, groggy, his vision blurring, people were bending over him where he lay sprawled on the sidewalk and he could hear a siren approaching.

"Just lie still, Mitchell," he heard a voice say.

Mitchell tried to focus on the face above him. "Jack?" he said, recognizing his old friend on the police force. "I tried to call…"

Jack squatted down closer to him. "The call came through that you started, Mitchell, and they heard your muffled cry when you were hit. From what we've seen here, you interrupted a theft in motion. We found part of the base of the Mountain Musician statues already dismantled. Whether the thieves planned to try to take those big statues down in full or to only remove parts of them we'll never know. However, they fled when they realized someone had seen them. They had a lookout hidden in that inset area of the realty doorway and probably another on the other side of Main, maybe even one on Miller. We can't know. They'd left by the time we got here and found you."

Mitchell tried to clear his head to see better, but he felt himself beginning to waft toward unconsciousness again as he moved and his chest hurt like the dickens.

"Did you see anyone clearly?" Jack asked. "Recognize anyone or see a car or van parked nearby?"

Mitchell shook his head, which really hurt. "No, I just saw the shadows of two men in dark clothing."

The ambulance, siren screeching its approach, roared up beside the curb and Mitchell soon found himself being ministered to and loaded for transport to the hospital.

He reached out a hand toward Jack before they put him in the ambulance. "Call my mom," he said. "Don't let her hear about this from someone else. Tell her I'm okay."

Jack nodded. "I'll do that right now."

The next hours were a blur of arriving at the Haywood Regional Medical Center, the area hospital that served Waynesville, Clyde, and other small towns in Haywood Country. Mitchell was able to communicate some basic information on arrival and provide ID, knowing his mother would show up soon to give any additional information needed.

With a hit to his head and losing consciousness, a battery of assorted diagnostic and imaging tests were ordered and then other checks and scans given for the hit to his chest. Mitchell's mother arrived not long after to sit with him whenever she could in the ER and now in the room they'd finally put him in.

He'd slipped off to sleep for a short time and woke now to see his mother sitting in the chair by his bed.

"How are you feeling?" she asked.

He tried to grin. "Like I got beat up by a couple of thugs."

As he reached for some water by the bed, his mother got up to get it to hand to him. When she did, she leaned over to kiss his forehead. "This scared me, son."

"Where are the kids?" he asked.

"Glaydean Sterling came over to stay with them. You know she and Neal and their kids live right next door. She knows the house and she knows the children well. Her three children Taylor, Kirby, and Sharon are in and out of our home all the time, as are Mackenzie and Charlie at her house. Tomorrow is Sunday; she and her husband Neal will see to the children until we get back home. They're good neighbors."

"Did you call Nannie V and Mimi?"

She raised her eyebrows. "No, not at this hour of the night. In the morning will be soon enough—certainly before the newspapers hit their houses." She smirked. "I imagine you'll be painted quite the hero, interrupting another theft of city property in Waynesville."

"Do you think that's what was in progress?" He tried to remember what Jack had said.

"Yes. The police found signs they were trying to detach those fifteen-foot steel statues on the corner of Miller Street. Can you believe that? I can't imagine how in the world they planned to haul those big things out of town."

Mitchell struggled to focus his memory. "Jack said they might have only planned to take some part of them away. "

She shook her head. "Well, I suppose that might have been possible. If the sculptor had fitted and welded pieces together to make the statues, they might have been able to dismantle parts of them in some way, but it's shocking to think about."

"Because it's art?"

She frowned at him. "Because it's one more ugly theft with still no one knowing why these things are happening." She sighed. "You could have been killed, Mitchell."

He saw her put a hand to her face, noticing tears on her cheeks.

"I'm okay, Mom."

She crossed her arms in annoyance. "You've had a minor concussion. You will have a head bruise and pain for a time. You had dizziness, loss of awareness. I heard all those medical people mumbling about this. It almost took a year off my life, believe me. But they say it wasn't a serious head or brain injury now." She closed her eyes for a moment. "That hit to your rib cage caused bruising and a little crack in one rib, but no major breaks and no injuries to internal organs. Despite an array of bruises and scrapes from the fall, you'll heal with some rest after a short time. You were lucky."

"And blessed."

"Well, that, too, of course."

"Have they caught anyone related to the theft? Did anyone see any of the thieves or their car after?"

She shook her head. "No, but Jack Salter came by the hospital when you were having some tests to check on you. He said he'd be back in the morning to talk to you, to see if you remembered anything else."

"When do I get to go home?"

"I imagine after some more checks they'll release you tomorrow or no later than Monday afternoon."

He rolled his eyes. "I have appointments Monday and a training session at the store."

She gave him a steely look. "Someone else at Quinlans can handle all that or it can be rescheduled. I'll call Norma and ask her to phone Rosamarie and Kent. They can all handle things, Mitchell—you know that—and you'll need to rest at your place or at mine for several days. So don't be thinking you'll be going straight back to work anyway. You took a hard hit on your head and to your chest."

Mitchell glanced at his wrist, not seeing his watch there. "What time is it?" he asked his mother.

She glanced at her own watch. "Nearly six now."

"Why don't you go home to be there for the kids when they get up? You know they'll be upset, even with Glaydean there. It might bring back bad memories." He watched her hesitate. "I'll be fine, Mom. And I need to sleep a little before they come in here again to poke something else into my IV."

She reached for her purse. "All right. I don't want either of those children to start having nightmares again. We went through enough of that in the past and I don't want them to start clinging to us, crying and afraid, every time we need to go somewhere either."

"We've been through some rough times." He smiled at her.

"This is only minor stuff in comparison, Mom. Don't worry about leaving me."

"Well, I'll come back later, when my mother or Nannie V can come to stay with the children." She paused. "If I can bring Mackenzie and Charlie that would probably be better. Then they'd see you are fine."

"That's a good idea." He winked at her. "Bring me something to eat, too. You know hospital food isn't anything to write home about."

She came over to kiss him on the cheek before she left. "Rest and get better," she said, leaving a little waft of her floral cologne on the air as she left.

With the room quiet now, Mitchell closed his eyes and soon drifted off to sleep.

After breakfast and more poking and prodding by one of the doctors on weekend duty, a change of bedding, and a trip to the bathroom with help from one of the nurses, Mitchell leaned back against the pillows again. "Hospitals are a pill," he mumbled to himself.

He'd hunted up one of those music channels on the television earlier, which now played in the background, covering some of the routine hospital noises. It gave him a little peace, too. He hated the erratic beeps, intercom announcements, and constant sounds of machines in the hospital. The confinement and the dependence. Looking out the window, he saw blue skies and sunshine, provoking him further that he couldn't be outside. He'd never been a good patient.

A knock on the door got his attention, and Laura looked in the doorway. "Can you have company?"

He grinned. "Yeah. Seeing you makes my day." She wore a soft blue knit shirt, white slacks and sandals, her familiar purse draped over a shoulder. And her smile gave him a healthy jolt making him glad to be alive. He knew it could have gone worse for him.

She handed him a box, which he opened, discovering several homemade Danish pastries, the rich filling oozing out of them.

"Thank you, sweet woman," he said, reaching in the box to pick one to try.

"I stopped by Kandi's Cakes & Bake Shop on my way over to the hospital. I remembered you liked their pastries."

"I love them." He looked across from her. "How did you learn I was here?"

"Your mother called me." She leaned forward, anxious now. "I'm so sorry you were attacked like that. Are you all right?"

"I will be with a little time. I just got a banged up head, bruises, and a slightly cracked rib. I'll heal, thankfully. The guy who hit me sure landed a strong punch or two, I can tell you that." He took a big bite of the apple-filled pastry.

"Tell me what happened," she said.

He told her the story, around eating the pastry.

"Why did you walk home alone at that time of night?" She looked puzzled.

He grinned at her. "I've lived in Waynesville all my life, and walked home to my old home on Church or to my own apartment hundreds of times at night after a show or event or an evening at a friend's place." He hesitated. "This time I'd been over in Asheville to a bachelor party with Rob. He did some drinking; I didn't. He'd driven us over to Asheville in his car but I drove him home. He only lives over on Welch, a few blocks away, so I decided to walk home. It was a nice night. I wanted the exercise. That wasn't an out of the norm thing for me to do, Laura."

"I suppose." A smile tweaked her lips. "But I imagine you would have read me the riot act for doing the same thing."

"You know it's more dangerous for girls to be out at night alone." He frowned. "You arguing with me on that point won't change the facts about it."

"I just hate that you were hurt, and your mother is right, too. It could have been worse and much more serious."

He winked at her. "Well, you see God was watching out for me." He finished off the pastry, licking his fingers after. "Set this box inside the drawer there by the bed, if you would. I don't want one of the nurses to see it and fuss at me."

Her eyes widened as she got up to put them away. "Should I not have brought these?"

"No. You definitely should have brought them. I enjoyed every bite of that pastry and they haven't put me on any kind of restrictive diet, just fed me pretty bland food so far."

"Your mother said you might get to come home today or tomorrow after your doctor is sure you're all right." She hesitated. "She hopes you'll come stay over at the house."

He wrinkled his nose. "I'd rather stay at my place but it might be better for the kids if I stay at the house. They tend to get overly alarmed if anything happens to Mom or me, if we get sick or hurt. It's pretty stressful for two little kids to come to terms with losing their parents suddenly one night in an accident. It took some time for us to work our way through and past that." His eyes moved over her. "If you'll come see me, it will make it better."

She smiled. "I'll see what I can do. I already told your mom I would stay with you and the kids on Tuesday and Thursday nights when she teaches her class at the college. She's also worried about leaving you for her day classes when the children are in school, but she says Nannie V or Mimi will stay with you then."

He rolled his eyes. "I'll only need a few days to a week to heal up and get back to normal. Hopefully less."

Another knock came at the door, letting Jack in to ask him more questions. Laura left and the day was soon filled with more visitors and the ongoing arrival of flowers and plants until the room looked like a dang plant nursery.

As the afternoon moved on, some serious pain kicked in. Mitchell's head ached and it hurt to cough or sneeze. Like overdoing on a hike, various aches and pains arrived from the hits he'd taken and the fall to the hard sidewalk last night. The ongoing company all day kept his mind and time occupied but by evening he was, admittedly, worn out, and a little glad his doctor decided he wasn't going home until the next day. The doctor was waiting for one or two final test results and keeping a watch on Mitchell's condition.

Mitchell had to tell Jack and another officer again today that he hadn't seen the face of the man who hit and knocked him out, that he'd been looking down at his phone when the man jumped out of the doorway at him. "He hit fast and quick," Mitchell told them. "And the other men working around the statues were totally hidden by the darkness and the shadows of the trees."

The police were glad another theft was stopped, of course, but frustrated to have no further leads or witnesses. And no explanations as to why the thefts continued to happen.

The kids, who did get to come to the hospital briefly, were excited about the write-up in the newspaper, featuring his name and photos. Mitchell, however, was only sorry he hadn't seen anything more to help find the individuals continuing to cause trouble around town.

Rob showed up late in the evening. "Man, I feel like this is my fault."

"Why, bro?"

His cousin shrugged, pushing back the ball cap on his head. "Because I was drinking and you had to bring me home and then walk home."

Mitchell shifted in the bed to get comfortable. "You and I have walked around Waynesville since we were kids at night and we never had a problem. Besides you offered to let me drive your car to my place. You said you'd walk over to pick it up the next day."

"My mom said I should have insisted you take the car, and she read me the riot act about drinking."

Mitchell laughed. "We did go to a bachelor party. I was the odd one to not even have a drink, and you weren't drunk Rob, just not fit to drive. Quit worrying about it. Stuff happens sometimes. I'll be all right."

They talked and visited for a time and then another nurse came in, signaling it time for Rob to head home. "If we ever find that guy that hit you, maybe we can beat the snot out of him," Rob said before he left.

The idea sounded appealing right then when coughing, deep breaths, or sneezes hurt like the devil.

CHAPTER 13

$\mathbf{L}$aura glanced at her calendar. Two weeks had passed since Mitchell was hurt. Admittedly, it frightened her that Mitchell was attacked so near their apartments and businesses on Miller Street. She'd found herself more cautious walking around town in the evenings ever since, even while knowing it unlikely she'd run into any problems at the times of night when she was out.

Mitchell had healed rapidly from his injuries, but he'd been cranky to be out of work almost a week, impatient about the forced rest. She'd stopped by the house to sit with him a time or two and she felt glad, along with him, when he got to move back to his own place.

Now on a lovely spring evening, Laura closed the shop and headed upstairs to her apartment. As she sat down on the sofa to relax for a while, she got a text from Mitchell on her phone. "Hey, I'm outside your back door entrance. Can you open the alarm so I can come up? I brought you something."

Laura released the lock for him and then opened the door of her apartment as Mitchell bounded up the back stairs carrying a cardboard box.

"What's in your box?" she asked as he followed her inside.

"Dinner, for one thing." He went to the kitchen, put the box on a side counter, and pulled out a casserole dish. "I left the office early today to go to my grandmother Mimi and Frances's house to mow the grass for them. They gave me this casserole for dinner as a thank you. I thought I'd share it with you. Have you eaten yet?"

She shook her head. "No, I just got off work and was resting after a big day at the shop." She peeked under the aluminum foil at the casserole, still warm with its aroma slipping out into the room to tantalize her. "Ummm. This smells wonderful. What is it?"

"Mimi calls it The Sisters Secret Sausage and Potato Casserole." He laughed. "That means it's one of Mimi and Frances' recipes. Mimi told me it had smoked sausage, frozen shredded potatoes, sour cream, onion, cream of chicken soup, and cheese in it. She also said all I needed to make a meal was to add some green peas or a salad."

Laura turned to the refrigerator. "Fortunately, I have frozen peas in the freezer; they'll only take five minutes in the microwave. We can set the table while I cook them."

They busied themselves putting plates and silverware on the dining room table. While Mitchell poured iced tea, Laura got a loaf of wheat bread out of the old breadbox with roosters on the front of it. The breadbox had been her mom's, and Laura loved it.

When the peas were ready, they filled their plates in the kitchen and carried them into the dining room. Before Mitchell sat down, he walked back to a table by the front door and returned carrying a floral gift bag stuffed with pink tissue.

"What's this?" she asked as he handed it to her.

"A little bird told me that tomorrow, May 20th, is your birthday, so I brought you an early gift," he answered, sitting down. "You can open it before we eat."

"How sweet of you to get me something. Thank you." She dug a card out of the gift bag and two books wrapped in tissue. Opening the card first, she smiled over the sweet verse and Mitchell's scrawled signature. In an envelope inside the card, she found a plastic gift card with a picture of Biltmore on the front.

"It's a season pass for you for Biltmore Estate and Gardens in Asheville. I thought if you could get off from work tomorrow I'd take you to the house and the Floral Festival so you can see the gardens in bloom. I know you haven't ever been to Biltmore, and it's a beautiful time to visit."

She put a hand to her heart. "What a lovely gift. I've heard everyone talk about Biltmore and I've been wanting to go!"

He grinned, obviously pleased.

"This is so nice of you!" She jumped up to hug and kiss him. "Thank you. Thank you."

He kissed her back. "I admit I checked with Nolan and Rita to see if they would cover the shop for you tomorrow. They said they'd be glad to. Rita said to tell you she planned to bake some banana bread for you tonight for a birthday treat. She and Nolan also said for you to be sure to come down to see them before you leave so they can wish you a happy birthday, too."

"I'll do that. I'm so excited!" She sat back down and then looked at the paperback books wrapped in tissue.

"Those are books about Biltmore, telling about the Vanderbilt family that built the estate and about how the gardens were created. I thought you'd enjoy looking through those before you go. I put a Biltmore map in the bag, too, that I saved from one of my last visits."

"This is the most wonderful gift. I don't know what to say."

"Well, let's eat dinner and then I'll tell you more about our day tomorrow."

They settled in to eat dinner, Laura asking excited questions now and then while they ate. When they finished, Mitchell opened one of the books to show her a picture. "This is George Vanderbilt and his wife Edith. George bought thousands of acres near Asheville in the late 1800s, built a grand home, and then contracted Frederick Olmsted to create his gardens. The gardens cover thirty acres and the estate over 8,000 acres. The gardens at Biltmore are always pretty to walk through but especially in the spring. We may have missed the glory of the tulips already but the azaleas will be gorgeous. I think you'll love seeing the house and walking around the grounds and gardens."

Mitchell spread the Biltmore map across the table. "We'll enter here." He pointed to the road leading into the estate. "Then we'll drive to the parking area and walk up the road to the house. It will take us most of the morning to tour the house—it's big and has two hundred and fifty rooms—but we'll head outdoors to see the grounds and gardens after. When we get tired, we can sit on the lawn to eat a small picnic in front of the Diana statue looking toward the house. I take the kids there when we go to Biltmore. I can carry a backpack with a couple of bottles of water and a light lunch."

He smiled at her. "I don't want us to eat too much for lunch because I made reservations for dinner at the Biltmore Inn Restaurant."

"I heard that's a very elegant place. Won't we need to dress up?"

Mitchell pulled out his phone to look it up. "Uh, oh. It does suggest nice attire at night—slacks, collared shirts for men, dresses or blouses with skirts or pants for women, and nice shoes." Mitchell frowned. "But it's hot out now. I'd planned to wear shorts and good walking shoes tomorrow. There's a lot of walking around the gardens and grounds and through the estate house, too."

Laura smiled at him. "Won't we drive to the restaurant afterwards?" She pointed to the map. "It looks like it's at some distance from the house and gardens. Maybe we could take extra clothes and change in the lounge or something."

"That's a good idea. I'll call to see if that would be all right." He started looking for the restaurant's number on his cell phone.

"Do you want some coffee?" she asked

"Yeah, that would be good." He dialed the Biltmore while she fixed the coffee and then he walked into the kitchen to bring their dishes from the table. "The lady at the restaurant said there are several restrooms we can change in, that it would be fine."

"Good. I certainly didn't want to tour the Biltmore grounds in dressy clothes."

After they finished cleaning up in the kitchen, they carried their coffees into the living room to sit down and relax.

Laura glanced through her Biltmore books and studied her map while they sipped their coffee. Mitchell had put some music on in the background. They'd grown comfortable with each other now,

Mitchell reading the newspaper with his feet propped on the big coffee table.

"Are you sure you've recovered enough for a big day out tomorrow?" she asked, curling one leg under her on the sofa.

"I'm fine, Laura, and the doc gave me a full release." He glanced back at his newspaper again. "You know, there's still no word and no clues as to who has been doing the thefts around town, but there hasn't been another incident since I was attacked."

"Maybe that scared them off, the idea of getting caught."

"They may be lying low because of that." He ran a hand through his hair. "Rob and I can't figure out any reason for the thefts, though. There has to be a reason."

"Maybe, but there isn't always a reason for everything."

"You could be right." He looked across at her, and Laura felt that old familiar attraction kicking in.

Mitchell grinned. "I don't know the reason why this humming in the air begins every time I'm with you either, but I do enjoy it."

Laura looked down at her lap, a little embarrassed.

"Once when my dad and I were sitting in the den at home talking, my mother came through the room, stopping to pick up things here and there, sending Dad a little smile. He forgot the thread of his conversation entirely, just watching her. When she left the room, he looked at me and said, 'Ever since the first day I met your mother, she's knocked me for a loop. Makes me forget what I'm thinking or doing.'"

He smiled over the memory. "As a teenager, I thought it was a nutty thing for Dad to say. It made me roll my eyes. You know how kids are. But now I know exactly what Dad was talking about." He moved in closer. "You mean more to me every day, Laura. I hope you know that."

Mitchell leaned in to kiss her then and to whisper love words to her as they wrapped themselves up in each other. Music from the radio played softly in the background, enhancing the mood. The musky lime scent of his cologne drifted across her senses, his hands moving over her in a magical way, and she loved the way he feathered kisses across her face, her neck, and in her hair, thrilling her.

Mitchell always sent lovely jolts of feeling through her whenever they kissed, whenever he held her, and sometimes when he simply looked at her across the room or gave her one of those suggestive smiles of his or a wink. Laura had never felt this way about anyone else before in her life, and she knew she was falling more and more in love with Mitchell Quinlan every day.

"You hear that song playing—'Like the First Time?'" he whispered. "I think of you whenever I hear it. Because it always feels like the first time whenever I'm with you, like the first time we met. I wish I could tell you or show you how much you mean to me. I'm so glad I found you…so glad."

Laura pulled away after a few more minutes, feeling Mitchell's hands growing more aggressive, hearing his breathing becoming more ragged. Somewhat like sensing when she needed to pause on an upholstery piece to study it, to not make a mistake in the work, she sensed when she needed to pause with Mitchell, when things were starting to rush out of control. She put a hand to his face when he started to move in again.

"It's time to stop," she whispered, pulling back from his arms, trying to steady her voice.

He sat back after a minute, closing his eyes, steadying his breathing.

She always worried he'd be mad when she drew things to a halt.

"I look forward to tomorrow," she offered after a few minutes, hoping to introduce a new subject.

He smiled finally, his breath steadying. "We'll make it a good day," he said, standing up. "And I'd better head home."

He went to the kitchen to retrieve the casserole. "I'll take the last of this casserole with me, too, so I can clean up the dish and get it back to Mimi and Frances."

"Tell them how much we liked it and that I'd love the recipe."

"I'll do that." He paused at the door. "I'll come pick you up about nine if that's okay."

"That sounds good."

His eyes moved over her for a minute. "I'll blink the lights for you when I get back to my place," he said, his voice softer. "If you see an extra blink, you'll know how much I wished I didn't have to leave."

He slipped out of the door and Laura sat back down on the sofa to take a few deep breaths. She certainly understood that feeling and she wasn't surprised to see that extra flick of the lights later. Their feelings were certainly growing more intense.

After tossing and turning for a time, Laura finally fell asleep and woke excited the next morning about the day ahead. Rita and Nolan brought her a little gift for her birthday, as well as the banana bread. Laura unwrapped the present to find a cute carved rooster and hen, each about five to six inches high, both painted colorfully and a perfect size for her apartment.

"I love this little rooster and hen," Laura said, keeping an eye on the street out the window. Mitchell had called to say he'd pick her up in front of the shop soon and to be watching for him.

"Nolan and I saw them last weekend at the Farmer's and Craft Market that's opened out on the highway. They looked like something you'd like." Rita gave her a hug.

"Zack Barnwell carved those out of white pine. He's a good hand with a knife," Nolan added.

"He is obviously very talented and I know exactly the spot for these in my kitchen window." She saw Mitchell's Bronco then slowing down in front of the store.

"There's Mitchell," Nolan said, spotting his car, too. "You run on and have a good day. We'll set these gifts in your office and we'll take good care of the shop, too, so don't worry."

"Thanks. I hope you two have a good day, too," she said, grabbing her purse and a small tote bag, with her extra clothes in it, from the chair by the door. Slipping her purse over her shoulder, Laura ran out to Mitchell's car. It had been a long time since she'd enjoyed a special birthday. And she loved knowing Mitchell had planned it just for her.

CHAPTER 14

Mitchell still remembered that jolt of feeling and the intense physical attraction he felt the first day he met Laura in early March. Since then, he'd kept expecting the feelings to diminish, skeptical about quick attractions. Instead, his feelings for Laura had continued to grow and sweeten over the months. He still thought it the dangedest thing how it all began, something he never thought would happen to him. But crazy or not, like it or not, he'd fallen head over heels in love with Laura O'Dell, and the more he came to know her the more he loved her. She haunted his thoughts and tormented his nights, and she interfered with his work focus and thinking. Soft, sweet, and pretty, she aroused all his deep protective feelings, too, as well a barrage of heady sensual needs he continually tried to tramp down. Who knew that love could be so good and torturous at the same time?

His heart lifted now as he pulled up in front of Laura's shop and saw her all but skipping out of the door. Smiling, so beautiful, and obviously excited about their day ahead. He figured a girl with an upholstery shop would love a grand and beautiful house full of antiques like the Biltmore. Remembering how often he'd seen her gush with pleasure over every spring flower and shrub popping up around Waynesville this spring, too, he knew she'd love the gardens, as well.

Mitchell had wanted to create a happy day for Laura, with so little family around to help her celebrate. He felt pleased to see how excited she was about the day.

"How old are you today?" he asked as she slipped into the car, shut the door, and began to buckle her seatbelt.

"Twenty-six," she said. "And it only seems like the other day I was excited about turning sixteen so I could get my driver's license."

"Feeling old?" He teased.

"Not even a little bit. But definitely happier."

"This has been a good move for you to Waynesville," he said, heading out of town to the freeway that would take them to Asheville.

"It has. I love it here, but I admit I woke up this morning thinking about my sister. We always had a lot of birthday fun growing up." She touched the necklace she wore above her yellow knit shirt, paired with navy capris today.

He glanced toward the necklace. "It looks like that necklace has your name on it."

"It does. It was a gift from Georgina when I turned sixteen. She was in college by then, our mother gone, and Dad wasn't ever very clever about gift buying. It seemed lovely to get something this personal from her. I went to Georgina's college to stay one weekend not long after that to hear her sing solo in a big choral concert the school was giving. She was so gifted and I felt so proud and special to be there."

She sighed. "Not long after that she took off, left school, and ran away with Chance Richardson. Dad and I couldn't believe it. She was well into her junior year and only had another year of school to graduate." She shook her head. "I still can't figure out why in the world she would do that."

"I guess she fell pretty hard for him."

"Obviously. He is handsome and he sings well, but I think she got caught up in the whirlwind of his dreams."

"Maybe everyone with a gift or talent yearns for big success. Even when you aren't gifted growing up, you fantasize about being a big movie star or singer. Didn't you?"

She giggled. "Maybe. I had some movie star crushes, I admit. Girls do, you know. I pinned up a few pictures in my bedroom and dreamed over them."

"Mackenzie already has a crush on a few stars herself."

"I saw a photo in her room." Laura pulled a pair of sunglasses from her purse to slip them on. "I've been hearing her talk about summer already, excited for school to be out. She was telling me about some camps she hoped to go to."

"She and Charlie both went to camp last summer and want to go again." He accelerated to pass a slow-moving vehicle as they headed east on the interstate. "It's sort of tradition for girls in our family to go to Skyland Camp for girls in Clyde. The camp has been operating for over one hundred years. Both my grandmothers, my mom, and Alise went there as girls."

"That's the camp Mackenzie mentioned."

He tapped a finger on the steering wheel. "We're a big camp family. I always went to Camp Caroline, the boys' camp in Brevard. Dad went there, too, when he was a kid and Charlie went last year and loved it. Charlie and Mackenzie will probably go to the Girl Scout and Boy Scout camps nearby for a week, too, and to Bible School at the church later in the summer. Usually, they enjoy Bible School a second time at their grandmother Mimi's church. They'll be busy this summer and that's good. Mom still works in the summer and teaches a few summer classes. It's getting harder now for Nannie V or for Mimi and Frances to keep up with both the kids for more than a day to help out. Mackenzie and Charlie can be a handful and they need to be kept busy and doing things."

Laura crossed her leg and Mitchell's eyes flicked over the motion.

"I really enjoyed meeting the kids' grandfather Sam Jacobs when he came through town earlier this month. You were still at your mom's then." Laura smiled across at him. "Mackenzie and Charlie are really excited about going to Sam's beach house at Tybee Island for a week at the Fourth of July. I think your mother looks forward to it, as well. Sam was talking about a riverboat cruise they planned to take to watch the fireworks from the water."

Mitchell frowned, remembering that conversation.

"What's causing that frown?" Laura asked, always quick to pick up on his emotions.

He shifted traffic lanes to stay on I-40 east to Asheville, avoiding answering her question for a minute. Their turn to the Biltmore wouldn't be too far ahead.

"Do you not want them to go to Sam's again?" Laura pushed the issue. "Something's bothering you."

Mitchell sighed. "I was at the house this time, still recovering, when Sam came for one of his weekend visits. I kept noticing some ways he and Mom acted together."

She turned to him in surprise. "You think they're interested in each other?"

"I don't know about Mom. I can't read her as well. But it seemed obvious to me Sam is interested in my mother."

She laughed. "Well, that's a thought-provoking situation. But I guess it's all right They've both lost a spouse, are alone." She grew quiet for a moment. "Do you not like Sam Jacobs for some reason?"

"Sam's okay, a good man. It's just hard to think about the idea of them as a couple somehow."

Laura nodded. "I remember a few years after my mother died, my dad went out a few times with a woman in our church. It sounds ugly to admit it, but I felt glad when nothing came of it. I liked the idea of my mother and dad together in my mind. I wasn't sure I wanted to see anyone else come into our family picture. My dad and I were really close, too."

"Well, I guess you know the awkward feeling then. It seems weird to me, as well, seeing some man making moves, even if subtle, on my mom." He shifted his car into the turn lane. "We're almost at the Biltmore now. There's the sign ahead." Mitchell smiled at her. "I hope you're ready for a fun day."

"I am," she said as they started up the long drive into Biltmore. "Look at this beautiful forest land we're driving through—and oh, my goodness, look at the azaleas along the road. They're simply gorgeous. I can't wait to see everything."

Mitchell stopped at the reception center and then moved on

through the admission gate to the designated parking lots near the Biltmore house. Later in the day, they'd drive over to the Antler Village and Winery and then to the Biltmore Inn and Restaurant, which sat in the northwest corner of the estate property.

As they got out of the car, Laura draped her purse over her shoulder and Mitchell strapped a lightweight pack around his waist, containing two small bottles of water and some snacks for a lunch later. They found the walkway to the house then and Laura started oohing and aahing as the grandeur of the big French chateau came into view. It was truly a stupendous place, more like a castle, and even Mitchell looked forward to walking through the Vanderbilt home again.

After they toured the house, which took about two hours, they came back out into the May sunshine to begin walking the trails in the garden areas. Because Mitchell had been here so often over the years, he knew the prettiest places to take Laura.

"There are over twenty miles of trails here," he told her. "We'll hit the highlights of some of the nicest spots today. We can come back and see more another time since we both have season passes now. I like to bring my bike over here to ride, too."

"Oh, I'd love that. I used to ride a lot around Amory and I brought my bike. It's in one of the storage rooms in the back of the shop."

He grinned at her. "That's good to know. We can ride around downtown in Waynesville and on some of the bike trails nearer home, too. My dad loved to bike. I rode a lot with him, hiked and fished with him, too. He really loved the outdoors."

"I've enjoyed the hikes you've taken me on, like the trail to Purchase Knob, high up on the mountain behind Maggie Valley. It was gorgeous there and the views were incredible. I also loved the day we went with Rob and Becky Ray to see all those waterfalls in the Pisgah Forest area—Looking Glass Falls, Moore Cove Falls, Cove Creek, and Sliding Rock Falls."

"That was a good day. We'll plan another day like that soon." He pointed ahead. "Here's our first garden trail."

Mitchell walked Laura around the Shrub Garden Path near the house and then down the long stretch of green lawn to the Diana statue under a wooden gazebo. They settled on the grass to rest and eat their lunch there, chatting about all they'd seen and enjoying the day. After a lunch break, they walked back toward the house again and into the landscaped gardens in front of the Conservatory.

In the Walled Garden they didn't find many tulips still in bloom with May nearly gone. "Last month it would have been stupendous here," Mitchell told her. "There are more than 80,000 tulip bulbs in this four-acre garden."

Laura took his hand. "Well, I can look forward to seeing them next year. But look at all the incredible flowers here now. What a beautiful, beautiful place this is. I can't imagine what it must have been like for the Vanderbilts to live here or for their daughter Cornelia and the Vanderbilt grandchildren to play here on these wonderful grounds. Think what glorious and imaginative games they must have invented on these garden paths."

She pointed at a wall ahead. "What are those heavenly purple and white blooms draped over the wall? I've seen them in other places already, too."

"Those are wisteria. I'm not a flower guy, but mother knows her plants and flowers well and has educated me some over the years."

They cut through to the historic Rose Garden next. "There are nearly two thousand roses here in over a hundred varieties." Mitchell gestured around. "Most are not in bloom now, but some are. I read that the World Rose Society gave this place a Garden of Excellence award. A lot of these roses have thrived here since the 1800s when Biltmore was created."

Laura started down the garden's pathways. "We'll definitely have to come back here when the roses peak and go to Junaluska's Rose Walk, too."

After wandering around in the Rose Garden, which also included some beautiful statuary, they took time to go inside the glass-roofed Conservatory so Laura could see the hothouse flowers, like orchids, in bloom, and then walked outside again to admire the terraced butterfly garden.

There was no one way, or best way, to tour the Biltmore property, but Mitchell had mapped a route out in his mind to follow that he thought Laura would enjoy today. With this in mind, he led her next on the quarter mile Spring Garden Path and then down the winding Azalea Garden Path to Bass Pond. They stopped to rest briefly by the pond on a pretty bench before starting back again.

"I loved the bridge at the end of the lake with the big waterfall tumbling behind it," Laura said as she looked across the lake scene before them.

"There's a great story related to that bridge at the dam." Mitchell crossed an ankle over his knee. "A man decided to propose marriage at that beautiful spot but accidentally dropped the diamond ring over the bridge into the pond at the bottom of the falls. The ring wasn't insured yet so he was distraught and sought out some of the Biltmore gardeners to help him find it, but nobody did."

"Oh, that's sad."

"It was sad, but later, the Biltmore staff kept looking for the ring, and using an underwater metal detector, they actually found it for the couple, creating a happy ending to an otherwise unhappy event."

Her face lit in a smile. "I'll think of that whenever I see that bridge now."

"I always do, too. Come on. We need to walk back toward the house now to see the rest of the gardens." He stood and offered her a hand as she got up. "Are you having a good time and not growing too tired yet?"

"I'm having the best of times and no, I'm not that tired. In fact, I can't wait to see what's next."

Near the house again, they explored the Italian Garden with its pools, statuary, waterlilies and beautiful koi fish. It was always a spot Mitchell enjoyed.

"I wonder how long it took to create a place like this?" Laura asked

Mitchell paused to look back across the gardens and then toward the house. "I imagine any of the gardens we've seen are an ongoing work in progress. Think of all the gardeners we saw working today. But I did read it took workers six years to build the house, which is kind of amazing considering its size and that this North Carolina area wasn't very well populated in the late 1800s."

She glanced around with pleasure. "I can't tell you what a wonderful day I've had."

"Well, it isn't over yet." He glanced at his watch. "It's four now, but we have time to drive to the Farm by Antler Village so you can see the animals. That's always one of Mackenzie and Charlie's favorite places to go. The kids will have a fit if I don't take you to see some of the animals, like the goats, lambs, chickens, and the draft horses."

Mitchell took her hand to start toward the car. "At Antler Village there are some shops and the big Winery, too. You know I don't drink, but you're welcome to sample some of the wines, while learning more about how the wine is created. You'll probably like the arts and crafts shops in the Village, like The Barn Door and a home accents store called Traditions." He moved around a group of tourists talking. "Of course, the kids' favorite place is the Creamery with its ice creams, shakes, and sundaes."

"It sounds like fun."

"There are walking trails near the Antler Village area, too. In late summer there is a mile-long sunflower patch along the greenway. Mom always loves to come to see that."

"What time is our dinner reservation?"

"It's at six in the Biltmore Inn Restaurant not far behind Antler Village. We'll plan to get there early so we can slip in the restrooms to change and put our clothes in the car before going in to dinner."

Mitchell pointed out more sights they'd missed as they walked toward the parking lot. "There is another big restaurant at Biltmore, too, called the Deerpark. On another visit, we'll go there to eat. It's less formal and has buffet options at certain times. It's pretty with views looking out over Biltmore's farmland."

After finding their car, Mitchell drove them to explore the Antler

Village area and at five thirty, after a long day, they arrived at the Biltmore Inn. They took the tote bags they'd brought with them into two of the restrooms, changed and cleaned up a little before coming back to meet in the lobby.

"You look beautiful," Mitchell said, walking a partial circle around her and admiring the soft blue dress she wore. "How did you keep that dress from getting wrinkled?"

"It's knit and doesn't wrinkle easily if you fold it right. The blue color looks like those beautiful flowers we saw today, doesn't it?"

"Yes, it does." He noticed she'd taken her hair out of its ponytail and put it up in a pretty twist in the back. Moving closer, he caught a whiff of that citrus scent she always wore, too.

She gave him a kiss on the cheek. "You look nice yourself in that gray jacket and slacks with your crisp white shirt."

Mitchell winked at her. "Now that we've finished complimenting each another, let me take our bags back to the car. You can wait for me here." He gestured to some sofas in the lobby. "I won't be long."

He returned quickly and they were soon seated in the restaurant at a lovely table by a window with stupendous views across the estate grounds. The tables were draped in pristine white linens, the gold upholstered chairs elegant and comfortable, and the rich Oriental rug covering the dining area especially stunning.

Laura looked around in appreciation. "This is a tasteful and refined place. It fits the ambience of the whole day, don't you think?" She looked down at the menu the waiter had brought. "What should I order?"

Mitchell smiled. She was always so amenable about food choices. "The seafood entrees are really good here, so I'm planning to order the trout with peas, carrots, ham and a basil emulsion."

She leaned forward and whispered softly, "What is a basil emulsion?"

"A sauce for meat or vegetables to give them a burst of flavor. It usually has olive oil, fresh basil, and garlic in it. It's good for dipping bread in, too."

She flushed. "I don't often eat at elegant places."

Mitchell glanced at the menu again. "Do you like scallops?"

"Oh, yes," she replied.

"You might like the scallops with sweet corn succotash, crispy okra and a little lobster butter sauce." He pointed to the item on her menu as he read the words.

"Oh, that does sound good." She smiled.

"I'd say anything you ordered here would be good, Laura. I plan to order us both a small salad to begin, too. I'm hungry after our long day, aren't you?"

"Yes, and I'm tired, too, but in a happy way."

Passing on the waiter's offer for wine or alcoholic drinks ahead of dinner, Mitchell asked for coffee instead. He still needed to drive home from Asheville, and he thought it would give both of them a lift after a long day.

It was nice to spend this lovely time with Laura after their good day and it seemed easy to imagine the pleasure of a life with her now. He watched across the table as she talked with animation about all they'd seen while they shared dinner.

"I simply itched to feel some of that beautiful upholstery material used on the furniture in the house. Can you believe how gorgeous it was?" She leaned forward, her face still rosy from a day in the sunshine. "Some of those lush bedspreads in the estate bedrooms were simply opulent. I wonder if any of those are the original fabrics? And did you see all those books in the library? Can you even imagine how many books are in there?"

Not sure which question to answer, Mitchell said, "I can see why you'd love the rich red upholstery on the chairs in the library. And I read there are more than 10,000 books in that library. Supposedly, Vanderbilt read over eighty-one books a year, too, so the library wasn't only for show. It was used and loved by the family."

"I simply can't stop thinking about it all, and this dinner was wonderful." They'd finished nearly everything now, and the restaurant was bringing a dessert for Laura's birthday, a piece of chocolate cake and ice cream, drizzled with a caramel sauce.

Laura giggled then. "I keep thinking about that poor man who dropped the engagement ring over the bridge. Bless his heart. He must have been so embarrassed."

"Do you ever think about getting married?" he asked.

She hesitated, surprised. "I suppose everyone hopes to when they meet the right person, don't you?"

"I do." His eyes met hers. "Do you think you've met the right person?"

He saw her eyes slide away and a blush steal up her neck.

"I'm asking because I'm blessed to believe I've found that person and I'm wondering if those feelings are mutual." Mitchell kept his eyes on her. "Nannie V told me that God knows when you're ready for exactly the right person to come into your life, when you're ready for the responsibility of commitment and for loving with faithfulness. She said at that perfect time He will send the right person your way."

"That's a lovely thought." She took a breath. "I love how you've come into my life, to make me feel joy and see the sun again when I saw so many clouds before."

He reached across to take her hand. "I'm in deep love with you, Laura. I've never said that to a woman before. I like the vision of spending my whole life with you. Can you see me being a part of your future, too?"

Her voice grew soft. "I knew the first time I saw you that I'd found someone special and you've become, like that scripture in Solomon, someone my soul loves. Perhaps the moment we first met, we knew we were looking at our future."

Mitchell took a breath. "I'd like to marry you, Laura. I know it might seem like it's too soon to ask you after only three months, but my heart feels really sure." He kissed her hand before releasing it. "What do you think? Do you think you could live your life out with a guy like me? We don't have to get married right away or anything. But my heart really wanted to speak out and maybe get this settled between us. I wanted you to know how I felt and what I hoped for between us. Would you feel okay if we got engaged, if we got pledged?"

She put a hand to her heart. "My answer is yes, Mitchell. It's like you heard the dreams of my heart. I'd like to get engaged, and I'm so thrilled you can envision me in your future. I hope I can make your life happy."

Mitchell blew out a long breath. "I am a happy and relieved man to hear you say that." Impulsively he got up to walk around the table to kiss her. "I don't care who sees. A man can't get engaged to the woman he loves without kissing her."

The couple at the table next to them raised their wine glasses in a toast, smiling, and a small smattering of applause moved around the tables nearby.

The waiter came with dessert and fresh coffee then, breaking the moment and giving them both a minute to catch their breath.

"What will your family think about us getting engaged so soon?" Laura asked after the waiter left.

"They'll be thrilled. Are you kidding? Mimi and Frances said the other day I'd better get smart and grab you up before someone else found you."

Laura laughed. "That's sweet."

"Mother, the kids, and Nannie V will be pleased, too. Sometime in the future I want us to also make a trip to possibly meet some of your family in Alabama and Mississippi. Do you think any of them might come for the wedding?"

Her eyes widened. "Mitchell, let's don't race too far ahead too soon. We don't have a ring yet and we haven't talked about a wedding date at all."

Mitchell winked at her. "I can take care of the first." He reached into his jacket pocket to take out a small velvet box. "See what you think of this."

He watched Laura open the box, her eyes widening with pleasure at the ring there.

"I knew you loved silver things, so I thought you might want a ring in white gold. That round sparkly diamond felt like you somehow, too. Do you like it?"

"I love it," she whispered.

"You can try it on," he pressed.

A little dazzled, she pulled it out of the box to slip it on. "Oh, look it fits perfect. How did you know my size?"

He grinned. "I snooped in your jewelry box one night at your apartment. One of your rings had the size in it."

She held out her hand, admiring the ring. "You've obviously been thinking about this for some time."

"I have, in a lot of ways." The look he passed her then made her blush.

She turned her hand again to see the lights sparkle off the diamond. "I'll probably be admiring this for days and finding a million reasons to hold out my hand so everyone will notice it."

He laughed. "I'd say the news will get around quickly, and knowing Mother, she'll want to plan a little engagement party. Her friend Benny Fritz is a wonderful photographer. I'm sure Mom will be pushing us to let him make some engagement pictures."

"I don't want to rush too fast with everything," she said. "Can we wait until fall or after to plan a wedding? To give us more time? There will be a lot to talk about. A lot of people to share with, and a lot of plans we'll need to make." She smiled. "I'd sort of like for us to take our time, savor it all and enjoy preparing for the changes ahead without feeling rushed or pressured."

"You think you might change your mind?" His mouth quirked in a smile.

She waved a hand at him. "No, but there is so much to think about. You've already been considering it, Mitchell, but I'm still a little overwhelmed."

"I imagine you are."

She reached across the table to lay her hand over his. "You planned this whole lovely day for me knowing you had this special ending in mind, didn't you?"

"Well, yeah. I guess I did, but I wasn't sure if I wouldn't chicken out at the last minute." He shifted in his seat, a little uncomfortable with his words. "It's a big moment asking someone to marry you, and I knew it was a little soon to do so."

Her eyes moved to their dessert. "The ice cream on my birthday dessert is starting to melt."

He laughed, glad at the change of conversation. "Well, then let's enjoy it. They brought us two spoons and two forks."

The evening grew lighter and happier then.

On the drive home they decided to tentatively plan for a time in October or November for a wedding date, and Mitchell agreed that since her apartment was the largest, they could live there at first and then look for a home later. Both of them wanted it to be downtown so they could walk to work, and they decided it would be fun to get Becky Ray to start looking for options for them in the next year or two.

Mitchell felt like a huge area of his life was suddenly resolved and, in an odd way, he also felt as if a big hole in himself—he'd hardly known was there—was now comfortably and happily filled.

Like Laura said before they both said goodnight later, "It's a happy thing to find the other half of yourself that you needed but hardly knew you were searching for, isn't it?"

Mitchell sent up a little thanks to God on his way home that everything had worked out so well.

CHAPTER 15

The months slipped away in what felt like a happy daze after Mitchell proposed at the Biltmore. It was late July now on a Saturday morning. Laura had just finished her breakfast and was looking over the newspaper, while drinking a second cup of coffee. The paper was full of the news of the annual Folkmoot International Festival, which was starting in Waynesville and would continue around the area in a ten-day festival spread.

Mitchell was out working with others this morning getting ready for the Parade of Nations down the Main Street of Waynesville and Laura was meeting him later, along with his mother, Mackenzie, and Charlie, in front of the Arts Council to watch it all. She glanced over the paper's write-up about the other events that would occur as a part of this big festival.

Laura's cell phone rang and she picked it up to answer it, soon hearing Lillian Greeley's voice. "Laura, this is Lillian. I hope it's not too early to call. I remembered you always get up early, even on the weekends. Work habits are hard to break."

"That's true, and I'm already up and dressed, sitting at the table drinking a cup of coffee and reading the newspaper. How are you and Bobby?"

"Oh, honey, we're both fine," she answered. "I just had you on my mind this morning and wanted to call to hear your voice. Bobby and I are so happy about your marriage. I can surely see God's good hand in this for you. We wanted to let you know we've decided to take our vacation trip near that time this fall so we can come to your wedding."

Laura put a hand to her heart. "That is so sweet of you. Did you get the campground names I sent you?"

"Yes, and we've already checked them out online. We'll get a definite reservation time set up at one real soon. We hope to also come a little ahead of the wedding, so we can catch a visit with you and see your shop before you get too busy."

"I'll look forward to that and to seeing you both again."

"Tell me about what's been going on with you since we last talked. I know you had a little engagement party and that you and Mitchell took a trip to see some of your family."

Laura settled back in her chair for a catch-up visit with Lillian. "Mitchell's mother Evelyn had an informal engagement party for us in her pretty back yard. She called it the *Welcome to the I-Do Barbeque*. I laughed when I saw the sign. She'd painted the "O" in the word "do" to look like a big engagement ring. We had such a good time celebrating with our friends and family there."

"I hope I'll get to meet Mitchell's mother and others in his family you've talked so much about."

"I'll make sure that you do."

"Did you enjoy seeing your family again, Laura, on your trip?"

"Yes, I really did. They liked Mitchell and he got along so easily with all of them. He pushed for us to make the trip, wanting to meet my family, since I'd met his. So, we took a week off to visit everyone. We drove first to Dothan, Alabama, to my Aunt Dorothy and Uncle Curtis Bowman's home. They insisted we stay over with them. We got there late in the day after a six-hour drive from Waynesville and enjoyed visiting that evening and part of the next day, before leaving again."

She got up to pour a little more coffee as she talked. "I don't know if you remember, but my Grandmother Ida, Daddy's mother, moved from Montgomery when my granddad died and bought a little house beside Dorothy and Curtis's brick rancher. It gives her independence, having her own place, and Aunt Dottie and Uncle Curtis are right next door. She gets to see their children, and the grandchildren, when they come to visit. She really loves that. Dottie and Curtis's three kids were much older than Georgina and me, since Daddy married late. We never got to know them well. Did you ever meet any of Daddy's family?"

"I remember your daddy's mother Ida. She and your grandfather used to come here to visit when you and Georgina were small. If I recall, she was a right outspoken woman, almost offensively so, but skillful with a needle. Didn't she and your grandfather run a little furniture repair and upholstery business in Montgomery before?"

"Yes, they did. That's where Daddy learned upholstery. My mother claimed it was Grandmother Ida's sharp tongue and critical ways that pushed Daddy to save to buy his own place in Amory— in a town a good distance from his parents."

Lillian chuckled. "Well, some people can surely be a little tactless and less diplomatic than we'd like. I remember Ida O'Dell felt she had a right to tell everyone else how to live their lives. She was the type who believed that whatever way she did anything was the way everyone should do things. Your father certainly had his moments with her, I can tell you, and whenever she came to the shop, she was full of opinions and criticism for how we did things and how she could do them better, of course." She hesitated. "Did she act ugly to you when you visited? Say something mean she shouldn't have?"

Laura shook her head at the question. "No, not toward me, thankfully, except to suggest I shouldn't have moved so far away from my people. She surely had words to say about Georgina and her life though. When she pushed to know more about where Georgina lived now and what she was doing, I sort of side-stepped the question to say we'd lost touch, that I didn't know where she was living right now. Mitchell jumped in to help with that and moved my Grandmother on to a new subject."

"The more I hear about that man, the more I like him." Lillian paused. "Did you go down to Mississippi next to see your Mama's people?"

"We did. Mitchell planned originally to stay in motels near both families but neither would hear of us doing that. My mother's brother Uncle Tom and his wife Aunt Deidre insisted we stay with them in Gulfport. Tom is an attorney and their home is a fine gracious one. I've always enjoyed going to Uncle Tom's. He's very fun loving, likes to cook out, and always plans side trips to make visiting him more memorable. He and my Aunt Deidre live near the coast, so we all spent part of the next day enjoying the beach with them, which was a treat. Uncle Tom has a boat and he took us out to Ship Island, to see old Fort Massachusetts, and to enjoy the wildlife and pristine beaches there."

"Wasn't Tom the one who had a bunch of boys?"

"Yes. They had three boys, Tommy Junior, Dale, and Bryan. The boys were older than Georgina and me and all handsome. As young girls, we naturally noticed that. I got to see pictures of the boys and their families while there and got updated on their lives."

"If I remember right, your mother's parents Rodney and Ann Baylor live near there, too. Did you see them? You know I remember them really well because your granddad was the pastor at the big Methodist church downtown in Amory for about five years. That's when your dad met your mother Carolyn and they got married."

"I always forget how far back you and Bobby go with our family."

"Honey, we came to work for your father not long after he bought that old building, helped him fix it up and start his upholstery business. He was older, and still unmarried, when he met your mother." Lillian stopped to laugh. "I always think his sharp-tongued mother scared off any girls he dated seriously before."

Laura couldn't help giggling.

"Your daddy went to that Methodist church, where your Grandad pastored, and he met Carolyn there. He sure did love her and I think her warm and joyful spirit, and the music she brought into their home playing the piano, giving lessons, and playing at the church was a blessing to Mason. Carolyn was talkative and friendly, too, always had a smile and hug for everyone."

"I remember that about Mother. Her parents are both warm and loving people, too. They live near Tommy at a Methodist

Retirement Center in Gulfport. They came over and spent the whole first evening with us after we arrived. It was good to see them again. After Daddy died, I worked so hard to keep things going and to learn the business that I didn't get to see any of my relatives much."

"Well, I think it's a sweet thing your Mitchell pushed to make that happen for you. He's a man that knows the importance of family and keeping ties strong."

"That's true." Laura agreed. "On our way home, he added another treat for me, too. We detoured slightly to Gainesville, Georgia, to see my best friend Elizabeth Donaldson, from my school years, and her husband Lee. She was Elizabeth Blackwell before. You may remember her. Her parents still live in Amory."

Lillian laughed. "I sure do remember that child and her nice family. You two came into our shop many a summer's day, with your cute little ponytails and short sets, giggling. I know Irma and Ralph Blackwell, too. They go to our church and I went to Elizabeth's wedding. You were her matron of honor, if I remember right."

Laura was always surprised at Lillian's detailed memory of people and events. "You're right. I was in her wedding, and she's promised to come to be the matron of honor when Mitchell and I marry this fall. Gainesville is only about two hours from Waynesville. I didn't realize it was so close, and we're hoping to see each other more often now."

"Does Elizabeth have children yet? I remember she was crazy about the little ones at our church, loved to keep the nursery and work with the kids in Bible School."

"I'd forgotten that, Lillian. Elizabeth and Lee don't have children yet but she's the director for a childcare center not far from their home. Lee is a high school basketball coach, loves sports and the outdoors. They recently bought a house near a finger of Lake Lanier and close to their schools." She paused smiling. "Mitchell and Lee really hit it off. I didn't know until we visited that Mitchell played basketball in high school. "

"Marriage is a journey in which you're always learning things about each other, not only before the day you say 'I Do" but for all the years afterward, too. You'll find that's true with your Mitchell as you go along. I have with Bobby."

"Well, Mitchell can't wait to go back to Lee and Elizabeth's for a weekend. They have a little boat, and Lee and Mitchell want to do some fishing. I've promised to help Elizabeth go thrift shopping around Gainesville to look for furniture for their house. If any of the pieces need recovering, I can bring them back to the shop."

"It sounds like everything has worked out real nice for you in moving over to Waynesville. Bobby and I are so tickled about it all."

Laura took a breath. "You know I have both of you to thank that I'm here at all. You pushed on me to consider a move, to search for a shop someplace other than Amory, to make a change in my life."

"Well, honey, we could see you were restless and unhappy about so many things. It seemed to me Amory had started to be a place of sad memories and problems for you." She paused. "I kept praying and praying about it, and then that day when I found you crying, it seemed to me like you just needed a change."

"Well, thanks for the push. It's been a happy change."

"You're a sweet girl and deserved some happiness."

Laura heard Bobby calling her in the background.

"Honey, I need to go now. Bobby and I are driving over to the Sullivans to look at some pieces they want us to reupholster for them. I'll talk to you again soon, and we'll look forward to seeing you this fall."

They hung up and Laura sat thinking back over their conversation. These truly had been happy days getting the new business started, falling in love with Mitchell Quinlan, becoming wrapped up in his world and friends. She'd started making new friends of her own, too. While doing an upholstery job for Allison Tate, they'd become friends. Allison was new to Waynesville and had moved here after marrying Drew Tate. She'd started a small business downtown called Good Scents, selling lotions, soaps, oils, and related crafts. Drew had his accounting business near her shop.

She and Mitchell had double-dated with the couple a few times, and sometimes Becky Ray and Mitchell's cousin, Rob Killian, came with them. Lately, Kent, who worked with Mitchell, and Paula Clancy had started joining them, too. It was fun to have a whole group of couples-friends to share good times with.

A short time later, Laura walked to Main Street to find Evelyn, Mitchell, and the children, sitting in lawn chairs on the sidewalk, ready for the parade to begin.

"We brought you a chair and saved it for you," Charlie announced.

"Thank you," she said, as Evelyn lifted her purse from the chair so Laura could sit down. Laura glanced across at Mitchell, who'd just arrived, too. "I imagine you've had a busy morning."

He nodded, drumming his fingers on the armrest of the chair.

Laura noticed the gesture. "Is anything wrong?"

"Someone took down the string of International Flags draped in front of the courthouse last night—six of them, one a US flag. It's an embarrassment."

Laura glanced down the street. "There are still flags along the road."

"Yes, they didn't bother those, only the ones in front of the courthouse." He rubbed his neck in annoyance. "The parade travels down Main Street to end with a performance for all the elected officials right in front of Haywood County's Historic Courthouse. The flags always hang overhead behind them as a backdrop, attached on a long wire between two of the courthouse porch pillars."

Laura bit her lip thinking about it. "This is the first time for another theft since…"

"Since I got attacked in May," he interrupted. "Everyone thought that finally put an end to all this."

"I'm so sorry."

He raised his eyebrows. "It's not your fault, but everyone is certainly upset to see this ugliness show its face again."

"Did the theft happen during the night as before?"

"Yes. Only during the night could someone have even pulled this off. There was too much activity during the day yesterday and into the evening hours. There were too many people around, too."

Evelyn leaned toward Laura. "This festival is a huge event with thousands visiting and with all the international dancers and performers traveling from abroad. Mitchell is right that it is an ugly embarrassment to the city for another of these petty thefts to occur just now. It will be especially obvious, too, since videos and hundreds of photos are snapped at that location at the end of the parade."

"Listen Grammy!" Mackenzie called, pointing down the street. "The parade is starting."

The elaborately dressed dance troupes and regional visitors soon appeared, giving everyone downtown their first look at all the colorful performers that would be a part of this year's festival.

"How beautiful!" Laura exclaimed, her mouth dropping open with excitement.

Most of Laura's experiences with parades had been local ones for Christmas or the Fourth of July with floats, bands, cars, and fire trucks so she was immediately captivated with the gloriously costumed dancers swirling and dancing down the street. She couldn't help pointing and leaning forward with excitement, just like the children, at the incredible show walking right down their Main Street, the dancers often stopping to sing and perform for the public with the wonderful flavor of international musical sounds in the background.

"I knew you'd love it," Mackenzie said, sending her a smile.

"I do," she agreed. "It's wonderful."

Sometimes, the dancers swept spectators out to dance with them or interacted with the audience in a fun way. A group of women dancers from India wandered among the women onlookers to put appropriate *bindi* marks on their foreheads. Evelyn got a small black dot to indicate she'd been a married woman, now widowed, while Laura got a yellow *bindi*, appropriate for an unmarried girl.

After the women passed, Evelyn leaned toward Laura to say, "*Bindi* marks show a woman's marital state. Young unmarried girls in India can actually wear a multitude of *bindi* colors, except for red, for married woman, or black for widowed ones," Evelyn added. "They often paint rows of small dots above their eyes, too, to be festive. There's a lot of symbolism behind the *bindi*, but here at the festival it's only for fun."

Laura's attention was caught by a new group of dancers coming down the street now, the women twirling and swirling their sumptuously decorated long skirts, the men leaping around them and then squatting low to the ground to kick out their feet.

"This is a Ukranian group and the dance is a Hopak dance, from the Ukraine verb *hopaty* that means to jump," Evelyn told her.

"It looks like a Russian Cossack dance to me," Mitchell put in.

"In Russia that's what it is called," his mother replied. "The dance is much the same in both countries."

The fun of the parade continued for some time, a treat to watch.

"This is simply spectacular," Laura said to Evelyn. "How did this festival begin?"

"Waynesville started this event," she explained. "A Waynesville surgeon saw a folk festival when traveling in England and came back with the idea of starting an international folk festival here. The festival, now nearly forty years old, has hosted many thousands of performers over the years from hundreds of countries."

"I think Mitchell said it lasts all week, too," Laura commented.

"Yes, it does. The festival started last night with opening events here in Waynesville, but events are now held in nearby cities, too, like Asheville, Flat Rock, and Cherokee. Most of the ongoing events and shows are indoors and fee based, but the parade and the International Day next Saturday, which lasts most all day, are free to the public. The festival officially ends, after the International Day, on Sunday with a Candle Lighting performance and ceremony at the auditorium at Junaluska."

"How many of the events do you attend?"

Evelyn smiled. "Mostly I'm working during the entire time. The tourist traffic is intense during the festival, and volunteers are always needed in the Arts Council. I have showings and demonstrations at other galleries, too, and I am on the festival committee, so I'm usually helping with one thing or the other the whole time."

"I'm sure it's a mammoth project to plan and orchestrate a festival of this size."

"Look at the new group coming," Mackenzie pointed with excitement. as a colorful new group of performers caught their attention. This group slowed to encourage parade watchers, mostly children, into the street to join them in a circle dance, and Mackenzie and Charlie were thrilled to be chosen.

At the end of the parade, Evelyn took the children with her to the Folkmoot Friendship Center for more activities while Mitchell and Laura folded up their chairs to carry back to Quinlan's.

"I hope you don't mind joining Mom and the kids at the Friendship Center for more celebrating. The kids will be disappointed if we don't go for a little while at least," he said, as he tucked away their chairs in the storage room. "I think you'll enjoy it."

"I'm sure I will," she said, following him out to his car.

"There will be youth activities, face-painting, dance lessons, and artisans sharing pottery, beadwork, and jewelry. There will also be food vendors with baked goods, ice cream, and some international cuisine. We'll stay a little while and then slip away to catch dinner."

They drove to the Folkmoot Friendship Center and enjoyed taking the children around to see the booths and activities going on. At five when Evelyn loaded up two very tired children to head for home, Mitchell said goodbye to various friends and then they walked to Mitchell's car.

"I thought we'd go eat at Clyde's not far from here," he said as they got in the car. "It's a great old-fashioned diner with home-cooked comfort food. The food is really good with daily specials and great local vegetables. I don't think I've taken you there yet. Will Clyde's be all right with you?"

"It will be fine," she assured him. "And I think you're tired, too."

"Frankly, I'm wiped. We worked late last night getting things ready for the parade and then I was out again early this morning."

They drove on to the restaurant and a short time later were

seated and began looking over the menu.

"What do you usually order?" she asked.

"I usually get one of the daily specials, a meat with three vegetables." He pointed to the options on the menu. "The fried chicken is great and you can pick any three vegetables you like with it. I think I'll get green beans, carrots, and creamed corn tonight but, believe me, everything here is good."

She studied the menu for a minute. "I'll have the same," she said.

He smiled at her. "You're always so easy to please in a restaurant."

She grinned at him. "Maybe, but I'm not easy to please with upholstery work. I'm very picky there."

They visited over dinner, talking about the things they'd enjoyed during the day. Laura told Mitchell about Lillian calling and he caught her up on the theft that had occurred.

"I keep wondering what in the heck they've been doing with all that stuff," he said, frowning. "The police haven't found a single clue to any of this either. It's frustrating, and I admit I'm taking all this more personally since I got attacked in May. I worry something worse may happen to someone."

"Maybe they'll find some clues after this," Laura suggested.

"I hope so." He paid their bill and then they made their way to his car to head home. "I'm going to go crash after I take you home," he said. "I'll probably be busy much of this week, too, with things related to the festival. And next Saturday you'll get to enjoy the big International Day. The next weekend, though, I thought we'd take off on Saturday to go hike a trail in the Smoky Mountains. What do you think?"

"That sounds fabulous," she said.

"Well, hunt up some comfortable hiking boots between now and then if you don't already have some," he added, as he dropped her off at her door with a kiss. "I'll pick you up tomorrow for church. This Sunday Mimi and Francis have invited us all to their house for lunch. We try to do one grandmother or the other every month to avoid rivalries."

"I'll look forward to going to Francis and Mimi's place again.

Those two keep me laughing every time I spend time with them. They are a hoot."

Mitchell gave her another kiss and then laid his lips against her neck. "I look forward to the time when we don't have to say goodnight at the door. Won't it be great to snuggle up all night with each other?" He nibbled at her ear as he said it, making her giggle.

"It will," she admitted.

"Well, I'm glad we moved the wedding date up to the first Saturday in October. I'm not really loving this waiting anymore."

She threaded her hands through his hair. "The date is only about two months away now. That's not long."

He took a deep breath. "Well, tonight it seems like forever."

As she climbed out of the Bronco, he added, "Watch for the lights, and I can assure you that you'll see that extra blink tonight, too."

Smiling, Laura let herself into the back door. This had been a fabulous, memorable day she'd treasure for a long time.

CHAPTER 16

Two weeks later on a lovely sunny day in early August, Mitchell and Laura headed to the Great Smoky Mountains for a day of hiking. From Waynesville, Mitchell drove toward Maggie Valley and turned to follow Highway 276 to Cove Creek Road, a narrow rural road that climbed over the Cataloochee Divide Mountain range before dropping to the Cataloochee Valley below. At the national park entrance at the bottom of the hill, Mitchell continued straight ahead into Hwy 284, an old dirt and gravel road.

"This part of the Smoky Mountains lies on the far western border of the mountains," Mitchell told Laura. "Many settlers once lived in the Cataloochee Valley and the old roads and trails they created lattice through the area. I'm taking you to hike on one of my favorite trails today called The Little Cataloochee Trail. It's a 5.2-miles long hike, about ten and a half miles round trip, so I thought we'd only walk a portion of it today. Unless you hike often, ten to eleven miles can wear you out and leave you with sore muscles the next day."

"I'm looking forward to this so much and glad it's a pretty day today."

Mitchell glanced toward Laura as she spoke, excited, peeking out the window at everything along the way. She wore brown shorts, a pink T-shirt that matched her pink lipstick and cheeks, socks and boots, her hair tied up in a ponytail. "You're a beautiful woman," he said.

Her eyes turned to meet his, soft honey brown eyes. "I'm glad you think so, but I'm just a regular brown-haired, brown-eyed girl."

"Whoever told you that missed really seeing you. Was it your sister?"

Her glance away from his eyes gave him the answer.

"I've seen your sister's pictures. She's pretty but no more so than you, Laura. From what I've heard you're a lot nicer person in every way, too."

"So, tell me about the trail," she said, changing the subject.

"You'll see it soon. It's an old settlers' roadbed. I'll tell you more about it as we walk along. I like it because it's a culturally rich trail. Many families lived near this road through Little Cataloochee and there are remnants of their lives all along the way—old cabins, a church, cemeteries, and more. I often wonder what it might have been like to live here, to walk or ride horseback to church or school every day, to live so simply. Eleven houses used to sit off the trail we'll be walking along, four log ones and seven frame ones, plus barns, smokehouses, corncribs and other buildings. Here and there you'll see evidences of the settlers if you look closely—crumbling walls, rosebushes they brought and planted, patches of daffodils that bloom in spring, apple and fruit trees, old fence posts."

He laughed then as his Bronco hit a rutted hole in the road. "Despite how great this trail is, not many people hike it because they hate this piece of rough road leading to it. I don't know why the state of North Carolina doesn't repair it. It's a harsh, bumpy, stomach-bouncing drive."

Laura gripped the handle above the door as Mitchell hit another pothole. "I notice we haven't passed any cars on this road."

He chuckled. "I'll bet you ten bucks we won't see a single one either."

After a time, Mitchell turned into a small pull off near the beginning of the trail. They locked the car, put their waist packs on, and started down a slope that soon flattened out to wind into the valley. Although the road was narrow, it was wide enough for them to walk along side by side. Mitchell pointed out trees and sights along the way, even a few wildflowers beside the path.

"It's really quiet and peaceful here," Laura said.

The trail wound up and down, in and out, and soon came, at about a mile, to the intersection of the Long Bunk Trail. Not far past that intersection a side trail led to the right.

"We'll turn on this side route for a few minutes." Mitchell pointed up the pathway. "It leads to the Hannah Cabin built in 1864 and a family cemetery."

The rustic cabin, with its long roof, brick chimney and covered porch, came into view in a few minutes.

"What a lovely setting." Laura looked around in pleasure. "Do you know about the family who once lived here?"

"It was the home of Martha and John Jackson Hannah, early settlers to Cataloochee. The park took all the land here in the 1930s, but one of the Hannah's sons became a forest ranger and stayed on at the cabin for over thirty years. Many of the other Hannah children went on to become well known in the Western North Carolina area." Mitchell gestured to a big tree near the cabin. "See that old apple tree there? In the fall it will be covered with apples. I sampled some on an October hike and I read that the Hannah family had a big orchard here once."

Laura walked to the porch to look inside the old cabin. "We're so used to homes with a lot of space, but big families lived in these small cabins."

After exploring around the cabin, they walked on a short distance further to the Hannah family cemetery with over fifty graves scattered across a green hillside. Mitchell and Laura walked around to study some of the 1800s gravestones and inscriptions and then walked back to the main trail again.

The path soon led to a bridge crossing over Little Cataloochee Creek and then wound into a flat area where they spotted old walls before climbing uphill and around a ridge. At two miles, Laura pointed ahead. "Oh, look at that pretty old white church on the hillside."

"That's the Little Cataloochee Baptist Church," he said. "We can go inside. On special days services are still held here."

As they walked up the side path to the church, she asked, "Why is everything here called Little Cataloochee rather than just Cataloochee?"

"Well, this was sort of a smaller isolated community, on the other side of Noland Mountain. Many of the people who settled here didn't want to live in the larger Cataloochee area and made their homes here instead, calling it Little Cataloochee."

They explored the old white church with benches and a pulpit still inside and then wandered around the cemetery before moving on. "I thought we'd hike for another mile to the Dan Cook Cabin and eat our lunch on the cabin's porch before turning around to come back," Mitchell said. "That would make our roundtrip hike about six miles. Is that all right with you?"

"That would be great." She stopped to prop her boot on a log to tighten a shoelace. "I hope we can come back to Cataloochee to hike more of the trails later, too."

"We'll do that."

Laura pointed out another rock wall and some fence posts along their path.

"All of this middle section of the trail, called Ola, was once the center of the Little Cataloochee community." Mitchell stopped to look around. "It's hard to believe now, but a good-sized commercial area thrived here with a general store, a blacksmith, post office, gristmill, and other buildings. The Messer family owned the store and several other prosperous enterprises. They were more well-to-do than many in Little Cataloochee. I've seen pictures of the big white two-storied frame home they lived in." He grinned at her. "It's said that Mr. Messer had the first car in the valley, too."

Her eyes widened. "Did he drive it down this tiny, narrow road?"

Mitchell laughed. "I guess he did and probably on that rutted road we followed to the beginning of the trail. Mr. Messer and his sons made the coffins for the valley, too," Mitchell added as they hiked on. "I read if people were too poor that he gave them a coffin without pay."

"I think people depended on and helped each other more back

then," she suggested.

"Probably."

They walked on through the old settlement area, the path switching in and out along the way. Laura spotted an old rose bush and the remains of earlier flowers.

"Have you ever driven through a ghost town?" she asked.

"Do you mean a town with ghosts or just a town no one lives in much anymore?"

"The latter," she said. "There are many little towns like that in Mississippi and around the South, towns that time has simply forgotten. They always make me feel sad, sort of like walking through this place, knowing a big community of people once lived here, built homes, worked and raised families but now are gone."

After another half mile the trail began to pass more fence posts and rock walls, signaling the Cook homestead ahead. They spotted the log cabin on the left, sitting on a small rise, behind split rail fencing.

"The Cook cabin, like many of the others here in Little Cataloochee, was built in the mid 1800s," Mitchell said as they walked up the hill for a closer look.

To their surprise another couple walked out of the cabin as they grew nearer. They had walked in from the southwest end of the valley, first following Pretty Hollow Gap Trail. Mitchell and Laura visited with the couple, Sylvia and Jake French, for a while, who both lived in Sylva and worked at the college nearby in Cullowhee. After they left, he and Laura explored the cabin and then sat on the front porch to eat their lunch.

A half mile after they started their hike back, Mitchell heard a deep rumbling in the sky. Stopping at a clearing where they could see the sky better, he saw thick dark clouds gathering in the east.

"Uh, oh," Laura said. "That doesn't look good. Where did those clouds come from? The sky was totally clear and blue before."

"It may pass over," Mitchell studied the darkening sky a minute longer. "Little storms pop up around the mountains now and then. But if it starts sprinkling, we have rain ponchos in our waist packs.

We'll be okay."

The sky darkened more ominously as they walked on, the rumbling increasing with streaks of lightning beginning to flash across the sky. About halfway back to the church it began sprinkling, soon increasing to a steady downpour. They stopped to dig out their ponchos to put them on, the rain pelting down heavily now, with lightning streaks zigzagging closer and thunder booming right behind it, seeming to shake the ground.

Mitchell took Laura's hand, seeing her eyes widen with alarm. "Let's walk fast and head to the church," he said. "It isn't far now. I think we should take cover there until the worst of this passes. Then we can walk the other two miles back to the car."

"Good plan," she said, her voice a little anxious.

Despite their ponchos, the rain seeped in as it beat down on them. They were both glad to see the white church ahead in a few minutes, sprinting up the path to let themselves inside and shutting the door quickly behind them. As if angry to see them escape, a huge flash of lightning crashed right near the church with a deep roar of thunder following it, all but shaking the walls.

"Whew! Where did that storm come from all of a sudden?" Mitchell pulled off his poncho, shaking the rain off it and hanging it over the back of a pew. As he took off his waist pack he pulled out a bandana. He wiped the rain off Laura's face, helped her out of her poncho, and then kissed her. "Are you okay?"

She glanced toward one of the church's side windows. "I think so. A rainstorm is scarier in the mountains than back at home, isn't it?"

"It can be." He looked around the church. "Let's go up to the front of the church near the pulpit and sit on the floor against the wall, where we can stretch out our legs. We still have water and snacks left from lunch."

"You just ate lunch a short time ago."

He winked at her as they settled onto the floor. "I guess storms make me hungry."

She giggled. "Well, then I'll eat the rest of my snack bar."

They ate for a few minutes, listening to the rain pound on the church roof and to the thunder rumbling around them.

"I'm glad we were close to this old church when the storm moved in," Laura said after a few minutes. "I hope that other couple got back to their car safely. Was there a place along the other end of the trail where they could shelter?"

"They might have found an old cabin or barn on the way back, but nothing as nice as this church. The Cook Cabin is about midway along the trail, so they had a two-mile return on their end, like we did, plus another mile down Pretty Hollow Gap to their car." He crossed his ankles. "That section of the trail is rougher than the portion we hiked in on. It climbs up and over Davidson Gap and then crisscrosses the stream a couple of times before ending. Those stream crossings will be muddy if the storm hit there as hard as it did here. They might have a wet hike back but they'll be okay."

"I hope so." She smiled at him. "Tell me another of your stories about someone in this area."

Mitchell stopped to think. "If we had walked to the other end of the trail, where Sylvia and Jake were heading, we'd have come to Turkey George Palmer's old homeplace. He was quite a character from the stories I read. He taught the mountain people how to find ginseng to sell and earn cash—which is illegal now, of course— and he was famous as a bear hunter, killing over a hundred bears. He insisted on being buried in a steel coffin instead of a traditional wooden one, too, claiming the bears would take their revenge on him and dig him up otherwise."

She laughed. "Why did they call him Turkey George?"

"He built a pen to trap wild turkeys once, but when he tried to go in to catch one, they all attacked him viciously. Evidently the story got around and folks started calling him Turkey George after that."

"You know a lot of great stories," Laura said leaning back against the wall.

They fell quiet for a time, listening to the storm outside.

"What are you thinking about?" Mitchell asked.

Laura glanced around her. "Sitting in this church reminds me that whenever I wanted to talk to God as a little girl, I'd walk over to the big church where we went every Sunday and go sit inside on one of the pews to pray. I prayed there about whether to leave Amory and move here."

"Did you get an answer?"

She wrinkled her nose. "Sort of. I opened a Sunday bulletin, that I found on the floor while waiting, and the verse on the front of it said to seek and you'll find. You know the one."

"I do."

"Well, it seemed like a sign when I was asking God if I ought to look for another location at all." She brushed back her hair. "It was Lillian who pushed me to do that. I don't think I'm naturally very adventurous. Are you?"

"I can be, but like you my life has been spent mostly in one place. I wonder if people who move around a lot in their lives become naturally more adventurous, more eager to seek out changes?"

"I don't know." She flinched as a big crash of thunder shook the church again. "It's nice to be safe in this church right now though."

She paused. "I learned about God in church but I gave my heart to the Lord at a church camp I went to with Elizabeth one summer. It had a pretty chapel sort of like this." Laura turned to give him one of her smiles. "When did you give your heart to the Lord or have you ever had a special experience like that?"

He thought for a minute. "The first time was at church in Bible School, but I was young. The next time was after my dad died. I got mad at God for losing him. Then Nannie V helped me, talked with me, and prayed me through that difficult time. I sort of renewed my vows to God then. Got right with Him again."

Laura twisted her hands in her lap. "Your Nannie V had a candid talk with me one day about where I stood with God. She said she'd be glad to talk with me about faith anytime I needed it. She told me it was important for a couple to develop a strong relationship with God to get them through all the years of marriage, raising kids, and all the ups and downs life brings. She asked me pointed questions to be sure I'd really given my life to God, gotten truly saved."

"That sounds like my Nannie V. She's been a help to me in growing my faith." Mitchell leaned his head back against the wall. "I guess the fact that she never doubted, always stood strong, helped me out. She always defended God when I tried to blame Him or when anyone else blamed Him for life's sorrows He never brings. I remember she made me read the scriptures with her that talk about our adversary and how he works to bring the hurts, losses, and troubles of life. Her faith life is a good example to follow."

Laura sighed. "I like it that we talk about God and pray together, Mitchell. I wouldn't have thought once that was important but I do now. You've helped me to be more comfortable talking about faith and in praying out loud. Thanks for that." She hesitated. "I was raised more with the idea that religion was personal, private, and that you didn't need to share about it. Praying in my family was something you did quietly on your own. I guess it seemed more of a Sunday thing most of the time."

"Well, even in my house with my parents it was mostly that way. But Mom and Dad had their moments of sharing."

"I've never really talked with a boyfriend about God and faith."

Mitchell turned to grin at her. "I certainly didn't have talking about God and faith in mind when I knew we'd be holed up in this church in the middle of nowhere in a storm. But our faith talk sort of took the edge off my passions."

He laughed as Laura's eyes widened.

"But not that much," he said, moving in to kiss her well.

"I don't hear the rain anymore," Laura said after a few moments.

Mitchell cocked an ear, listening. "I think it might have stopped, and we should probably head back to the car before any darkness falls." He stood and helped her to her feet and then drew her close against him. "Every time I'm with you, life is new and sweet, Laura. With you I'm always thinking to the future, toward tomorrows, rather than only for the moment. That's different for me; I wanted you to know that."

Laura leaned her head against his chest. "You know how once

you said a song always made you think of me ..."

"'It Feels Like the First Time,'" he interrupted.

"Yes, well I think of you whenever I hear 'What A Difference You've Made In My Life.'" She leaned up to kiss him again.

"Honey, I'm going to make a lot of differences in your life before we're done." He laughed over his words and then went to get their ponchos. "Our hiking trail will be different, too, going back, probably muddy and slick in spots. Watch your step as we walk along. Give me your hand in any rough places and at the bridge."

As they headed out, Mitchell thought again about all the coincidences that had brought them together. Maybe the old saying was true after all: *What's meant to be will always find its way.*

CHAPTER 17

Two days later on Monday, while Laura looked through fabrics in the shop, trying to pick out upholstery options for a customer's favorite chair, her phone rang. She glanced at the number, and seeing it was Mitchell answered. "Hi, Mitchell."

"Hi yourself. How busy are you this afternoon?"

"I just finished upholstering the last of a set of dining room chairs and was picking some fabric options for Mrs. Greenlee's chair now. I went to her house to see it yesterday, and she's coming to the shop tomorrow to look at options. But I don't have anything definite scheduled from now until close. Why?"

"Can Nolan and Rita cover so you can drive down to Hazelwood with me? I need to run by the Blue Ridge Bookstore to pick up a couple of books for Mother's birthday coming up. I thought you could help me. I know you and Mom trade books now. After that, I need to swing by the Barlow's office about 4:30. Reed wants to talk to me about adding a couple of part-time workers to his construction crew. After that I thought we could stop on the way home to eat supper at the Haywood Smokehouse. It's a little after three now."

"Let me check with Rita and Nolan." Laura laid her phone down, checked with the Nolans in the workroom, and then came back to pick up her phone again. "They'll be happy to close. I'll walk over in a few minutes to meet you."

Hazelwood, one of Waynesville's outlying communities, lay only a short distance from the main part of town. As downtown

Waynesville grew, Hazelwood had grown and expanded, too, and most of the larger franchised stores, like Walmart, Lowe's, Belk's, and Best Buy, sat in the Western North Carolina Town Center, and other businesses and small shops could be found there, too. Blue Ridge Books on Hazelwood Avenue had moved from a downtown location to Hazelwood to expand its business. The bookstore sat not far off South Main Street near the Folkmoot Center and a cluster of local businesses and churches.

"I love this bookstore and the people in it are so nice," Laura said as they pulled up near the store to park. "They not only have books but magazines and newspapers, and gift items. I want to get some decorating magazines while I'm there."

As they walked from their car over to the store, Mitchell said, "Blue Ridge Books started in 2007 downtown and later Jo Gilley and Allison Lee bought it. I've helped them with part time employees a couple of times. I called yesterday to ask them to put back a couple of books they thought Mom would like. She shops at Blue Ridge so often they know her favorite authors. You can look through the books they picked out to help me decide which ones to get and suggest others, too."

After Laura happily spent time helping Mitchell decide on a few books for his mother and picking out a few magazines for herself, they drove to the Barlow's business office not far from the Smoky Mountain Expressway. A sign over the door read: Barlow Construction, Renovation and Rentals.

"The Barlows' office doesn't look like much," Mitchell said as he parked the car, "but they have a pretty prosperous business. Reed, his brother Crockett, their dad Obion, and Reed and Crockett's sons do contract work all around this area, own a passel of rental homes, and buy, fix up, and sell properties, too. The Barlows look like down home boys but they're all smart and savvy."

Laura agreed with Mitchell's assessment about the Barlows' office. She itched to get her hands on some of the old chairs in the waiting room, covered with faded gray, dusty Naugahyde, some with rips in the upholstery as well.

A stern-looking woman, with dark mannish hair, wearing a loose faded shirt and worn jeans, sat at a desk in one corner of the room. Laura noticed the woman's desk and the file cabinets around it were piled with papers in a helter-skelter fashion.

The woman offered a nod to Mitchell. "Reed said to tell you to go on back to his office when you came in." She gestured toward a door near her. "You know where it is down the back hall." Her eyes studied Laura. "It ain't much of a place for a girl."

Mitchell grinned, not seeming to notice the woman's lack of diplomacy. He turned to Laura. "It would probably be best if you wait out here. I won't be long talking to Reed." He glanced toward the woman. "Laura, this is Leona Barlow, Reed's wife, who keeps this office running smooth and keeps Reed out of trouble."

Her mouth twitched slightly.

"Leona, this is Laura O'Dell. She bought Bennett Renfree's upholstery business."

"I've heard of her." She nodded at Laura and then glanced back at Mitchell. "You'd best get on back to see Reed. After your meeting he needs to head to one of our sites for a problem that's come up."

"We won't be long," he assured her.

She nodded again while Laura glanced around, trying to decide on the least worn, and least dusty, chair to sit on.

After she settled down, Laura made an effort to initiate conversation with Leona, but she got few if any return comments for her efforts, and mostly frowns as the woman shuffled papers on her desk and entered data into an old computer.

Laura looked around for a magazine to leaf through but found only an old newspaper under a used coke can. She glanced through it anyway for something to do. As the minutes slipped by, she could feel Leona sending glances her way every now and then as if she resented her even sitting in the room. It was also hot in the waiting area, too, and without thinking Laura soon fanned herself with a piece of the newspaper.

"The air conditioning went on the fritz this afternoon," Leona said, startling Laura with her voice after such a long space of silence. "We got somebody coming to take care of it tomorrow."

Laura smiled. "It's always hard when that happens."

Leona didn't answer.

Looking around, Laura saw a restroom door across the room. "Would it be okay if I use the restroom?" she asked.

"It's clean if not fine," she replied. "I opened the window in there earlier to let some air in after the AC went out."

"Thank you." Laura draped her purse over her shoulder and headed into the restroom, glad to escape Leona.

After using the bathroom, which was admittedly clean, she washed her hands and stood for a moment, reluctant to return to the waiting room. She fished in her purse for a lipstick and then heard voices outside the window as she did.

"Did you tell Durwood we're on again for next Monday night, a week from today?" one deep voice asked.

"Yeah, and Porter's coming with us, too. Daddy thought we might need extra help on this one," a second somewhat raspy voice replied.

"We're only going after them old lion statues on either side of the entry to the mayor's fancy subdivision, Harper. Daddy said two other of them crooks live there, also."

Laura's eyes widened and she looked around in panic. This wasn't a conversation she needed to be hearing. Her eyes flew to the window, glad to see it a high one that no one could see into from outside. She couldn't see the speakers either. Afraid to move and make noise, she stood frozen in place trying to decide what to do.

One of the men laughed. "Dang, Gideon, I don't know what Daddy and Reed are going to do with all that stuff, and I wonder sometimes if it's making a flip of difference to what happened to us."

"Well, there wasn't any justice done through it all, Harper. We took a huge financial hit from it and even Grandaddy said we ought to get some revenge at least and bring that bunch of crooks some embarrassment."

The other man chuckled then, too. "It's been sort of a lark in some ways, hasn't it? And the only trouble we've had was with that man the one night."

"He's all right." The other man's voice dimmed, as if moving away from the window. "Come on. We got to get over to that site where the boys found them bats in the house and figure out how to clear them out."

Laura could hear them move away then, a truck starting up not far from the window and then driving off.

After a little more time to be sure it was safe to come out, Laura walked back into the office and sat down. She took a long, deep breath, trying to calm down and wishing Mitchell would come back soon.

"You all right, girl?" Leona asked, startling her. "You sick? You look a little pasty."

She glanced at Leona. "I do feel a little funny. I hope I'm not coming down with something," she decided to say.

Mitchell came out then, Reed following him.

"Nice to see you again, Mitchell," Reed said with warmth. He smiled at Laura. "Nice to see you again, too, girl. I came by your shop one day to chat with Nolan about a show we had coming up. You and I met then."

Laura realized he looked familiar. "Yes, it's good to see you again, too, Mr. Barlow." She managed a smile.

Reed winked at Mitchell. "She's a pretty one, boy."

He turned to Leona. "I'm going over to that site with the problem. The boys are already there. I'll see you back at the house later."

Leona nodded as Reed headed out the door.

As Mitchell turned to leave, Laura stood, too.

"I hope you feel better," Leona said, startling Laura again.

As she climbed gratefully into Mitchell's Bronco a few minutes later, he asked, "What was that about? Are you feeling sick or something? You do look a little pale."

She took a breath and closed her eyes. "I'm all right. Let's just leave, okay."

He lifted an eyebrow and then shrugged and started the car.

"Well, it's not far to the Smokehouse. You're probably hungry. It's after five now."

Laura tried to decide as they drove to the restaurant if she should tell Mitchell what she'd heard. It sounded like the men talking were planning another of those thefts. Did she even want to get involved in this or get Mitchell involved? He'd already been hurt once. Laura knew the thieves could turn violent. She thought back over the conversation she'd overheard carefully. Didn't one of those men say his daddy's name was Reed? Did he mean Reed Barlow, the man Mitchell just met with?

"Are you sure you're okay?" Mitchell asked again as they arrived at the Haywood Smokehouse. "We don't have to eat out. I can take you home if you don't feel good."

Laura forced a smile. "I'm all right. It was just hot and stuffy in that office. Leona said the air conditioning had gone out."

He nodded, getting out. "Yeah, I remember Reed mentioning it. He had a big window fan running in the back in his office. Loud as the dickens, but it kept the place cool."

Following him into the restaurant, Laura decided not to talk to Mitchell yet about what she'd overheard. She wanted a little time to think about it first, and seeing the restaurant busy and full already, she didn't want to talk to him about any of this where anyone could overhear.

They chatted over dinner, talking about Evelyn's upcoming birthday and the family's plans to celebrate. Mitchell told her some funny work stories and updated her on things Mackenzie and Charlie had been doing since they got back from the beach. Laura tried to join in as much as she could, making comments and asking questions.

As they came out of the restaurant later, Mitchell said, "I love to come to this restaurant. They have the best barbeque, ribs, and brisket and the smell of the smoker hits you as soon as you pull in the parking lot." He took a deep breath. "Makes me hungry all over again."

"I enjoyed my barbeque and the sides were good, too."

Mitchell backed the car out of the parking lot and they soon cut over to South Main Street to head back downtown. Laura looked out the window, thinking.

"Are you going to tell me at some point what's wrong?" Mitchell said as he pulled into the parking area behind Laura's shop and apartment not long after. "You picked at your dinner. You made a sweet effort to keep up a conversation, but it was obvious your heart wasn't in it. What's wrong? Did Leona say something to hurt your feelings? She's a tough, businesslike woman, not always diplomatic, certainly not talkative, but underneath she has a good heart."

Laura closed her eyes as he turned off the car motor. "I overheard the conversation of two men outside the bathroom at the Barlow's place. You know the air conditioning was out and Leona had opened a window in the bathroom to let some air in. The window sat high on the back wall, so people couldn't see into the bathroom or out, but I could hear the men talking outside."

He studied her. "Did they curse or something? Talk nasty? A lot of the guys who work for the Barlows are a pretty rough bunch."

She shook her head. "No, that wasn't it."

"So what upset you?"

Laura sighed. "Let's go upstairs and I'll tell you. I've been trying to decide ever since we left the Barlows if I should tell you or not, but I think I need to talk to someone about this. I don't know what to do about what I overheard."

"Well, you've got my curiosity up now." Mitchell grinned at her as they let themselves in the back door to head up to Laura's apartment.

As she unlocked the door, he asked, "Got any ice cream? I'd love some ice cream with coffee."

"I have fudge ripple ice cream in the freezer," she answered.

"One of my favorites," said Mitchell, heading toward the kitchen. "You dish some out for us and I'll start the coffee."

A little later they settled onto the sofa in the living room. Laura picked a pillow up to hug it. She'd skipped the ice cream, nervous, but Mitchell was enjoying his.

He propped his feet on the table and then put his empty dish down. "Ice cream is especially good after something spicy like barbeque. Are you sure you don't want some?"

"Yes, I'm fine."

"Come on and talk to me, Laura. It can't be that bad." He grinned. "Did you hear someone plotting a murder or a crime or something?"

Annoyed at his humor, she snapped back. "Actually, I did."

He put a hand on hers then. "I'm sorry. I hope you'll share with me. I promise not to make any more jokes."

She took a deep breath. "Leona, as you said, is a tough, uncommunicative woman. I kept feeling like she wished me anywhere but sitting in her office. I finally asked if I could go use the restroom to just take a break from her for a few minutes. I lingered in there, dreading going back, and then suddenly I could hear two men talking outside the window. They must have been coming out from the back of Barlows or something to the side parking lot there."

Mitchell waited now for her to continue.

"I can still hear their words. The first man, who had a deep voice said, 'Did you tell Durwood we're on again for next Monday night?' Right after that, the other man said yes, and told him someone named Porter was coming with them, too. Then he added, 'Daddy thought we might need extra help.'" Laura sighed. "I didn't know what they were talking about, Mitchell, but then the man with the deep voice, the other guy called Gideon, said they were going after the lion statues on either side of the entry to the mayor's subdivision. Gideon called the other man Harper. He said his Daddy said that 'two of them crooks' as well as the mayor lived in the subdivision."

Laura turned to Mitchell. "I got scared then. I stayed really still in the bathroom, not wanting those men to know someone heard them." She hugged her pillow tighter. "I didn't come out until I heard their voices fade away and a truck start."

Mitchell frowned. "Are you sure that's what you heard?"

"Yes." She scowled at him. "Do you think I'd make something like this up?"

"No, but maybe they were only joking around or maybe you didn't quite hear their words right."

Irritated, she said, "Do you know anyone named Gideon or Harper? Those are odd names."

Mitchell looked away from her. "Was that all you heard?" he asked instead, not answering her question.

"No. The man named Harper said he didn't know what his Daddy and Reed were going to do with all that stuff." She paused. "He also said he wondered if it made any difference to what happened to them."

Mitchell closed his eyes.

Watching him, Laura asked, "Do you think they were talking about your friend Reed Barlow? They were outside his business. The man Harper made it sound like his Daddy and Reed were friends or at least working together in some way."

"This is hard to believe, Laura," Mitchell said.

She knew her mouth dropped open. "You don't believe me?" she asked. "Why is that?"

"I know these people. They're good people," he answered. "I think you got something wrong, thought you heard something you didn't."

In a very quiet voice, she said slowly, "Why in the world would I make up anything like this Mitchell Quinlan? I know what I heard. The man Gideon said they were mad because no justice had been done and they wanted revenge."

Mitchell rubbed his arm. "I really think you got something mixed up."

Laura leaned forward. "Tell me who these people are. I can tell by the way you're acting that you recognize the names."

He drank some of his coffee, stalling. "Reed and Leona have a son named Gideon. Reed's brother Crockett, who works in the business with them, has three boys named Durwood, Porter, and

Harper. The Barlows have always named their kids odd names. Reed and Crockett's father's name is Obion."

Laura watched Mitchell's face. "And you don't like thinking Reed and Crockett Barlow, and their sons, might have been behind the thefts around Waynesville?" She said the words carefully and saw his jaw twitch.

"They're the kind of guys who would joke around about stuff like this, even joke like they were going to pull off a theft." He wouldn't meet her eyes. "But they wouldn't do it. You don't know them."

Laura crossed her arms. "You may not know them as well as you think you do. One of them called all of this a lark and said the only trouble they'd had was with that man one night." She emphasized the words. "That man was you, Mitchell Quinlan."

Mitchell stood up. "This just can't be true. Something is off with this."

Laura looked up at him. "What is off is that you don't want to believe this or believe me. That hurts, Mitchell. I think you should go home now. I made a mistake in confiding in you. I thought you might be concerned with me that these men planned to do another theft of private property next Monday night. What if someone else gets hurt this time? Is it worth protecting your friends if that should happen?"

She got up and walked to the door to open it for him. "You go home and think about this. I'll think about it, too. But I will tell you right now that my conscience won't allow me to do nothing between now and next Monday night."

Laura all but pushed Mitchell out the door then.

"Don't do anything until I can do some checking," he said, catching the door before she could shut it. "Give me one day to think about this. One day before you call anyone else or tell anyone else. Will you promise me that? Please, Laura. Just one day. These are people I know and care about."

She glared at him. "I thought you cared about me, too. But I didn't hear you worrying once about what might have happened to me if those men had heard or seen me. Or what might happen yet if Leona puts two and two together from something one of those men says, knowing I was in the bathroom. I could be in danger."

Laura pushed him into the entryway. "I'll give you the one day even if I shouldn't. You think about this tonight and stop by my office after work tomorrow. I promise you I will go to your policeman friend Jack Salter about this if you don't come up with any better ideas. It's wrong to let those men, even if they're your friends, steal public statues next Monday night and not do anything to stop them. You know that's true, Mitchell. I'm disappointed you don't see that and that you doubted what I heard."

She slammed the door and locked it then, and when she heard the downstairs door close, she went back inside and cried.

CHAPTER 18

Mitchell drove back to his apartment with his mind in a whirl. Surely Laura hadn't heard that conversation correctly. She was in a restroom, the men outside. Maybe she got the names mixed up. It was easy to forget details. She'd gotten upset and scared, too. He knew that could cloud judgment. He let himself in the back door of Quinlan's and walked upstairs.

In his apartment, he slumped on the couch trying to think. Surely Reed and Crockett Barlow couldn't be involved in criminal theft. He'd grown up around the Barlow family. He and his dad had gone fishing with Reed, Crockett, and their boys, sat by the bank or out in a boat with them all day, listened to their stories and jokes. The Barlows lived in the country at the end of Allens Creek Road. With thousands of acres of wilderness beyond them, all the Barlows tromped through the woods and over the hills in the mountain area nearby. They knew the good streams and hidden spots for fishing, the best places to hunt.

His dad grew up with Reed and Crockett and had always been especially close to Reed since they were the same age. Granted his dad came from a more cultured background but he'd respected Reed's savvy, his humor and common sense. He often sought Reed out for advice, and when life at Quinlan's got tough, he took off to the Barlows to find someone to go fishing with him or he got permission to cut through their property to head into the wilderness around the reservoir. It was the Barlows who taught his dad hidden trails that led to special spots where the fish bit good.

"Laura can't be right about this," he said out loud. His eyes moved to photos of his dad on the bookshelf across the room.

"What should I do, Dad? This is Reed that Laura thinks she heard something about. You know the Barlows have always been an independent bunch, not always coloring inside the lines in their business or their lives. But this? Surely, they wouldn't do this. There has to be another explanation."

His eyes moved to a picture of his mother and dad then, and more memories flashed back through his mind, of the day Reed and Crockett Barlow brought his dad home after he had a heart attack near the reservoir. They'd been so kind, so strong when he and his mom needed it. Even Obion and Leona had come with them.

"Dad, I don't know what to do," Mitchell said again.

Restless and fidgety, he got up to walk into the kitchen, looking for a cola or something to drink. For once, he almost wished he was a drinking man. But he knew too well drink caused more problems than it solved. It wasn't the answer.

He slumped back onto the couch, trying to clear his mind. Still in shock.

Seeming to hear his Nannie V's words in his mind, Mitchell tried to pray, but he couldn't seem to even find the right words for prayer.

Getting up to pace the room now, he spotted another picture, one of him with Laura, laughing at their engagement party. He winced. "I really hurt her, not believing her. Gosh, she was mad. I don't ever think I've seen her mad like that."

Going to look out the window toward her apartment across the street, he imagined he would be disappointed in her, too, if he'd confided something and she'd doubted his word about it. Oddly, he remembered in that moment her telling him how when she hadn't known what to do about whether to move or not, whether to look at places outside Amory, that she'd gone to the church to pray. She said she opened a Bible and read the words seek and you'll find.

Trying to remember those words now, Mitchell hunted up

his Bible. He found the scripture finally in Matthew, using his concordance: "Ask, and it shall be given you; seek and ye shall find; knock, and it shall be opened unto you. For every one that asketh receiveth; and he that seeketh findeth." Mitchell stopped, thinking. "That's what I need to do—seek and research until I find the answers. If the Barlows are involved in this there has to be a reason. Finding that will help me know what to do."

He got up and headed down the hall to his upstairs office. "That's my answer," he said, talking out loud again. "If the Barlows have been wronged somehow, I'll find it out." Surely there will be something in the newspapers if they'd been involved in any lawsuits or problems related to their business. If not, he could go to the library tomorrow and research more. He'd done it often enough for Quinlan's, researching businesses or people, searching out their problems and their past. This was something he knew how to do.

Glancing toward the living room, he thought about flipping the lights to let Laura know he was thinking about her. But she was mad. She probably wouldn't be watching, and until he had some facts and answers he had nothing to say to her that would fix things between them right now. He'd see her tomorrow when he knew more.

The next day, near five o'clock, before Laura closed the shop, Mitchell cut across the street to her front door, purposed to show up before she could lock the door and refuse to see him at all. He wouldn't blame her for it.

He opened the door and stepped into the vestibule.

"Well, you're prompt." Laura's voice said from her office.

"Yes, and I owe you an apology," he said, standing in her office doorway and looking at the business-like face she wore.

Seated behind her desk, she didn't answer, simply watched him.

"Can I take you out to dinner to talk?"

"No. We can talk here. Nolan and Rita already left. It's time to close." She glanced behind him. "Lock the outside door if you would."

He did and came back into her office, taking the chair across from her desk.

Mitchell took a breath, trying to decide how to begin. "I was shocked and upset last night with what you told me that you overheard. If someone told me something like that about my mom, the kids, or anyone I love fiercely, like I love you, I think I would have probably acted just the same. I'm probably loyal to a fault. It's difficult for me to believe or accept when someone I care about has done wrong. I get mad. I don't want to hear it. I'm not reasonable then. It's something I need to work on."

She waited, listening.

"I wrestled with myself when I got back home last night. Upset. A sweep of memories about the Barlows, especially Reed, crowded my mind." He hesitated. "Reed Barlow and my dad were staunch friends, different men in many ways but fiercely loyal friends. I grew up spending time with the Barlows, going fishing and hunting with them on the reservoir and the streams near their place outside Hazelwood. They were a rough bunch in some ways, but Reed and Crockett's boys helped toughen me up. They taught me understandings only kids growing up out in the country usually know. Can you understand that legacy of friendship with them?"

"Yes. I've seen you can be a loyal person," she answered. "To some."

He winced but forced himself not to respond to the obvious dig. "My dad fished at the reservoir and on the streams and creeks with the Barlows often. Especially when he needed a break from the annoyances of the business. He went there to fish the day he died. Reed and Crockett were too busy to go with him that day, but when Reed came in and saw Dad's car still parked at the back of their property, he and Crockett went looking for him."

Mitchell closed his eyes, hating the memory. "They found him slumped dead by the bank where he'd been fishing. They could have called for someone to come retrieve him, but they didn't. Reed and Crockett carried him out themselves and brought him home to my mom and me."

"Should they have done that?"

"Most people wouldn't have, but the Barlows have always done things their own way, followed the old ways. Like you and I were talking about in Cataloochee while hiking. They brought Daddy home to us. Their dad, Obion, came, too, even Leona. They helped us and ministered to us at a hard time. I doubt police or emergency crews would have done what they did. Mother and I have never forgotten it."

"I understand how you'd feel gratitude toward them. Were they the only people who knew where your dad was that day?"

"Actually, yes. When dad took off, he kind of liked to get away." Mitchell thought back. "Dad told the Barlows where he was going, of course. He wasn't irresponsible about taking off into the mountains alone."

"And these memories of the Barlows made you not want to believe any ill of them? What do you think now, Mitchell?"

He made a face and rubbed his neck. "It took last night until the late hours and more time in the library today, digging through data and old newspapers, for me to get some answers that made sense to me."

"What did you learn?" she asked.

"You may not know it, but a lot of the area around Waynesville is geologically faulty, subject to natural landslides. Usually, if this is known, people don't build on lands most likely to be unstable. However, sometimes there are problems not foreseen. About twelve years ago, a rural development not far from where the Barlows' office is started having problems of this sort. Residents began finding cracks in their basement walls and driveways, holes and crevices in their yards. Some geologists were sent out to investigate and found that a slow, gradual landslide was moving down the hillside in the development."

"That must have been scary for the people involved," she said.

"It was. To shorten the story, after a time, it was decided some of the homes were unstable and vulnerable, and the people were forced to move out. Suddenly, those home owners had worthless assets, houses condemned to be demolished, and their insurance agents wouldn't cover the problems that incurred nor would the city."

"Did the Barlows have homes there?"

"Not then, but there's more to the story."

He watched her brows furrow. "Is this going somewhere, Mitchell?"

"Yes, I promise it is." He crossed an ankle over his knee. "As time went by, people kind of forgot about the landslide. Nothing else happened and the other people who had homes in the area never experienced any further problems."

She sent him a patient look. "And?"

"And the Barlows picked up a couple of homes in the area, fixed them up, and rented them out. People were still reluctant to buy in the subdivision, or at least some were, but rentals worked well. In a foreclosure, Reed and Crockett picked up a house that had sat empty a long time, fixed it up, and put it on the rental system with their others. Then the town came and told them the house was unsafe, even though there hadn't been any problems for over twelve years. The battles started then between the Barlows and Waynesville. The town cut off water and power to the property, disagreed with surveys showing there'd been no further landslide damage. They wanted the Barlows to demolish the house, because it was still a condemned home. A back-and-forth legal fight began that lasted for over a year, but with every appeal the Barlows lost. I imagine Reed and Crockett lost a lot of money through it all with legal fees, buying and fixing up the property, then being unable to rent or sell it. They were stuck, like the homeowners all those years ago."

"Why didn't the Barlows know about this house? They're in the building business. They owned other homes in the area, like you said. Wouldn't they have researched any house they bought ordinarily? Found out about it in the foreclosure purchase or when they attained building permits to remodel?"

He sighed. "I don't know all those answers from the data I

studied. I do know the Barlows have their own code of behavior about things. They don't like dealing with government any more than they have to. It's a mountain thing passed down, I guess."

She crossed her arms. "Are you trying to tell me they can be excused from all these thefts because they got mad at the town of Waynesville about a property dispute and a house?"

Mitchell winced. "You make it sound pretty dumb."

"It is dumb, Mitchell. I'm sorry if they suffered loss and weren't dealt with fairly in a legal dispute, according to their point of view. I didn't exactly think it fair the government wanted to come in and tear down my father's business property. I kept thinking surely there was another route the road could have taken. But no matter what any of us who lost our businesses thought, the government put the road exactly where they planned. By imminent domain they made us all sell and vacate. I made out better than many who had mortgages and debt, but I still lost a place special to me. And even though I sometimes felt it was wrong, I didn't take revenge on the town of Amory."

"It's not exactly the same thing."

"No, I'm aware of that. But it was similar. Life is full of unfair things. You don't take illegal actions because you get mad at the government, or at anyone, without paying the consequences." She shook her head. "Prisons are full of people who chose to handle problems in the wrong ways, Mitchell. Despite all that happened to the Barlows, they did not have the right to start a petty series of vengeful acts toward the city."

He frowned. "But at least I understand why they would do such a thing. Before I couldn't imagine it at all." Mitchell ran a hand through his hair. "The Barlows are the types to take an eye for an eye, a tooth for a tooth, to right their own wrongs."

She sat back in her desk chair. "Okay, I gave you the day you asked for to think about this. I promised you I wouldn't talk to anyone else until you had your day. Now you've obviously looked into the matter and found a possible reason why the Barlows are doing these random thefts. Now my question is what do you plan to do about it?"

He didn't answer for a moment.

"Come on, Mitchell, unless they suddenly have some sort of Come-to-Jesus moment, as Lillian calls it, and decide to repent and put everything back, something has to be done. We can't stand by and let them commit another theft or we become a sort of accessory to the crime."

Mitchell sat forward. "Look, I'm glad you said that about them putting everything back. If you'd give me another day, I'd like to talk to Reed and suggest they do that. I don't really think he's considered what might happen to him, Crockett, and their boys— even to their dad, who is old now—if they get caught."

"You're kidding?" She looked stunned. "Mitchell, they've already attacked you once because you interfered, not even meaning to. They might really hurt you if they think you know and that you're the only one who does." Her eyes widened. "Or if they realize I was involved and overheard Gideon and Harper talking, they might hurt me as well."

He shook his head. "They'd never do that."

"And you're willing to risk my life over that assumption—and your own?"

Annoyed, he said, "Well, what do you suggest?"

"I would suggest going to your friend Jack Salter. Tell him what we heard, let them be at the lion statues well hidden on Monday night, and if the Barlows come to thieve again, they will catch them in the act."

Mitchell looked down at his hands. "Then I will have it on my conscience that I sent the family to prison. The town is angry over this. Some of the property they took is valuable. It won't be possible for the Barlows to get a simple slap on the hand for this."

"Should they get only a slap on the hand? They've stolen an expensive American flag and International flags from in front of the courthouse, they removed a historic bell from in front of the school and a town statue honoring a military hero, plus they entered a homeowner's private property and stole his vintage car. In addition, they tried to remove part or all of the two musician sculptures on our street, and they attacked a citizen who unfortunately ventured into the area at the time." She shook her head in exasperation. "Mitchell, I'm sorry these individuals you care for have committed these crimes, but I'm not ready to excuse them."

He leaned forward. "You said you heard one of them say he didn't know what they were going to do with the stuff, which means they probably still have it stashed somewhere. Maybe they planned to put it back after a time, once the joke was over, the revenge past. You said you heard them say they wanted to embarrass the government. They've done that. If you hadn't heard what you did, they might have put all this back in a week or two, piled it on the courthouse lawn at night or something. But if we step forward in the wrong way, they won't have the chance to do that."

She shook her head. "Do you really believe that?"

"If it had been anyone but the Barlows, I'd have said no. But I can remember in the past them playing jokes around town. Perpetuating a little trouble in foolhardy fun but making it right later. I could tell you about school pranks the Barlow boys played. No, they weren't ever right, but I'd hate to see them all imprisoned for this." Mitchell put his hands on Laura's desk and leaned forward. "I don't think I could live with myself turning them in without at least giving them a chance to set it right."

She sighed. "We're both taking a risk doing this, Mitchell."

"I won't tell them you had any part in this. Reed went out back once when I was in his office. I actually went to the other bathroom off the hall while he was gone. I told him I was going to step in there a minute. I can tell him I heard Gideon and Harper talking. The window was pushed ajar there, too. They opened windows about everywhere they could that day. It's hot in August without air."

She leaned her head back resigned. "What's your plan? I can see you're purposed to do this. I can't say I like it, but I understand it in part. However, I want to know every aspect of your plan, when you plan to talk to the Barlows and where, and I expect you to come right back afterward to let me know what happened and that you're all right."

Laura paused. "I'm still mad at you but I don't want to see you hurt. Do you hear me? Tell me how you plan to keep yourself safe."

"I'm going to call Reed and ask him to meet me in the morning at the Huddle House down in Hazelwood. It's a favorite spot of his. He used to meet my dad there and me sometimes, too. I'm going to tell him I need to talk to him about something personal. We'll be meeting in a public place, and only Reed will be there. I know him better than any other of the Barlows. I think I can talk to him."

"What about the Monday night theft planned?"

"Naturally I'll expect them to call that off."

She interrupted. "I drove over to that subdivision on my lunch hour. It's called Lyons View, probably named after someone. But the statues seem to echo the name. The big lions are old cream-colored statues, really beautiful, sitting on either side of the walls before you drive in the subdivision. The streets are full of gracious homes, like your mom's and Nannie V's. It's wrong for them to come and take those statues away to spite only a few people. Did you learn who else lives there that they're angry with?"

"Yeah, the town attorney Henry Briggs and the Development Services Director of the Planning Board, Daniel Hooper, both live there and both attend most all the town meetings. They were heavily involved in the landslide case and decisions about the property."

Laura shuffled some papers on her desk. "I can't believe grown men could be so petty. It reminds me of those old western movies where ranchers fought each other in nasty, vengeful ways—damaging one another's property, getting even in almost childish ways. I guess movies are more real-to-life than I thought." She crossed her arms again. "What about all the stolen items?"

"I thought I'd suggest they should all be returned to the city before next Monday and an anonymous call made to pass that knowledge along. It might be easier for them to take them all to one place and unload them. The Barlows have some big trucks, closed ones, too. I'll leave it to Reed and the family how to handle that. But I do plan to tell him I will report it if everything isn't returned. With all of them helping, they can take everything back over the next days. They won't be dismantling things this time. They can work faster."

"What if they get caught?"

He shrugged. "That's their risk to take, just like they took risks to remove everything. It's a better risk option than prison." He got up and walked over to look out the window. "Besides, if one of us heard one of the boys talking, who else may hear something? Luck always runs out when thieves push the limit. The Barlows made their point a long time ago. It's time for this to be finished."

"Mitchell, this is not a plan I like, but considering the relationship of the Barlows to your family, I'm hoping they won't see you as a threat and make you pay in some way for this. I'd hate for their vengeance to turn on you."

"I've thought about that, but I owe a sort of debt to Reed and his family. I need to give them the chance to set this right, to avoid getting caught and prosecuted. The Barlows are risk takers who, amazingly, seem to get away with things. Not ever big things. Just little stuff like this. Borrowing someone's boat to go fishing. Spending the night in an empty cabin up in the woods, that isn't theirs. Helping themselves to a snack from someone's outdoor freezer. Taking the clothes away from some girls skinny dipping and dropping them further down the path so they'll find them later."

He saw Laura's mouth twitch over the last.

"They went too far on this, though, but I don't think they really realize it."

"One day something may catch up to them, Mitchell."

"Yes, that's true, but at least I won't be the one to catch them." He turned to her. "Do you want me to take you out to eat now?"

She shook her head. "No. I'm still upset with you. I need some time to settle down over all this. You didn't want to trust and believe me. That hurt, Mitchell."

He turned to her. "I was wrong, I've apologized, but I can't go back and act differently now. All through our lives, Laura, situations are going to come up where one of us acts impulsively, says something he or she shouldn't. We're going to hurt each other sometimes, disappoint one another by our actions and words. But my parents taught me that the important thing is that you apologize with a true heart and try not to inflict that hurt again. That's all I can offer you right now. I wish I could turn back the clock so I hadn't hurt you. You've had enough hurt to deal with this year. I hate to think I added to it by doubting you."

"Your words help," she said. "But I'll feel a lot better tomorrow when you come by here to show me you are all right and that your meeting with Reed Barlow went as you hoped it would. I doubt I'll sleep well tonight for worrying about it."

He gave her a little smile. "Mimi loves to quote Erma Bombeck about that: *Worrying is like a rocking chair. It gives you something to do, but doesn't get you anywhere.*"

She scowled at him. "This isn't a very good time for jokes, Mitchell."

He lifted his hands. "I was only trying to bring a little humor into the situation."

Laura stood up. "I know worrying is not helpful, but I can't lie and say I won't be troubled until I know you're safe." Tears filled her eyes. "Even when I'm mad at you I love you. I don't want anything to happen to you."

Mitchell went over to take her in his arms. "I'll be fine, Laura. Remember, I've known Reed Barlow all my life. I'm sure our conversation won't be a welcome one to him, but I'll be fine. You just keep me in your prayers that I'll say exactly the right things."

"I will," she said, letting him out.

At eight the next morning, Mitchell walked into the Huddle House to find Reed already settled into a booth in a back corner. Mitchell stopped at the booth to look at him before scooting onto the opposite bench.

"What's the matter, boy? You got some girl in trouble or something? Don't know what to do about it?"

"No, it's not that sort of problem."

"Well, spit it out so we can talk about it. I ordered breakfast for us, and here's the coffee coming now." A waitress stopped to put it on the table.

Mitchell glanced around glad to see no one sat at any of the tables close to theirs. He drank some coffee, gathering his courage, and answered, "I know what you did, Reed, you, Crockett and the boys. I heard Gideon and Harper talking about it outside the office when I was there Monday. The window in the bathroom was open. Sound carries."

Reed grinned. "And what did you hear that we did, boy? We Barlows are always up to something, according to most folks."

Their breakfast came and Mitchell got a minute to decide what to say next. "Let's start with these to clarify things." He pulled a pile of folded papers from the waistband of his jeans and laid them beside Reed's plate.

Reed opened them and began to leaf through them while he ate. The papers were printouts of news articles and other write ups about the property disputes the Barlows had been involved in, ending with the last appeal lost this winter.

"What do you have your nose in this for?" Reed asked after a while. "I don't see it's any of your business."

"It's not," Mitchell agreed. "I wouldn't have gotten my nose in it if it wasn't for what's happened since. I knew on Monday there had to be a reason why the Barlows were trying to bring embarrassment to the town."

Reed leaned across the table and his voice dropped to a dangerous low. "Son, I'm fond of you, but the accusations you're flirting with are testing my fondness. And once again, whatever our business is with anyone isn't yours to stick your nose into."

Mitchell took a breath, trying to think how to reply. "If I could hear about this, Reed, others could, too. And others might carry it to a higher authority."

Reed glared at him. "You planning to do that?"

"I don't expect to need to. After I thought it out, I felt sure you, Crockett, and the boys were only pulling a few pranks. I heard Harper say you still had the stuff so I decided you meant to return it soon, once the joke was finished. I knew you were a smart man and wouldn't want to see your son, Crockett, his boys, or yourself go to prison over something this petty."

Mitchell saw Reed stiffen and clench his fists, but he went on. "I came today to suggest you return everything sooner than later. I have a feeling the word may be out. If I learned of it, others will. I'd suggest getting everything returned before Monday and obviously disbanding any other plans for Monday. It will be easier putting it back with nothing to dismantle. You can even dump it all in one place. But it would be a shame for someone to find it now and trace it back to you and yours."

"You got a lot of nerve," Reed hissed, adding a few expletives to the words.

"No, actually I've got a lot of love." Mitchell lifted his chin. "I love you and your family and I owe you, Reed. I could have just walked away with this knowledge but it would have been wrong. If you all got caught, I'd have felt it was my fault that I didn't say anything. I couldn't live with that. If I'm pushing this it's because I think it's time there was an end to it before someone gets hurt."

"It might be you." Reed sent Mitchell a steely look.

"It might be." Mitchell offered a grin then. "In fact it already was."

Reed pushed his old hat back. "Dang, boy, that was a mistake. It was dark and Durwood doesn't know you like most of us do. I didn't even know it was you until the next day. I'm glad you weren't hurt worse. It would have been hard for your mother."

"It will be hard for my mother if anything happens to you, Crockett, your boys, or Obion, too, and it would be hard for me." He offered Reed another small smile. "Who would I go to if I got some girl in trouble?"

Mitchell saw Reed's lips twitch. "You need to get yourself hitched. I thought I heard you were heading in that direction, marrying that pretty little thing you had with you on Monday." His eyes narrowed then.

"Don't even think that," Mitchell said. "She's nothing to do with this. I'd never risk her. She's had a lot of pain herself. The government took her family business property by imminent domain. There wasn't a dang thing she could do about it."

"At least she got paid for it. We got nothing but ripped off."

"Why'd you buy a place up there you could easily learn had been condemned? That's the part I couldn't figure out. And how come when you got building permits to do repairs on the place, they didn't flag it. I couldn't figure out why after you bought the place, renovated it, and put it on the rental market that it took over a year before the town came after you. Where had they been all that time?"

He shrugged. "Just shows government inefficiency."

The waitress came to refill their coffee, and when she left Reed continued. "Over the years, we'd picked up a couple of places cheap in that development. Nothing further was happening with any slides but a lot of folks didn't want to buy there or wanted to get out." He grinned. "Dang, most people think now it was that big water leak back twelve years ago that caused all the trouble. All the engineering studies now are saying there's no real danger up there if they keep monitoring the slope off and on."

Reed stopped to drink some coffee. "That place we bought was supposed to be demolished twelve years back, but the homeowners cut out and disappeared. The mortgage went outstanding but the bank didn't want to mess with it and foreclose because they didn't want the liability or to be pushed to pay for demolishing. The county didn't want to pay either despite outstanding property taxes. So they all just let it sit there and rot. Weeds grew up, vandals got in and stole stuff. The place declined more every year. It was an eyesore and a danger. I got tired of looking at it and of hearing complaints about it from renters in places we owned nearby. I went down to the county office and told them I'd pay the property taxes and buy the place in foreclosure if they'd put it up. They did and I did."

"Then you knew the house's history?"

"Well, sure. I thought I might pull it down afterward just to see it gone. I got it cheap. But when we got to looking at it we found it was in right good shape, considering. So we decided to fix it up and rent it."

"How did you get the building permits you needed to do that?"

Reed rubbed his neck. "We sort of skipped that part. All that government stuff takes a blamed lot of time and money."

Mitchell almost smiled. "You skipped getting a building permit?"

Reed leaned forward, clenching a fist again. "Watch how much you put your oar in my business, son. I don't come downtown and tell you how to do things with your staffing business. Whatever ways you choose to run it are your ways. That courtesy should go both ways. You got that?"

He nodded. "I'm sorry your family has experienced this trouble."

"Well, it has been trouble. And it got nasty. We got insulted and royally screwed in one too many ways. It rankled us all. I can't rent the house now and it's looking like I'm the one that's going to have to take the blamed thing down after it sat, nobody doing anything or stepping up to deal with it, all these years. It's just wrong, you know."

In his mind Mitchell heard one of his father's favorite sayings that two wrongs don't make a right, but he thought better of voicing the words. So he drank coffee for a minute, staying quiet to let Reed think.

"I'd say it wouldn't go easy for us, like you said, Mitchell, if our pranks got found out. We've ruffled the feathers of a lot of important people in the city." He frowned at Mitchell. "I hate you knowing about this."

"I find my memory fades about a lot of things these days. Guess it's because I stay so busy." Mitchell shrugged, trying to hide a smirk.

He saw Reed's mouth twitch in a smile again. "Sometimes, forgetfulness is a healthy thing, boy."

"That it is." Mitchell looked out the window and changed the subject. "The weather report says it's supposed to be pretty and sunny all the rest of the week. Nice nights, too. No mention of any rain."

Reed didn't answer but he laid some money on the table and stood up. "I've got to get to work. You take care, son."

He paused and looked down at Mitchell. "Don't be out and about any nights this week real late, you hear?"

"I'll keep that in mind." Mitchell folded and stuffed the papers back in his jeans.

"Give me a call sometime and we'll go fishing," Reed said before he left.

Mitchell lifted a hand to him and then sighed with relief after he left.

He dug out some money for his own ticket, and as he got in his car he pulled out his phone and texted Laura. "All's well. Heading your way."

CHAPTER 19

Laura ran out the back door of the shop as Mitchell pulled up a short time later. She threw her arms around him as soon as he stepped out of the Bronco. "Oh, I'm so glad you're okay."

"I texted I was."

She pulled back, her eyes wide. "But someone might have followed you."

"Aw, I'm fine," he assured her, giving her a hug. "Can you take a break to talk? Are Nolan and Rita in the shop?"

"Yes, I told them you were stopping by, that I wanted to talk with you for a minute. Rita said to give you a piece of the banana bread she brought to the shop today."

"You know I love her banana bread. Did you eat breakfast earlier?" He glanced at his watch. "I ate some at Huddle House with Reed but my appetite was off."

"I felt too nervous for much, too." She wrapped an arm around his waist as they went inside and started up to her apartment. "I'll share a piece of banana bread and some coffee with you."

Mitchell stopped her on the dimly lit stairs and kissed her at length. "I'm glad you've decided to forgive me."

She traced a hand down his cheek. "I was so worried about you. I couldn't help it."

"Well, you can see I'm fine. More than fine now." He winked at her and kissed her again, wrapping her tight against him, easing away a little of her earlier tension of the day but sending a new sweet jolt of tension swirling through her.

"I'm glad we're getting married next month," he said in a husky voice.

"Me, too," she said, trying to catch her breath as Mitchell's mouth nuzzled a tender spot on her neck.

After a few moments, they walked up the rest of the stairs to her apartment.

"You will tell me everything, won't you?" she asked as she opened the door.

"Yes, I'll tell you everything." And Mitchell did, filling her in on all the details of his meeting with Reed, around eating a piece of Rita's banana bread.

"You see? Everything turned out fine," he said again, finishing his account. "Now the rest of the week will show an end to all of this—I hope."

"I hope so, too," she added, offering a smile, but inside Laura still worried that Reed Barlow or someone in his family would lean toward a different direction.

After Mitchell left, Laura walked downstairs and let herself into the big upholstery room where Rita and Nolan were working on furniture pieces with music from the radio in the background.

"Mitchell said to thank you for the banana bread, Rita," Laura said, walking over to look at the wicker love seat she was working on.

Rita glanced at the upholstery material she was starting to cut on her work table. "Don't you love this pretty floral fabric?"

"I do. I see Nolan's already working on one of the matching chairs, and I'll start the other in a few minutes." Laura picked up the rich floral fabric to study it.

"That's a good fabric for outside porch furniture," Nolan said. "I'll work on the wicker rocker when I finish this chair, and Rita's going to make pillows this afternoon for the whole set."

"These are all for the Iris Inn on Love Lane, officially called the Inn at Iris Meadows Bed and Breakfast." Laura smoothed a hand over one of the old chairs, not yet reupholstered. "The weather takes a toll on outdoor furniture but the veranda at the inn these chairs sit on is surely beautiful."

"We drive up to the inn sometimes to see the gardens around that place," Rita put in. "They're pretty, too."

Laura smiled. "When I was there picking up these pieces, big sweeps of black-eyed Susans and coneflowers crowded along one of the white fences. After seeing them, I took time to walk on one of the inn's pathways to see what else might be in bloom in August."

"Well, I'm glad the folks at the inn trusted us to recover this furniture." Nolan began cutting fabric for his piece in progress using the old fabric he'd already removed as a pattern. "A few years back we reupholstered a couple of period pieces from inside the house, too. That place is full of some beautiful antiques."

"Did you know one of the original owners was actually named Iris?" Rita asked.

Nolan laughed. "No. I just figured the name Iris Inn came from all the iris growing around the garden. It's a fine, grand Greek Revival house whatever its history. Bennett used to call it the Grand Lady of Waynesville."

Laura heard the front door bell chime as someone let themselves in the shop vestibule. "I'll go see who that is and check messages in the office before I get started on my chair."

"Go ahead. Do what you need to do," Nolan replied. "Redoing these wicker pieces is easy work, compared to some things. If you get tied up, or have other things to do, we'll start your chair."

Laura walked in the vestibule to find two local women interested in buying one of the pieces she'd reupholstered and put in the showroom window for sale.

"I love that cute little chair," the taller woman said. "It will be so nice for a reading nook in the corner of my bedroom and that sage green fabric will blend in perfectly with our bedspread." She paused. "I'm Darleen Oslo and this is Rebecca Watkins," she added. "We live out in the Lyons View area and we came into town to shop and have lunch today."

"I'm Laura O'Dell." Laura smiled, shaking both their hands. "I drove past that subdivision the other day. I loved the lion statues at the entry."

Rebecca laughed. "They have a history, those two, but I always laugh whenever I pass them. My two children named them when they were small and they'd always call out and wave to them whenever we drove in or out of the subdivision."

"Goodness me, I remember that, too. My Elsa picked it up from hearing your children talk about it when she was little." Darleen giggled. "I still find myself saying hello to Virgil and Flaubert. Wherever did your children get such names?"

"Remember their daddy, my Jimmy, teaches English Literature at the college."

"Well, I guess that explains it." Darleen turned to Laura. "Do you have any other finished pieces we can see? Rebecca and I would like to look at fabrics in your showroom, too. We both own a few older pieces in our homes we'd like to have recovered."

Laura spent the next hour working with the two women. She sold the chair that she'd originally found at a thrift store and recovered to Mrs. Oslo, plus a side chair to Mrs Watkins. In addition, she made two appointments for the next week to go look at furniture, at the women's homes, that they wanted to consider reupholstering.

The mail came as they left, and Laura leafed through it, still feeling a little anxious sometimes as she did, wondering if she'd hear from Chance Richardson again or get a note from her sister Georgina. So far only that one ugly note had arrived and she'd never heard anything further from either of them. It felt odd not knowing where her sister was or what she was doing, but Laura knew she didn't want to be mixed up with Georgina and Chance's style of living, their unkind ways, or their drug and alcohol problems.

Popping in to the workroom, she saw that Nolan and Rita had already started on the chair she'd planned to do, so she decided to catch up with orders, bills, and paperwork in the office. People kept stopping by throughout the afternoon, too, with the weather sunny and fair. Laura hoped it stayed nice all week. Mitchell had promised to take her on Friday to one of Waynesville's Mountain

Street Dances in front of the Haywood Courthouse. He said the town closed off the whole area for the evening and everybody brought lawn chairs and blankets to enjoy the entertainers, local bands, and clogging groups, as well as joining in, if they wanted to, with some square dancing. It sounded fun, and he and Laura planned to meet several of their friends there.

By Friday, when they joined their couples-friends, Rob and Becky, Kent and Paula, Allison and Drew, at a place they'd picked out on the courthouse lawn, all their friends could talk about was the news that the items thieved since Spring had suddenly showed up at the courthouse, obviously dropped off overnight. The staff and officials spotted them immediately as they pulled up for work, especially with a crowd already gathering nearby who'd spotted them on their way to work.

As Mitchell settled their lawn chairs into a place among their friends, Kent pointed to the front of the courthouse. "Look, Mitchell, the thieves even put the flag back up on the flagpole and hooked up the international flags over the courthouse steps."

"I can't believe those thieves did this," Paula said, leaning back in her chair. "It's so unexpected. Everyone assumed they stole the things they did to sell them for money, but obviously that wasn't true." She pushed a swath of auburn hair behind her ear. "The city moved the big militia man statue from the back parking lot to his base on the lawn by the courthouse today and took the old bell back to the Tuscola high school. I saw film coverage of it on the television news before coming here."

"I saw that coverage too," Becky put in. "The newscaster reported that the thieves parked the old 1950s blue Chevy, stolen earlier, right in the Mayor's private parking space in back of the courthouse."

Rob laughed out loud. "There was no key in the car to move it, either, so they had to call the car's owner Harold Jacobson to see if he had a spare. Fortunately, he did, and I heard he was tickled pink to come and move it from the Mayor's parking space to take it back home. All the people hanging around the courthouse cheered him as he drove away."

"I'd like to have seen that." Mitchell chuckled.

From what Mitchell had told her about the Barlows and their property dispute, Laura felt sure Mitchell wasn't surprised to hear Reed and the boys found one last way to make a little statement.

Laura glanced from their spot on the lawn to the row of flags fluttering in the breeze over the courthouse steps. "The city didn't take down the international flags yet today."

"No. They probably left them up as a sort of statement to people, that all this is finished now. People have been anxious about their properties and about getting out at night ever since you were mugged, Mitchell." Rob grinned at him.

"None of this makes any sense to me." Allison frowned, putting her feet on top of a cooler of drinks they'd brought. "Why would anybody take all this stuff and then bring it all back? It's just weird."

"My guess, like Rob said once, is that some group in the area had a grudge against the city for something and they did this as a pay back," Becky said. She turned to Rob. "Have any of the city officials, any of the department heads or aldermen, or the police ever figured out a reason why this happened at all? Or ever found any suspects?"

"Not that I know of," he answered. "If someone knows something, they're certainly not saying anything. Dad said they talked at several of the city meetings about potential suspects but it was always only talk. There was never any evidence or probable cause for this that anyone could see."

Drew reached into the cooler for a cola. "I'll bet someone in the city knows who's behind this but simply isn't saying. They may even know they wronged someone. Officials don't always make decisions in the best interests of all concerned but they do the best they can. It's hard to make everybody happy. I don't envy the job of city officials and politicians."

"Here, here," said Rob. "These days, too, it seems like there is less respect and appreciation for political leaders than in the past. People are quicker to criticize, to pick fault, to get hateful, even vengeful." Rob glanced at Mitchell. "You've been quiet in all this discussion."

Mitchell grinned. "As the man who was assaulted, I'm simply glad it's resolved."

"But it isn't really resolved." Allison made a face. "No one still knows who did this. And no one heard or saw anything last night when all these items were returned. Honestly, you'd think someone would have seen or heard something."

Her husband Drew laughed. "It's hard to see anything when it's pitch black at two or three in the night. And no one lives close around the courthouse square. There are only businesses here and they're closed at night. It wouldn't have taken a group much time to unload that statue and bell, put the flags back up, park the old Chevy, and then vamoose."

"Oh, look, the show's beginning." Laura pointed to the courthouse porch, which often served as a stage.

Laura imagined Mitchell was glad to see the show starting and relieved, as she was, to see a change of conversation. They'd talked about the return of all the items over a quick dinner earlier before heading to the courthouse to meet their friends. And both of them needed to be particularly discreet on this subject.

"Hurrah. It's the Waynesville Boys," Becky added. "One of my favorite groups. Nolan Harbeck can really pick the banjo like no one else, and those Barlow brothers, Reed and Crockett, can play the guitar and the mandolin and make those instruments really sing. I remember when I was a girl, their daddy Obion played, too." She turned to Mitchell. "Didn't he play mandolin as well sometimes?"

Mitchell grinned, looking toward the men warming up on stage. "Obion Barlow could play several instruments, and his wife Pearl could sing like a lark, too. I remember times at their house with my daddy as a kid listening to them. They taught Reed and Crockett to play and some of their grandkids, like Gideon you see up there playing bass."

"Well, the Barlows are all good people," Becky said, as the Waynesville Boys began singing an old song everyone loved, called

"Carolina in the Fall."

Mitchell sent Laura a happy smile and Laura offered up a silent prayer of thanks afterward at how well everything had turned out.

CHAPTER 20

In the next week all anyone around Waynesville could talk about were the thefts and the sudden return of every item stolen. Mitchell tried to stay busy with work and out of any ongoing discussions as much as he could. He had already taken a big chance talking to Reed as he did, sticking his oar in the Barlows' business, as Reed put it. It was risky to do that with the Barlows but, even looking back, Mitchell couldn't, in all conscience, see any other way he could have handled things differently and he felt right about it.

At the end of the week, on Sunday evening, he put any negative thoughts aside to gather with his family to celebrate his mother's birthday at Mimi's. Mitchell had warned Laura his fun-loving grandmother Mimi and her sister Frances created rather fanciful, somewhat silly parties, but he watched Laura's eyes fly open with surprise, nonetheless, as they walked into Mimi and Frances's back yard.

The sisters shared a charming one level green house with a white picket fence and a pretty tree-shaded yard on 4th Street. Tonight, a large hand-painted sign saying Neverland, hung over the covered back porch, with twinkling lights all around it.

"Welcome, welcome," Mimi called, coming out to meet them in a long, blue dress, reminiscent of Wendy in Peter Pan. On her hair was a coronet of colorful flowers, which incredibly had flashing lights on it.

"Oh, my," he heard Laura whisper. Then, looking around, her face lit in a delighted smile. "Why, it's a Tinkerbell party!"

"Yes, it is," Mimi replied leading them up onto the porch. "You musn't ever let yourself grow old, you know. Evelyn was acting a little grumpy about her age lately so I thought she needed a fun party." Mimi smiled. "She always did love Tinkerbell when she was a girl."

The Quinlan and Dawson family birthday parties were usually small, only for family, and their gatherings were traditionally held at Nannie V's house, Mimi and Frances's place, or at his mother's home. All always had a fanciful theme, too.

Frances came out the backdoor then, dressed in a similar rose-colored dress to Mimi's, bringing a pitcher of pink lemonade to put on a side table. "Oh, I'm glad you two are early," she said. "Put some of those lawn chairs out in the yard for later, would you, Mitchell? And put those wickets around for croquet. The children will enjoy playing." She giggled. "I rather think I will, too, as well. I used to be rather good at the game."

She greeted Laura as she walked up on the porch. "Good to see you, too, dear."

"Everything is so beautiful," Laura said, looking around.

Twinkling lights were wrapped over the porch's rails, posts, and arches and a big table sat near one end of the porch with chairs down both sides, with an extra at the end for the birthday person. The table tonight was covered in a bright chartreuse cloth with a pink runner down the middle, the center of the table loaded with bouquets of flowers with butterfly picks in them. At each place was a Tinkerbell paper plate and a chartreuse cup with a pink napkin sticking out of it.

"There are nine chairs here instead of eight," Mitchell noted. "I thought only Mom, the kids, Nannie V, you two, Laura, and I were coming."

Mimi came over to admire the table with them. "Well, Sam Jacobs came through on business, so we invited him, too, of course. He's sort of like family, being the children's grandfather."

Mitchell frowned a little, wondering what Sam would think of their fanciful gathering. "What's for the birthday supper?" he asked, deciding to change the subject.

"Frances and I decided not to fuss," Mimi answered. "We bought one of those nice honey-baked hams, made baked beans, potato salad, and a grape salad. With cake and ice cream that should fill everyone up, don't you think?"

"It sounds wonderful," Laura said. "And I love the Tinkerbell cake."

"Isn't that cute?" Mimi glanced toward the tiered cake on a decorated side table. "I didn't make it. I had that lovely little bakery downtown do it. I found the pretty music box with Tinkerbell on the top, though. It gave me the idea for the party and the girls at the bakery said they could put it right on top of the cake. The music box plays Frank Sinatra's wonderful song, 'Young At Heart,' perfect for Evelyn's birthday. I always want her to stay young at heart and young of mind, to always look ahead with joy at life. That's so important. So many people think and talk themselves old. I've never understood it."

Frances came out with another tray to put on the table. "Here, you two kids. Put your party hats on. Floral coronets for the girls and these cute felt Peter Pan hats for the boys. Mimi and I made them, easy peasy, with some green felt, a glue gun, and red feathers."

Mitchell saw Laura smirk as Frances settled a hat on his head.

"Well, look how nice those turned out." Frances patted his arm fondly and then turned to put a flower garland on Laura. "Aren't these little flower coronets going to look cute when dusk falls and the lights show up more."

Mimi glanced over at them from where she was putting favors around the table. "Don't forget those chairs, Mitchell, and the croquet wickets," she reminded him. "I put the croquet set right there by the steps. The wickets are hanging on the back."

Laura followed him toward the yard. "I'll help you," she said.

The sisters went back in the house to begin bringing out the food and Laura turned to Mitchell, giggling. "Your hat is sure cute."

He winked at her. "Watch your jesting, my dear, or I may not save you from the pirates, the Indians, or the croc." He enjoyed watching her laugh.

"Are your grandmother and Frances always this much fun?"

He nodded.

"It's no wonder your mother became so creative and an artist, after growing up with Mimi as her mother."

"That's true but, despite Mom's creative streak, she got my grandad's sound wisdom and his more serious nature. He was a physician here in Waynesville until he died. They owned a big house on the hill across Richland Creek, a pretty place, but Mimi doesn't seem to miss it since moving in with Frances."

"They look a lot alike," Laura commented as they began putting croquet wickets around the yard.

He turned to grin at her. "Didn't you know they're twins?"

"I didn't know that, but I should have guessed."

"They wear their hair the same and a lot of the time they still like to dress alike to go downtown to eat lunch or to shop. Those two are always into something. Full of jokes and stories, as happy as two clams."

"Will your mother be surprised at this party theme?"

He snorted. "Not hardly. She gave up worrying years ago over what sort of party themes her mother would come up with." He paused, putting out the last wicket. "Nannie V is more serious of nature, but my Dad was full of fun. He loved Mimi's parties and he loved Mimi. She gave him a new bicycle when he turned forty. He was crazy about it."

Laura glanced back toward the porch to wave at Nannie V, who'd just arrived. "It's funny, but it often seems to me like your mother is more like Nannie V."

"It's true, and in a lot of ways Dad, with all his outgoing, fun-loving ways, and hearty jokes, acted more like Mimi than his mom. I guess we all turn out in our own individual ways, despite our parents." They began to walk toward the porch. "Here come my mom and the kids."

The evening's party was nothing but fun and Mitchell enjoyed himself, playing with Mackenzie and Charlie, singing "Happy

Birthday" to his mom, watching her laughing and opening her gifts. Laura enjoyed herself, too, and Mitchell liked that. She fit in well with his family, and he knew she appreciated having a family to love and share with again.

Surprisingly, Sam Jacobs enjoyed himself, as well, acting easy and comfortable with the children, ready to romp and play with them. Sam was a handsome man, tall, broad-shouldered and fit, his dark hair lightening at the temples, his smile genuine. Mitchell felt glad to see he wasn't one of those serious, remote types that didn't know how to have a good time. There were moments, over the dinner table with everyone talking and laughing, when Mitchell saw Sam and his mother pass a look. He wondered if anyone else noticed.

Later as he and Laura left, his mother patted his cheek and hugged him. "I'm teaching a class in the morning downtown and Nannie V is keeping the children," she said. "Can you have lunch with me after my class?"

"Sure," he said. "How about one o'clock?"

"That should be perfect."

Mitchell dropped Laura off after the party a little later, both of them needing to do laundry and catch up on cleaning at their apartments.

He was tired, too. The week had been a strain. He wouldn't have admitted it to anyone, but he'd worried about confronting Reed Barlow and especially about giving him an ultimatum, no matter how tactfully. It wasn't something anyone who knew the Barlows would usually dare to do. Mitchell found himself a little edgy all of last week, too, not sleeping well, and even after the items were returned, it took another week for him to decide Reed or one of the Barlow family wouldn't play some sort of joke or prank on him for his interference. Or come to warn him about keeping his silence.

Now he finally felt better. The Monday staff meeting at work was an easy one, the day sunny and everyone in a good mood. He'd conducted the testing of several applicants that morning while Norma was tied up with payroll, and then, after a meeting with a new business owner, seeking retail help, he went to meet his mother for lunch.

She'd texted earlier and suggested they eat at The Patio, a bistro on Church Street. With the day fair, Mitchell walked over, and soon found his mother already settled at one of the courtyard tables outside. It was a pretty spot with ferns hanging from the rafters above and pots of flowers and plants scattered around on the old brick patio.

He leaned over to give her a kiss on the cheek before he sat down. "Did you enjoy your birthday?"

"I did. Mother sent me home with enough leftovers for tonight's dinner, so I won't have to cook. The children are excited they'll get to help me finish off the Tinkerbell cake, too." She laughed. "What did your Laura think of her first family birthday party?"

"Couldn't you tell? She had a fabulous time."

"I do like her, Mitchell. I think she will make you happy."

He nodded as the waitress came to take their order. His mother ordered quiche and a Caesar salad, Mitchell one of the Patio's roast beef melts with Provolone, grilled onions, and homemade potato salad.

They made a little conversation; his mother talking about her watercolor class that morning and a trip to Asheville when she took Mackenzie and Charlie shopping for school clothes. When their food arrived, they stopped to eat for a space.

"It's hard to believe school will be starting so soon. Mackenzie will be in the fourth grade this year and Charlie in the second." His mother gave him a small smile. "I still remember the day we brought those two little things home, four and two, not understanding what had happened to their parents, grieving, crying, and going through such a painful transition as they readjusted to a new life with us. It was hard."

"It was but they've thrived. They're happy and well now."

She picked at the necklace she wore. "It still hurts that we lost Alise and Hudson so young, that they won't get to see Mackenzie and Charlie grow up."

Mitchell tried to think what to say. "I'm glad Sam Jacobs, Mackenzie and Charlie's grandfather, could stop through to see the children, that he's made sure to keep a strong presence in their lives."

She glanced away, picking at her necklace again. It was obvious she had something on her mind.

"You want to tell me what's on your mind, Mom?" He grinned at her. "I hope with my wedding next month, you're not planning to have a birds-and-bees talk with me."

She looked up at him, an edge of tears in her eyes now, surprising him. "You so often make me think of your father. He would do that, know when I had something serious on my mind and then make a little joke to ease the moment. I miss him."

"Nannie V told me we're meant to always hold those we love in the memory of our hearts. I liked those words." Mitchell waited.

After a few minutes, his mother took a breath and said, "Sam Jacobs has asked me to marry him."

If Mitchell hadn't put his glass of cola down a minute ago, he'd probably have spilled it all over the table. He'd noticed a little interest between the two. But had it progressed this far? He tried to think what to say but couldn't seem to find any words.

"I know this might be somewhat of a shock."

He glanced up to find her watching him anxiously.

Mitchell finally found his voice. "I guess I'm hurt more than anything that you've obviously been developing a relationship with Sam for some time but haven't bothered to mention it to me."

She sighed. "I guess I should have talked to you about it sooner." She rearranged her silverware on the table, obviously nervous. "For all this time since Alise and Hudson died, Sam and I have only been friends. Good friends who'd both lost children. Sam was grateful I was willing to take the children. He couldn't, being widowed and traveling all the time with his work. But he wanted to build a good relationship with Mackenzie and Charlie. I always respected that, and I worked hard to help him have that opportunity, taking the children to his place at Tybee for vacations and visits, opening our home to him for weekends when he could drive up to Waynesville or when his travels brought him through the area and he could stop over with us."

"When did things change?"

"I'm not sure exactly. It's hard to pinpoint how friendship changes to something else. Looking back, I guess I suddenly felt a little difference in the air between us. I would notice him a little more keenly than in past and it seemed like he was noticing me in a similar way." She laughed then. "We both really tried to pretend nothing was different over the last two years. He never said a word to me, and I certainly never said a word to him. Neither of us wanted to risk hurting our friendship, our joint interactions with the children."

Mitchell rubbed a hand through his hair. "When Sam was here this spring, I caught him looking at you sometimes the way a man does when he's attracted to a woman. Not that I saw you look back at him in a similar way. But I noticed it and I wondered for the first time about all the time you spent with him when you went to Tybee to his place with the kids, when he came to our house."

She picked at her necklace again. "This spring when I took the children down for their break, we caught each other in some of those looks. The feelings were surfacing more, but we both kept pretending they weren't there. I kept thinking what in the world I would do if he ever said or did anything." She shook her head. "Honestly, I felt so stupid, like a silly school girl."

"I know the feeling." He grinned then.

"Yes, and I saw you had a relationship forming and I didn't want anything to interfere with that. But this summer when the children and I went down for the Fourth, Sam and I were sitting out on the screened porch after the children had gone to bed, both of us reading a book, enjoying the night sounds and the cool of the evening. Suddenly Sam just threw down the book he was reading, walked across to my chair, learned over me and said, 'I can't stand it anymore' and kissed me." She looked away, embarrassed. "Of course, then we had to confront and come to terms with things. That has taken a while and a lot of talk."

"What do you want to do, Mom? Surely you know I wouldn't stand in the way of any happiness you wanted. You've been alone a long time now. It's hard for me to wrap my mind around the idea of you being with someone else besides Dad though." He laughed a little. "Actually, when it's your parents you really never think about them that way very much."

"Yes, I know. Children always seem to see their parents as asexual beings."

"I suppose that's right."

She chuckled a little. "Do you know what Mother said to me last night when I went into the kitchen with her for a minute?"

"No, what?"

"She said, 'That man has the hots for you, Evelyn. That ought to give you a spark and make you feel younger.' I thought I'd wet my pants."

Mitchell couldn't help laughing. "Mimi always has been one to tell it like it is."

"Well, it made me realize people were noticing, that you and others would soon notice as well. Then with Sam wanting to move the relationship forward, I realized I needed to talk to those closest to me." She took another breath. "Sam has an opportunity to take early retirement with his company. He wants to do it. He knows I don't want to leave Waynesville or move the children, so, as he says, he can come to me now, and we can keep his place as a vacation home. It's paid for."

"When will this early retirement happen?"

"Not until the end of the year, and we want some more time together after that, for him to come to stay in Waynesville more often, for us to spend time together, to be sure all this will work comfortably and to let the children get used to the idea."

She gave Mitchell an anxious look then. "What do you think they will say or think about this idea? Will it upset them all over again, upset their lives and their security? I don't want that, Mitchell."

He realized then his mother was struggling not to upset the lives of those she loved, even if meant not pursuing her own happiness.

Mitchell put a hand across the table to take hers. "When I had the kids for the day one Saturday not long ago, Charlie said, 'I wish Daddy Sam and Grammy could get married' and while I was trying to figure out what to say to that, Mackenzie added, 'If they fell in love we could be a family all the time and not just on vacations.'"

His mother started crying then. "Those blessed children."

"You see, after losing Alise and Hudson, to the kids you're their mother, and Sam has become like their father. I don't think you have anything to worry about deciding to marry Sam except to wonder if it's what your own heart really wants."

She closed her eyes. "Do you think your father, Charles, would understand? I hate to think I'd hurt him even in the grave."

"I don't think you need to worry about that, either. How many times did he say to you that your happiness made his happiness? Follow your heart, Mother. The rest of us will come along happily."

CHAPTER 21

Later in August on a Friday afternoon, Laura sat in the showroom area of the Shop On the Corner with Evelyn Quinlan, the table in front of them covered with papers, scribbled notes, pictures, and fabric swatches.

"I'm so glad Glaydean Sterling wanted to take Mackenzie and Charlie with her three children to spend the afternoon at the pool today and that you had some free time to spare. We needed to go over and finalize all the plans for the wedding." She smiled across the table at Laura. "It isn't far away now, on Saturday October first." She grinned wider. "I told Mitchell it would be easy to remember his anniversary date, since it's on the first day of the month. His father was always getting our date mixed up."

"It's wonderful how much you've helped me with all this planning. I'm so grateful."

Evelyn looked at her over the top of the blue reading glasses she'd popped on. "My sweet girl, you've become like a daughter to me, helping to ease the hurt of losing mine, and I hope I've become like a mother to you, as I know you lost your mother."

Laura felt like crying at the words. "Thank you."

Evelyn winked at her then, reminding her of Mitchell with the familiar gesture. He planned to join them soon, but many of the details she and Evelyn could go over easily before he arrived.

"I love the colors you picked out for the wedding, all these soft dreamy mauves, silky materials for the dresses, muted gray tuxes for the men. It offers such a romantic feel." She laid out print-out pictures of the dresses for the bridesmaids, suits for the groomsmen, and a picture of the wedding dress Laura had chosen."

Laura's eyes moved over the pictures, loving the understated tones all over again.

"This dress you chose is simply lovely, too." Evelyn pointed to the picture of Laura's dress. "Simple, modest, with the lacey overlay material giving it an heirloom look. It's perfect." She studied the photo. "Are you sure you don't want a veil though? A veil can be so romantic when the groom lifts it up to kiss the bride."

Laura shook her head, giggling. "No. I just want that little floral headpiece I picked out with a long wisp of veil attached." She pointed to a picture of it. "The headpiece has a comb in it so I can tuck it in my hair in the back, and let the tulle drift down to my waist." She showed Evelyn the picture. "This feels more like me."

"I do like it and I like all the flowers you've picked for the bouquets, too, with the same mauve, cream, and dusty green colors. Honestly, everything is going to be simply beautiful."

Laura lowered her voice. "You know I needed to plan a simple wedding without a lot of expense. Do you think your family and friends will be disappointed? Would they have expected a more lavish wedding with one of those gala receptions afterward in a location besides at the church? In Amory, many church weddings still only have a receiving line and a simple reception after the ceremony with cake, mints, nuts, and a pretty punch. I like that myself. It seems sweet and intimate, but I've been to those grand upscale receptions with big buffets of food, a cash bar, and dancing."

Evelyn pushed her glasses up. "As you know our family doesn't drink and being around inebriated people has never done anything for me. It brings up old painful memories, as well. Frankly, I've never seen the point in spending a fortune on a wedding. The bride walks down the aisle and the ceremony takes thirty to forty minutes at best. I doubt few, beyond the bridal party, know if the bride's dress cost five thousand, five hundred, or fifty dollars. No one cares either if the church sanctuary is banked with expensive flowers and candelabras or with modest decorations. We're putting lovely nosegays alternately on the end of every other pew with a little tulle hanging below and draping that wooden arch the church has at the front of the sanctuary with tulle and flowers. On either side of it we're putting two fabulous ferns of Nannie V's tucked into big white pots—you've seen them hanging on her porch. Everything will be gorgeous."

She pulled a piece of blush mauve fabric toward her, piled among other swatches on the table. "Downstairs in the church fellowship hall, you and Rita have made lovely mauve tablecloths for the tables as well. I've always been pleased the church bought round tables for its dinners and events. They seem so much more intimate and are prettier to decorate."

"I found that whole bolt of soft mauve-pink fabric and a roll of tulle for a steal at a fabric outlet where I buy store supplies." She picked up a silk rose from a box. "I discovered all these mauve and cream silk roses online on clearance that we're using for the pew and table decorations, too."

"You're such a sensible and resourceful girl. I love that. Most people who are well-to-do, except the silly Hollywood types and those trying to impress others, are far more prudent with their finances than you'd think and they wear more understated clothing, too."

"So you don't think Mitchell or anyone else will be disappointed in anything?"

"Mitchell?" Her eyes widened. "Honey, we've had to economize and live judiciously ever since my husband Charles died. Especially after we took in Mackenzie and Charlie to raise. You see how many hours I work, teach, and paint around the children's lives, and Mitchell has worked hard to keep the business solid and going. People who own small businesses as we do, you included, seldom make a lavish income, but we're comfortable." She offered Laura a sly smile. "I've come to view discovering ways to be thrifty somewhat like an art form."

Laura laughed and then sent Evelyn another concerned look. "That's also why I worried about you doing the reception dinner the night before the wedding. It's expensive to cater and feed people. Can't I help with the expense of that in some way?"

Evelyn laughed. "Honey, I am hosting that rehearsal dinner in the tent in my large backyard, the same place I had the I-Do Barbeque engagement party. That tent, huge as it is, belongs to me. I bought it for a song from a group wanting a larger one and wondering what to do with their old one. I can't tell you how many times I've hauled that big tent out and gotten Mitchell and his friends to set it up for one party or another. I also have an assortment of those six-foot fold-up tables I snag anytime I see one at a garage sale. If I need extras, I can borrow them from the church. You might have noticed, too, that the chairs I use are a mixed assortment of wooden chairs I've bought at thrift shops and garage sales and painted white so they would all match. I keep the tent, another smaller tent I use for outdoor art events, the chairs and tables, all neatly stacked in that storage shed to one side of the garage. It looks like a third garage building outside, but it's loaded with my event chairs, tables, tents, and all my larger art supplies."

Evelyn picked up her bottle of water from the table to take a long sip. "So you stop worrying about my expenses for hosting the little reception that I've planned and simply pray it doesn't rain. I can move the event to the church fellowship hall if it does, but I'd rather not."

"You'll still need to think about feeding all the people who will be in the wedding or helping with it." Laura glanced at a guest list on the table. "That's about twenty-eight people."

Evelyn looked at the list, too. "Well, that small a number is no problem. I'm doing an Italian themed event with three large pans of manicotti. I can put that together and bake it the day before and reheat it before the reception. I'm adding a spinach, mandarin and strawberry salad with almonds sprinkled on it, a Tuscan white bean salad with tomatoes, olives, and white beans, along with French bread, and bottles of nonalcoholic sparkling rose to make everything festive. Really, Laura, I make everything ahead for my little events, and Nannie V, Mimi, and Frances, are helping me. They're each making a cake, so we'll have three selections. Everything will be lovely. Don't worry." She grinned. "I also hunted out a pile of Italian CDs so we can enjoy music in the background for a nice ambience. Rob has one of those players that keeps the music rotating and he's bringing it."

"You've worked so hard planning this."

"It's really been fun," Evelyn answered. "Haven't you enjoyed your part of the planning, too?" Seeing Laura nod, she pulled out another sheet of paper. "Let's look through this last wedding checklist to be sure we have everything on schedule."

They heard the chime on the front door then, and Mitchell came around the corner from the vestibule to join them. "Am I too late?" he asked.

"No, your timing is perfect. Come sit down. We're just getting ready to go through the last checklist to see what else needs to be done."

Evelyn began to read through the items. "Our date, Saturday October first at 2:00 pm is secure at the church. Laura and I have sent all the announcements out." She grinned. "It will be a crush at the wedding and the church reception."

"It's good we're only serving cake, nuts, and stuff then." Mitchell grinned.

"Hmmm." Evelyn looked down at her notes. "We do have those basics well planned but the ladies at the church, most in my women's group, asked if they can make trays of those little crustless tea sandwiches. They seemed most insistent. What do you two think?"

"You've brought their leftover sandwiches home from events before. They were pretty and tasted great." Mitchell turned to Laura. "Is it all right with you? People might like a little snack with their cake if it's there."

"If they really want to," Laura said. "And tell them we said thank you."

"I will." Evelyn paused again. "Additionally, the members of the Arts Council want to go in together to provide dipped strawberries. They've started a fund. I couldn't think of a reason to say no. Will that be all right with you, too?"

"People are being so nice," Laura said.

"Quinlans have lived in this town for a long, long time," Evelyn said. "It makes a difference."

"You've helped many times with other people's events, too, Mom," Mitchell added. "You're due to get blessed back."

She laughed. "I do loan out my big tent a lot!"

Mitchell glanced over her shoulder at the list. "The wedding party is set. The tuxes are all ordered for the men. My cousin Rob will be my best man. Kent from work and Drew Tate are groomsmen and Mike Wingate is coming in from Missouri to be the third."

"Wonderful," Evelyn said. "I haven't seen Mike often enough since he went out west to Logan University to their Doctor of Chiropractic program. Sally says he's been working at their campus health center in Chesterfield, where many of the students train, since he graduated. I wish he'd move back nearer to home and his family to work."

"Actually, I think he's talking to Neal Sterling about coming in with his chiropractic practice. The business has grown to be more than Neal can handle. Mike said Neal started talking to him about it at Christmas. Plus Mike and his wife Susan are expecting their first child. I think they like the idea of raising their children nearer to family. Susan's people are from Spartanburg not far away."

Laura tried to follow all this conversation.

Sensing her confusion, Evelyn said, "These are our neighbors on Church Street we're talking about, Laura. The Sterlings live next door to us; the Wingates live in the next house down. My husband and I were good friends with Bergen and Sally Wingate and our children grew up playing with theirs. Mike and Julie were about the same ages as Mitchell and Alise. You met the Wingates and the Sterlings at the engagement barbeque."

"Oh, I think I remember them now. Thanks for the reminder.

I'm still learning people."

Evelyn glanced at her list again. "Laura, are your attendants set and the dresses ordered?"

"Yes," Laura answered. "Elizabeth Donaldson, my best friend since childhood, is coming up from Georgia to be my matron of honor, and you know I asked Becky, Allison, and Paula to be my three bridesmaids." She looked down at the table and sighed. "It seems sad that I don't have any family to be in the wedding."

"I know you're thinking about your sister," said Evelyn. "But your grandfather, Pastor Rodney Baylor is coming in to give you away, along with his wife Ann, your Uncle Tom and his wife Deidre, all the way from Gulfport, Mississippi. Mitchell says they are flying in and renting a car at the airport. He offered to go pick them up but Tom insisted that renting a car would be easier since the airport is in Asheville."

Laura smiled at the thought. "They're staying over at Junaluska Thursday and Friday night. It's a Methodist Retreat Center and my grandfather and grandmother visited there when younger. They're eager to see it again." Laura picked up a sample of mauve fabric as she talked. "My Aunt Dorothy, Daddy's sister, and my Uncle Curtis are driving over from Alabama, too. It's only a six-hour trip, not as far to drive. They're staying Friday and Saturday with one of Curtis's brothers who lives in Sylva before going back. My Grandmother Ida isn't making the trip though. She's had some health problems lately and thought such a long trip would be too hard for her."

"So there you are, dear," Evelyn put in. "Your grandparents and two aunts and two uncles are coming to your wedding, so you will have family present." She glanced at her list again and then at Mitchell. "Laura and I have already talked about the wedding ceremony and the rehearsal dinner. She can fill you in. I confirmed with Rob's mother Bernice Killian that she will play the piano for the wedding. She plays for the church, and you know she's gifted." Looking to Laura now, she added. "Bernice said she'd already talked with you about the selections, mostly traditional pieces, with

'Pachelbel Canon in D Major' for the processional and 'Wagners Bridal Chorus' or 'Here Comes the Bride' as you walk down the aisle. Is that still good?"

Laura nodded.

"Our professional photographer friend, Benny Fritz, that did the engagement photos, is doing all the wedding pictures," Mitchell added. "Everyone knows to come to the church early so we can do them before the wedding, too. I hate those weddings where everyone has to hang around after the service before going to the reception because photos need to be made."

Evelyn began to chat then about a few extra points, little gift bags she and Laura planned to make closer to the wedding date for attendant gifts. She looked up with a smile from the papers in front of her. "I'm so tickled your friend Lillian Greeley, from Amory, wanted to help Rita Harbeck serve in the reception. It gives us a way to recognize them, since you're close to both. I've also invited Rita and Nolan, and Lillian and Bobby, to the rehearsal dinner. I'm pleased Lillian and Bobby could come over from Amory. I know you said they would be camping and staying for a week."

"I'm looking forward to meeting Lillian and Bobby, too," Mitchell added, beginning to tell his mother about the campground where they planned to stay.

While listening, Laura was distracted by someone peeking into the large showroom window, where she kept upholstered furniture pieces and decorative items to make the window more attractive to passers by.

Suddenly she gasped, her mouth dropping open.

Mitchell and Evelyn, seeing her face, glanced quickly toward the window.

"What's the matter?" Mitchell asked.

Laura tried to find her voice. "I think the woman looking in the window was my sister. She's moved out of view now, but I really think it was her."

Laura froze then as she heard the frontdoor bell and someone coming in to the vestibule.

"What am I going to do if it's Georgina and Chance?" she whispered.

"You'll bring them in here and we'll talk to them," Evelyn answered matter-of-factly. "What a blessing we're here today so you'll have support at this meeting if you need it."

Before Laura could get up, she saw Georgina walk from the hallway into the showroom. "Laura, is that you?" she asked.

Georgina paused in the doorway, putting a hand to her heart. "Oh, my goodness, it is you. I thought it was, looking in the window." She moved across the room. "Don't be so shocked that you don't stand up to give your own sister a hug. You're my family."

Somehow Laura stood up, and Georgina quickly wrapped her in an embrace. While they hugged, Laura kept glancing over Georgina's shoulder, wondering if Chance was with her, if he was waiting in the vestibule or would walk in the room any minute.

As Georgina stepped back, Laura finally found her voice. "Is Chance with you?" she asked looking toward the doorway again.

"No," her sister dropped her eyes. "I have a lot to tell you." She glanced toward Evelyn and Mitchell. "I can wait in the vestibule until you finish with your clients though." She gave Evelyn and Mitchell one of her million-dollar smiles. "I'm so sorry to interrupt."

"It's no problem. We're pleased to meet you." Evelyn stood and held out her hand. "I'm Evelyn Quinlan and this is my son Mitchell. We're been here talking about wedding plans, so I guess you might say we're sort of family, too. Mitchell and Laura are getting married at the first of October. We're so blessed life brought her to Waynesville and we've welcomed her, with our deepest love and affection, into our family here."

Laura watched Georgina's eyes widen. After a moment of surprise, she looked down to the floor in some embarrassment. "Well, that's really nice. Congratulations." She hesitated. "However, Laura and I still need to talk privately about a lot of personal things together." She stressed the word personal.

Mitchell walked closer, offering Georgina his hand in welcome.

"Whatever you need to talk about with Laura, I'm sure she wouldn't mind you sharing with us." His eyes narrowed. "There's nothing about Laura's past we don't know, Georgina."

"I see." Georgina raised her chin, stepping back. "It sounds as if you've heard only the bad things. That woman in the workroom, who came out to greet me when I came in the front door, must have heard bad stories, too. She frowned at me, when I told her who I was."

She turned to Laura. "I guess you've told everyone here my personal business and probably not many nice things about me either."

Mitchell gestured toward a chair at the table. "Why don't you sit down, Georgina? I can assure you Laura has shared many wonderful stories about the two of you growing up together in Amory, the good times you had, rich memories of your mother and father and the home you grew up in. She also told us about your talents and gifts and about how well you sing."

Somewhat disarmed by Mitchell's words, Georgina sighed and sat down. "Those are kind words, but I still feel uncomfortable sharing some of the difficult personal times I've passed through with people I don't know well yet."

"Well, here's the thing," Mitchell said, returning to his own chair. "I've come to feel very protective about Laura. I'm not willing to leave her alone in your company after the threatening letter she received from you and Chance in the past." A muscle in his jaw bunched. "It's illegal to send threatening letters in the mail. Did you know that? In North Carolina, it's a misdemeanor."

Evelyn straightened and cleared her throat. "Please understand, Georgina, that Mitchell and I would be concerned not to stay here with Laura because of that. I'm sorry if you wanted to talk with Laura alone, but I hope you can understand our feelings." She glanced toward the door. "Where is your, er ah… partner now?" She searched for the right word before finding it. "Perhaps he might want to sit and talk with us also."

Georgina blanched white at their words, her mouth dropping

open. Then she began to cry. "Chance is not with me. Actually, he's dead."

She began to weep openly then after shocking them with her words.

Laura tried to think of something to say.

Angry red spots came into Georgina's cheeks as she wiped her eyes and then looked around at them. "I don't know anything about any letters that Chance might have sent to you, Laura. I didn't even know he knew where you lived. I only found your address on an old scrap of paper in his stuff recently when packing to move." She crossed her arms, her eyes bright with tears. "It hurts my heart, Laura, for you to think I would write something hateful or threatening to you. I got hurt enough when you moved away without telling me where you were even going. I cried a lot over that."

"I think Laura had good reasons for all those actions," Mitchell put in.

Evelyn gathered up her papers and stood. "You know, now that I think about it, I believe I will go on home. I need to pick up the children at Nannie V's. It's getting late. Mitchell, I think you and Laura can talk about whatever else needs discussing without me." She looked at Georgina. "I'm sorry we've met at such a sad time for you."

Georgina lifted her chin again. "I know you think I'm a really awful person, but I'm not. Chance died in early May and my life is all different now. I have a good job, I'm going back to school to finish my degree this fall, and I'm married." She held up her left hand to show a ring. "I married a really nice minister who helped me to turn my life around. He's over at Junaluska at some meetings right now. I came here to look for the address I found in Chance's stuff. I told Warren I didn't know if Laura was really here or what it would be like when we got together again, so I thought I should come by myself first to see."

It was all Laura could do to keep her mouth from dropping open once again.

Unflustered, Evelyn said, "Well, that is very nice to hear. Perhaps you and your husband can come back for Laura and Mitchell's wedding. If you'll leave your address, I'll send you an invitation."

She walked over to give Laura a kiss on the cheek and then left.

CHAPTER 22

Mitchell grinned over his mother's neat escape. Obviously when she realized Chance was out of the picture and wouldn't be a threat, she decided he and Laura could handle the rest of Georgina's emotional overload without her. That's what it seemed like to him. Who would tell virtual strangers all she'd begun telling them in such a dramatic manner? Her take on things, too, was hardly realistic, seeing herself as a victim rather than recognizing she'd caused most of her own problems herself.

Laura glanced at her watch as she heard the jingle of the front door bell as Evelyn left. "I need to tell Rita and Nolan good night and close the shop," she said, standing up. "Mitchell, maybe you could get Georgina a cola or a water from the little refrigerator. I'll be right back."

"Would you like something to drink?" he asked as Laura left to lock up.

"A water would be nice." Georgina leaned back in her chair, crossing her leg as he came back with it. He noticed as he brought back the water and walked to sit down again that Georgina let her eyes move over him, with a little more interest than he cared to see. She was obviously a beautiful woman, as Laura often said, with a knock-out figure, blond hair with red highlights, and the sort of easy grace and sure confidence in her own body that some woman had naturally.

Studying him again, she asked, "Are you really going to marry Laura?"

"I am," he replied.

She ran a hand through her hair and shrugged. "It's hard to think of my little sister getting married. She was never very good at drawing and attracting the boys."

What a cat, Mitchell thought.

He picked up his water to take a sip. "You know, that seems hard for me to believe. Sparks lit up the room for me the first time I met your sister. I can't recall any other woman ever attracting me in quite that way."

She seemed annoyed at his response and then said, "Well, I regret you and your mother had to get involved in Laura's and my relationship. I still think it would be better if Laura and I talk privately now."

He ignored her request. "Did you really not know Chance wrote Laura a threatening letter?"

She squared her shoulders. "No, I didn't. I had no idea Chance even knew where Laura lived. It never dawned on me that he would look for her either. He was so mad when she left."

"As I said before, Laura had a lot of reasons for doing things the way she did. Good ones, too."

She tossed her hair. "You don't know everything."

"I'd say I know enough."

Laura came back in the room then. "Mitchell, if you need to leave, too, I'm sure Georgina and I can finish talking without you."

"No, I think I need to stay." He smiled at her.

He'd caught the strained look on Laura's face when she made the offer. Despite what she said, he knew she wasn't really sure she wanted to spend much time alone with her sister yet. He could certainly see why. "Besides, Georgina hasn't finished telling us her story yet," he said. "We want to know more about what happened to Chance, where's she's working, about her marriage and her school plans."

Georgina glared at him. "You need to know, too, that I was going through a very difficult time in my life last spring when Laura left." She turned to Laura. "You should have sensed things weren't really happy with me when Chance and I came to stay with you. It wasn't easy for me knowing that you didn't want us there either. I knew how you and Daddy felt about me leaving school and going to be in Chance's band. I really believed we could be good though, that we could really make it. But it was slower and harder than I thought it would be. Chance was so determined that the band and the music come first with us. Yet we never seemed to have enough money."

She looked away from them toward the window. "Often, we ran out of food and couldn't pay bills. Chance kind of handled it all by simply focusing more on his music, writing songs way into the night, practicing with the group till all hours. They all began to drink more, to smoke dope and do drugs and stuff. Chance said all bands did that, that it helped them loosen up, helped new songs to come, and fit the image. I guess maybe I thought that was just the way things were in the industry. I saw it everywhere at the clubs and places where we performed, with the people we hung out with."

Mitchell leaned forward. "I assume that when things went bad and you got evicted, you came to Laura's," he put in, making an effort to move the story along.

She turned to him. "Yes, sort of, and I hated the way Laura looked at us, acted like we were scum or something. Not seeing our dreams at all. I could tell she didn't believe in us, that she wanted us to leave. Chance was trying to save some money so we could get another place. His parents wouldn't loan him any more money. They were mad he dropped out of school and mad he hardly ever came home. They didn't like the band and they didn't like me. He took me to his home in Kentucky once but they treated me like dirt, really rude, like it was my fault things weren't going well for us or for Chance and the band right then. I told Chance I didn't ever want to go back."

"So Laura was the only person who would give you money anymore," Mitchell said.

She scowled at him, almost forgetting Laura was sitting right there listening along with him, her face still white with shock.

"You make that sound really mean, Mitchell, but Laura was my family. I thought she might believe in us and help us until we could get our break. Then Chance and I would have paid any money back that we borrowed."

"What happened to Chance?" Laura asked quietly.

"We moved back to Nashville after you left, got an apartment near the downtown music scene and Vanderbilt University. It was kind of a creepy place on the third floor but it was all we could afford. I worried when we moved back and after because our gigs weren't bringing in much money anymore. After we divided the money with the band every time, Chance and I didn't get much."

"How did Chance manage before you got together?" Mitchell asked.

"Chance and the band used to all crash together in some big apartment before I came along. He suggested doing that again, but I didn't want to live with all those men. They lived really nasty and I didn't want to become their maid and cook and everything." She sighed. "Chance and I started fighting a lot in Nashville when we went back in April. He was doing more drugs and crashing out and sleeping a lot afterward and I didn't like that."

Neither he nor Laura made a comment.

"One morning after we'd had a big fight the night before, I went for a walk down the street and discovered Vanderbilt's school of music was only a couple of blocks away. I didn't know before it was so close. I went walking through the lobby and the halls, sometimes hearing the music coming from the practice rooms, remembering how happy I'd been at Ole Miss. On a bulletin board I saw some job notices and remembered at Old Miss a friend got to take some free classes because she worked at the school. On a whim, I went to the professor's office, the head of the voice department, to see if I could apply. It was only a receptionist job in the department with a little secretarial work; I knew I could do that. They like people who look nice and have good communication skills for jobs like that." She smiled at both of them as if reminding them she possessed both.

"The professor's door was open and I just sort of walked in. His name was Dr. Thurston and he was really sweet to me. I found out there was a process to follow for jobs, but because he liked me, and learned I'd been a voice scholarship student at Ole Miss, he thought I'd be a good fit talking with incoming students. He helped escalate the process, made a couple of calls to the school and stuff while I waited, and I got the job right then. He even said I could take some classes starting in the fall or winter to complete my degree. I only need about a year and half to finish."

"I'm really happy you're going to get to finish your degree," Laura said, and Mitchell saw her smile with pleasure at Georgina.

Georgina wrinkled her nose. "Well, Chance wasn't happy about it. I thought he would be, that he'd be grateful I could help him by working, too. But he got mad and hollered and said I didn't believe in him. He got furious, too, because I didn't talk with him and ask him first. Can you believe that? Even when I explained how it happened, he wanted me to not take the job. I couldn't believe he was being so unreasonable and mean to me when I was only trying to help. He kept saying the job would get in the way of our gigs and shows when I needed to travel with them to sing. I suggested they could do more gigs nearer Nashville or that he could sing when I couldn't go like he did before I joined the band."

She shook her head. "He carried on and on about how this was like a betrayal and he called me some really mean names. I got mad then, too, and I said that it wouldn't hurt if we both got jobs. He really hollered and yelled more mean and ugly things at me then." She looked at Laura. "He said I sounded like you. He said you'd poisoned my thinking and belief in him."

"You know that's not true, don't you, Georgina?" Mitchell asked.

"Well, of course. But Chance likes to get his way no matter what, and things went totally downhill after that. I started getting up early for work every day, dressing nice. I had new people to meet, and was actually making money. Chance started wanting my money as soon as I got paid, but I said no, that I was spending it for rent and groceries. We had a big fight then and he went off more and more to hang out with his band friends, sometimes not coming home at night at all. I could tell he was drinking more, too, and doing more drugs. I knew it was bad but I didn't know what to do."

Tears came into her eyes. "I didn't have anyone to turn to that might help me to move out, no family or anything."

Mitchell could see the hurt and guilt streak across Laura's face. Georgina was certainly an emotional manipulator.

She leaned her head back and closed her eyes for a moment. "One day I came home from work and found Chance asleep across the bed. I thought he'd passed out again because he didn't hear me come in. But after a minute I noticed he was too still. I couldn't wake him up so I got really scared and called the emergency number."

She sighed. "An ambulance came and took him to the hospital and it was an awful time. I wasn't really his family so they acted funny about telling me anything. I didn't know a lot of his personal and health information that they wanted to know either, so they called Chance's parents from the information they found in his wallet. I sat out in the waiting room and cried, not knowing what to do. Then this really nice man came over and sat down to talk with me. He was an assistant minister at a big church downtown. He'd been visiting a church member at the hospital, and he talked with me and prayed with me and helped me."

Her eyes welled with tears. "His name was Warren Bratton and he saved me in that awful time when I didn't have anyone to turn to. When Chance died, because they couldn't save him from overdosing, Warren stayed to help me. Chance's parents came from Kentucky, all upset and crying, and they took over everything. They would hardly speak to me, like it was my fault Chance died. Warren was really kind to me then though."

She heaved a sigh. "I had some really bad days after that with Chance's parents coming to get his things to take back to Kentucky. They wanted Chance to be buried in their family lot. I didn't even get to go to his service. They took Chance's car away, too, the only one we had."

"It sounds like they blamed you more than they should," Mitchell offered.

"They did and they were really ugly to me. Fortunately, all the furniture in the apartment was mine that we brought from Amory so they couldn't take that. I was lucky too, that I could walk to the school for work, to the grocery and laundromat nearby. But I was all by myself and the guys in the band dumped me completely after Chance died."

"I'm so sorry Georgina," Laura said.

She sent Laura an anguished look. "If I'd known where you were, I could have at least had some family to talk to. But I soon learned Warren's church, the big Belmont Methodist Church he invited me to, was only a few blocks away, so I started going to church there. Warren and the other senior pastor started talking with me and helping me, and I started singing in the choir and I started getting better."

She stopped to offer them a small smile. "Mitchell, you may not know it, but I grew up singing in the choir and going to the big Methodist church in Amory. I don't know if Laura told you our mother played piano in that church or that she met my daddy there when my grandfather was a pastor at the church. I felt like I was coming back to my roots going to Belmont, back to a better place."

Mitchell wondered if Georgina had ever considered calling that grandfather or any other relatives during her hard time. He knew from visiting with them this summer that none of them had seen or heard from her since she started college and left home.

"I'm glad you're back in church and are singing in the choir," Laura said in a soft voice. "Mother would have been happy about that.".

"I've thought about that sometimes." Georgina offered Laura a wistful look. "Warren sings in the choir, too. He has a beautiful baritone voice, deep and resonant. We got to be friends. We'd go for coffee after choir, and sometimes to eat dinner after church on Sundays. He was really helping me with my faith and my life, and then somehow gradually over the summer we started to like each other more." She shrugged. "You know."

"When did you get married?" Mitchell asked.

"We were starting to talk about getting married near the end of July. Warren had a vacation coming up and he was wishing I could go. It wouldn't have been right for me to go with him not married though. He's not like that and I'm changed now, so we decided just to get married in the chapel in the church. There wasn't any point in planning a big wedding. Warren's parents live abroad right now, his father is with General Motors in Indonesia, and his brother is in the military at a Naval Base in San Diego, California. I didn't have parents at all, and I didn't know where you'd gone, Laura, so we just did a small private ceremony with church friends."

"Warren sounds like a nice person," Laura said, overlooking the subtle digs.

Georgina dug in her purse. "I have a wedding picture in my billfold." She found it and passed it around.

Mitchell saw a kind-faced, brown-haired man with hazel eyes, looking with fondness at Georgina. He hoped things would work out and that her feelings for Warren were what they should be.

"I wish you both happy." Laura smiled over the photo.

Georgina looked at her watch as she put her billfold back in her purse. "I need to go back to Junaluska. Warren came here for meetings with some people he knows about maybe coming for a Music Weekend later. Different groups attend for specialized workshops and learn about new anthems. Our choir director couldn't come to this pre-meeting so Warren offered. He likes the mountains. I agreed to come, too, because he told me Waynesville was right near the Junaluska Conference Center. I'd told him earlier I thought you lived here in Waynesville now and that we'd lost touch. I didn't tell him I really found the address in Chance's stuff." She shrugged. "If things had gone bad when we met again, I could say I didn't find you or something."

"Well, I hope we can meet Warren someday," Laura said with her usual graciousness. "I'm sorry about Chance—I really am—but I'm glad your life has been turning around to become happier."

"Will you come over to the Bistro Lakeside to have an early lunch with us at eleven tomorrow before Warren and I have to drive back to Nashville? It's four hours so we need to leave early. We both have to be at church tomorrow and in the choir. The restaurant opens at eleven though. We're staying at The Terrace Hotel, and the Bistro is on the third floor of the hotel." She hesitated, looking down at her lap. "I told Warren if I found you, I'd see if you would come to meet him. Will you?"

"Well, sure," Laura's eyes moved to Mitchell's with appeal. "I hope Mitchell will come with me. I'd like both of us to meet Warren."

He nodded. "We'll both come. Laura and I will meet you in The Terrace Hotel lobby and then we'll go to the restaurant together. You might ask Warren to call and make a reservation. Sometimes the Bistro gets crowded on a Saturday."

"Oh, I'll ask him to do that," Georgina said, getting up to leave. She went over to give Laura another small hug. "I'm so glad we found each other again and got things worked out. Family is important."

Mitchell pasted on a smile as she said these words. The fact that Georgina had not offered one single apology bothered him, but he felt sure Laura would still be happy her sister had found her. No matter what a person's family members were like, good or bad, kind or selfish, they were still your family.

CHAPTER 23

Laura heaved a huge sigh after letting Georgina out the front door and locking it behind her. Mitchell had walked to the door with her and he reached out now to take her into his arms and hug her.

"Are you okay?" he asked.

"I think so," she answered, moving to sit down on the small sofa in the vestibule.

He glanced at his watch. "Before Mom left she said for us to come over for dinner when Georgina left. She put a roast in the electric cooker earlier, and she also said she wanted to hear the rest of the story."

"I guess that will be all right," Laura said.

Mitchell leaned over to give her a kiss. "I know you're worn out from all this but we do need to eat."

Her lips twitched. "Well, you know we won't hear the end of it from your mother either if we don't fill her in on all that happened."

"It does read somewhat like a soap opera." He sent her a grin. "Can I call her and tell her we're on our way?"

"Sure. I'll get my purse and turn off the lights in the back rooms while you do."

At Evelyn's, they were met with the usual excitement and greetings from the children and Zoey. Laura hoped someday she and Mitchell could have a dog like Zoey, always so excited to see you. She squatted down to pet the little collie mix, talking to her and enjoying her enthusiastic welcome. Something about a dog or cat just cheered you up sometime after a bad day.

"You children come sit down," Evelyn said. "I have dinner ready." She gestured them to the table already set.

"Can I do anything to help?" Laura asked.

"No, no. Everything is done. I popped a shoulder roast in my electric cooker earlier this morning with carrots, potatoes, and onions, and then cooked some green beans after I came home. I put some quick biscuits in the oven, too. They'll be ready in a minute. Let's sit down and say grace before we eat."

Hearing Mackenzie's sweet little words saying grace and then listening to the warm chatter of the children talking about starting school again began to gradually ease Laura's tension away.

"Mackenzie is in the same class this year with Taylor," Charlie told them. "And my best friend Matthew is in my class."

Mackenzie's eyes lit. "Taylor is my best friend, Laura, and she lives right next door," she explained. "She went to the movies with us one Saturday. Remember?"

"I do, and she's nice."

Mackenzie nodded. "It's happy to have friends you like in your class."

They babbled on, Charlie telling jokes and Mackenzie showing off her fingernails, decorated with ladybug decals she and Taylor had pasted on them after school. The two children interacted with such warmth and affection, and Laura noticed this especially tonight. Her relationship with Georgina had always been different. Funny how she'd never really seen that before or recognized their affection as not as rich and loving as it should have been. She'd always been more the smaller planet circling her sister's sun.

As they finished dinner, Evelyn said to the children, "Since you already did your homework before dinner, you can go watch that new *Spy Kids* movie I picked up for you when I was out today."

"Is it *The Island of Lost Dreams?*" Charlie asked.

"Yes. That's the one you and Mackenzie said you wanted after watching the first one," Evelyn answered.

"Thanks, Grammy," Charlie and Mackenzie said almost in unison as they scrambled out of their chairs to head to the den.

Evelyn turned to Mitchell and Laura. "They've really gotten into detective and spy stories lately. Mackenzie has read *Harriet the Spy* and they've discovered a Disney series about *Mira the Royal Detective* among a few others." Evelyn carried the last of the plates to the sink. "Let's go take our coffee out on the porch. These dishes can wait. I'm dying to hear about the rest of your visit with your sister, Laura."

After settling into wicker chairs on Evelyn's screen porch, Mitchell and Laura took turns filling Evelyn in on the rest of Georgina's story.

At the end, Evelyn commented. "Honestly, like Mitchell said, your sister's life could make a great soap opera. Pardon me for saying that. I know she's been through her share of sorrows, too. It had to be traumatic and painful for her finding Chance dead like she did." She shook her head. "But she does have a way of landing on her feet."

Mitchell nodded.

Evelyn reached across to pat Laura's hand. "I know you must be relieved, dear, that your sister is out of that difficult situation. Being involved with a group doing drugs, hanging out in places like the ones she talked about, was dangerous."

"It always scared me that she was involved with Chance," Laura said. "It wasn't that I didn't believe in her, like she said. Her situation simply didn't feel right. I worried about her."

"You had a right to worry. I hope she sees that now."

Laura frowned. "I'm not sure if she does."

"I'm not either," Mitchell put in. "Not once did I hear Georgina offer an apology or a thank you for all you did. She always made it sound like it was just your obligation to help her in any way needed, no matter how she acted or what she did."

Evelyn looked out into the yard thinking. "Well, despite all this, Georgina seems to have turned her life to the good. She's married to a minister now. That certainly is a step up from her situation before and surely he will be a good influence."

"I don't mean to put in a negative word here but I still see that Georgina's focus is on herself," Mitchell said. "I hope she hasn't used Warren as a route out of her problems."

"Well, even if she has, perhaps his stability and morality will impact and change her," Evelyn replied.

Mitchell made a face. "Maybe. But in all her talk, I didn't hear any references to God, how He'd changed her, how He was helping her day to day. I didn't hear anything in her conversation about a growing depth of faith."

"But she's back in church," Laura put in.

"Yes, and that's good," Evelyn said. "We all have to start somewhere, Mitchell. A steady diet of church and living with a minister will surely have an impact. Let's be hopeful. Real faith takes time to grow. At least perhaps she's in the right environment now and certainly in better company."

Evelyn turned to Laura. "Did she give you an address for a wedding invitation?"

"No. With everything that was going on, I forgot to ask for it. I'll ask for her new address tomorrow." She hesitated. "Do you think I should ask her to be in the wedding? Everything is all set. I've already asked Elizabeth to be my matron of honor, Becky, Paula, and Allison to be the bridesmaids. All the dresses are ordered. I would feel awful to ask any of them to give up their place to Georgina."

"There's no need to consider that. Georgina should realize everything is already planned" Evelyn said. "It's enough to invite her to the wedding at this point."

"I agree," Mitchell added.

"What if she pushes tomorrow to be in the wedding?" Laura asked, biting on her lip at the thought.

"Then ask her to sing at the wedding instead," Evelyn suggested. "You said she's often done that in the past, that she has a beautiful voice. We haven't scheduled anyone to sing yet. That should make her feel special to be asked."

"Oh, that's a good idea, Mom." Mitchell turned to Laura. "I

know you hate not including your sister, now that's she come seeking you out. However, if she sang, she couldn't also be one of the attendants at the wedding, anyway. Why don't you ask her tomorrow if you want?"

Laura thought about their words. "It does seem like a good idea. I'll ask her. I hope Warren is a nice person. I do want Georgina to be happy. The two of us might not ever be really close, but we are sisters."

The next day, Laura felt a little anxious about meeting with her sister and new husband. She knew Warren had never met her, and depending on what Georgina had told him, he might have a distorted view about her. Her sister did tend to paint any story with her own brush, often touching up the truth.

She felt really pleased though as she, Mitchell, Warren, and Georgina sat getting better acquainted at a pretty table on the Bistro's balcony looking across Lake Junaluska.

"I'd forgotten how beautiful this place is," Warren said. "I came here for a retreat years ago, and I still remember the good times I enjoyed."

As he shared about it, Laura studied him. Warren seemed such a regular, genuine, and truly nice man. Laura found him easy to talk to, kind and thoughtful in his ways. Georgina acted different around him, too. Nicer. That was a positive.

Mitchell winked at her when both Warren and Georgina looked away from them at a pontoon boat skimming across the lake. He knew she'd been nervous about this meeting and he could tell she was relieved things were going so well.

When Warren turned back, Mitchell said, "My mother reminded me to ask for your address so she could send a wedding invitation your way. Warren, do you and Laura live downtown near the church or in one of the outlying suburban areas of Nashville?"

"We live downtown," he answered. "I bought a condo not far from the church in the Hillsboro-Belmont area when I moved to Nashville. I grew up not far away in Lebanon, so I've always lived around the Nashville area except when I went to college at the

Candler School of Theology in Atlanta." Warren stopped to drink a little more of his iced tea. "I work in several volunteer capacities at Vanderbilt as well as carrying my job at the church, so I felt I needed to stay in the downtown area."

Georgina's eyes lit. "Warren's condo—I mean our condo— is really nice. It's a lovely two-story in a brick building with two bedrooms, a nice living and dining room, kitchen and a shady little patio out back. It's further away from school for me, but I love it."

"Since I took Georgina further from her place near the campus, I bought her a little Honda after we married so she can get herself back and forth to school, run errands or shop." He sent Georgina a besotted look. It was obvious he'd fallen hard for her.

While the waiter stopped by to check on them, Warren wrote his address on the back of one of his business cards from church.

"When is the wedding?" he asked. "I'll put it on my calendar. I'm sure Georgina will want to come." He glanced at her with a smile.

She made a face. "Well, I thought Laura might ask me to be in her wedding. I'm her only family after all."

Mitchell jumped in to answer. "I regret we didn't connect with you in time to work that out, but you know how it is with weddings. Everything gets planned far in advance. The tuxes and dresses for all the attendants are already ordered." He smiled. "Laura thought maybe you might like to sing at the wedding instead. We haven't chosen anyone to do that and I'm sure it would make our wedding special if you'd like to sing."

"We would really love that," Laura added, feeling grateful Evelyn had come up with the idea last night.

"What a wonderful idea," Warren said.

He turned to Georgina. "You could sing that beautiful piece you did for Isaac and Marla's wedding last month, 'I Choose You.' I don't think there was a dry eye in the house when you finished."

"Well, it's not as though Laura was at my wedding," Georgina said with a pout. "But maybe I could think about it."

Warren looked at her with surprise. "You didn't even know where Laura lived at that time to invite her." He sent Laura an uneasy look. "Georgina explained to me you two got estranged while she was in that difficult relationship with Chance. It's hard when we get off on a wrong path in life, hard on the people on the path and hard on the people who know them. Georgina and I have talked about that a lot, haven't we, Georgina?"

She gave Warren what Laura well recognized as one of her fake smiles at his words. "Warren has been such a good help and counsel to me. I don't know what I would have done without him."

He looked pleased at her words and then turned to Laura. "I'm really glad Georgina chose to reach out to you and restore your relationship."

Not having any idea what Georgina had said to Warren about their relationship, and not wanting to say the wrong thing, Laura simply offered him a nice smile.

Warren pulled out his phone to check his calendar. "I don't see that we have any other commitments for that first weekend in October, Georgina. Don't you think it would be nice if we came to Mitchell and Laura's wedding? I think it would be wonderful if you sang, too."

Laura could see Georgina wrestling with the idea. "Well, I suppose I could." She fingered her napkin by her plate. "Ryann Darling wrote that song 'I Choose You.' It's had over twenty-five million streams and has been sung at thousands of weddings all over the world. It is a special song, but it does show best in a really big sanctuary like our church in Nashville."

"I think you'll find First Baptist here in Waynesville big enough," Mitchell said, and Laura heard the testy tone in his voice. "It's an old historic downtown church. My family helped establish it and we've supported its growth." He paused. "But you do as you feel led."

Seeing a little wash of displeasure cross Warren's face, Georgina rubbed on her wedding ring thoughtfully. "Well, all right. I know Warren loves Junaluska and the mountains and I'm sure he would like a chance to come over here again." She beamed at him. "We can stay here at The Terrace again, can't we? There might be a little fall color around the lake by then."

"It will be nice to stay here again." He gave her a beaming smile like a parent gives a child who has acted appropriately and done something nice.

"Let us know what sound equipment you'll need," Mitchell said to Georgina. "Naturally you and Warren will also be invited to the rehearsal dinner the night before with others who will be in the wedding."

He shot Georgina a softly mutinous glance. "I'm sure you'll be glad to see your grandfather Baylor again. He and your grandmother are coming from Gulfport with your Uncle Tom and Aunt Deidre, and your grandfather graciously offered to walk Laura down the aisle. I believe your Aunt Dorothy, on your father's side, and her husband Curtis will be here, too. I'm sure they'll all be pleased to see you again, to meet Warren, and to hear you sing."

Laura watched Georgina's eyes widen with surprise.

"I'll be pleased to meet more of Georgina's family," Warren said. He glanced at his watch. "I'm sorry to cut this time short but we do need to hit the road. I have a meeting at the church tonight and we both need to get up early tomorrow for Sunday School and to sing in the choir in the church service. We always attend both the 8:15 and 10:30 services so our Sundays are always busy."

Laura almost giggled at that comment, remembering how Georgina grumbled as a girl to even get up on Sunday mornings to attend Sunday School and church. She'd never been much of a morning person. Perhaps she was changing.

Mitchell stood and pulled out Laura's chair. "We'll look forward to seeing you both again in October. I hope you have a safe and good trip back to Nashville."

Before they said their final goodbyes outside the restaurant, Laura watched Georgina, when Warren's back was turned, put a hand on Mitchell's arm in an almost intimate way. Mitchell scowled and pulled away, and a few minutes later Warren and Georgina left to start their trip home.

Laura followed Mitchell out of the restaurant then and toward his car. "Thanks so much for coming with me, Mitchell," she said.

"Laura, like those Bible verses in Ruth, from now on where you go, I go. Where you lodge, I'll lodge, and your people will be my people." He grinned and then leaned over to kiss her, not caring who watched. "I'm so grateful I found you and that you're going to be walking with me through the rest of my life."

She smiled at him. "What brought that on?"

"Probably spending time with your sister and feeling a little sorry for her husband." He glanced across the lake, glorious under a blue skies day. "How about a walk around the lake trail? It's a nice day."

"It is." She tucked an arm in his. "I'd love a walk with you."

They took off down the paved walkway along the lakeside, passing the rose gardens, with many flowers still in bloom.

"The roses aren't as pretty now as last month," she said, stopping to lean over to sniff one of the more fragrant ones.

He nodded and after a few minutes asked, "So, what did you think about our visit with the Brattons? Did you like your sister's new husband Warren? Do you feel better about reconnecting with Georgina now? Are you pleased she will sing at the wedding?"

She wrinkled her nose. "Yes, to the first two questions. I think the visit went well and I do like Warren. I'd have to answer maybe to the next two questions. I do feel better about reconnecting with Georgina in most ways but I think I'm disappointed she isn't more changed. I guess I keep hoping for that." Laura slowed to look at another pretty rose bush still blooming. "I'm glad your mother had the idea of asking her to sing, but Georgina made me feel like she was doing me a royal and undeserved favor to say yes."

"Yeah, that irked me, too."

They moved on around the path, passing others also enjoying the day.

Laura paused to look out over the lake as they crossed over the dam. "Can I ask you something, Mitchell?"

"What?" He leaned on the rail beside her.

"Did my sister hit on you at the shop earlier as well as at the restaurant today before we left?" Laura saw his eyes widen.

"You noticed that?" He shook his head. "I didn't want to mention it with all you had to deal with."

"I hated to mention it, too, but I don't want there ever to be things between us. You know."

"Look, I didn't initiate anything …"

She interrupted. "You don't need to say that or apologize. My sister has been like that ever since we were girls. I told you she always flirted with any boyfriends I had, even when they were much younger than her. Georgina and I are five years apart in age, too." Laura hesitated. "I think Georgina simply likes to see if she can get men to notice her. To her, if someone doesn't admire and notice her, it's like a challenge to her in some way, unless she doesn't like them."

"I feel sorry for Warren for that." Mitchell shook his head. "He's really besotted with her and blind to any of her faults. He can't read her at all, he's so taken with her."

They moved on around the trail and walked out on a long pier into the lake before moving back to the pathway again.

"Do you think Georgina will change, living with someone really nice like Warren?"

"I don't know. We can hope and believe for that, for her sake as well as his. People do change. Maybe being in church will help her to change, draw her into a deeper place of faith. Right now, it seems like church to her is more of a social activity, an avenue where she can perform and get recognition—perhaps even attention."

He hesitated. "I worry that Warren is more a meal ticket to her than anything. She was in a rough spot when Chance died, left to her own resources and left to totally make her own way. Some people rise to new strengths at a time like that, to new fortitude and character, and some look around for another person to lean on, to carry them. They don't seem to mind using people if it's advantageous to them."

"Won't Georgina be grateful for that in Warren? That he was there to help her when she so needed it? That he fell in love with her despite all the mess of her past? As a minister, even an assistant minister, he might have been reluctant to get involved with her."

Mitchell took her hand in his as they walked. "Sweet and nice people are sometimes the last to see when other people are self-serving and not as good or sincere as they try to appear." He leaned over to kiss her cheek. "You, Laura, are one of the truly nice people in the world. I hope you'll always stay that way."

"You're a very nice person, too, Mitchell."

"Well, let's both stay that way then. I feel so happy to be marrying someone like you, to not be getting involved with someone like…." He hesitated.

"Like my sister? It's okay for you to say that. I'm not like her."

"I'm grateful for that." He squeezed her hand as they walked on. "We're going to be really happy, Laura. I'm so glad we found each other." He pointed toward the big cross on the hill. "Maybe we have God to thank for that, too."

"Believe me, I remember to thank him often." She stopped to sit down on a bench to tie her shoe and asked, "Are you starting to feel okay about your mom and Sam now?"

"I'm doing better with it." He sat down beside her. "Sam and I had a couple of good talks. I told him he could stay in my old apartment later after Christmas when he retires and until he and Mother set a date to get married."

"That was nice of you. Will you miss your place, moving in with me?"

"No, the benefits of moving in with you are too good to be missed." He sent her a lecherous look before speaking again. "Nannie V has been talking to me about us possibly moving into her house later. She told me she said something to you about it."

"Only generally. But where would she move?"

"I think she's starting to look around, for something smaller on one level, like Mimi and Frances have. She has a big property and a big house to take care of, but I told her not to hurry. We'll be fine in the apartment. It's close to our work. If we bought a house, I'd want it to be downtown, like mom's, or Mimi's and Nannie V's. I like walking to work, being near the downtown. It feels like home to me, but I'd consider moving outside of town if it was what you really wanted."

She reached out to touch his cheek. "You're so sweet, but I like being downtown, too. I admit I've been walking around the little downtown streets near our shops looking at houses myself." She looked down at her lap. "We'll need a house, don't you think, when we have a baby?"

"That is a pretty picture to think about in every aspect." He grinned at her again as they got up to walk on. "I'm counting the days now until October, you know."

She sent him a small smile. "Me, too."

CHAPTER 24

On October the first, Mitchell stood looking at himself in the mirror in his apartment. This was his last day as a single man. After today he'd be committed to care for another as well as himself for the rest of his life, to think of her needs, her joys, as equally important to his own. He paused over that thought. It wasn't as though the concept was totally new to him. He'd moved home to be a support to his mom when his dad died. When Alise and Hudson were killed, he'd stepped up to take the role of father, along with his mom, to help raise two lost and grieving children only two and four.

He reveled in finally getting back to his own apartment here a year ago when the kids grew older and settled into school. He'd fixed the place up, started getting together again with his single friends more, but he quickly realized he was different.

"Dude, you act like an old married man now," one of his friends had joked one night. "Lighten up."

It took a while for Mitchell to realize he couldn't turn the clock back. Life had changed him. When he'd grumbled about it to Nannie V one day, she patted his cheek and said, "Son, you simply stepped up and became a man early. You're way ahead of the pack; that's all. They'll catch up in time."

Eventually accepting what life was, he'd moved on. You can't go back in life, only forward. He threw his heart into his business, his family, new friends, the town he loved. He even deepened his faith, in part with Nannie V's help. He envied the calm, deep place of trust and fellowship with God she held. Thinking of that he felt glad Laura was a person of faith, too, and had what Nannie V called a Seeking Heart.

Not that he was thinking about having a prayer meeting tonight or anything on his wedding day. He had eager physical feelings toward Laura. She'd stirred him since the first day they met. It was still incredible to remember how that jolt hit him out of the blue. He'd never believed in stuff like that happening before Laura.

Glancing at his watch, Mitchell took a last look at his "single self" in the mirror, winked, and headed for the church.

After parking his car, he stopped to glance into the sanctuary as he walked into the church's big front doors. Everything looked pretty with the flowers and that tulle material on the pews, a matching white runner down the aisle, and more tulle draped over a wooden arch at the front, decorated with flowers. Laura would be pleased.

Mitchell found the wedding party gathered and ready to walk outside for a few photos before heading into the sanctuary for more.

"You look very handsome," Laura said, turning from talking with Elizabeth, who was dressed in a filmy, pinkish dress. He tried to recall what Laura called that color? Blush mauve or something? He couldn't remember exactly but his tie, the handkerchief in his pocket, and the boutonniere flower Sally Wingate came to pin on him matched it.

Sally, his mother's best friend, was helping today to coordinate everything with the wedding. Mitchell's eyes moved to follow Laura as she walked across the room, her dress a drift of white and lace, her face flushed and pretty. Her hair was tied back and twisted somehow in the back, with flowers and a sweep of that white tulle hanging down to her waist.

He caught up to her as they all began to walk outside for photos. "You look unbelievably beautiful," he whispered to her, wishing he knew something more creative or original to say. "You simply take my breath away."

A little smile twitched her lips. "Those are sweet words."

She leaned toward him, tempting him with that familiar citrusy, floral scent reaching out to tantalize him. But as he leaned closer toward her, his eyes on her lips, she put a hand to his chest, as if straightening his tie, and whispered, "We can't do that here right now."

Mitchell almost laughed. She could read him so well.

The photographer, Benny Fritz, herded them further outdoors to stage photos with trees, flowers, benches and such, making them all laugh at some of his photo ideas.

As Benny snapped photos, Mitchell thought back on the good times he'd enjoyed last night at the Rehearsal Dinner with his friends Rob, Kent, Drew, and Mike Wingate. All Laura's bridal attendants had come, too, along with family and friends, either in the wedding or helping with it. The weather had been perfect for an evening out of doors and everyone enjoyed the ease and informality of his mother's themed *Vive la Difference Italian Rehearsal Dinner.*

"I really had a great time last night," Mike said after they posed for a photo shot. "I got a chance to talk to Neal again about working at his clinic. Sally and I are going to move back to Waynesville after Thanksgiving."

Mitchell thumped him on the back. "I'm glad to hear that, Mike. I've really missed my fishing and hiking partner."

"I'm looking forward to more of that, too," Mike said, before the photographer herded them into the church for sanctuary pictures.

"Doesn't my Grandad look wonderful in his tux?" Laura whispered to him between some family photos. "I'm so touched he wanted to come and give me away. He seems so pleased to be here."

"All your family are nice people," Mitchell said, but then frowned to himself. Georgina texted yesterday that Warren had gotten tied up with some situation at the church. She said, unfortunately, they had to miss the rehearsal dinner but would drive in this morning to arrive before the service. Somehow it annoyed him how nonchalant she'd been about it, although Laura had acted very understanding.

When the pictures were finished, the wedding party broke into groups, the men heading to get ready for the processional in one place, the women to freshen up in another.

Mitchell's mother grabbed his arm as he started out of the sanctuary. "Come walk to the fellowship hall with Laura and me for a minute. We want to check to see if everything is set up and if Rita and Lillian need anything."

He followed them to the big fellowship hall, decorated today in the theme colors of the wedding. Sparkling lights were draped around everywhere, pots of flowers placed here and there, and the wedding cakes and refreshments all laid out.

"Wow," he said, stopping to look at the big three-tiered wedding cake with fancy swirled icing and silky roses stuck around on it.

"Look at the groom's cake, too." Laura pointed to a second multi-layered chocolate cake with fudgy icing dripping over its edges.

"It looks great." His eyes moved to another huge white sheet cake to the side. "Good grief. How much cake do we need?"

"A lot," his mother answered. "I told you the church would be packed today. Lillian and Rita will cut the sheet cake first, and offer pieces of the groom's cake as well, until you two do a bridal cake cutting of the wedding cake."

Side tables were already loaded with refreshments they planned to serve, and Mitchell knew more food would be brought out from the kitchen after the service.

Rita and Lillian came over to greet them. Both were dressed pretty and smiling but Mitchell caught an edge of concern on Rita's face.

He lifted an eyebrow at her.

Her eyes moved to his face with an anxious look and then to Laura's. "I hate to be saying even a word to trouble your joy on a day like this, but Nolan came down a few minutes ago, worried. You know he and Bobby, Lillian's husband, are starting to seat people in the church, and Bernice Killian has already begun to play at the piano to entertain folks while they wait for the ceremony to start."

Lillian shook her head and interrupted. "And your sister Georgina isn't here yet. Bernice is anxious over it. They were supposed to talk together before she started playing the piano so the transition would go smoothly before Georgina went up to sing. Because Georgina couldn't get to the rehearsal last night, Bernice assumed she'd come early today. Isn't it just like that girl to be irresponsible and worry people?"

"Do you think anything has happened?" Evelyn asked. "Sometimes the interstate over the mountain gets clogged or there is a wreck. Has she texted or called?"

"She didn't call or text before we started the pictures," Laura answered, biting her lip anxiously. "I put my phone away after that."

Mitchell scowled to see Laura unhappy. "I still have my phone with me, and Warren's cell number is in it. I'll call to check on them." He pulled out his phone and found Warren's number, and when Warren answered, he said, "Hey Warren. It's Mitchell. I'm calling to check to see if you and Georgina got caught up in a traffic problem on the interstate or something since you guys aren't here yet."

A short silence followed, and then Warren blurted out his answer in a rush. "But we're not coming. Georgina said she notified you about a month ago when her school scheduled a Concert Choir performance at Vanderbilt in the Turner Recital Hall for tonight. They had practices last night and today. Georgina has a solo part in the program, and the show is for school, so she felt she couldn't say no about participating and performing with the college. We hated to miss the wedding but Georgina thought she shouldn't bail on a performance at the school, just getting started in the program and all. I'd put her on the phone right now but she's already at the school."

Laura's eyes filled with tears, and Mitchell felt like biting into a nail.

"Didn't you get Georgina's message last month?" Warren asked. "She told me you did."

Mitchell took a breath, hating to answer, but he wasn't going to lie to Warren about this. "Georgina texted yesterday on Friday morning that you had a situation at church that had come up so the two of you couldn't come for the dress rehearsal and dinner last night. However, she said you were both driving over this morning and would be here in plenty of time ahead of the wedding for her to sing."

He heard Warren's breath catch in confusion. "But that doesn't make sense. Why would she say that? Are you sure about this?"

"I'm sorry, Warren, but I was with Laura when she got the text. Georgina made it clear she would be here to sing."

"I don't know what to say," Warren said. "Why would she do this?"

Mitchell heaved a sigh. "I'd say it's her little revenge to Laura for leaving Amory without telling her this spring. She made it clear to us she'd been angry about that. She never seemed grateful for all the money Laura loaned to her and Chance or for letting them stay with her for months without helping around the place in any way to clean, cook, or do yard work or errands. Georgina seemed to feel it was their right to stay and be taken care of. They made life pretty difficult for Laura. There's a lot more to the story, but this isn't the time to tell it." He paused, trying to bank his anger. "You tell Georgina that she scored, left her sister in the lurch, and made her cry on her wedding day. I hope she feels good about that."

To Mitchell's surprise, Rita snatched up the phone. "You tell her, too, from Rita Harbeck that we have some fine singers right here in Waynesville, North Carolina, who love Laura and will be singing with joy and love at her wedding to make this a special and memorable day for her and Mitchell. You remind her that he who laughs last laughs best … and that we'll all be laughing and having a fine and better time celebrating with Mitchell and Laura without the likes of someone like her here." She hesitated and took a breath. "I heard that you were a minister so maybe you can talk to Georgina and let her know that this was a cruel, childish, and sinful thing for her to do."

"Ma'am, I'm really sorry for this," Warren said.

"Well, I don't have time to talk about it anymore right now so I'll tell you goodbye. But I feel sorry for anyone who would do an ugly thing like your wife did." And she punched off the connection.

"Way to go Rita." Lillian all but danced a jig. "That selfish girl just can't seem to quit causing hurt to people. I told Bobby that I kept hoping she'd have a Come-to-Jesus moment and get her life straightened out, but apparently it hasn't happened yet."

"Poor Warren," Laura said, sniffling. "I really feel sorry for him."

Evelyn glanced at her watch. "Rita, do you really think you and Nolan might sing something? Do you know a selection that would work for a wedding? We don't have much time here."

Rita smiled. "I sang with the Waynesville Boys this summer for an outdoor wedding on the mountain at Purchase Knob near Maggie Valley. Up there we couldn't take instruments easily, so we sang a pretty piece *A cappella,* without instruments, called 'You Raise Me Up.' It will be a fine and good selection for today, and the Barlows are here, too. At least I know Reed and Crockett are. I'll go see if they won't help us out. We all sang together on the mountain before."

She went over to hug Laura. "Don't you let this ugliness be hurting you today, you hear? This world is full of folks that aren't all they should be, that seem to take a nasty pleasure in hurting others, but the world is also full of good folks that want only joy and happiness for you. So you go pretty up your face and get ready to walk down that church aisle smiling and glad for this day."

Rita turned to Lillian. "I think with Sally's help, and the help of those other church women earlier, that we have everything about ready here until after the wedding. Can you finish up without me, Lillian? I need to run upstairs and round up the men to sing."

"I'll be fine," Lillian said.

Mitchell gave Rita a hug. "This is so good of you. Even if you sing by yourself, Rita, I recall very well that you have one of the prettiest voices I've ever heard."

"Well, aren't you sweet to say that as well as handsome in that fine suit." She laughed then. "Speaking of suits, wait until you see how fine Nolan and the Barlows look today. Most folks haven't ever seen how good those men can clean up."

Mitchell grinned. "I'll look forward to that."

Rita hustled out of the room then and, looking after her, Lillian said, "I sure do like that woman."

"So do I," said Evelyn with a big smile. She turned to Laura. "You listen to those wise, sweet words Rita offered to you and run on up to join the girls to finish getting ready to walk down the aisle."

Lillian came over to give her a hug. "You sweet girl, you're just as beautiful as can be today. Bobby and I are so proud to be here to see you get married, and we're so happy you're marrying into such a fine family and to such a good man. You listen to Evelyn and Rita and cast this worry and hurt off and go enjoy your day. Don't you give that girl the satisfaction of spoiling your day even for one little inch, do you hear me?"

"Okay," Laura said, smiling now and hugging Lillian back.

Evelyn turned to him next. "Mitchell, you need to go find the other men and check in and then you need to head around with the minister to be ready to come in the church at the right time. It's twenty minutes before two now. We're just about ready to host a beautiful wedding."

His mother was right, of course. And as far as Mitchell was concerned, everything found a way to work for good. He'd worried since this summer that Georgina might find some snotty way to try to diminish Laura's joy today. He couldn't help wondering either what story she'd spin to Warren about this in explanation. Surely the man, by now, was beginning to get a wake-up call about the woman he'd married.

A little later, standing outside the door to the chancel at the front of the church with the minister, Mitchell listened with near reverence to hear Rita and the Waynesville Boys sing Josh Groban's lovely song "You Raise Me Up" with their voices in sweet harmony. The minister had told Mitchell earlier that the Barlows still had some instruments in the back of their van from a show last night, so Reed brought in his guitar, deciding to strum a little, and Crockett added some extra richness with a touch of mandolin.

To Mitchell's surprise, when they finished, Reed spoke up in front of everyone in the church. "Ya'll all know there was a little mix-up and the singer couldn't get here. This wasn't the piece printed on your program, but we hope you liked it. If you don't mind, I'm thinking I'd like to sing one more song for this couple getting married here today. It's an old favorite of mine and it's one I know Mitchell's daddy purely loved."

They started singing an old Elvis song then, "Can't Help Falling in Love." Mitchell felt sure his mother was shedding a tear or two over the words. His dad had loved that song and it had been a special one to him and his mother. To Mitchell, the words were especially sweet to hear today because he hadn't been able to keep from falling in love with Laura from the very first.

When the music finished, the groomsmen seated his mother and Laura's grandmother. And then the processional began, with an excited Mackenzie scattering roses down the aisle, Charlie proudly carrying the ring behind her, and then Laura's attendants walking slowly in on the arm of his groomsmen and best man, smiling and pretty in their wispy long dresses, carrying their bouquets. He realized, watching it all from down front, why people planned days like this to marry. To carry the rich, warm memories of it all through the years of a lifetime.

Bernice started the opening notes of a change in song then, to announce it time for the bride. Everyone stood, and Laura began to walk down the aisle, her fingers tucked in her grandfather's arm, her bouquet a glory of soft colored roses, her face now wreathed in smiles. Surely he was the luckiest of men to have found her. Seeing her always lifted him, raised him up like the song said. And like the old Elvis song, he found himself falling even more in love with her all over again, simply looking at her.

From the audience he caught Reed Barlow's eye, who winked at him. He'd come back in the summer to thank Mitchell in his own way by inviting him to spend a day fishing on the lake with him and Crockett. Reed had never said another word about that morning when Mitchell talked to him at the Huddle House. Mitchell expected he never would, but it wasn't forgotten.

Later in the day after a good reception and a scattering of bird seed thrown over them as they left the church, Mitchell and Laura set out on their honeymoon, after stopping a few miles down the road to pull over and untie some of the junk hooked on the back of the Bronco and to clean off the windows.

He glanced across at Laura as they drove down the freeway. She wore a simple, tasteful flared dress in that mauve color of their wedding now, keeping up the theme for the day. The color was pretty on her, the knit fabric one she told him was good for travel and wouldn't wrinkle on the drive.

Mitchell grinned at her. "How does it feel to be Mrs. Quinlan now?"

She sent him a mischievous look. "It has a very nice ring to it." She looked down at the travel brochures in her lap. "There are so many beautiful places I hope we can visit in Savannah."

"I hope you're not disappointed we're only going to Sam Jacobs' house on Tybee Island for our honeymoon week."

"Why should I be? And how lovely of him to offer it," she answered. "I also think it was sweet of you to offer him your apartment for the week while he worked his North Carolina territory. He said it kept him from staying in motels and meant he could spend more time with your mother and the kids."

She pushed her hair back behind her ear. "You know I've never been to the east coast, to Tybee Island or to Savannah. I'm so excited. But with the late start we got after the wedding, and with the drive over six hours, it will be late when we get there. Too dark to see anything and not much to do except go to bed."

"Oh, honey, don't diminish that thought." He laughed. "I'm thinking that's going to be the best part of the day." He watched a blush steal up her neck.

"That's not what I meant ..." Her words drifted off, embarrassed.

He sent some sweet talk her way then, words you wouldn't want someone to write down, and then leaned over to kiss her as the traffic thinned, letting his fingers trace up her bare leg under her skirt. "I have a fine new license and permit to do all sorts of lovely new things with you, Mrs. Quinlan."

"Well, certainly not in the car on the interstate," she said, pushing his hand away with a grin. "I'd like us to get to Georgia safely and not get pulled over for indecent exposure or anything."

She tucked her dress back down around her knees, while Mitchell laughed again. "Laura, we're going to have a sweet good life." He looked across at her. "You're not still hurting over what your sister did, are you?"

"I think I've spent more time feeling sorry for Warren than for myself." She sighed. "I've been in his place before."

"I've wondered, too, how he'll handle being lied to like that," Mitchell said. "I imagine they've had some words. Even a kind man like Warren doesn't like being lied to so he ends up embarrassed and feeling like a fool."

"I hope Georgina will change. Do you think she will?"

"She might. People can change." Mitchell passed a slow-moving car, thinking for a minute. "Every day we get the opportunity to create our own legacy, you know, who we are for that day, and for the next day after it, and what we'll be remembered for. My daddy called it 'our little portfolio we'll carry to heaven' that will determine whether we get the job God has planned for us right away or not. For some a little remedial time might be needed first, and if the portfolio is bad enough, and not at all like it should be, some may find themselves with an unfortunate alternate destiny, getting a job and an end they don't really want—and for a very undesirable employer."

She laughed. "I wish I'd known your dad."

"Well, we can keep the people we've loved alive, remembering and telling good stories about them."

"I don't ever want to have hurtful stuff like Georgina's in my portfolio."

"Well, I'd say we're both bound to make some mistakes and do some things we regret. There's a long journey of life ahead. What we do about those mistakes matters a lot, whether we seek out forgiveness and then try to make things right with people we've hurt."

She leaned toward him. "Let's always try to do that, Mitchell, love each other, talk things out, not be too proud to say we're sorry when we hurt each other."

"I want that, too, Laura." He sent her a foxy grin. "And I'm looking forward with great expectation to all the ways a married couple become one."

She blushed again. "Honestly, Mitchell."

"Honey, this is just the beginning of a long, sweet journey in every way between us. I'm eager for every little bit of it. For the rest of time, we'll be choosing joy and choosing to love one another. I can't imagine anything better."

A Reading Group Guide

SHOP ON THE CORNER

Lin Stepp

About This Guide

The questions on the following pages are included
to enhance your group's reading of
Lin Stepp's *Shop On The Corner*

DISCUSSION QUESTIONS

1. Laura O'Dell is having to give up her family's business, called the Shop on the Corner, as the story begins? Why? What is imminent domain? Where is Laura's shop located? What kind of shop is it? How did Laura learn this business? The government is giving her a fair buy-out deal, but she is still upset about moving and can't seem to decide on a place. Have you ever had to move away from or to give up a place you loved?

2. Laura's sister Georgina is staying with Laura as the book begins. When did Georgina and her boyfriend Chance come to Mississippi? Although Laura was pleased originally to learn Georgina was coming for a Christmas visit, why is Georgina staying on at length a problem? Where is Laura living now, and why did she also have to leave her house when her father died?

3. Georgina's dream is to become a big singing star with Chance Richardson and his band the Mississippi Ramblers. What did she walk away from to follow that dream? How is that decision working out? Georgina has borrowed money often from Laura, and she claims Laura should be happy to help her to achieve her dreams, adding "It's not as though you're going after any dreams of your own to understand." How did you feel about Georgina when she made statements like these?

4. Lillian and Bobby Greely have worked at the Shop on the Corner almost since the day Laura's father opened it. How are they a help and encouragement to Laura in this hard time of her life? How do they feel about Laura's sister? What do they

encourage Laura to do as the set date to vacate the shop property grows closer? How does Laura feel about their idea? What does she find as she researches and looks for potential shops in other small towns? What factors sway her decision in deciding on a big life change and move?

5. Mitchell Quinlan has had some of his own difficult times to walk through. What business is he running as the book begins? What happened to his father that put him in charge of the business at such a young age? What types of services does Quinlan Staffing Services offer in Waynesville, North Carolina? What do you remember about Mitchell's three employees Rosemarie, Norma, and Kent? After the loss of his father, Mitchell's sister Alise and her husband are killed in a car wreck. Who takes in their two small children Mackenzie and Charlie to raise? How is Mitchell a help to his mother Evelyn in that time—and still a help? What type of work does Mitchell's mother do?

6. Nolan and Rita Harbeck come to Mitchell's business hoping he will help them gain employment at the new Shop on the Corner opening across the street from Quinlans. How does Mitchell know the Harbecks from the past? Why do they want him to help them with an introduction to the new shop owner and why do they want to work there? Why are the Harbecks an especially good fit to work at Bennett Renfree's former business that Laura bought? Does Mitchell agree to help them out?

7. After work, Mitchell heads over to the Shop on the Corner to meet the new owner, take a welcome gift from Quinlans, and recommend the Harbecks. What unexpected event happened when Mitchell met Laura O'Dell at her door a little later? Have you ever been suddenly attracted to someone like that? Was Laura affected in a similar way? Wanting some more time with Laura, Mitchell impulsively invites her to go eat dinner with him. Where

does he take her? How did that meeting go? What did they learn about each other?

8. Mitchell is surprised at his sudden strong feelings and so is Laura. Neither Laura or Mitchell are typical of most young people in their twenties. What factors have caused them to be more mature and serious? What were you like in your twenties? How was your life similar or different from Mitchell and Laura's? Do you think tragedies and family problems can push young people to grow up more quickly? An old saying says: Hardship can make or break us. How have the hard times in Laura's and Mitchell's life impacted them? Did you experience any events when younger that made you different from most of your peers?

9. The Saturday after Mitchell meets Laura, he has breakfast at his mother Evelyn's house and plans to take his niece and nephew to the movies and out for the day. Why does his mother encourage him to invite Laura along? Does she go? How does their day at the movies, out to lunch, and to the local park with the kids work out? Who did they run into and share dinner with later? How did Mitchell and Laura's evening end in a romantic moment? Did you think Mitchell's way of blinking the lights to say goodnight to Laura romantic?

10. At dinner with Becky Ray and Mitchell's cousin Rob Killian, you learn about some pranks that have been going on around Waynesville. First, pranksters stole the American flag at the courthouse and raised a Jolly Roger pirate flag in its place. What is the latest crime involving a historic school bell? When are these crimes occurring? Why are they upsetting to the town? What did you learn about Waynesville and its history in the early chapters of the book? Have you ever visited this city in Western North Carolina? What do you remember most about your visit?

11.   As Mitchell and Laura's relationship moves along, he is troubled that she is holding out on telling him more about her past. Why hasn't she confided in him more? What has been happening with Laura's sister since she left Mississippi? In a phone call, what does Lillian tell Laura about Georgina and Chance that upsets her? How does this situation end up causing Laura to open up and share with Mitchell? How does Mitchell help her with the guilt she's carrying? Do you think Laura did the right thing leaving as she did? What would you have done in her situation?

12. Mitchell is blessed to have a warm and happy family, despite their tragedies. How does their love and warmth, extended to Laura at this time in her life, help her? How do you like Mitchell's family members—his mother, niece and nephew, Nannie V, Grandmother Mimi and her sister Frances? How are they a help to Laura as the book moves along? Which of Mitchell's family members did you especially enjoy in the book and why? What joys or sorrows have you known with your own family?

13. In this story, you get to enjoy many of the places and events that are a real part of Waynesville and western North Carolina. Mitchell takes Laura walking with the children at Lake Junaluska., a beautiful conference and retreat center only a short distance from Waynesville. He takes her to a city park, downtown to several restaurants and shops, to art galleries, and to enjoy the International Festival held in Waynesville every year. Have you ever visited any of these area sites or events? The couple also go hiking with friends and later, on their own, to hike in the Cataloocheee Valley area of the Smoky Mountains, the home of many early Appalachian settlers. What trail do they hike? What happens while they are hiking that gives them both a scare? Have you ever been caught out on a mountain hiking trail in a storm?

14. For Laura's birthday, Mitchell takes her to the Biltmore House estate in nearby Asheville. Did you enjoy visiting Biltmore with them? Have you ever been to this 8000-acre estate, grounds, and gardens in the Blue Ridge Mountains? What question did Mitchell ask Laura at the end of their day in the restaurant? What was her answer? Who later shows an interest in Mitchell's mother Evelyn and asks her the same question?

15. The thefts of historic items around Waynesville continue. A statue and an old convertible, that the mayor always rides in for parades, are both stolen. Yet, still there are no leads as to who is committing these crimes or why. What happens to Mitchell one night when he is walking home from his friend Rob's? What does he hear and see? What occurs before he can complete his phone call to the police? Where does Mitchell end up and what did he interrupt that night?

16. On a later day, Laura goes with Mitchell on errands and to Reed Barlow's business in Waynesville. What does Laura overhear there about the ongoing thefts? How does Mitchell react later when she shares with him what she heard? The next day, what does he propose doing about the issue to Laura? What happens when Mitchell meets with and confronts Reed Barlow? How is the situation finally resolved? Do you think Mitchell did the right thing? What would you have done?

17. The summer progresses with Mitchell and Laura making wedding plans. While discussing plans with Mitchell and his mother one day, Laura suddenly sees her sister at the window. When Georgina comes in, what do you learn has been going on in her life? What has happened to Chance? What has occurred in Georgina's life since? What is she doing in North Carolina at this time? Georgina, now married to a minister named Warren Bratton, claims she has changed totally in her life. What positives

do you see and what negatives make you still wonder how much inner change has really occurred?

18. Mitchell and Laura's wedding in early October is a happy time until Georgina puts a kink in Laura's day by not showing up to sing at her wedding as promised. What happened to Georgina and why didn't she come? What explanation did her husband Warren offer? How do Laura and Mitchell's friends and family rally to make the day turn out happy for them? Who sings instead of Georgina? Did you like this unexpected story ending? Where did Laura and Mitchell go on their honeymoon? Do you think they'll have a happy life?

Books by J.L. and Lin Stepp

The Afternoon Hiker
Discovering Tennessee State Parks
Exploring South Carolina State Parks
Visiting North Carolina State Parks
Coming next -- Traveling Georgia State Parks

Books by Lin Stepp

The Smoky Mountain Series

The Foster Girls   *Tell Me About Orchard Hollow*
For Six Good Reasons *Delia's Place*
Second Hand Rose   *Down by the River*
Makin' Miracles   *Saving Laurel Springs*
Welcome Back   *Daddy's Girl*
Lost Inheritance   *The Interlude*

The Mountain Home Books
Happy Valley
Downsizing
Eight at the Lake
Seeking Ayita
Shop on the Corner
Coming Next --- The Red Mill Bookstore

Christmas Novella
A Smoky Mountain Gift
In When the Snow Falls

The Edisto Trilogy
Claire at Edisto
Return to Edisto
Edisto Song

The Lighthouse Sisters Series
Light the Way
Lighten My Heart
Light in the Dark
Coming Next
The Light Continues

About The Author
Lin Stepp

Lin Stepp is a native Tennessean, businesswoman, and educator. A *New Your Times, USA Today, Publishers Weekly*, and Amazon bestselling author, Lin has twenty-four published novels out now, including her twelve beloved Smoky Mountain novels and five Mountain Home books, all set in different Tennessee or North Carolina mountain locations, a novella in one of Kensington's Christmas anthologies and six South Carolina coastal novels, including her three Edisto Trilogy books and three releases in the new Lighthouse Sisters series.

Lin and her husband J.L. also write regional guidebooks, including a published Smoky Mountain hiking guide and TN, SC, and NC state parks guidebooks, all filled with hundreds of color photos. Writing and adventuring are her joys and more novels set in the Smokies and at the beach are on the way, as well as more colorful regional guidebooks. Lin's title *Claire At Edisto* was the *2019 Best Book Award Winner in Fiction: Romance*, sponsored by American Book Fest and her novel *Welcome Back* a finalist in the *2017 Selah Awards*. Lin enjoys speaking for events, festivals, libraries, and book clubs. And she loves reading, hiking, exploring out of doors, and keeping up with her readers. Look for her pages on Facebook and Twitter and follow her monthly blog and newsletter, too, that you will find on her website at: *www.linstepp.com*.